G000122774

NEVER 2 RETURN

This novel is a work of fiction.

All names and characters, businesses, events and incidents, are fictitious. Any resemblance to actual persons, living or dead, or incidents other than references to events or organisations in the public domain, is purely coincidental.

ONE

Max's love affair with Hong Kong had just ended with a bump. To be precise, with a blow from the butt of a Beretta handgun to the base of his skull. Now he lay almost unconscious on the plush carpet in his hotel suite. Two other men were in the room. The eldest was visibly agitated as he paced in circles waiting for someone to answer his call from his mobile phone. The younger man who had administered the blow, had holstered his handgun and now knelt beside Max to frisk him, turning a few possessions out of his pockets and claiming his mobile phone and some cash. The other man was suddenly connected and spoke Cantonese very quickly into his phone .... then listened .... then spoke again ..... then signed off.

"Mr Liang says to take him to Horizon One at The Tempest. He said you should sedate him – you will know what to do."

Without speaking, the gunman reached into his linen jacket, removed a small plastic box that he flipped open to reveal a tiny syringe. He unsheathed the needle, tapped it, squirted it once at the ceiling then pushed it into Max's right arm.

Max had fallen in love with Hong Kong on his original trip nearly five years ago in 1995. Its energy and enterprise rubbing shoulders with its history and traditions - even the smells - all played their part in his seduction. That trip was also his first overseas project for his uncle's security company, Briggs-Buchanan Security or BBS. Max's task had been to install a top-of-the-range security system throughout The Celestial Hotel in Kowloon and The Tempest Hotel on Hong Kong Island. With a total of over eight hundred rooms, each requiring a new keyless entry locking system, along with the ancillary support services, the two hotels afforded a highly profitable contract.

But much had changed over recent years. Briggs-Buchanan had been through very turbulent times resulting in the prefix 'Briggs' being dropped from the name and now more than ever needing the sort of contract that Max was supervising.

Ownership of The Celestial and Tempest Hotels had also changed hands soon after the British handed the dependency back to Chinese control in the summer of 1997. Max heard rumours that the previous owners had upset some powerful people in Beijing so were forced to sell all their Hong Kong property - with the emphasis on *forced*, by some accounts.

Max had brought his current dilemma on himself. Yet again his short temper and intransigence had won over his better judgement. He had started to argue with his client within days of arriving the previous week. The new owner of both hotels - a dapper, diminutive Chinaman named Zem Liang - seemed to take a dislike to Max the moment the couple first met. They just didn't click. Mr Liang resented having to use a British supplier, but the security systems update was contractual so Max was despatched from London to supervise the work to be undertaken by one of Mr Liang's local suppliers. A supplier with absolute loyalty to Mr Liang but absolutely none to Max or Buchanan Security Services. Their mutual mistrust had come to a head tonight when Max threatened to leave the project. A heated discussion had become a row that had become physical until the pistol butt of one of Mr Liang's henchmen had put an end to the argument and Max's consciousness.

Max woke over an hour later. He was in another suite in another hotel, cable-tied into an upright chair. His head throbbed which he assumed to be related to his circumstance, but he could move it so concluded that nothing was broken.

The door opened and Zem Liang walked into the room with another minder. He and Max stared at one another.

"I'm sorry it has come to this Mr Duncan. It's not how I like to do business but you have given me no choice. You should know that we can't let you leave the programme before it's complete. Mr Feng tells me that he will need you here for about another week. During that time you will be kept here in this suite. Mr Feng will come here for project meetings or he will phone you here. You on the other hand, will not be allowed to make any calls out. If your office contacts the hotel, they will be informed that you are safe and well but indisposed. You can order any food and drink on Room Service. Do you understand my rules?"

Max said nothing, partly in defiance but also because his mind had just latched onto what, until this moment, had been a serious and potentially embarrassing problem. Now it suddenly offered retribution. Only when he checked the inventory of the hardware that had arrived from the UK, did Max realise that the control systems were still equipped with old non-millennium-compliant boards. They had not been upgraded to avoid the impending problems from what had been recently named The Millennium Bug. In a little over seven months from now at midnight on 31ˢᵗ December when 1999 would become the year 2000, the old timing boards would fail and chaos would ensue. Once Max had realised his oversight, he had immediately phoned his office to get new replacements couriered out to Hong Kong. He was planning to replace the old boards surreptitiously once the upgrades arrived so no-one would be any the wiser. Problems averted. Mr Liang repeated:

"Do you understand my rules Mr Duncan?"

Max gave a single nod of his head.

"Good." And with that, Mr Liang exited.

Max knew precisely why he was here. The room had one of Buchanan's highest grade remotely-controlled security systems that included a concealed video surveillance system. Max would be closely watched for the duration of his incarceration.

To his and his captor's surprise, Max became a model prisoner. His more usual gritty demeanour softened as he relaxed into the imposed sedation of his luxury cell. He had regular meetings and more regular phone conversations with Mr Feng, the owner of the contractor company responsible for implementing Max's instructions for the installation of the new equipment.

The replacement boards that had been so essential for the safe completion of the project a few days previously, arrived during the week. No-one but Max knew the contents of the package that was sent to his room from reception. Aware that his minders may take an interest by means of the surveillance system, Max checked the package then blatantly pushed it aside as if it were of no consequence. He eventually opened it under his bedsheets in the middle of the night, removed all the

Buchanan Security Systems identity then placed the remains of the pack in his laptop shoulder bag the next morning.

Eight days later, Max was told to prepare to travel. 4th June – now less than seven months to his retribution date. Max smiled as he considered the outcome.

Mr Feng shook his hand with surprising sincerity and wished Max: 'Bon voyage' then bowed slightly and exited the suite. An hour later Max was frog-marched to a waiting car, driven to the airport and handed an airline ticket for a Cathay Pacific flight that would depart in a little over an hour.

'*Clever,*' Max thought. '*No time to arrange anything more than my departure.*'

He set off at a pace into the airport with his backpack over one shoulder and a laptop bag on the other. He relaxed as he checked in his rucksack but he still had to dispose of the two timing boards before encountering the security and the x-ray machines in the departure area. That problem was solved when he noticed a chunky batterymobile heading in his direction pulling a trailer containing open rubbish bins. Max headed towards it, removed the anonymous package from his shoulder bag then dropped it into one of the bins as the truck passed, without breaking his step.

Now to departure. But as he turned, his eye fell on something that stopped his progress instantly. A petite pea green straw Derby hat. A speck of vivid colour amid the hues of beige and grey. The very same hat that had first caught his attention when its owner arrived on his flight as his plane stood on the tarmac at Dubai Airport on Max's outward flight to Hong Kong almost three weeks ago.

On that encounter, Max had been dozing in his seat when his attention was first drawn to the green hat then to its owner -

a stunningly pretty oriental lady in her mid-twenties who stopped at the end of his empty row, hoisted her small shoulder bag into the overhead locker and settled into the aisle seat two from his. She then removed her hat to reveal straight black hair that perfectly framed her face. Max was not normally a great observer of the opposite sex, but now this fellow traveller who had arrived in his space at two o'clock in the morning, had captivated his attention. He surprised himself by how he was drawn to her. He leaned over the vacant seat to introduce himself by name to which the lady replied with:

"I'm Jia." Then she giggled. "It means 'beautiful' in English."

'How could your parents have known when they named you at a few weeks old,' was Max's immediate thought. Their ensuing conversation was little more than small talk until Jia suddenly asked:

"Why did Mrs Thatcher agree to give back the whole dependency?"

It threw Max. He had no answer, not knowing anything about the politics of Hong Kong. Jia was clearly engaged by the subject and explained some of the history that moved to a string of tirades about the Chinese government's shortcomings. After a break, she apologised for her outburst with an explanation that Max later recalled having included something about her membership of a movement relating to the Tiananmen Square massacre in June 1989.

Eventually the need for sleep got the better of Max who apologised, pulled up his mini pillow and dropped off into an uncomfortable slumber.

That had all happened some three weeks ago and had been committed to Max's distant memory. Now he was experiencing the same frisson as he had on their first meeting. The diminutive lady was standing with her back to him but it was definitely Jai with the pea green straw Derby and jet black straight cut hairline. Only as Max made his way towards her for another brief encounter did he doubt his conviction. The lady ahead of him was heavier with a fuller waistline than Jia's petite form. But at that moment she turned and their eyes met. It was certainly Jia, but she immediately turned away; then she stopped and turned back. Now at a distance of five or six metres, the couple stood looking at one another. No words, just staring. Jia knew that Max would soon become aware of the horrific circumstances of her extra weight. Not hers but the lumpy bulk of a body belt and tabard packed with explosives under her loose raincoat.

"Hi Jia."

"Max....You must leave. Go. Please go." Jia was mouthing the words more than speaking them. Her eyes were now pleading.

"Please....Please go."

Jai started to walk backwards slowly. Max feared that he knew what was happening. He instinctively took a few steps forward to maintain their contact, but then he stopped and almost shouted the words:

"Please don't do this, Jia. You can do more for your cause alive."

It was too late. Jai suddenly screamed something in Chinese. People nearby stopped then a realisation resulted in panic. There was screaming. People started to run. A ripple moved from those close by who had heard Jia's yell. That caused more panic across the concourse as people tried to get away, stumbling and snatching up small children.

9

Jia was now holding her raincoat wide open for all to see her body belt and tabard. She shouted again:

"I am doing this for the people who died in Tiananmen Square. Ten years ago today. Thousands of protesters were killed by the same murderers who now control your lives in Hong Kong." Then she screamed: "Murderers!"
Max didn't move; standing statuesque as everyone around him was running in panic.

"Please Max... I don't want to hurt you. Get behind that pillar please."
Max continued to watch Jia, defiantly staring stony-faced, hoping his presence would affect her decision. Only as he watched Jia put her hand inside her raincoat pocket and mouth the words..."Good bye" ...did he move. He glanced around for cover, saw the pillar nearby and dived full length across the shiny marble floor towards its shelter.

KABOOM!

TWO

Max's direct flight arrived at Heathrow two days later. He was shattered, agitated, nervous and upset. Not from the incident with Jia as much as from news that he had received when he eventually phoned back to London while he waited for his flight to be rescheduled after the bomb-blast then the subsequent interviews by the police who knew that he was the last person to speak to Jia.

Making a call home to tell everyone in London that he was okay was Max's priority but without any local currency he was dependent on making a reverse charge call; a slow and complicated process from the other side of the world. When he eventually heard his aunt's phone ringing....and ringing...he was at first a little confused then reassured. He knew from his last call more than a week previously, that his uncle Dennis was unwell again and spending time in bed. If no-one was at the house, he must have made a full recovery and was perhaps back to work. So Max started the process again to call Buchanan's. The call was answered by a young lady's voice that Max didn't recognise. She sounded hesitant before agreeing to accept the *collect* charges.

"Hello, Buchanan Security Systems, how may I help you?"

"Hi. Thanks for paying for the call. Who are you?"

"This is Buchanan Secur…"

"Yes I know - I work there," Max interrupted in an irritated tone. "Who are you?"

"Oh sorry. I'm a temp."

"Can you put me through to Dennis please - Dennis Buchanan?"

There was silence. Max broke it.

"Hello."

"Yes, hello."

"Is Dennis in the office?"

"Er, no."

"Okay," Max stated slowly, containing his diminishing patience. "Then Ari Sumeer in Technical please."

"Sorry, who did you say you were?"

"For God's sake. I'm Max Duncan, Dennis's nephew. I work there but I'm in Hong Kong - working."

There was another silence before:

"Oh God…. I'm really sorry to tell you …but… your uncle's died …I think it may have been last week, from a heart attack …… Everyone is at his funeral today. There's no-one here except me to take messages. I'm so sorry, I can't tell you any more than that …Sorry."

Max reeled away from the phone, panting for breath. This was impossible. No it wasn't, was it? His uncle had been unwell recently but not dying, just unwell with an occurrence of his heart condition when Max left. When he last phoned, Dennis was stable, just *'under the weather'* Molly had reported. *'Nothing to worry about,'* his aunt had assured him.

Max mumbled his thanks to the temp and hung up the phone mechanically then slid down the wall and sat deep in remorse. He didn't realise that tears were rolling down his cheeks.

Max hadn't slept on the flight. Now back in Heathrow he had to face the phone call to Molly. He used the last of his sterling to call his aunt's house number from the most private phone booth that he could find.

The conversation was as difficult as he had imagined. Molly burst into tears as she heard Max's voice before scolding him for scaring her with his absence. When she calmed, she listened to Max's very brief potted excuse for being out of contact. Max was profuse in his apologies that Molly put into context with:

"Max, darling, there was nothing you could have done. Nothing any of us could have done. A heart attack, pure and simple. It had been a possibility for so long that I thank my guardian angel that I had Dennis for as long as I did."

"I'll drop my bags at my flat then I'll come straight over. I should be with you in a couple of hours."

"No don't do that. I won't be here. We are all going to the solicitors this afternoon to hear Dennis's will being read."

"What?! A will being read? Already. Really?"

"Yes, I know. Very odd, but it was one of Dennis's last requests. My only hope is that it's so unlike him that perhaps there will be a surprise – some revelation to sort all the ghastly financial problems. Some buried treasure somewhere that I don't know about, perhaps."

"Yeah, perhaps."

THREE

Under normal circumstances, Tessa Chapman would have considered the reading of a will to be one of the easiest of her professional tasks, but today would be different. No easier for her than it was about to be for her clients.

Dennis Buchanan was Miss Chapman's first new client in her first month at her first practice in London. For that alone she would probably never have forgotten him any more than she would her first love. But from that introduction began a switchback journey to the heights of Briggs-Buchanan's success in the eighties to the ear-popping fall between ninety-four and ninety-seven. As Dennis Buchanan's solicitor, then representing the Briggs-Buchanan Group, she had fought numerous battles on his behalf; from the normal range of minor legalities to large litigation cases. Then there was the steady stream of copyright infringements against their security systems and eventually the battle with Jack Briggs when the business partnership split.

Dennis Buchanan needed her support, or at least he needed the protection of a good lawyer. He was a designer, a computer wizard ahead of the game, but he was no businessman. Jack Briggs on the other hand, was a marketing man through and through with an American's natural flair for spotting the main chance then exploiting it to the full. For a while their partnership worked remarkably well. They had made a lot of money and Briggs-Buchanan was certainly one of the leading suppliers of high-tech security control equipment anywhere in the world. Dennis had never paid much attention to the scale of his achievement but Jack Briggs loved it and played it for all it was worth, jet-setting his way around the world like playing the tables at a huge international party at which the entry requirement was wealth, fame or both.

Whilst Briggs-Buchanan's success was due in great part to Jack's astute approach to business, so too was Dennis's demise. Jack's shrewdness extended to the partnership agreement that he originally drew up and later used to take the lion's share of the beast they had created.

When the split came and she realised the consequences for Dennis Buchanan quicker than anyone, Miss Chapman saw her task was to protect her oldest client. But try as she might, everything turned against them. Dennis Buchanan's luck just seemed to run out. Fighting Jack Briggs in the US courts was never going to be easy or cheap and it cost Dennis Buchanan very dear – in time, money and finally his health. After the sale of Briggs-Buchanan, came the shock waves from two bad investments in Taiwan, a negligence case against the newly formed Buchanan Security Systems, followed swiftly by the debacle at Lloyds of London during the mid-nineties. Dennis was a 'name' at Lloyds with a substantial nest egg investment that cracked open and haemorrhaged money he no longer had. In just three years of the very worst luck, it seemed that everything he had worked for was gone. At least he had managed to keep his house – some of the 'names' hadn't.

When Dennis's heart problems were identified two years ago, the pressure had already taken its toll. But Dennis Buchanan was a fighter and refused to let his health slow him to a standstill, it just made him pace himself. However much Molly nagged, Dennis would not give up work. His breaks from the business had got longer recently but Molly sensed that work gave him a purpose that gave him a strength, so she stopped pestering and supported his passion as she had everything else in Dennis's life.

As Tessa Chapman turned the pages of his will, those present in the room could not have failed to recognise the precision with which he had organised his modest estate. With Molly was a small assembly of immediate family-members that included her daughter, Samantha, from her first marriage.

Tap-tap. The door to Tessa Chapman's office crept open, halting her flow of words. Her assistant, Jayne, peeped in as all heads turned.

"I'm sorry to interrupt, Miss Chapman, Mr Duncan has just arrived." She moved aside to let Max's tall dishevelled frame pass her.

"Come in Mr Duncan, please take a seat." Tessa Chapman gestured to a chair by the panelled wall. In all the years she had worked with Dennis Buchanan, Miss Chapman had no reason to meet so many of his family. Now she was struck by a genuine warmth and closeness that existed between them. Every member of the group acknowledged Max with a smile, a wave or a wink. Molly Buchanan reached across from her chair to touch his arm and mouthed a silent:

"Thank you for coming, dear."

Max couldn't be anywhere else today. He owed everything to Dennis and Molly. His life had taken a series of unexpected twists and turns since the loss of both his parents when he was fifteen. On the 21st December 1989, Gerry and Sonya Duncan boarded a plane at Heathrow airport to take them on a pre-Christmas weekend break to New York to celebrate their twentieth wedding anniversary. But Pan Am flight 103 only reached Scotland when, above the little town of Lockerbie, a bomb blew the plane out of the sky and into the world's headlines.

Max took his parents' deaths as badly as any sensitive fifteen year-old would do. But added to his loss was a deep sense of guilt. His parents had planned to take their break the previous week but put their arrangements back when Max was rushed into hospital with suspected appendicitis. By the time the doctors signalled a false alarm and diagnosed stress-related tension, his father had already re-booked their departure – to the 21st December.

Max was staying with his auntie Molly and uncle Dennis when the disaster happened. When the family's affairs were resolved, it was decided that Max would stay on and live permanently with his favourite relatives. But he didn't make it easy for them at first. With no brother or sister to share his burden, Max shrunk into a shell of remorse and guilt. He became unpredictable and prone to flashes of anger that could be triggered by the smallest incident, causing him to flare up with red-eyed rage. Not the constant gas burn-off on an oil rig, more a smouldering forest fire that flashes into life in an instant to engulf everything in its path. Only Molly and Dennis's undying patience with Max's evident pain and mood-swings, eventually paid dividends and brought their nephew round to some sense of normality.

His only positive act in those early months was to change his career path. His father had always wanted him to follow a profession, by which he meant the law, politics or the military. Max had been horrified by the choice but at fifteen had known only that he wanted to do something with computers. Several of his friends had the same idea at the time, but even then, Max showed a rare talent and aptitude.

After the tragedy, in the midst of all the grief, Max suddenly announced that he wanted to go into the army. At first Dennis and Molly thought it was a passing phase, to follow one of his father's wishes for a career path, so they agreed to help where they could, assuming that anything positive that suggested a future for their nephew must help him to get over his loss. But Max never wavered. He saw it through, entered as a trainee officer at eighteen and so began a promising career.

To his surprise, Max actually enjoyed some of the mindless unquestioning obedience and routine. And he was good at it, winning recognition early for his stamina and aptitude for the more physical activities; so much so that it was suggested he move to a Commando regiment. Everything was proceeding in that direction until his medical report included: '...*his psychological profile shows similarities to those of a manic depressive*'. The message was clear and the Commandos could not take the risk. The rejection would have been a greater blow to Max had it not been confirmation of his own suspicions – and had he not just discovered that the Army used computers and would allow him to work with them. To begin, it was at a level that hardly tested his ability but once his talent was recognised he was re-directed to the Air Corps where he learned to fly helicopters and began work with some serious high-tech guidance systems.

By the age of twenty, Max seemed to have his life and career in good order until he went to Germany on manoeuvres. There he met Hannah and fell completely and utterly in love. Hannah's feelings were never expressed. Perhaps Max was a passing novelty. But by the time she moved on and left Europe for college in California, the damage was done. She had touched senses and raised emotions within Max that he had suppressed for many years. Max was okay and handled the split with a new maturity and a review of his future that was not to involve the armed services. Within three months of meeting Hannah, Max was planning to buy his release from the forces with his parents' inheritance that was being held in a trust fund. Two weeks after his twenty-first birthday he was a civilian once again; one week later he bought a small flat with the remainder of the money and two days later began working for his uncle at the fledgling Buchanan Security Systems Ltd.

As Max sat in the panelled room listening to Tessa Chapman reading his uncle's words from sheets of paper, he felt a surprising calmness wash over him. Max had worked for his uncle for almost five years, helping where he could to rebuild a phoenix from the ashes of his old partnership. Within their family they had a special closeness born of their mutual passion and genius with computers. Whilst the rest of the family viewed Max simply as one of their relatives, Dennis also thought of him as a workmate who became a soulmate. Dennis had all the power dressers he needed in his sales department but he and Max produced the goods – the security systems that would once again lead the market.

"....and Buchanan Security's affairs will continue to be overseen by Scrimiger & Co, with power of attorney remaining with Tessa Chapman." She glanced up momentarily to catch some of the eyes of her audience, as if for approval. "Jim Wandle will remain as Managing Director and Max Duncan's current trial placement as head of 'Systems and Development' is hereby confirmed as permanent. Details of Max's salary and precise instruction are enclosed." Tessa Chapman produced a padded A4 envelope that Max assumed she would pass over to him but she gestured to it as she placed it on the desk in front of her then made no effort to hand it forward.

As Tessa Chapman finished her reading of the will everyone glanced to one another for a lead. After a few moments, Molly Buchanan, looking drawn and tired, stood up and thanked Miss Chapman for her help who in turn thanked everyone for coming then called Jayne on her internal telephone, asking her to show her guests out. Max made his way to her desk and picked up the padded envelope. He turned to catch Tessa Chapman's eye but she was already watching him as she shook hands with each of her departing guests. Her body language made her intentions clear to Max that she didn't want him to take it.

"I'm sorry to keep you Mr Duncan," Tessa Chapman apologised once they were alone in the room. "It's just that your uncle gave me a message for you when I handed this to you. He told me that you were the only person to hear these instructions." She looked for a sign that Max understood the significance of her remark. Max looked intrigued as he waited for the punchline.

"Uhu, right," he mumbled to break the silence. "Go on."

"He asked me to tell you *'never to return'* – and that you would *'understand when you opened the package'*."
Max looked vacant. It clearly made no sense now.

"He told me never to return?"

"That's right. He was very precise about those words."

"He didn't say to where? Or from where…or when? Just that I shouldn't return?"

"Apparently so. Just 'never to return' and that it would make sense when you read the contents of the envelope…. Sorry I can't help more than that."

Max arrived home as the sun was setting. In another age Max's studio flat in the Earls Court area of London would have been termed a 'garret'. Furnishings were sparse, ill-matching and functional. Comfort appeared to be a very low priority, as was order and cleanliness. That was, all apart from the bank of computers and related hardware that was neatly installed under the raised sleeping area. Where the majority of sitting rooms are arranged around a television, so Max's flat gave the centre of attention to his computers. Even his one comfortable chair was positioned to allow him to watch the TV and his computers processing data simultaneously.

Max removed the padded envelope from his bag immediately he arrived home. He moved to his make-shift desk, ripped open the envelope and tipped out its contents. The only thing to emerge was a double CD in a clear plastic case that clattered onto the surface of his worktop. Max picked it up, looking for some identification but there was nothing. He opened the box to find two standard CD-ROM discs marked '1' and '2'. Nothing more. On the inside of the white insert, inside the lid, there was a note in Dennis's shaky handwriting – MAX – FOR YOUR EYES ONLY – OPEN IN PRIVATE.

Max continued to check the CD wrapper, intrigued by the lack of identification. He peered into the envelope then pulled out a single sheet of company headed paper with typed notes on one side and a small brass key held in place with a single strip of electrical tape on the reverse. Max checked the envelope again. It was empty. He turned to the notes. A simple business-like letter with a series of bullet points outlined his new salary and package of benefits and allowances. Max read them quickly and registered surprise at his uncle's generosity. But he was more surprised at the lack of any personal message – and no reference to his instruction '*never to return*'. Apart from the hand written note on the CD cover this had all the sensitivity of an internal memo.

Max turned to his bank of computers, threw a few switches then made his way into his kitchenette while the kit performed its warming-up procedures.

He opened the fridge and removed half a bar of chocolate and a bottle of mineral water that he swigged as he walked back across the room. He tapped a few more keys to move the program on before removing the number '1' CD from its case as he sat down in front of the screen. He dropped the CD into the tray, closed it and moved the mouse over the mat at speed, running quickly through the set-up procedures. Click… click… click… password. The program on the CD was password-protected.

'Must be important,' Max thought as he automatically typed 'd1bd1bd1b', the password derived from Dennis Ian Buchanan's initials that they usually used for low security work. Nothing happened.

Max tried again with 'm4dm4x' that Dennis sometimes used for their joint projects. But zero. Max stared at the screen in the fading light.

"Come on Dennis, you're not making this easy." The words were audible in the quiet of the flat. Max leant back in his seat.

"Bloody hell Dennis…" His mind hunted for inspiration. Logic told him it must be obvious, surely Dennis wanted him to get into the program, it must be something they both used. He tried a couple of company passwords but wasn't surprised when he got no response.

Password… password… password. It sat on the screen tantalising Max. He pushed his chair back and fell forward onto his folded arms, his chin on the desk just inches from his keyboard. Nothing was coming to him. Why would Dennis do this? Why give him a disc that he couldn't access? Of course he wanted him to access it but why not use one of their passwords?

Max felt exhaustion getting the better of him as he reran the activities at the solicitors; was there a clue there? ….. Of course there bloody was!

Max's eyes opened wide. In a split second he was sharp, awake and sitting up. He thought for a moment then tapped the keys 'n e v e r   t o   r e t u r n'. At the touch of each key another asterisk traced onto the screen. He tapped the 'enter' key, certain that the program would now open. But again, no reaction from the machine. He was shocked so repeated the exercise in case he had made a typing error – but got the same result. Max was convinced that this was the password – he just had to type the right combination of letters and spaces . . . and numbers. He tried substituting the 'to' with the number '2'. That didn't work. Neither did the addition of spaces between the words, nor the substitution of cap letters. Max was stuck – perhaps this wasn't the password after all.

'Must be,' he told himself. He jotted the words down on a piece of paper and stared at them, looking for inspiration.

Dong! With the abruptness of a clock chiming, the revelation struck Max. Dennis still referred to the *Enter* key as the *Return* key as it was on earlier computer keyboards. Max typed feverishly: 'n e v e r t o' then hit *Enter* but his energy was again sapped when nothing changed. Try again. He repeated the exercise with the number *2* replacing the word *to*. Enter. . . The screen cleared instantly then carried on its warm-up routine.

"Yes!" He was in. "Never 2 Return… Dennis you bugger – this better be important," Max whispered to himself as the computer whirred with life. He started to crunch on a chunk of rock-hard chocolate until the first image appeared on his screen. It froze Max's jaw mid-chew.

"Hi Max – surprise surprise eh? Bet you didn't expect to see me again so soon. I told you I'd leave you something special in my will didn't I…?" Max fell back in his chair, his eyes wide open, transfixed by the image on the screen – the image of Dennis Buchanan sitting rigidly in an upright chair talking to him. His uncle looked very uncomfortable and very unwell – worse than Max remembered seeing before he left for Hong Kong. His words came slowly with apparent effort.

"I wish I could be with you right now Max, if only to see your face. But if you're watching this, it can only mean one thing…well two in fact. First, my poor old ticker has finally given up as I know it soon will. I know it's only a matter of time now..." He brought a glass with a straw up to his mouth and sucked for a moment. It seemed to give him some relief. Max's face grimaced as he shared Dennis's evident discomfort.

"And it means that I haven't seen you to...well, to say goodbye. You've just left for Hong Kong on the hotels' upgrade and I sense that by the time you return, this will have to be my 'goodbye'. I'm sorry Max. I have been told that I'm far more ill than we thought and I'm not telling Molly because I know she'll worry more than I want."

Max's eyes were now so full of tears that he couldn't see the screen. He squeezed his lids shut. The clear salty water flowed down his cheeks into his scraggly beard. He made no effort to wipe them away.

"I just wanted to say 'thank you' my dear friend… Thank you for all your help and love over these black months… years. I hope you know what strength you've given me. Without your help… well, it would have been harder, if that's imaginable. I just wanted you to know that, in case I can't tell you in person."

Max now wept aloud. He reached forward to touch a key to freeze the action on the screen. His body was shaking, his face distorted, as he wiped his eyes with the back of his wrists. He sniffed deeply, then reached to his keyboard to continue the program.

"Now to some unfinished business." Dennis thought for a moment as if considering his words. "But listen to me Max, what I'm going to tell you now is for real. Only one other person knows anything about it, so if you want no part in this, that's perfectly fine. In fact, the more I think about it, the dafter you'd have to be to get involved." He sucked on his drinking straw. "I've started something I can't finish – so as usual you're the only one I can turn to." Another drink to moisten his mouth.

"You remember I talked to you a while ago about the feasibility of building a 'sleeper' program into our systems…? Well I've done it!" He smiled as if knowing Max's reaction to the statement. Max just frowned.

"In fact, you were more help than you knew…After that conversation, I rebuilt the sniffer exactly as you suggested and it worked, Max…It works brilliantly…So now I've got the system installed and it's just waiting for me to go and get my money back…*our* money back." Dennis took another slow draw on the straw. Max blinked for the first time in a minute then re-adjusted his stare at the screen, as a cat assesses a distant bird.

"That's right Max. This was never just an exercise. Right now it's installed in a safe deposit box in New York - at a branch of the First National Credit Bank. Now that's a name you know from three years ago. You worked on the installation in London but I handled New York…and that's where that thieving bastard, Jack Briggs, has got a stash of his ill-gotten gains. You may recall how he got so close to their CEO. That's why he's got his valuables there – but it's not important why it's there – it's there, so is my sniffer, monitoring the bank's systems and waiting for me to walk in and take some of my money back – the 'Geraldine Diamond Collection', to be exact. It's valued at over £2,000,000 now. He keeps it in the same vault as I've installed my sniffer, monitoring the entire system just as we discussed – just waiting for me to go in and steal back some of the money he shafted off us."

Dennis took a brief break.

"Well, I know that's never going to happen now, so it's over to you Max…Everything you need is here – well almost; the entire layout of the bank, the systems, everything is on these discs. But you'll need help at the other end. The contacts you'll need to help you in New York are on here as well. My contact over there is someone I've known from way back. His name is Bo Garrick – you can trust him. But he's put together a small team I don't know. At the end of the day, just remember, they're doing the job for the money, not for you or me." He sucked at the straw.

"Just in case you go along with this lunatic plan, I've taken the liberty of sorting out an alias for you. So you'll soon be receiving a passport and business cards in the name of *'Alex Slater'*. You work for *'Astrodome Games'*- another old client.

"My box is in the name of *'Daniel Slater'*. At the bank, you'll be checking your dead dad's possessions. You're 'Alex Slater' from the moment you book your flight until you get back home when he'll vanish into thin air... So no-one here should know where you've gone.

26

"You know this isn't for me, Max - it's for Molly, bless her. She knows nothing about this, any more than she is aware of quite how ill I am. I have been trying to buy time, but that's about to run out. Meanwhile, I've left such a bloody mess, I know that. So, if you do it, Max, you have to use the money to help your aunt. For sure she needs it." He paused to gather some energy.

"That's it. I'm so sorry to land this on you, Max. If you do it, take lots of care - everything by numbers. Use your military training…..And if you don't go near it, well that's understandable, but please do what you can to help your aunt. I love you both so much……. Goodbye."

The screen froze then transformed to a set of icons and lists that sat stationary awaiting instructions. So did Max. He was hunched in a pool of cold computer light in the dimly lit flat. For a full thirty seconds, Max's crouched figure was motionless staring at the screen, thinking his way around what he had just heard. Then he gripped the mouse, moved the cursor to one of the icons and clicked. The screen opened to reveal a computer illustration of a First National Credit Bank. Max immediately moved the mouse to animate the image. With the character of a computer game, the program 'walked' him through the front door into the bank, then through the corridors with signs and graphic notes flashing onto the screen to explain points about security cameras, fire escapes and the like. Max moved the program faster until he was in the safe-deposit vaults. New icons appeared down the side of the screen. Max clicked on one. More information opened – what appeared to be wiring diagrams. When the disc ran out of memory, Max replaced that disc with number '2' and the process continued. New symbols, charts and graphic displays burst into life on the screen. Max was taking their meaning at a glance. Faster and faster, now not studying what he was looking at, just registering the sheer scale of the information that Dennis had included. Max was hypnotised by everything he could find. His eyes darted over the screen as his hand moved the mouse around the mat. Max's face was fixed into a broad grin that eventually burst into a laugh.

"The hidden treasure – hidden in a bank vault in New York …. Huh - Dennis, you're a nutter - a complete bloody nutter."

FOUR

Max had never been a morning person, but today was easier than most – ironically because he had hardly slept since the early hours – repeatedly replaying Dennis's message and his program in his head, trying to grasp its full significance.

He arrived at work before nine and was surprised to find an internal message already on his computer when he switched it on. The MD wanted a meeting at ten o'clock.

Jim Wandle had been headhunted eighteen months earlier from a competitor company. He arrived as Buchanan's new managing director with high hopes and an equal energy level, determined to build it once again to a market leader. But the markets were changing and he was becoming more realistic in his expectations. Max hardly knew his MD and spent no social time with him, but word was that he was finding the financial pressures on Buchanan's very difficult to handle and may even be looking for a new job if the company didn't begin to turn around soon.

"Morning Max – come in." Jim stood to welcome him into his office then to Max's surprise, reached forward to shake his hand. "Congratulations!"

"On what?"

"Our new Head of Systems and Development."

"Oh that? Yes, thanks. I assume you knew before I did – that Dennis had confirmed the position."

"Yeah, but he also said he wanted to announce it to you himself…Well, you know, as best he could. You know how he liked to spring surprises."

"Yeah, didn't he?"

"Which brings me straight to the point." Jim's tone changed as he gestured for Max to take a seat. "You're Head of Department now and that brings new responsibilities, along with the new pay packet. You understand that?" Max said nothing, but nodded once.

"I hope you and I can work together and…well, see some improvements and make some changes - for the better, of course. Some of these changes will be operational and some will have financial implications. The fact is…" He stopped to consider how to say the next bit, adopting a familiar pouting expression that always irritated Max and reminded him of a fish.

"The fact is, Max," he continued, "we have to run a tighter ship than ever and I'd prefer you to be on my side in this, okay?" Max shrugged, not knowing to what he was supposed to be agreeing.

"I'm running late right now, so I'd like to pick this up tomorrow and go through a few points, but I thought it only fair to say as soon as possible that I was shocked by the contents of the package Dennis left you."

Max was taken aback.

'*Jim Wandle knows about the CDs? Dennis said only one other person knows about it – but why Jim Wandle? Is the company going to finance the bank robbery in New York?*'

"You seem surprised at that," Jim Wandle suggested.

"Yeah, you could say that."

Now Jim was surprised by Max's reaction.

"Why?"

"To be honest, I'm surprised anyone else knows about it."

"Knows about it? Don't you think it's my job to know?"

"No."

"Max – are we talking about the same thing here? I'm talking about your new salary and benefits package that Dennis left you in his will."

Max was so tired that reassembling his thoughts to be sure that he hadn't said anything stupid in the last few moments, took several seconds.

"Of course, what else?"

"Are you alright? You look awful – worse than usual. You sleeping okay?"

"Yeah, I'm okay."

Jim Wandle looked at his watch that he wore on the underside of his left wrist.

"I'll come to the point. We can't afford it. Sorry to be brutal, but as usual your uncle was too generous with money we don't have. I'm sorry, but I can't agree to give you everything Dennis left you. If I did, I'd have Dave Fisher and Sally Longada and…well, they'd all expect the same. It's too dangerous. So, I'd like you to accept this slightly reduced package." He passed Max a single sheet of paper with typed notes, then stood up and began tidying his desk, dropping files into his briefcase.

"Let me know tomorrow. If you agree, I'll get it in place for your next pay packet. If you don't, we'll talk about it, but I need your help with this Max." He snapped his briefcase closed. Max didn't have time to give his reaction, although he sensed his irritation.

'How dare you question Dennis's wishes – especially his _final_ wishes,' he thought to himself. But Max was still reading

the typed notes as Jim swept past him on his way out of the office.

"See you nine-thirty tomorrow."

Back at his desk, Max found a padded envelope embellished with a 'FedEx Mail' sticker. Not unusual. Max opened it without much consideration as he watched emails dinging onto his computer screen. Only as he tipped out the contents of the envelope did he pay it his total attention. A polished new British passport fell into his hand. Max checked that no-one was watching then furtively flicked to the back page to see himself staring out. All other identification related to a certain *'Alex Thomas Slater'*. Another shake and a small pack of business cards fell from the envelope onto the desk, identifying Alex Slater as a *'Sales Executive'* of *'Astrodome Toys and Games'*.

Max got away from work early and was home before six. All day his mind had been on the CD case that never left his shirt pocket. So many questions were now occurring to him that he wanted to check the program in detail.

As he dropped his keys on a table near the door, he was surprised to see the light on his answerphone blinking to signal a message. He seldom remembered to switch it on – if someone really wanted him, they could let it ring for long enough to switch it on themselves.

"Hello…? Max, it's me, Molly. Can you call me when you get in please dear?" …Pause… "Thank you."

Max thought it strange. He couldn't remember the last time, if ever, his aunt had left a message on his phone. Was it his imagination or did she sound upset? He tapped two keys and listened to the chirrup of bleeps auto-dialling. He felt uncomfortable, as if he was going to hear bad news.

Telephoning Molly still reminded him of some of the anguished calls over recent months, as Dennis's health faltered in harmony with his finances.

"Hello?"

"Mo – hi love, it's me, Max. I got your message – you okay?"

"Yes, I'm fine…It's so good of you to call." But she couldn't go on. She tried to contain her tears, then gave up and they poured out in uncontrollable sobs.

"Molly..." Max wanted to console her, but couldn't think of anything to say. "Molly, come on…what's up?"
Molly calmed herself enough to speak again. "I'm so sorry, Max. I'm all right now," she said with little conviction.

"I'll come over. I can be there in about an hour."

"No, no, no." Molly had renewed vigour. "Not tonight... but…can you come tomorrow? Please."

"Tomorrow?"
A pause. Molly broke the silence.

"I'm sorry, I shouldn't ask – I'm sure you must be very busy at work."

"No, it's okay. I'll be there. You sure I shouldn't come over tonight?"

"Yes, really. As long as you're here by about nine in the morning. I'm sorry - I wouldn't ask, but…."

"I'll be there," Max interrupted. "But you're worrying me, Mo. You sure you're okay now?"

"I'm certain. I'll explain everything in the morning... Goodnight now."

"Goodnight."
Max replaced the receiver slowly. He felt anxious and considered phoning straight back to insist that he went over tonight, but then his attention returned to Dennis's CDs. He

33

began to load one of them into his computer, mechanically tapping the keys with little enthusiasm until the now-familiar menu appeared. Immediately, Max sensed himself being drawn into its grasp once more. He began to step through different strands of the program slowly to register exactly what was there. It was evident that much of the content was collected from company sources. Dennis had accumulated a mass of information on the bank that would have been generated when they were working on the installation three years earlier. But there too was a mass of new information, some of it in such detail that Max was shocked at the amount of time and effort Dennis must have spent working on it in secret. And it was so logical. As Max moved through the program, it seemed that Dennis had considered every possible detail. All the questions that had come to Max during the day, were answered.

Max had assumed that the key on the notepaper was to open Jack Briggs's deposit box. So he had questioned why the cloak-and-dagger dramatics were necessary when all he had to do was to pretend to be Jack Briggs and walk in and empty the box. But it was not to be so easy. The key opened Dennis's box in the same vault, which contained an elaborate sniffer system that was monitoring all computer data within the building. Dennis had installed a transmitter in the bank's own security system that the sniffer in the vaults was reading every minute of the day. With that data loaded into Max's computer, combined with the programs on the CD, Max would be able to take total control of the bank's security system and move around as he wanted within the building. A dummy program on one of the CDs allowed Max to simulate a dry run, step by step through the process, from a forced access point on the roof, all the way to the bank vault and out to a secure loading bay. Max was conscious that this was unreal. It had all the character of a computer game with the same ability to transfix a player in its hypnotic grip. He knew that it wasn't a game, but still Max was hooked. He played it and won. It took him a little over fifteen minutes from breaking into the bank from the roof, to driving through Manhattan with his £2,000,000 diamond collection in the back of the van.

Max stood up, walked across his kitchen and took a yoghurt from the fridge. He hardly diverted his attention from the screen that he had returned to the original menu of icons. His eye went to a collection of graphic tablets labelled 'image', 'personnel' and 'fence'. He clicked on the first.

"You're going to have to change your image, Max!" Max spluttered on a spoonful of yoghurt as Dennis appeared on the screen and spoke straight to him.

"You've got to access the sniffer that you will find in my deposit box. But…well, frankly Max, you will arouse too much attention if you turn up…well, not looking smarter than usual. You've got to play the role of a Brit with a deposit box in a Manhattan bank, so look like it and act like it. That means a shave and some smart clothes…Oh yes - and best lose the earrings."

Dennis immediately disappeared from view, his image replaced by two look-alike impressions of Max in his new persona. His mug shot had been retouched with shorter hair and no beard. Beside it, a full-length view of Max in a blazer, polo neck jumper and slacks. A caption identified it as *MK 2 Max*. He could not have stretched his eyes wider open, as he stared at the screen in bemused amazement.

"Good grief, Dennis. We can do better than that – I look like Roger Moore."

He finished his yoghurt quickly and clicked on the 'Crew' icon that brought up a line of four mug shots. Max clicked the mouse on one and a file of information on 'Bo Garrick' replaced the other mug shots. He scrolled quickly through Mr Garrick's CV. It gave all vital details – background, specialist skills, personal statistics and contact phone numbers. It also profiled him as someone with an inclination to kill anybody who crossed him in the past, resulting in a prison record in two American States. Max wondered how Dennis knew such a character and how he could be so certain that Mr Garrick could be trusted, but the program gave no clues. Max opened the other files on Gus *The Bus* Cleveland, Sammy Samms and Michael Gavini. A mixed bunch of which Bo Garrick was team-leader and thus, Max's point of contact. Max returned to his details and read them carefully. He looked at his watch – it would be early afternoon in New York. Max reached across to his telephone and pulled it close to the screen. He wanted to try dialling Bo Garrick's phone number to prove that he existed. It would be further proof that this was all for real. Max pondered for a while, then suddenly began to tap out Bo Garrick's home phone number. A few seconds, a few rings and an answerphone gave an abrupt response in a slovenly New York drawl, but didn't give his name. Max hung up, sensing a relief that he didn't have to explain the reason for the call.

'So the number's real enough - and that may have been Bo Garrick,' Max thought to himself.

He leaned back in his chair and swivelled it to his thinking position that enabled him to put his feet up on the desk and stare out of his window, past the street lamp, between the buildings to the underground station. He sat almost motionless for a full ten minutes replaying everything through his head, then thinking through the entire process of the bank raid, step-by-step with military precision. It all *seemed* to work, almost too easily. Dennis had been so thorough with the parts of the program that Max could check that he had to assume that the rest would be just as reliable. But Max knew there would be only one way to prove it. Perhaps, with more preparation and planning, more checks on the gang in New York, maybe he could go over and do his own recce in a few weeks, depending on his workload at BSS.

FIVE

Sleet was driving at forty five degrees into the entrance of Wimbledon station as Max emerged just after nine o'clock the next morning. Two number ninety-three buses, that he needed to get to Molly's house, were pulling away in procession from the lights across the station car park and, not surprisingly on such a foul morning, the taxi rank was empty. Nothing for it - he scraped his hair back into a ponytail and hunted in his pockets for a band, but instead found a scarf that he tied around his forehead as a bandana, then turned up the collar of his trench coat and set off on foot.

He arrived at the elegant mock-Tudor house close to Wimbledon Common some twenty minutes later and was grateful for the shelter of the porch as he rang the bell then unwrapped his coat that had taken on much of its own weight in rain water. In the house, Jasper, Molly's cocker-spaniel, began to bark at the door.

"It's all right Jasper…It's me…Good boy." But nothing changed. Jasper continued to bark, but Molly didn't arrive to let Max in. Max waited for several minutes in case she was in the bathroom. When nothing happened, he rang the bell again then pushed open the letterbox to see Jasper in the otherwise empty hallway. He called:

"Molly, it's Max!… Molly, you there?" Still she didn't appear. Jasper had calmed down a little, but Max sensed he was agitated and that added to Max's concerns.

'*She must be in, she knows I'm coming,*' Max thought to himself. He wrapped his coat around him again then dodged out of the porch and made his way around the side of the house, peering through the rain-drenched windows for any sign of his aunt. This set Jasper off again as he tracked Max's path from inside the house, scampering from room to room barking constantly. The poor light outside made it more difficult for Max to see into the kitchen and dining rooms which were both in darkness.

'*She hasn't been up yet – she must still be in bed*,' Max reasoned. '*But why? She must know I'm here, with all this noise.*' The realisation suddenly panicked Max. He must get into the house, now. Perhaps the patio doors would be open at the back – or maybe a window. The rain began to drive with new ferocity as he tackled the high gate at the side of the house that was always kept bolted from the garden side. His heavy, wet coat made the task of jumping to grasp the lintel nearly as difficult as the effort needed to drag himself up the flush face of the wooden door. As he sat for a moment on the top to catch his breath, he was unaware of the twitching bedroom curtain in the neighbouring house and only vaguely aware of an approaching police car with its siren wailing. Max was too focussed on the challenge of getting into the house to pay it more attention. As he pulled his leg over the lintel and dropped to the ground the other side, the small police car skidded to a halt at the entrance to the drive. The driver had seen the briefest movement of Max, but it was enough to fire the two officers into action in pursuit.

Max was systematically trying all the doors and windows that he could reach at the back of the house as the two policemen began to tackle the barrier of the locked gate. Still oblivious of their presence, Max had seen a first-floor window ajar and was considering his ability to climb a drainpipe against the speed of smashing a ground floor window.

One of the policemen was over the gate and wriggling the two bolts to open it for his partner to follow as Max kicked a brick loose from the path and wrapped it in his sodden sleeve to protect his hand. He was about to launch it at the glass beside the lock of the patio door as the two policemen rounded the corner of the building, causing Max to jump back with surprise.

"Hold it right there!" the younger officer ordered. Max had already frozen his swing.

"You're under arrest!" the older policeman added. Then, to Max's increasing astonishment, they began to remove riot batons as if expecting a confrontation.

"This is my aunt's house," Max tried to explain in a tone that should have conveyed his surprise at their aggression. "I think she's ill – I've got to get in," he added.

"Oh yeah, you can prove that can you?"

"Prove what – that my aunt's ill?"

"Identification – you got some identification," the younger officer chipped in.

Max considered the request for long enough to realise that he had nothing on him.

"Nope," he replied; then immediately swung the brick that he still gripped in his soaking wet sleeve. The first blow rebounded from the glass, leaving only a cracked scar, but instantly, Max swung it again with increased effort. The brick hit the same mark a second time and the glass cascaded onto the conservatory floor as a million little fingernails, sending Jasper scurrying away, yelping with fear. It coincided with the full weight of the younger policeman hitting Max so hard in a flying tackle, that the pair left the ground momentarily then hit it again locked together with Max breaking their fall. It knocked all the wind from his body, but not before Max had landed a defensive blow with his elbow that made firm contact with the policeman's cheek.

"Aargh – you bastard." The policeman yelped, recoiled for an instant then threw himself forward onto his forearm that was now pinning Max's head to the ground. The second policeman arrived and added his weight by kneeling on Max's neck.

"You're under arrest you fucking Hippie!" the younger officer shouted as he scrambled to fit handcuffs and began reciting Max's rights. "You don't have to say anything, but..." Max's anger was fuelled by frustration.

"For fuck's sake," he tried to yell. "Don't be stupid." Max could hardly speak or breathe with the weight of the two men pinning him to the patio slabs that were awash with puddles of rainwater. "Do you idiots really think I'd break into a house with you here if there wasn't a good reason? You've got to let me go. I've got to find my aunt."

The younger officer was more concerned about a trickle of blood that the rain was washing down his cheek as the other was searching Max's pockets. But now, Jasper returned to the scene and ventured out to join the fun. At first, he ran around the group barking with such effort that his body vibrated. Then, after the first flush of cautious excitement, he calmed down and ran up to Max to lick his face.

"Hi Jasper – good boy," Max managed to say whilst flinching from the dog's saliva and bad breath. This had more effect on the police than all Max's protestations.

"Come on, get up," the elder officer ordered. They pulled Max to his feet. "What's your name?"

"Max Duncan. My aunt who lives here is Molly Buchanan. This is her dog, Jasper."

"Can you prove *any* of this?"

"Oh for God's sake…," Max sighed with exasperation. "Look, if you won't let me go, then one of you go and look for her. I think she must still be in bed. It's the door facing the top of the stairs." The policemen were clearly considering the suggestion. "For God's sake – go on will you? Or let me go."

"I'll go – you keep him here," the elder officer instructed his junior.

"Wipe your feet on the mat and don't drip water everywhere," Max ordered. Then, to his surprise, the officer did shake water off his jacket and wiped his feet after crunching through the pile of shattered glass.

Less than two minutes later and he returned. Max could see immediately that something was wrong.

"Get the cuffs off him Dean," he ordered, then to Max: "Sorry sir, she's… she's in a poor way. I've called an ambulance, it's on its way."

"She's alive?" Max was distraught and fighting to free his hands of the cuffs.

"Oh yes, but she's barely conscious."

Max discarded the handcuffs the moment they were released and raced into the house, dropping his coat inside the door and wiping his feet briefly on the mat.

Upstairs, Max entered Molly's bedroom cautiously, almost reverently, not knowing what he would find as he pushed the door open. To his relief, Molly tried to turn to him, but she was so weak that she fell back into the pillow.

"Molly, it's Max. Come on Mo, talk to me, Mo." Max had no idea what was best for his aunt at this moment, but he sensed that he shouldn't let her slip back into sleep.

"Mo. Come on Mo," he urged. He sat on the bed looking at her pasty pale face and rubbing her frail hand. She looked so distant. Beside the bed, Max noticed a small brown bottle of medicine with its lid beside it. He picked it up to check the label then realised that the bottle contained pills, but the label showed a name that meant nothing to Max. It was half full.

"What are these, Mo? Have you taken these?"

"Sleeping pills," she managed to say slowly, with evident effort.

The doorbell rang downstairs and Max heard the policeman open the door to, what he assumed to be, the ambulance team. But it was the elder policeman's head that appeared above the top stair to call Max away from the bed.

"What's happening? Where's the medics?" Max asked.

"I think you better come down, it's someone asking for your uncle, I think."

A stocky skinhead in his late twenties with a thick neck and thicker East London accent, was standing at the door.

"Can I help?" Max asked.

"You Dennis Buchanan?" the skinhead asked after checking the name from some sheets of A4 paper on a clipboard.

"No. He *was* my uncle. Who are you – why d'you want him?"

The skinhead readjusted his shirt collar with a shrug, looked slightly awkward and flashing a glance at the two policemen hovering in the background.

"I think you better read this 'cos I've got to collect money or goods to cover this." He handed Max the top sheet of paper – a standard official document from 'North London County Court', with a number of details overtyped. Max had never seen such a document but didn't take long to register that the court was giving a company called T.A.V. Tronics the right to *repossess goods or property to the value of £4,243-78 including court costs'.* The goods appeared to be some specialist computer equipment.

"Look, there must be a mistake, my uncle would buy stuff like this through his company. You better go and check your facts. Get back to me later, okay?"

The skinhead smirked in response.

"I don't think so pal, this is *later*. This is collection time. The money – that's cash or bank draft – or goods to the value. End of. Simple as that."

"Not now. I'll sort it out, but not now."

"Yes, now!"

Max's attention was diverted over the skinhead's shoulder.

"What the hell's that? Is that yours?" He was looking at a box van reversing down the drive.

"Yeah," replied skinhead.

"Well get it out of here, there's an ambulance on its way that'll need to get in. Go on get out of here. Leave me your card or something. I've told you I'll deal with it later."

"And I told you I can't do that, pal."

"Don't '*pal*' me. I don't need this right now. Go on, fuck off." Max could feel his anger welling up. He knew this was a danger sign and tried to close the skinhead out, to put some distance between himself and this irritating man on his aunt's doorstep. But as he tried to shut the door, Skinhead put out his arm to keep it open. This was too much for Max. He reached through the gap and grabbed a large ring in the man's right earlobe and twisted it fiercely. The skinhead yelped with the pain and shock then immediately removed his hand from the door to pull Max's hand free. But Max was too quick for him. He put his foot into Skinheads chest and kicked him off the step then slammed the door closed. Max had moved so quickly that neither of the two policemen could react fast enough to prevent it. Now they were on Max as he turned from the door, each gripping one of his arms to restrain any further outburst. Their movement to Max set off Jasper who growled then began to bark at the group. Behind Max, Skinhead began banging on the door then shouting through the letterbox. The elder policeman took Max into the kitchen as the younger one pacified Skinhead and told him to wait in the truck while they sorted things out.

"I wanna charge him. Fucking assault - you tell him - you was a witness - I'm fucking serious - you tell him," Skinhead complained vehemently.

In the kitchen, the older officer calmed Max down enough to explain the stark facts to him. As a bailiff with a County Court Order, Skinhead had the legal right to demand payment or to repossess enough of Dennis's possessions to cover the debt. He checked the details on the paper and pointed out that the original invoice was nearly eighteen months old.

"Not a good day for you sir," the younger officer stated as he joined them. "One assault charge and one for resisting arrest before ten o'clock. Good going that."

Max barely restrained himself from a burst of expletives. The elder officer was more supportive, told his subordinate to wait in the car then explained to Max very calmly that he couldn't stop the bailiffs from carrying out their task except by paying off the debt right now. He then explained that he had to file a report and needed Max's full details, which he wrote slowly into a notebook. "You'll probably get off with a warning on the 'resisting arrest' charge," he explained.

Max couldn't believe this.

"And what about your assault on me? You and your mate attacked me without provocation, remember?"

45

"Of course you're at liberty to make an official complaint, sir," the officer stated as he closed his notebook. "But don't you think you've got enough on your plate at the moment?"

During the next half an hour, Max moved through the motions of clearing up the mess that surrounded him at the house. By the time the ambulance arrived, Molly was starting to brighten up noticeably. She was reluctant to leave but Max insisted, with the added assurance that he'd visit her in hospital this afternoon. He then negotiated with Skinhead's boss by phone to give him a couple of hours to get the money, during which time the truck and its two occupants would stay on the drive as a threat if Max failed. Then Max called an emergency glazier to repair the smashed patio window.

Max's lifestyle was cheap to run, but then he had never earned much money to support it. Arranging the banker's draft for £4,243-78 cleared out his current account and tipped it a little into the red. He wasn't unduly worried as he assumed it would be a temporary situation, reimbursed by Molly as soon as this misunderstanding was sorted out.

He was back at the house ten minutes before his deadline to pay off Skinhead who threatened that Max "*hadn't heard the last of this*" as he signed a receipt then spun the truck wheels on the gravel drive for additional affect.

Max arrived at St George's Hospital just after three o'clock – later than he'd intended, thanks to the emergency glazier – but he found Molly's ward with comparative ease in the sprawling complex. Sister McMahan was in charge and was pleased to report that Molly was recovering well from what appeared to be an accidental overdose of sleeping pills.

"Not serious," she explained. "In fact there was no need to get her into hospital – she had virtually made a full recovery before she arrived. But I think your aunt has learned her lesson." Then she added: "The sleeping pills haven't done any harm, but did you know that your aunt has very high blood pressure - alarmingly high?"

"No idea," Max replied. "Is it serious?" He was concerned.

"Hopefully not, but we should keep her in overnight to monitor it, then we'll pass on a full report to her GP. He, or she, will decide on the best course for her."

"Thank you. Does she know about this?"

"Only that we're keeping her in to check her full recovery."

"Thank you."

Molly certainly seemed to have fully recovered as she greeted Max in her little gloss-painted room. She was full of remorse and kept apologising to Max for her stupidity.

"You know you frightened me this morning, Mo," Max stated.

"I know. I know. I'm so sorry, I forgot how many pills I'd taken. They don't work as well as they used to."

"How long have you been taking sleeping pills?"

"Since Dennis's last relapse - a few weeks, I think."
Max blew air through his teeth and thought about the situation.

"You've got to promise me that you'll stop taking them now or I'll worry that it could happen again."

"I'll try," she said with little conviction. "But I'm not sure I can sleep without them now. I promise I won't be so stupid again, though."

"You know those people at the house this morning had come to collect some money that Dennis owed? You knew they were coming didn't you? Why didn't you tell us – even last night you could have told me – why Mo?"

Molly shrugged.

"Don't shout at me Max, you don't know how difficult this is for me." She was fighting back the tears again. Max slid along the bed and hugged her.

"I know – I'm sorry. But you've been worrying about it so much that you can't sleep. All I'm saying is that I wish you'd told Sam or me about it before. We'd have sorted it out for you. It wasn't such a big debt – certainly not worth making yourself ill for."

From Molly's reaction to this, he sensed he was going to hear bad news. Molly didn't reply immediately. She was considering how to tell Max the next bit.

"I wish it was quite that simple." She false smiled wearily.

"What do you mean?"

"That's not the only debt. If only it was. I had no idea when Dennis was alive – he always kept the problems from me – he never brought them home from work - old fashioned, I suppose. Of course I knew things were really bad when he sold the villa, then the glider and his Bentleys, but I never really knew the full extent and that was a long time ago now. But since he died, I've been sorting through his affairs and opening his post." Molly had to hold back tears again before she continued. "It's very serious, Max. I had no idea and this is just from the first few days. I dread what I'll find or what will arrive at every post. I've found so many statements for old bills, reminders, solicitors' letters – even court orders for debts that go back years, some of them.

"I paid some already and have started to agree time to pay others, but my income now is so small that it takes a long time and some people don't want to wait."

"And you knew that they were sending the bailiffs today?" Max asked.

Molly nodded her reply as she fought to hold back tears, then gave up and sobbed aloud.

"I'm so sorry that you had to sort it out."

"You should have let us do it before, Mo. You know that don't you?"

"It's not your problem or Samantha's. I've got to do it myself."

"No you haven't. How much more do you think there is to pay?"

Again Molly considered her answer – she thought about lying, but wanted to tell someone at long last.

"So far, from what I've pieced together, the total is over £90,000."

Max drew in his breath as he rubbed his eyes.

"Ninety thousand! And there's no money to cover it?" Molly shook her head. "What are you living on? Dennis must have a pension, what about his investments?" But Max knew the answer as he asked the question.

"He cashed everything in to sort out the problems years ago – even his pension. Buchanan's now gives me £200 a week. But it won't pay the old debts."

"Molly, you know that I'm not the person to advise you about money - you need to speak to an accountant – how about Sally Longada at Buchanan's?"

"Oh no, I'd be too embarrassed."

"Well we'll find someone, but you know they might say you've got to sell the house."

"I know that'll sort it out," Molly said with apparent certainty.

"You do?" Max was surprised.

49

"Oh yes – that would raise more than enough to pay the debts and buy a little flat here in Wimbledon after all the debts are paid off."

Max was sensitive about asking:

"So…why haven't you done it before, Mo - or mortgaged the house? It would end all this grief."

"When his heart problems were diagnosed, it changed Dennis's attitude about a lot of things - not surprisingly I suppose - and he began to confide in me more when he knew that time was running out." She wiped her eyes with a tissue. "He told me a bit about the problems and I suggested we could sell The Gables but he wouldn't hear of it. In retrospect, I think we should have mortgaged then to pay off everything. I don't know why Dennis was so against that or the sale, now I know the scale of the problems, it makes no sense. But some months before he went into the real decline, Dennis told me he was working on a project that would sort out all our problems for once and for all. He was sure it would make a lot of money. He never told me more about it and I didn't ask so I guess he couldn't finish it. But, well, I was just hoping there was something in his will that would shed some light. Some hope – grasping at straws I suppose. But there was nothing, as we now know."

"Hence the sleeping pills." Max suggested.

"Yes," Molly nodded despondently.

Max had agreed to spend the night at Molly's house to look after Jasper until Samantha brought her mother home from hospital in the morning. He sat in the kitchen with a cup of tea and few distractions for his thoughts as the chimes from the grandfather clock in the hall slowly signalled five o'clock. He ought to phone the office before everyone left, to explain his absence all day. He walked through to the phone in the hallway and dialled Buchanan's number by the light from the kitchen. Max was exhausted and didn't want a long conversation, so he asked the receptionist to pass a message to Jim Wandle that he'd be in tomorrow afternoon once his aunt was home, in case his MD wanted to reschedule the meeting they missed today. Max then asked to be put through to his department to collect any messages. A colleague, Ari Sumeer, answered and reported that Jim Wandle had been tutting all day that Max wasn't in and no-one knew where he was. Then Ari ran through a short list of unimportant messages, until he mentioned the name 'Garrick'.

"<u>Bo</u> Garrick?" Max asked with a start as soon as he registered the name.

"I'm not sure – he just called himself 'Garrick' – and said to tell you he'd called, when I said you weren't here."

"An American, right?"

"Yeah."

"But he didn't leave a number?"

"No, sorry."

"Okay, thanks Ari – I'll see you tomorrow."

Max's exhaustion had vanished. He had only thought about the CD fleetingly all day when Molly mentioned Dennis's plan to settle their debts. Max had instantly realised that Dennis must have been referring to the CD program and the bank heist. Now Max was totally focussed on it again. New questions flashed through his thoughts – how did Bo Garrick know Max? How did he have his phone number? Dennis must have briefed him before he died. But why was he calling? Was there some problem?

The more Max thought about the call, the more he became frustrated that he didn't have Bo Garrick's phone number with him. The CD was hidden back at his flat, but that was less than an hour away - a two hour round trip.

He was back at his flat before seven o'clock which would be the afternoon in New York. Max had the information on his screen in minutes of walking through the front door and immediately started dialling Bo Garrick's home number that he had called previously, only to get the same recorded message. He started again, this time dialling the mobile number. It rang three times.

"Yeah." The voice was the same as the answerphone.

"Err...hi, who's that?" Max asked.

"Who's you?"

"Is that Bo Garrick?"

"Who is that?"

"My name's Max Duncan – you called me in London."

"Hold on – I can't hear." There was a pause. "What you say you're called – 'London'?"

"No, Max Duncan," he shouted. "You called me. I'm in London."

"Right." Sudden recognition from Bo Garrick and relief for Max who was beginning to doubt he had the right contact. "You at your office?"

"No, I'm at home."

"I'll call you back in ten minutes – I got all your numbers."

Max replaced the phone slowly then stepped away from his computer. He began the mechanical routine of making a cup of tea. It was the most ordinary thing he could think to do in this bizarre situation, but his mind was locked into the conversation he was about to have with a thug called Bo Garrick about the prospects of robbing a bank in New York.

The telephone didn't ring for nearly twenty minutes. When it did, Max physically jumped in his seat.

"Hello?"

"Who's that?"

"Max Duncan."

"Okay kid, so what's the plan? When you coming?"

"I don't know...I've only just received...er...the instructions from Dennis. You know Dennis is dead, do you?"

"Yeah, course. Tragic – good man. So what you gonna do then?"

"I'm not sure yet. I've got some problems here right now. I thought I might come over nearer the end of the year."

"End of the year? I don't think so."

"Why not?"

There was a pause.

"What d'ya get from Dennis?" Bo Garrick asked.

"Err... Instructions – for repossessing some property in New York," Max replied cautiously.

"Well, in your *instructions* didn't Dennis tell you that we've got till the end of August to repossess the goods?"

"No, why?"

"I dunno why – you're the brains sonny boy. You got the *instructions*. I was just told to expect this to happen before September or it couldn't happen. I think you better re-read your *instructions* then get back to me. And don't call my house, use the cell phone – leave a message if you have to an' I'll get back to you. Take my advice and get your ass in gear – these things take time to set up and it's running out – right?"

"Yes, right." Click...brrr. He was gone.

Max was left in his own little world with his computer screen and his muddled thoughts. Why the September deadline? Not the Millennium Bug this time. A few taps to find 'Schedule' in the menu. He clicked it open and read: 'DEADLINE: 31st August 1999'. The explanation was there and it came down to battery power that could only be reliable until the end of August. After that, the system was on borrowed time and some of the computer functions would be adversely affected by lower power.

"Bugger," Max murmured to himself.

SIX

Max wasn't familiar with six o'clock in the morning on a normal working mid-week day, so registering it on the alarm clock in Molly's guest room took a few moments, by which time his brain had begun to fill with the thoughts that had made him restless all night. He re-arranged his body to stare at the ceiling and began to replay the entire scenario of the CDs, Molly's revelations, his worries about her future and the conversation with Bo Garrick. As barking mad as Dennis's plan appeared, Max had to admit that he seemed to have thought of every angle. Dennis would. That was his way, but then, he'd never planned, let alone pulled off a bank heist in the past. Pause for much more thought.

Max got up before seven and had finished a frugal breakfast by half past. As eight o'clock chimed on some distant church clock, Max and Jasper were striding out across Wimbledon Common, enjoying each other's company and a beautiful, clear crisp morning. From the top of the hill near the windmill, Max tried to calculate how far he could see – twelve, fifteen miles perhaps. London seemed so far away from here – he felt like an observer, uninvolved with the lives and bustle and claustrophobia of the city over there. Max pulled the tail of his coat under his bottom and sat on the summit as Jasper snuffled along last night's rabbit trails with his stubby tail revolving like a propeller. This was the perfect antidote for Max's worries. He sensed that it was a precious moment that would end soon, but for the few minutes that he could sit on his hill, removed from the reality that faced him as soon as he returned to the house, to work, to contact with the rest of the world, Max was at peace. He breathed in the fresh air and a fresh sense of well-being. And with it, his perspective cleared and he began to shuffle his thoughts into a priority list. He surprised himself at how easy it suddenly became to rationalise everything that had been in such a muddle just an hour ago. His choices now seemed simple - help Molly to sell her house and clear her debts, then carry on his life as if he had never received Dennis's CDs - as if they had never existed; or go to New York, meet up with Bo Garrick, check out Dennis's equipment and see where that leads him. *If* everything went to Dennis's plan, he would have the resources to solve Molly's problems at a stroke and make himself very wealthy into the bargain. But it was a big *if*. Even if he got away with it, he would still have committed a major crime, but if he didn't… Max stopped himself thinking about such an outcome with the assurance to himself that he wouldn't attempt it if he was not convinced that the plan was absolutely water tight. More immediate obstacles were Max's workload at Buchannan's and his lack of funds to pay for the trip. He now knew that Molly was not about to reimburse him for the money he had paid to the bailiff and Max was not about to ask her to. His coffers were empty and anyway would not have covered the cost of everything in Dennis's plans. Then there was the time he would need to take off work. Even for the recce, to visit the bank to test the equipment and to meet Bo Garrick, would take the best part of a week away from Buchannan's. Max knew he couldn't, or shouldn't, afford to take it. He was at a vital point in the development of a new product that the company needed to start selling as soon as possible. Their first mass-market product for the automotive industry that could change the fortunes of the company overnight. It was Max's project that would stop if he was not at Buchannan's to supervise it; and slippage in the schedule even of one week could jeopardise some big potential orders.

Despite the strength of the arguments that Max was finding *not* to get involved, he became conscious that two thoughts kept re-emerging as he reordered his choices like the tiles in a Chinese puzzle. The first was inspired directly by Dennis, who, in a moment of frustration once quoted a line from the film, One Flew Over The Cuckoo's Nest, that had apparently made a deep impression on him when he first saw it. Max had never seen the film but Dennis described how the hero's fight against complacency throughout the story was summarised towards the end when he loses a bet to pick up a slab of stone, but taunts his onlookers with: "Well at least I tried!" It became a standing maxim for Max and his uncle who would quote the line whenever they tried something new or inventive at work that ultimately failed. Now the expression took on a new poignancy in Max's considerations. And that led to the second thought that kept bugging Max, *'Could I live with myself if I don't give it a try?'*

"Right!" he eventually shouted to the sky and Jasper and himself as he stood with a rejuvenated energy.

"Let's go!"

At three-thirty, Max knocked on the door to his MD's office.

"Come in... take a seat, please." Jim Wandle was signing some papers, but Max recognised the frosty response that he had expected. Jim finished with his papers, pushed them aside and retrieved a file from a drawer which he opened.

"I got your message this morning so I know why you were away yesterday, but it would've been a politeness at least, to let us know earlier."

"Yes, I'm sorry."

"Right. Well now we have some things to sort out - have you considered my reduced pay and benefits package?" Max hadn't given it a moment's thought since he left this office two days ago. He tried to recall the contents and remembered that they still offered a considerable improvement on his existing pay.

"Yeah," he found himself lying.

"And?"

"That's cool." Max shrugged.

"Good…very good. I'll get that sorted for the end of the month. Well that's a good start, because as I indicated Max, we need to work together on a few things to improve the systems here." He averted his gaze from Max across the desk, his eyes moving first to the view from his window, then to the papers in front of him.

"I'm sure you know that money is very tight. Our backers are putting considerable pressure on us and…well, we have to begin making a profit very soon if we're going to survive. I've been looking at all our procedures throughout the company, so don't think I'm singling you out. But, well, R and D has always got too big a share of our cake. Last year it was over six per cent of turnover. I know Dennis's philosophy was that our systems had to be leading edge – but, well, I can't agree. We've got to sell what we've got first and we've already got some excellent systems. So, from now on we're only going to fund research and development work from earned profits." He stared at Max for a reaction. "Do you understand what I am saying?"

"No, not exactly," Max hesitated.

"What I'm saying Max, is that I'm putting all R and D work on hold."

"From when?" Max asked abruptly.

"From now. We have to consolidate…for the immediate future."

Max was incredulous.

"Are you joking? What about Podium? That's six month's work. You're just going to scrap it?"

"We'll park it up until we've got the resources. Until we make the profits to re-invest."

"How long's that?"

"I don't know – but I'd guess six months, minimum."

"Six months? You think we can just pick up where we left off after six months? What about the Ford and GM contracts?"

"Yes, what about them?" He pulled a copy of The Financial Times from his briefcase as he spoke, then turned it to Max. "We don't have any contracts yet, but apparently Adlime Systems do. Ford have announced today that they're installing the Adlime system in all their top-end models." Max only glanced at the small paragraph that Jim had pointed out on a folded page of the newspaper.

"So what about GM – or the rest of the car and truck manufacturers? You're bottling out because of one announcement by one possible customer."

"No Max. I knew this was coming at the start of the week so I've been speaking to the rest of our potential customers for Podium - *when* we can deliver it. Within two months we'll have missed the boat. And your best estimate is four, perhaps five, with a following wind – and we both know that's optimistic. The Ford announcement will rush the other big boys into following suit – they'll have to. And we don't have anything to offer them right now. So, I'm going to cut our losses on Podium as it is and rethink it for the after-sales market, but not until we can afford it. It's not cancelled, it's postponed."

Max couldn't think of anything to suggest.

"What do I do meanwhile?"

"You'll have to handle installations – you've done it before."

"Yeah, when I was training-up someone on one of my new systems – I'm not an engineer."

"No, believe me, I'd rather you never went near a client." Max thought about his remark for a moment, uncertain how he should take it.

"I beg your pardon?"

"Well, look at you, Max. Do you really think you represent this company properly on-site - when you meet clients? I don't think your appearance is acceptable for a technician; even less so, now you're supposed to be management. You're going to have to smarten up."

Max stared at his MD for several seconds.

"Any more air you want to clear?"

"Yeah, actually there is, since you ask – your time-keeping sets a bad example as head of department. Look what happened yesterday, not even a phone call till the end of the day. From now on I want you here by 08.30 in the morning with the rest of your staff, not at whatever time you care to drift in."

Another pause.

"So what you're really saying is that '*you're in charge now – Dennis no longer has any influence – that you want things to change – you want me out*'. Right?"

"No Max - well not entirely – three out of four perhaps. I don't want you out, as long as you sharpen up, smarten up and… well, help me – do things my way. You could be a great asset to this company and I think you will be when we get things in better shape. For Podium when it happens and other plans I've got in mind when finances allow. But now I need you to come with me on this." He stared at Max waiting for a reaction.

"I might want to take a holiday. I've got time owing – any problems with that?"

Jim was surprised at the abrupt change of subject.

"No, no problem – probably a good idea. You look tired. Will give you time to reflect on the situation. When do you want to go?"

"Soon."

"Okay."

"And, if I do, I'd like an advance on my salary please?"

"Shouldn't be a problem, it's the end of the month in two weeks – can you wait that long?"

"No, I meant a few grand in advance – ten perhaps."

Jim frowned. "Ten grand? That's quite a holiday. You are joking?"

"No."

"Max, have you been listening to me. The whole point of this conversation is to try and impress on you how tight our finances are. Have you the vaguest idea about cash flow? You must realise that we are not selling many of our bigger systems at the moment, so where do you think our money comes from? I'll tell you – it comes from Inter-Finance who is bankrolling us. And they're getting very twitchy about the one-way street that is our cash flow – it's all going out and too little's coming in. So I have to cut our outgoings."

"Do I take that as a 'no'?" Max asked.

"You do." Then, after a moment's silence, Jim softened the blow. "I think we owe you something for the mess up in Hong Kong, so I'll advance you this month's salary to help you out – and at your new higher rate, but that's my best offer. Max considered the situation for a moment.

"Thanks......Was there anything else?"

"No, Max – I think that's it for now. Can you let Julie know the dates you will be away as soon as possible? She'll put it in the system and let me know as and when."
Max stood up, carefully replaced his chair in front of Jim's desk.

"By the way, Molly's home from hospital – and she's okay, so I'm afraid she's still on the payroll. Thanks for asking after her, by the way." Max turned and left the room without waiting for a response that anyway was not forthcoming.

In the time it took him to walk back to his desk, Max had decided to go to New York. He spent the rest of the morning organising the trip, getting the advance on his month's pay from accounts, then hunting down the cheapest fares and equally frugal accommodation. Then he left a message on Bo Garrick's message service saying he'd be in New York on Friday night. Only at the last minute did he think to telephone the American Embassy to check that he didn't need an entry visa in his new passport.

By the end of the afternoon, he had put everything in place that could be organised from work and tidied up the loose ends in his department. At five-thirty he packed his bag, scribbled a note with his holiday dates, effective immediately, then dropped it onto the desk of Jim Wandle's secretary as he left the building.

SEVEN

'*New York, New York – so good they named it twice. We'll see.*' Max's mind wandered as he watched the raindrops racing to form deltas across the windows of the bus as it rumbled towards Manhattan from JFK Airport. He was tired and hung-over from the flight, so content to let his eyes drift in and out of focus between his reflection in the bus window and the lights of the city beyond, that twinkled in the blackness like a frogman's wetsuit in moonlight.

Max always remembered his arrivals in New York like this – late at night, raining, tired from the seven hour flight. He'd never needed to use public transport before, previously making the journey in a taxi paid by a client, but not on this trip. His funds, or lack of them, was just one of the problems that Max had grappled with during his flight. His thought processes at thirty-five thousand feet, aided by the view of a graduated blue void from his window seat and a steady flow of vodkas and tonic from an attentive stewardess, had alternated between a genuine excitement for the adventure ahead and the thought: '*what the hell am I doing here?*'

The flight had given Max more uninterrupted thinking time to consider what exactly he was about to do than he had so far managed in one sitting. That brought a list of new obstacles into his mind. The answers to some, Max felt certain, must be somewhere on the CD, but he dared not look into it on the plane with his nearest neighbour just inches from his left shoulder. Other concerns would be answered once he met Bo Garrick and had visited the bank. Max had come to realise that his time in the army had taught him a few valuable lessons for civilian life, of which, only formulating a plan once in possession of all available reconnaissance information and data, was one.

At 11.15 pm, Max stepped from a cruising gypsy cab that he'd used to complete the last mile of his journey to The Alamo Motel in Elmhurst. A grating across the door gave Max an anxious moment until he noticed a night bell beside it that offered hope of life the other side. He pressed it forcefully. Max didn't want to stand out in the rain with his rucksack and a shoulder bag advertising him as a visitor, for longer than necessary.

Suddenly the door behind the metal grating opened a few inches. Max adjusted his eye line down to a small girl who stared at him through the gap.

"You Mr Slatter?"

"Mr *Slater*, yes," Max replied, correcting her pronunciation of his new pseudonym. "Can I come in?"

"Please," the girl added as she disappeared for a moment. Max checked around him, considering what a bizarre scene this must be to any witness. But he was alone as he watched the grating lift on a motor, before the girl returned to hold the door wide for Max to enter.

"Thank you," he said distinctly to the girl who was already re-setting the defences.

"There's your key, your room's on the second floor, bathroom's next to the stairs. Breakfast's served in there from seven." She pointed through a door to a darkened room. "Now you must sign this book."

Max duly obeyed the order, bid the girl goodnight and made his way to his room without seeing evidence of another living soul in the building.

The next morning, Max was woken at some time before ten o'clock by a knock on the door and the voice of the same small girl that greeted him the night before, warning him that:

"Breakfast finishes in fifteen minutes!"

'*What is this place?*' Max thought as consciousness streamed into his head. '*This is weird. I'm staying in a hotel run single-handedly by a child of nine or ten!*' He thought for a moment. '*Perhaps she's a mature dwarf.*' But he dismissed the thought. '*Maybe this is what you should expect at one of the cheapest hotels in New York.*'

As Max became fully aware of his thoughts, he rolled onto his back to stare at the ceiling of his little room. '*Time to concentrate,*' he told himself, knowing that The Alamo Motel wasn't important in his plans. He should only be here for a few days before he either moves up town if the job is going ahead, or if it isn't, he'd be flying back to England. Even before he left London, Max had thought vaguely about the way in which he should conduct himself here in strange surroundings, with strange workmates and the strangest of projects ahead. On the plane he had convinced himself that the solution was to treat everything as close to a military exercise as possible. Precision-planning, absolute attention to detail and fitness. These were the disciplines he understood, that would give him the best chance of success – and survival. So that meant starting the day with breakfast for a change.

"Ah you must be Mr Slater," was the greeting as he walked into the little breakfast room. A lady in her late thirties, perhaps early forties, with a swarthy complexion and striking features, put down a tray of plates to shake Max's hand and show him to a table.

"Good morning, I'm Luisa. You slept well?"

"Fine, very well thanks." Max was quite taken aback by the warmth of the reception and somewhat reassured to know that there were adults in the hotel, although the two men at other tables chose to ignore him.

"You want coffee? We have pancakes or I can cook you eggs and ham. What would you like" Luisa offered.

"Just coffee please." Then Max remembered his resolution to eat better than his normal minuscule diet and added: "And the eggs and ham please. Thanks."
Luisa smiled, showing perfect white teeth, then gathered up her tray of plates and disappeared to the kitchen.

"You met my daughter Becky last night," Luisa volunteered when she arrived with the fried breakfast.

"She works long hours," Max said, before thinking it might be insensitive.

"She helps when she has to." Luisa's tone had changed slightly, a little edgy, Max thought, but he passed over it.

"This smells wonderful, thank you very much." Another smile and Luisa turned away to one of the other men demanding her attention.

Max wasn't comfortable using the payphone in the hotel to contact Bo Garrick, but didn't want to spend time walking the streets looking for one. So before returning to his room, Max made the call to Bo Garrick's mobile number where he only got to message service. He considered his options for a moment, then called the home number that he had been told

<u>not</u> to use –'but hell, this could take all day otherwise,' Max reasoned to himself.

"Ello!" Came the abrupt reply on the home number.

"Mr Garrick – I've been trying you on your cell phone – I'll try again." Max immediately hung up before hearing a response. He waited about a minute and dialled the mobile number again.

"Ello! Who's that?"

"Max Duncan."

"Okay, okay, where are you?"

"New York. One of the hotels you told me about - a motel in Queens."

"Okay, we need to meet. Where in Queens?"

"In Elmhurst – on a main drag into town."

"Queens Boulevard?"

"Yeah, that's it."

"Right, The Alamo, good - that's perfect. Make your way to a restaurant named Santini's near the Island Expressway intersection. You'll walk it in less than ten minutes. Ask for Sonny - tell him you're meeting me. I'll be there in forty-five minutes. Okay?"

Max checked his watch,

"That's fine. I'll see you there at eleven thirty. Oh, by the way – my name's Alex Slater, right?"

"Yeah, whatever."

"It's important – Alex Slater."

Santini's Restaurant was only notable by its anonymity. An unremarkable Italian restaurant in need of a makeover. Max arrived a few minutes early and checked it over from the other side of the main road before entering at the appointed time.

67

"Hi, I'm looking for Sonny," Max announced to the teenager laying a table by the door. The youth turned and waved an arm towards someone with his back to them behind a small bar.

"Hi, are you Sonny?" Max asked the back.

"Yeah." The man answered then turned and inspected Max over half glasses. "And you are…?"

"My name's Slater. Bo Garrick's meeting me here and told me to ask for you."

"Uhu. First I've heard of it," Sonny said as he turned away to continue with his chores. "You wanna coffee?" he asked.

"No thanks," Max replied as, behind him, another customer arrived. Sonny looked over his glasses to the door.

"Looks like your date's arrived," he said, then laughed. Max turned to the door to see the bulk of a large man silhouetted against the morning light outside. As the door shut, Max could make out the features of a clean-shaven fifty year old man beneath a black trilby hat which he removed to reveal short-cropped hair, a little greyer, Max thought, than the image on the CD. He wore a dark suit, white shirt and blue tie. This didn't fit the slovenly image Max had gained from their brief telephone conversations. Max was first to speak.

"Mr Garrick? Alex Slater." He held out his hand which was taken by the man's large paw.

"Hi, I'm glad to see you here," he responded, whilst quickly inspecting Max from head to foot, before turning his attention to Sonny. They passed a few greetings as old friends that hadn't seen one another for a while, then Bo announced:

"We need to use your room upstairs for some business, okay?"

"Sure. You want a beer or coffee?" Sonny offered.

"Coffee'd be nice," Bo replied.

Sonny busied up a filter coffee from a jug on the Gaggia then handed it to Bo who winked his thanks.

"Okay Mr...Slater, follow me." Bo set off across the restaurant and addressed Max over his shoulder. "You're not what I expected."

"Nor are you, sir." Max replied.

In the upstairs room, Max and Bo Garrick sat opposite one another at the end of a large dining table.

"So what you got for me? I wanna know everything - what you want and what's in it for me – shoot."
Max had prepared his presentation for this moment in his head and mentally adapted it to Bo's request.

"Before Dennis died, he'd been working on a plan to rob a bank's safe deposit vaults here in New York. It's First National Credit on 28th Street. Its existing security system was installed by Briggs-Buchanan a few years back. It was state-of-the-art at the time, but now, Dennis has produced some new programs that'll override the one in the bank. And that's what he's left me. To cut a long story short, I can get us into First National Credit Bank's vaults, any time we choose, by using Dennis's new programs." Bo Garrick made no response, so Max continued. "I'm only interested in the contents of one box that we'll open first once we're in the vault. You – you and your team - can have the rest. That's your payment. My plan is to do the raid over a weekend which should guarantee you enough time to open every one of the other boxes, if you want." Max stopped and waited for a reaction.

"Is that it?"

"In a nutshell, yes. But...um, I'm afraid there's a buy-in cost to you and the others to cover my overheads."

"How much?"

69

"$10,000 each," Max replied nervously. Bo only raised his eyebrows a little in response, suggesting that he carried such a sum around with him as small change.

"Okay, okay. Much as I understood from Dennis…all except the advance payment."

Max was surprised.

"What did he tell you?"

"That he had some device that could guarantee entry into a bank somewhere in Manhattan. I dunno which one and I didn't know it was safe deposit boxes he was after. Problem is you never know what you're gonna get 'til you're in, then everything has to be fenced. There's always a bit of cash, but the rest takes time to convert." Bo thought about his own remark for a moment. "Okay, okay – what proof you got that you can deliver?"

Max picked up his rucksack and pulled out his laptop computer. Bo watched with interest as Max set it up, dropped the CD in and used the unique password to open the program before stepping it through the preliminary procedures. Max moved straight to the walk-through animation of the bank, assuming that this would make the most impressive demonstration. Then he swung the laptop around to face Bo.

"Do you know how to operate something like this?" Max asked.

"No idea. What you showing me here?" Bo responded abruptly. "Why don't you show me, eh?"

Max realised that he'd embarrassed Bo who had no idea about computers and didn't appreciate having the weakness exposed.

"Sorry Mr Garrick, let me do that." Max got out of his seat and moved to the other side of the table to sit beside Bo, who was now putting on a pair of glasses with precise care.

Max changed his approach, realising that he would have to adopt a slower pace. He closed down the program and flicked the CD out of the small computer then held it for Bo to see.

"Dennis created all the information printed on two CDs like this. They're packed full of everything we need to gain access into the bank."

Bo tilted back his head and squinted at it through his glasses.

"Is that right?"

"Yeah - and it'll talk to a bit of equipment that Dennis has installed in the bank. Together, they'll get us in and out almost as easily as if we had keys."

"Is that right?"

Max dropped the first disc back into the tray and shut it into the laptop, then moved into the program.

"Look, this is the bank." Max began to demonstrate the walk-through animation and quickly became aware that Bo was engrossed in the moving computerised images. "Here, you try it – if you'd like to," Max suggested cautiously. "Just put your finger on here and move it whichever way you want to go." Max put Bo's large hand into position over the mouse, then held it for long enough to demonstrate the movements. As Max removed his hand and Bo realised that he was in control, his face lit up. His more usual scowl stretched away to an open-eyed smile. It was like witnessing a child making his first unsupported moves on a two-wheeled bicycle. This wasn't the reaction that Max had ever envisaged, but he was relieved nonetheless. Bo was transfixed and made muted giggles as he moved through the bank. And at the first sight of one of Dennis's notes about the security cameras, Bo let out a:

"Wah – what was that?" Then he read it aloud. "Security camera 4B. Fixed head. Manual switch from central station."

Max leaned back in his chair to take in the strange scene of this great bear of a man, huddled at the end of a big table in a big dining room, completely absorbed in Max's little laptop. Max knew at that moment that he had just won over an important ally.

"Brilliant - fuckin' brilliant!" Bo eventually declared as he leaned back from the computer some ten minutes later, after Max had demonstrated a few more of the facilities on the disc. Bo sat for a moment staring at the screen, slowly removed his glasses, then offered Max his big right hand.

"Count me in." He shook Max's hand with a crushing force, then reached into the inside pocket of his overcoat to produce a cell phone. "Here, you'll need this. It's a pay-phone thing – you have to top it up but it can't be traced by the cops. That's the number," he said, pointing to a label stuck to the back. "And these are some instructions…and a charger." Then from another pocket he produced something that Max couldn't see until Bo placed it on the table in front of him. It was a short-nosed 38 millimetre handgun.

"Take this." Bo instructed.

Max was so shocked at the sudden and unexpected idea that he would need to carry a gun that he found himself blurting out:

"I'd rather not – thank you," with the suggestion in his voice that Bo had misjudged him. Bo shrugged as he removed it from the table and replaced it in his jacket pocket.

"Well you be fuckin' careful walkin' round here with something so valuable. And don't go out after dark – you understand me, Max…Alex, or whatever your name is?"

"I don't plan to," Max replied.

Bo considered the situation for a moment.

"Right. So what's next?"

"I need to meet the rest of the team, to explain the plan to everyone. And I need your money 'cos I've got to buy some things for the job. Then I have to move hotels and change my image."

"Yeah," Bo agreed, glancing at Max from head to foot in one movement just as he had when they first met.

"And from now on, with the crew, I'm Alex Slater – okay?"

"Yeah, yeah."

Bo seemed to be distracted, his thoughts elsewhere.

"Hold on." Bo produced another cell phone. From their end of a series of calls, Max could hear Bo trying to arrange a meeting with the rest of the gang for later in the afternoon. Three calls, one person-to-person and two answerphones.

"Four o'clock here this afternoon. Don't worry, I'll get them, we'll all be here." Then Bo remembered. "Oh, you won't know about Sammy – Sammy Samms – one of the original team I put together for Dennis, but he's in hospital – got a stomach ulcer, would you believe? Worries too much. I told him he worries too much, now he's got a fuckin' stomach ulcer. So he's in hospital – so we have to count him out. But my nephew'll stand in for him. He's a bit of a Turk, but he's a good boy and he learns quick. He looks after me - drives for me an' that. I used him last month on a job already. His name is Joey – Joey Garrick - my brother's boy. No record and sharp as a stiletto. Okay with you?"

"If you vouch for him. 'You know the job, so you pick your squad' - army expression."

EIGHT

4.00 pm. Max, Bo, Gus Cleveland and Michael Gavini were back in the room above Santini's Restaurant. Max's first impressions of the others? Gus (who everyone called *Bus*) was bigger, blacker and quieter than his profile on the CD suggested; Michael (who everyone called 'Mickey') was wiry and alert with a ready smile that could have passed him off in a hundred professions other than the one he had chosen. So Max, who Bo had introduced as Alex Slater to the small gathering, was relaxed about the group so far, but it was still one short. Bo stood apart from the others dialling a number on his mobile phone.

"Joey – where are you?......... Well get your ass over here quicker, we're all waiting for you." He hung up and turned back to the group. "He'll be here in five minutes. We can start without him."

"No, we'll wait, then I'll only have to say everything once." Max responded quite abruptly. Bus and Mickey both looked immediately at Bo, expecting a reaction.

"You're right," he said after a moment. "Let's get some coffees up here while we're waiting. Mickey, get some coffees."

Mickey duly obeyed the order without question, arriving back in the room a few minutes later with a tray of drinks and Joey Garrick in tow. Joey greeted Bus with a high-five hand slap before hugging his uncle who then introduced him to Max, again as Alex. It occurred to Max that the expression *'flash bastard'* fairly summed up his first impression of Joey.

74

"Right, you can begin," Bo instructed as he pulled up a seat and started spooning sugar into his coffee.

Max stood up. Knowing that Bo had already briefed the group about the basics of the plan, he assumed to move on quickly.

"Right, you already know that the plan is to rob a bank – well, safe deposit vaults, actually, in the First National Credit Bank on 28th Street. I can get us all in using a special computer program to override their security systems. I'll come back to that in a minute. The plan is to go in on a Saturday night and start work in the vaults from seven-thirty hours on the Sunday morning. There are three hundred and ten boxes, so at two minutes per box, plus all the other manoeuvres – which includes creating a mock break-in to disguise our true entry method – I calculate that you have between ten and eleven hours work to clear every box starting with the single box that I've come for. The rest are over to you." Max glanced at Bo who was evidently agreeing with Max's summary. Max began to hand out some sheets of paper.

"This is a plan of the premises. It shows the entry and exit routes…"

"Hold on!" Bo interrupted. "We don't want drawings on paper. Show them the computer stuff you showed me. Get it set up an' I'll show them," he ordered. Max considered for a moment, then removed his laptop from its bag and began to open the program on the disc.

"This is fuckin' brilliant this is," Bo pronounced to the others. "This is technology." He waved a big finger to reinforce his point. "There's a lesson here for us. Technology, that's the future. No fuckin' explosives an' stuff on this job, we got modern technology on our side here. Fuckin' brilliant."

One minute later Max had the walk-through program lined up on the screen then turned the laptop to Bo who took over the controls and began to demonstrate it gleefully. The tone of the meeting was established. The others appeared to be as impressed with everything they saw and heard about the plan as Bo had been earlier in the day. Max's confidence had also grown as he was carried along by the group's evident wave of excitement for the job. That was, until the mention of the buy-in fee.

"Ten grand! For what?" Joey was first to voice his thoughts. The reaction caught Max by surprise this time. He stared at Joey with a quizzical expression.

"Sorry?"

"I'm not paying no fuckin' ten grand. What for eh? You need us as much as we need you's how I see it. What you gonna do without us eh, whistle up another team?"
Max gauged the silence of the others to be an expression of their agreement.

"So that's how you see it is it Joey?" Max asked. Joey said nothing, but shrugged then glanced around at the others, evidently feeling that he'd won the point. Max considered that this had the makings of an argument that he could lose, especially if it developed into a stand-off between him and Joey – or worse still, between him and the group.

"Forgive me, Joey, I'm new here in New York, you know that, so I don't know how you do business here, yet. And you're absolutely right, ten thousand dollars a head is a lot of money. So I *should* explain why I'm asking for it." Joey still wore the expression of defiance, but Max pressed on. "Okay, for now let's put aside the fact that I'm just presenting you with the easiest access route any of you will ever get into a bank. Then there's the time, effort and cost involved in producing this." Max was removing the CD from the laptop. He held it up. "Now I'd estimate that the programs on these discs took a minimum of five hundred hours to produce. And since my company charged my uncle's time at £150 an hour – what's that, nearly $250 – that puts the value of these bits of plastic at well over one hundred thousand dollars." Max was playing with one of the CDs. He put it carefully on the table in front of Joey. "Hard to imagine that, isn't it? Those little pieces of plastic, worth so much? But they're not worth a dime – without me. No-one else can even open the program, let alone operate it, because it's got a unique password and I'm the only living person that knows it." Max picked up the CD and replaced it in the laptop.

"Then there's the return on your investment. I'm asking for a total of forty thousand dollars, right? A raid on safe-deposit vaults in London a few years back, was estimated to have netted £6,000,000 - that's over $10,000,000.

"So that's what I bring to the operation that I think justifies my cost. But, as I said Joey, let's put all that aside for the moment 'cos there's a more important problem right now… and that's me." Max paused for affect before continuing.

"Just look at me – do I look like someone who's got a safe-deposit box at a bank here in Manhattan?" Max held out his arms to show his dishevelled state. "Of course I don't. But I do look like someone staying at the cheapest hotel in Queens. And that's not going to get me into the bank to check out the kit in my father's deposit box very easily, possibly without the bank doing extra checks on me which should make my visits good and memorable. And I don't think that's what we need, do you?"

"Well that don't take no forty grand!" Joey responded abruptly.

77

"Okay, okay – that's enough." Bo entered the discussion with the air of an elder statesman. "Have you got ten grand?" he asked Joey directly.

"Nope. So I guess that counts me out, don't it? You want me to leave right now?"

"No, I want you to shut up a minute Joey," Bo instructed with a patronising tone, then turned to the others. "Bus, you got ten grand?"

"No - five, maybe six tops."

"Mickey?"

"Give me a few days an' I'll get it. I don't wanna miss out on this Bo. But no-one said nothing before about us having to pay or I'd have got it, no problem."

"Okay, okay. I'll tell you what I'm gonna do – I'm gonna fund it and I'll take the cost out of the profits from the job – plus a hundred percent interest from each of you. So, you all get the normal split minus twenty grand. Any problems with that?"

A few glances were passed across the table, but an air of relief prevailed. Joey couldn't contain himself.

"You really gonna pay forty thou' up front before you've seen anything?"

"No, I'm coming to that," Bo replied as he addressed Max. "How much do you need?"

"I need what I'm asking for – forty grand," Max replied.

"No you don't. I asked what you *need*, not what you *want*. You've done enough homework on this job to know that."

"Ten thousand, perhaps twelve," Max admitted.

"Right, you'll have two grand on Monday morning. That'll buy you some decent clothes. You can get yourself smartened up an' move up town. Then I'll pay you twenty-five grand when we've checked out the stuff at the bank, if ..." He emphasised the word heavily then repeated it. "...*if* it all checks out an' *if* you convince me that the job can go ahead just as you've said. Then the last thirteen thou' you'll get after the job's done. You'll need that cash for your hotel bill up town by then." Bo leaned across the table to Max and lowered his voice a little. "That's how we do business here - cautiously. I think your price is fair, but I'll pay for what I get, as I get it. You understand?"

"Sure." Max replied.

"So do we have a deal?"

"Did you say '*we'd* check out the bank'?"

"Yeah, you and me – you got a problem with that?" Bo sat up rigidly.

Max glanced around at the others that now sensed confrontation. "Well, with respect Bo," Max ventured cautiously, "you're hardly anonymous."

All eyes turned to Bo. He said nothing immediately, just sat contemplating the remark.

"No. He's right," Bo suddenly announced. "Mickey, you'll go with him – no-one remembers you from Jack Shit. 'Anominus' ought to be your middle name." Bo let out a burst of raucous laughter. Mickey looked awkward, but said nothing as the rest took Bo's lead and enjoyed the moment at Mickey's expense. Bo turned back to Max.

"Right, that's the deal – take it or leave it," he announced with evident frustration.

"Fine." Max replied.

"Good, so now can we get on with the briefing?"

NINE

Sunday morning was dead time in Max's schedule now that he had already met with Bo and the others. But he got up early enough for breakfast, went for a walk in the balmy morning air to sharpen up his thoughts, then returned to his small room to work at his computer. He needed to remind himself of some of the details of the task ahead of him. This was important thinking time. He had only been in New York for some thirty-six hours and he was already a day ahead of the rough schedule that he had planned. That was good as it was going to generate some essential funds tomorrow morning, but Max was also aware that the project was picking up its own momentum, making it more difficult for him to walk away from the robbery if he wanted to. He sensed that this was no longer an option, providing the kit in the bank checked out; and he would know that within the next couple of days.

Max hadn't worried about lunch, but just after three o'clock there was a knock on his bedroom door.

"Mr Slater, it's Luisa. You want something to eat?"
Max answered the door to find Luisa holding a small tray on which was a plate of sandwiches and a bottle of beer.

"Luisa, hi." Max was surprised by the scene that greeted him. *'No-one said anything about Room Service,'* Max thought to himself.

"You haven't eaten since breakfast an' you won't find restaurants open round here on a Sunday. You like cheese?"

"Yes. That's extremely kind of you."

Luisa handed Max the tray and smiled flirtatiously with her whole face.

"I'll collect the tray later," she told him, then flashed another smile as she departed.

By nine o'clock Max had long since grown weary of his computer and was lying on his bed reading, accompanied by a violin concerto drifting softly from his portable radio-cassette player. A gentle tap on his door was again followed by Luisa's voice.

"Mr Alex, are you there?"

For no apparent reason, Max felt uneasy. He thought for a moment, closed his book and slowly answered the door. Luisa looked more striking than normal in a bright floral dress and her black hair loose onto her shoulders save for two combs at the sides.

"Hi Luisa. Have you come for your tray?"

"Yes, but I brought you this at the same time." She was holding two glasses of beer. Max smiled.

"*Two* beers?"

"Yes, one is for you and one for me. I thought you might like some company while you drank it." By which time, Luisa had pushed her way past Max into his little room. Then she noticed his computer and papers on the floor. "You still working?" she asked.

"Yes." Max hoped Luisa might take this as a hint to keep her visit brief.

"You shouldn't work such long hours," Luisa chided, then sat down on the bed and offered one of the beers to Max as he perched himself beside her.

"I could say the same to you," Max responded.

"I have no choice. I have a hotel to run and Becky and my stepmother to look after."

"Your stepmother as well?"

"Yes, she's in a bedroom upstairs. She had a stroke last year."

"You have no help here?"

"A lady comes half days during the week – she's all I can afford. But we only have ten rooms."

"But no husband or boyfriend?"

"Not now. Becky's father left when she was two. He didn't like the work here an' I refused to keep him any longer. Lazy man. So I sent him away an' we haven't heard from him since then."

"Why do you keep the hotel, it can't be easy for you?" Max asked as he realised that he had begun to enjoy Luisa's company.

"It was my father's. He came here from Mexico to marry my stepmother when I was fourteen. He left it for me when he died. It has big mortgage, but I pay it every month no matter what, so one day I give it to Becky – if she wants it. That's all that is important, so she has security when she is grown up." Then Luisa changed her tone and looked directly at Max for the first time during the exchange. "So I do whatever it takes to keep the hotel – you understand?"

"I think so," Max replied.
Luisa smiled.

"I wonder if you do," she added as she reached the short distance to touch Max's hand that rested on his thigh. She squeezed it lightly, then ran her palm along the inside of Max's leg and back to her glass in little more than a single movement. Max was aware that she was talking again, but he had switched out of the conversation. He was still enjoying his involuntary reaction to Luisa's touch – his mind had drifted onto another plain more in harmony with the violin music than with Luisa's voice. He gazed at her, his eyes moving over her features, her raven hair and the curve of her neck, her mottled brown eggshell shoulders, her slender arms and poorly manicured fingers holding the perspiring beer glass. This was a strange sensation that Max hadn't experienced for such a long time – and he liked it. He became aware that Luisa had stopped talking and was staring at him as if she was expecting a response.

"I'm sorry," he said as he switched back into the conversation.

"I asked if you have a girlfriend." Luisa evidently repeated.

"No, not at the moment."

"But you like girls?"

"Oh yes."

"Good." Luisa smiled as she reached out and touched Max's leg once again, but didn't remove it this time. "Because," she continued, "for my very special guests like you Alex, I can provide my special services - at a little extra cost." She stroked Max's thigh. "You understand?"
Of course he did.

"Yes," Max replied, then immediately took a drink from the glass to avoid Luisa's stare. He had just been propositioned with such ease, that Luisa might have been offering to deliver a morning paper. But there was no misunderstanding and Max didn't know how to handle the proposal. The sensation of embarrassment now added to Max's mix of emotions. He was hot and knew that he was blushing, then found himself blurting out:

"She's a lovely girl - Becky. You must be very proud of her. I've got a niece almost the same age, called Rebecca - we all call her 'Becky'." Max made the briefest eye-contact with Luisa, consciously trying to speak and behave calmly, but knowing he was failing to control either.

"I've got a photo. Do you want to see it?" Max removed his hand from Luisa's light grip, reached across to his bag and removed a wallet from which he produced two photographs then held one for Luisa to see.

"That's our Becky," he announced.

Luisa was amused by the coincidence. As Max put the photos away, he became aware of a need for some remark to fill an awkward silence. Nothing occurred to him before Luisa spoke.

"I think I'll go now."

"Really?" Max responded with evident surprise as they both stood up. "Must you go? Did I say something to upset you?"

"No, no, no," Luisa replied with a sincere warmth, then reached up and touched the side of Max's face with the tips of the fingers of her right hand. "You're a very nice man, Alex." She leaned forward, pulled his head gently down to hers and kissed his cheek. "And you are a very handsome man. You should smarten yourself up, then you get many girlfriends here in New York."

Max looked into Luisa's dark, smiling eyes.

"I might just do that." He unlatched the door and held it open for Luisa to leave, then closed it behind her and leant his back against it.

"Bugger," he sighed as he reflected on the last few minutes and how badly he felt that he had handled the situation. But more surprising to him were the emotions that he had just felt. Twice in a few weeks his emotions for attractive women had been aroused. *'And look how one of those ended,'* he thought to himself. He shuddered as he pictured Jia's beautiful face pleading with him in the last moments that he saw her. But perhaps she had awakened his latent attraction to the fair sex. Otherwise, why had he just become so attracted to Luisa? And what had he done to drive her away? His thoughts were confused but he knew with crystal clarity that he wanted to follow her, to talk to her again, to look into her big dark eyes and to smell her cheap perfume. And he wanted to do it now. At that moment, his eyes fell on the tray that Luisa had supposedly come to retrieve. It gave him the perfect excuse. He picked it up, checked that he had his room key in his pocket, then opened the door. As he stepped into the hallway, he just saw the swing of Luisa's colourful dress as she entered a bedroom at the other end of the corridor.

TEN

Monday. If all went to plan, this would be Max's last day at
The Alamo Motel. With Bo's advance payment, he could buy
some new clothes later today and move up town in the
morning.

By nine o'clock, he was sitting in the breakfast room on a
seat by the wall that gave him a clear view of the small room
and the door to the kitchen. Max had wanted to free his mind
of last night's meeting with Luisa, but as he arrived for
breakfast and realised that he would see her, he sensed a
nervous anticipation. He wanted to measure her reaction and
his own when they met this morning. So imagine Max's
disappointment when Sandra, as she was to introduce herself, a
chubby fifty year old with a fixed grimace and the beginnings
of a beard, emerged from the kitchen, approached Max's table
and demanded to know his order. As he waited for her to
return, Max became aware of Luisa's voice behind him in
reception, talking to someone who had just arrived. He was
instantly excited, until the mention of Max's name in their
conversation and the realisation that the other voice was that of
Joey Garrick, proved a total distraction.

Max left his seat in the dining room and walked the few
yards to the reception. He only glanced a polite smile at Luisa
as he passed her to greet Joey who turned away into a corner
then pulled an envelope out of his black bomber jacket.

"Here, this is from Bo," Joey stated as he slapped it into
Max's chest.

"Thanks," Max responded.

"Don't thank me – it's Bo's money."

"I was thanking you for delivering it," Max qualified with a sigh. "Joey, do you have a problem with me?"

"I ain't got no problem – you got a problem?"

"Only if your attitude threatens the job."

"Good, that's all right then, cos Bo wouldn't have me on the team if he thought I was going to mess up - and I work for Bo. Get my meaning?"

And with that, Joey pushed past Max who had lost his appetite and returned to his room to prepare for his shopping trip.

By mid-afternoon, Max had completed the task and was sitting in a cab on his way back to The Alamo Motel sporting a new haircut, a new leather briefcase and a new suitcase containing enough new clothes to partly fill a wardrobe at The Roy Hotel close to Fifth Avenue where he had reserved a room from tomorrow lunchtime. He was surprised at how tiring the exercise had proved. He lounged in the cab breathing in the aroma of new materials and tried to remember the last time he had bought an entire new outfit. It must have been over ten years ago when he became the proud owner of his first pair of 501s and a lookalike Giorgio Armani suit during a similar expedition down Oxford Street in London. But more surprising to Max now, was how he couldn't wait to get back to the hotel to try everything on again – another sensation he hadn't experienced recently.

The small mirror in his bedroom at the hotel didn't give him much idea of his total new image, but it did remind him that his scratchy unkempt beard didn't suit the new look. It would have to go.

'Blimey!' was Max's first reaction as he viewed the clean-shaven ceramic face that looked back at him from the mirror in the communal bathroom. It was such a novelty that he viewed it from every angle, running his fingers over the smooth skin and through his short hair. "Yep - I'd believe you were a man of means if you turned up at my bank," he told his reflection.

The scale of his transformation was emphasised a few minutes later when he was on his way back to his bedroom. He was just about to unlock his door when, behind him, Luisa, who had just arrived on the landing carrying an armful of towels, immediately challenged him.

"Hey, what you doing there?" Max turned and looked straight at her, but to his surprise, her aggressive tone didn't change. "What you doing up here?" She obviously didn't recognise him and assumed he was an intruder.

"Luisa, it's me – Alex Slater," he told her in a tone of voice to match his bemused expression. Luisa stepped back and checked Max with a sideways glance then clutched a hand to her cheek and let out a shriek of laughter.

"Oh my God!" she exclaimed as she began to take in Max's total new look. "Oh my God."

"You approve?" Max asked.

"I can't believe it's you – it's incredible."

"You told me I should smarten up and…well, I think you were right."

"Incredible."

Max was about to unlock his bedroom door, but turned back to Luisa.

"You know that I'm leaving tomorrow after breakfast?"

"Yes, I'll have your bill ready – no problem."

"Thank you. But before I leave, I think we have something to…" Max had realised this was a rare opportunity to catch

Luisa on her own and wanted to clear up some loose ends that had been troubling him since their conversation last night. But as he began to search for the right words, his flow was interrupted by Becky's voice from downstairs…

"Mummy - I'm home!"

Luisa responded.

"Okay," she called back, then returned to Max: "Sorry, go on."

"No, it's no problem."

The Roy Hotel, close to Fifth Avenue and Central Park, is little more than a thirty-minute taxi ride but light years in character from The Alamo Motel in Elmhurst. Max arrived, checked in and took up residence in one of the hotel's 'character rooms' soon after midday on Tuesday afternoon. His mixed feelings about leaving The Alamo and Luisa began to fade in direct relation to the mileage clicking up on the meter of the cab that carried him across Queensboro Bridge into Manhattan.

Max had made an appointment at First National Credit Bank to access Dennis's safe deposit box at 4.00pm and arranged to meet Mickey Gavini outside five minutes earlier. That gave him plenty of time for a final rehearsal with the program, which he did at his desk in his plush, designer bedroom. Max assumed he would have limited time with Dennis's box so would have to work quickly at the bank if he was not to arouse suspicion, so he timed his run-through once again. Eight and a half minutes, with no complications. *'Under ten should be fine,'* he thought to himself.

At 3.15pm Max packed away the laptop into his new briefcase, ran a new electric razor over his chin, then slowly dressed in his new outfit with all the precision he had once devoted to his army uniform.

He left the hotel in plenty of time for the short journey by cab and was relieved to see Mickey hovering on the kerb outside the bank as he arrived. Mickey looked a little furtive, Max felt, but was otherwise suitably turned out in a sober grey raincoat. They greeted one another with a nod and made their way to the entrance.

"Let me do all the talking," Max instructed. "You keep as quiet as possible. We don't want anyone to remember us. You don't need to use your own name, by the way. I do, but you can use anything you like."

"Like what?"

"Like anything - it doesn't matter – Donald Duck for all I care - as long as you can remember it. Okay?"

"Okay."

Max explained their business to a receptionist at a desk near the entrance, who politely asked each of them to fill in a card requiring a few personal details for security purposes, whilst she located the clerk who would look after them. Max filled out his card and sat taking in the view of the bank interior that he knew intimately from the program.

"Mr Slater, good afternoon," said a tall, smartly dressed man who looked like a bank clerk. "I'm Mr O'Donnell. I'm sorry to have kept you waiting,"

"Good afternoon," Max replied as he stood to shake hands. "This is my colleague…" Max suddenly realised that he had forgotten to check Mickey's alias. He waited for Mickey would fill in his name, but he said nothing.

"Hello…" Mr O'Donnell reached forward to shake Mickey's hand. "…Mr..?"

"Gonzo." Mickey eventually offered.

Mr O'Donnell made no reaction, but over his shoulder, Mickey may have caught the briefest expression of astonishment on Max's face as he registered the name.

"Welcome to First National Credit Bank, gentlemen. Have you been given S20 cards to fill out?" Mr O'Donnell enquired. They both handed over the cards, then Max picked up his briefcase and prepared to set off towards the vaults, so by the time Mr O'Donnell suggested they go, Max had already taken a few steps in the right direction.

"You've been here before, Mr Slater?" Mr O'Donnell observed.

"No I haven't. Sorry – after you."

Mr O'Donnell made polite small-talk as he led them through the bank, during which time, Max took the opportunity to explain that they were here to check the contents of his departed father's deposit box and might have to copy out some information from documents that should be there.

"That might take a little time," Max added.

"That's no problem, Mr Slater. Please take all the time you need."

As they were walking across the concourse, Max had become aware that his new leather-soled shoes were sliding on the marble floor. He thought no more of it than that until, as he took two steps down to a corridor of offices, his grip went and he slipped off the second step, twisting his ankle badly before he could regain his balance. Mr O'Donnell grasped Max's arm and showed due concern as Max winced with the pain. Mickey jumped forward to take his other arm.

"I'm all right, really." Max assured them. "It'll walk off," he added in hope rather than conviction. It was already smarting. Mr O'Donnell directed Max and Mickey into a small room with a table, two chairs and some bland blue wallpaper where they were to wait while Mr O'Donnell retrieved security box 163 from the vault.

Mickey helped Max to the chair behind the desk, then he brought the other one across from beside the door. They both sat to attention awaiting Mr O'Donnell's return. Hardly moving his body, Max began to check for cameras, his eyes moving systematically around the small room looking for the mirror, light fitting or grill that might disguise a hiding place. He knew there was no surveillance installed when Dennis made his program, but he couldn't take any chances. It took him no time to realise that the room was clean. He turned to Mickey and shook his head.

"Gonzo?" he sighed. "I don't need to ask where you got that from."

Mickey replied in a loud whisper.

"You said to use a name I'd remember. Gonzo's my favourite Muppet – always has been."

Mr O'Donnell knocked instinctively as he walked back into the room. He showed only a hint of surprise at the weight of the box. He was too professional to pass comment, but simply left the room after explaining that they could use the bell button on the desk to summon help or to let the guard know when they had finished.

Even before the door closed, Max was retrieving the small brass key from his trouser pocket at the end of a silver chain that he had bought on his shopping trip for the purpose. As he pulled the box across the desk to him, he was conscious of his heart rate increasing. He stared at the box before bringing the key to the lock and inserting it with gentle precision. One-eighth of a turn, then it stopped. Nothing happened. Max panicked. He and Mickey exchanged glances.

"What's the matter?" Mickey wanted to know, but Max said nothing. He tried again with the same result. '*No!*' Max closed his eyes for a brief moment as if in prayer, then he removed the key, inserted it again more firmly, placed his hand flat on the lid and pressed it down to release pressure from the lock. He turned the key once more. This time it travelled through a quarter turn and under his left hand he felt the lid pop as the lock loosened its grip. The two men sighed as one, with relief. Max's heart was still racing as he lifted the top of the box to reveal its contents for the first time in nearly a year. His eyes moved over the mechanism quickly. It looked exactly as he expected – exactly as the diagram on the CD. The components that had been state-of-the-art over a year ago already looked dated. Two batteries wired in series, the computer, receiver, a large mobile telephone and a complex aerial – all packed into the available space as neatly as the engine under the bonnet of a high performance car. The only evidence of any life in this strange device was registered by two glowing L.E.D. lights, one red and one green. Max's eyes were moving around the apparatus at speed, taking in everything that he only knew from the CD. Mickey was out of his seat, staring over Max's shoulder with eyes transfixed.

"Is it doing anything?"

"Not right now."

"No. Didn't think it was … Why not?"

"I've got to send it some…" Max's attention had darted back to the coloured lights. His heart rate sank as he remembered that only the green one indicated 'power', the red signalled a fault somewhere in the circuits. He knew instantly that there was a problem that he must identify before he could do anything else.

"What's up?" Mickey asked.

"Don't know."

"Can you sort it?"

"Mickey, shut up – please, I've got to concentrate," Max ordered. He unlatched his briefcase, pulled out his laptop and had it set up in a moment, then connected it to the computer in the box by means of a short grey umbilical lead. He then produced the CDs in their plastic case from the inside pocket of his jacket, inserted the first into the computer and rhythmically tapped his unique password onto the keyboard out of Mickey's eye line. He continued to work fast, moving through the program with his eyes scanning the screen at speed. He stopped abruptly – he'd found the problem. He studied the screen for a few seconds then used the mouse to move through some strands of his program. Within a further minute, Max sat back to assess his work and concluded that he had solved the problem. The red light was out. To his relief, the fault only concerned the transmitting system via the mobile telephone, so whilst it would soon prove essential to Max's plans, until now, it would not have affected the unit's performance. Max glanced at his watch.

"Okay, problem solved. We're back on track," he announced. But then an uncomfortable thought occurred to him. He immediately diverted to another part of the computer program that Dennis had included to self-diagnose faults, then he scrolled through some lists on the screen until his fears were confirmed. The word 'battery' was flashing as it arrived in view.

'*Shit!*' Max thought to himself, but showed no outward signs to Mickey that would suggest he had just discovered another problem that may not be so easily solved. He clicked on the flashing word, which was instantly replaced by a graphic scale indicating the batteries' energy levels. It showed that there was hardly any life left in them. The whole system was designed to run on little more power than that consumed by an electric clock, so the large batteries were more than adequate under normal circumstances to power it for one year as Dennis had planned. But the LED light may have been draining power for months. Ironically the very component incorporated to warn of problems, had caused one greater than that which it was registering. And changing batteries, or even gauging their life-expectancy, was not covered in Dennis's instructions as that was never part of his plan. Max couldn't believe that Dennis could have overlooked this when he had been so thorough about everything else. Max glanced at his watch, then back at the scale on the screen.

'That may be enough power to keep it running for a month, or it may run out tomorrow,' Max thought to himself. He had no way of calculating it. And in changing the batteries there was a tiny chance of scrubbing or contaminating part of the program without him realising until it was too late. Max checked his watch again. Six minutes and he hadn't started the real work that he had come to do.

'Right' he told himself. *'I need more data before making a decision.'* He enlarged the relevant area of the battery-indicator on the screen and noted that it showed a fraction over 3.2 on the bottom of the scale. He'd check how much power was used by his activities over the next few minutes and if the indicator had moved too far down the scale, he'd have to take a chance and change the batteries, but if not, he'd leave well alone. Now he had to get on before Mickey got more inquisitive, or worse still, anybody came to check on them. Anyone looking around the door while he had the computer set up would tumble them at a glance. Max pressed ahead with his tasks, nervously listening for footsteps outside the door but

showing no signs of panic that Mickey might report back to Bo.

"Right, Mickey – this is crunch time," he suddenly declared. "If this bit works, we're in business. If it doesn't, well, that may be the end of the job."
Mickey was out of his seat again and focussed on the components strewn across the table. Max was connecting his mobile phone to his laptop.

"What I'm doing now is simulating the connection from us on the outside of the building to the kit here in the bank vault, right?" Mickey nodded. "When I call it up on this phone, if that light comes on, we have the connection. Then, it should download a pile of data onto the screen." He looked at Mickey who nodded without blinking in case he missed anything on the screen. Max glanced at his watch, blew air through his teeth and tapped seven numbers into his mobile phone. He checked them carefully against those on the screen of the laptop, then, with his pulse racing, he pressed the green *OK* button. Four eyes moved to the small LED light that would indicate the connection. The next four seconds seemed considerably longer. Then, with the ferocity of a laser in Max and Mickey's imagination, the tiny orange light flicked into life. Before either man could react, the laptop began to whirr as it connected with the apparatus a few inches away, then began downloading information. Four eyes now watched the screen of the laptop fill with information, slowly at first, one or two lines at a time, then at great speed, tranches of typed lists and diagrams sprawled down the screen so fast that it was impossible to register any detail until it suddenly stopped.

"Oh my god…" Mickey uttered under his breath.
Max just blew out his cheeks then laughed nervously with the relief. He took hold of the mouse and began scrolling through

the lists to check what was there. He glanced again at his watch, fumbled in his briefcase for a clean disc which he pushed into the computer quickly to record the information on the screen.

"Well Mickey, that's a mega result, that is. I think we're on."

Mickey's turn to blow air as he stood back from the computer without taking his eyes off it.

"Fucking right. That's…that's…fucking right."

"We gotta get out of here." Max said soberly as he glanced at his watch. Twelve minutes since they arrived – was that all? Not bad, but no point pushing their luck. He began to pack up the security box and was about to break the connection with the laptop when he remembered to check the battery level again. Max was still so excited by the results of the connection that he hardly registered that the level had dropped below the 3 mark on the scale. But he *did* register it and understood only too well that if a few minutes use could have such an affect, he would have to install new batteries before the raid.

Two minutes later, Max pressed the bell for assistance. He felt a warm glow of relief as he and Mickey waited the return of Mr O'Donnell. He was still absorbed by the program, still elated by the way the equipment had worked. Now the prospect of testing the entire plan and apparatus for real, excited him. He reflected on the superb detailing of Dennis's planning that made his oversight with the batteries so much more surprising. Max knew this was going to be a thorn in his side and that he had every reason to worry about it, but right now his sense of euphoria was much stronger.

Max's thoughts were interrupted by a knock on the door and the entrance of a black guard in uniform followed by a young man in shirtsleeves.

"Mr Slater, Mr Gonzo?" the guard checked.

"Yes."

"Mr O'Donnell sends his apologies. He's tied up, but has asked Mr Sands here to return your box while I show you out."

"Fine – thank you." Max started to stand, but collapsed back in his chair with a loud yelp as the pain from his strained ankle shot up his leg. Max had completely forgotten about the injury while he was sitting still, but now the reminder was vicious. The guard and Mr Sands hovered, wondering what to do for the best as Mickey helped Max onto his good foot.

"I think I've sprained it," Max told them, but then wanted to play it down to avoid any fuss. "I'm sure exercising it will help."

Mickey picked up Max's briefcase and raincoat.

"Let's go."

A few minutes earlier, on the street outside the main entrance, an armoured Brinks Mat truck had stopped by the sidewalk as it did on most weekday afternoons at about this time. No-one took any more notice of the two guards wearing helmets and body armour, than they would on any other day.

Precisely two minutes and thirty seconds later, a Yellow Cab drew up behind the truck. Three men in their mid-twenties, each carrying a sports bag, left the car and walked towards the bank. So what? Nothing unusual. But this was to be the finale to several month's rehearsing and planning for a raid that was due to net the gang more than $100,000.

The gang was equipped to use force if required, but the plan was based on the simple concept that neither Brinks Mat nor its client banks would endorse their personnel - or worse still, their customers - getting hurt for the sake of a few thousand dollars. So a fast, brutal assault on the two couriers inside the bank, as they left with the full transit cases, would result in their compliance - without response or retaliation. This was the model that the gang had already trialled on two occasions at out-of-town banks resulting in a combined haul of almost $30,000. Today's raid was to be the big one. The same routine but with a far bigger pay-out. They knew that for certain because an aunt of one of the raiders worked at the bank and was advising them on the Brinks Mat schedule and the best day on which to get the largest haul. So the odds on success favoured the gang. But this was central Manhattan with more police, more public and more traffic to hinder the escape. The gang had replaced their previous muscle car getaway chariot of choice, with a stolen Yellow Cab. Once in the Manhattan traffic, it was indistinguishable from the other nine-thousand plying for business in the city. Their getaway today would be sedate and unrushed.

The tension in the gang was palpable as they mingled with the lunchtime crowds on the sidewalk. The plan now was for one of the gang to watch for the couriers to leave the inner fortified area in the bank. They would be hit when they were most vulnerable as they walked across the concourse to the main entrance doors. A swift, noisy attack as the gang took instant control of the area, ordering the couriers to their knees at gunpoint. A second raider would cut the chains on the safe boxes with bolt cutters while the other gang-member controlled the customers and the access through the front entrance. The entire action, from the first crowd-controlling shot into the ceiling of the bank to the car racing from the scene, would be over in less than ninety seconds - as it had been on both the previous trial raids.

The three raiders had now stopped near the front doors. One of them took up station in the entrance, staring into the dimly-lit central concourse, while the other two hovered a short distance away, watching the sidewalk. After just a few seconds, the first youth reacted abruptly and called back to attract the attention of the others.

"They're coming," he hissed in evident surprise, then turned back to squint again into the low lighting in the bank foyer. "Yeah, let's go!"

They instantly sprang into action, pulling masks, firearms, bolt-cutter and some canisters from sports bags which they then discarded. The first youth thought he had seen the Brinks Mat guards starting to leave the bank, just as he had witnessed on the previous reconnaissance trip. But as his eyes adjusted from bright sunshine to the low light inside the bank, the nervous youth had mistaken a customer wearing a bus driver's uniform, for one of the guards. As the gang rushed in, they quickly realised their mistake. They could see their real targets the other side of the armoured glass panels still filling the transit boxes. At that moment, their plan fell apart and they had to make an instant decision to leave empty-handed or cobble together a plan B. At about the same moment, the lady at the reception desk saw them and screamed a warning that triggered a chain reaction underlined by panic from customers, bank staff and the raiders alike.

One raider fired his shotgun into the ceiling, but instead of freezing the tension as intended, it accelerated the atmosphere towards chaos. Another raider threw or dropped a smoke canister that skidded across the stone floor before hitting a wall and igniting. From behind their masks, the would-be robbers screamed orders at all around them, effectively raising the tempo to a state of hysteria in most of the customers. They were ordering everyone to lie on the floor with no apparent plan except perhaps to trade money for the lives of their hostages.

This scenario had developed within moments. So fast that Max, Mickey and the guard, who were now making their way painfully slowly out of the vaults, were unaware of the scene that would greet them the instant the guard opened the heavy door onto the concourse, using his security pass. To the gang's good fortune, one of the raiders was just the other side of the door and immediately thrust a gun into the guard's face the moment he emerged. The youth screamed at the guard to lie on the floor, then turned to Max and Mickey who had dropped the briefcase and already had their hands above their heads. The raider shouted his order for them to lie face-down which Mickey instantly obeyed, but Max was in so much pain that he knew the action of getting to the floor was going to hurt. In the few seconds Max took to consider how best to approach it, the raider lost patience and held his handgun to Max's head, shouting through his mask:

"Get down - now! On the fucking floor - now!" at the top of his voice.

Over the next few days, Max would be asked repeatedly why he did what he did next and Max's answer would be the same every time – *"an instinctive self-defence reaction, probably still there from army training"*. What Max would fail to admit was that it was also driven by one of his flashes of red rage when the gunman threatened him at gunpoint. So as the masked raider held his pistol to Max's head, shouting into his left ear, Max erupted. He brought his left arm down so hard and fast that it knocked the youth's gun-hand away for the split second needed to follow through with his right fist. Max delivered his second blow straight from the shoulder, smashing it square into the raider's face through his plastic mask. This punch landed with such force that it knocked the youth off his feet and sent him crashing backwards into a pillar. The impact shook the gun from his hand. It clattered on the marble floor no more than a foot from the guard who instantly pounced on it, aimed it at another gang-member across the concourse and let off three rounds in less than a second. At least two of the shots found their target who screamed with the pain as he was thrown backwards by the impact. The third raider turned towards the guard and fired off a burst of shots that ricocheted off a wall and the pillar that Max now used as a shield. As that youth made his dash for the door, the guard fired two more rounds from his prone position on the floor. One of the shots hit the man on the shoulder. He screamed loudly with the pain, but his momentum carried him on until he burst out through the front doors onto the street. A moment later, the Yellow Cab raced away from the sidewalk into the heavy Manhattan traffic.

In the bank, an eerie silence lasted for several seconds before the relief that followed the drama manifested in an out-pouring of emotions. Max was still standing with his back to the pillar that had shielded him from the flying bullets. He looked down on Mickey who was pressed flat into the stone floor and the guard who was pulling himself to his feet, obviously in a daze, trying to appear in command but failing to focus his eyes.

"Are you okay?" Max asked.

"Yeah," the guard responded without conviction. "You?"

"Yeah, okay."

The guard was shaking off his lethargy.

"You're a cool dude… What a team, eh?.... Butch and Sundance, you and me." The guard lifted the wrist and felt for a pulse of the raider who lay motionless close to Max's feet.

"Well he's still alive," he pronounced after a moment then went to check the other body. Mickey was on his feet, brushing himself down.

"What the fuck was that about?"

"Listen." Max drew Mickey to him and spoke in a hushed voice. "You can't hang about. You have to get out of here, first chance you get. If the police do a check on you with the name Gonzo, we're in trouble."

"Yeah, right."

"Make your way to the entrance, slowly, before the police arrive. I'll catch you and Bo later, but make sure you tell Bo about the result. Go on."

"Sure - I'm gone." In the confusion, no-one took any notice of Mickey as he slipped out through the gathering throng of spectators at the entrance.

The bank staff had emerged from their side of the reinforced barriers to comfort customers in the concourse. Chairs were produced and plastic cups of water were being offered from trays. At the far end of the area, an authoritative manager had used Scotch tape to truss the hands and feet of the raider who the guard had shot. Max wanted to leave, but knew he would have to stay until he had given a statement. Just as he was thinking that the police were taking a long time, there came the wail of sirens heralding the arrival of the avenging cavalry. The scene that had settled into comparative calmness, moved up a gear once again. Strutting uniformed policemen, flashing lights, barked orders. The guard, whose name Max had noted from his identity card as Jason Winchester, had found a seat for Max who now sat apart from most of the action with his briefcase on his lap. Jason the guard had assumed the role of intermediary between the police and bank personnel, providing his eyewitness account along with a

103

guided tour of parts of the bank. A photographer began flashing shots of the scene while medical teams hovered, awaiting permission to deal with the two raiders who still lay where they were felled.

Max was fascinated by all the activity which, apart from a member of the bank staff offering him a beaker of water, he had watched undisturbed for the last five minutes. Eventually, from the throng of people across the concourse, Max became aware of a man and woman approaching him. At first he assumed they were police officers coming to take his statement, until the lady introduced herself as she handed Max her business card. In that moment, the fears that Max had been harbouring for the last few minutes were confirmed. His act of defiance had attracted the very attention that he knew full well he should be avoiding.

"Hello, I'm Gaynor Rubitz from The New York Times," the lady announced.

'Bugger' was Max's instant thought. He knew the implications immediately and they were not good. A newspaper had the story and had him identified as being in the centre of it. So much for his low-profile.

"My colleague here tells me…sorry, this is Donald Ying…"

"Hi." Max deliberately avoided giving his name but responded when Donald Ying reached forward to shake his hand.

"Aaagh." Max recoiled with pain. He hadn't realised that his right hand was now badly bruised from punching the raider with such force.

"Are you all right?" Ms Rubitz asked.

"Yes, I hurt my hand, that's all."

"Was that when you hit one of the gang?" Ms Rubitz asked as she pulled a small tape recorder from her bag, flicked it on and held it to Max's chin. Max was wondering how she knew about the incident but Ms Rubitz anticipated it.

"Donald was here in the bank when the robbery - attempted robbery - happened. He told me all about how you foiled it single-handed - well, you and a guard."

"Yes, he's over there. He did the real work – shot two of the robbers. One's there and the other got away, but he hit him. He's your hero. Look he's just there." Ms Rubitz's interest in Max was not to be so easily deflected.

"Yes, so I understand, but you were unarmed and you took one of them out single-handed. That's what I'm interested in. Where did you learn to do that?"

"S'cuse me ma'am." A uniformed policeman had approached the group and now interrupted. "Any of you people not here when the raid took place?"

"Well I wasn't," Ms Rubitz volunteered. "But I'm from The New York Times." She flashed her press identity.

"You'll have to leave. You shouldn't be in here. We have to clear the area of anyone who wasn't a witness."

"But officer, I'm a reporter, please," she protested.

"No. Out - now!" He obviously wasn't about to negotiate. Ms Rubitz tried another tack. "How long will this take? This man's injured and needs to see a doctor." The officer turned to Max.

"Is that right? D'you get hit?"

"No - well, sort of - it's my hand." Max held it out and flexed it.

"I'll get one of the medics to see you, then we'll take your statement an' let you get out of here." Then to Ms Rubitz: "But you ma'am – out, now!"

Almost immediately one of the medical crew inspected Max's hand, pronounced no breakages, rubbed in some cream to reduce the bruising and applied a loose bandage. With the clearing-up operation now well underway, news of how Max and Jason the guard had foiled the raid, began to spread amongst everyone in the bank. Max was shown into a private room away from the attention of the staff who kept approaching him in the concourse to congratulate him or to offer him endless cups of coffee, tea, water or something to eat. Even the police officer who took his statement couldn't resist departing from the standard questions.

"You know you broke that guy's neck when you hit him?" he told Max in an admiring tone.

"No, really?"

"That must have been one helluva punch. I'd love to have seen that. Where you learn to do that – you a boxer?"

"No... I guess from the army."

"Is that so?" Then the officer returned to his notes as he reflected. "I'd love to have seen that punch. Evander Holyfield never broke no-one's neck with a punch, that's for sure."

As the officer was finishing his questions and Max was hoping that he could leave for his hotel, there was a single loud knock on the door followed by the appearance of a tall, dapper gentleman with Brylcreemed hair and a blue suit.

"Excuse me interrupting, are you Mr Slater?"

"Yes," Max confirmed.

"Gee, I'm glad I've found you. I'm Dan Attaway, the manager of the bank." He stepped forward to shake Max's hand before noticing the bandage. "I've been told what you did, but I didn't know you had sustained an injury."

"I'm fine, really."

"Well please accept mine and the bank's sincere thanks. We must get you some medical attention."

"That's not necessary. It's only bruised. The police medical people have already checked it, thank you."

"Well the least we can do is to get you home – as soon as the police have finished taking your statement."

"I've finished here sir," the policeman confirmed.

"Good. Well I've got one of our cars waiting outside to take you wherever you want to go now," Mr Attaway offered.

"That's kind of you. I'd like to go back to my hotel, please – The Roy on 54th West." Max stood up carefully, collected his briefcase and started to walk. His ankle felt noticeably better – he assumed, from the enforced rest that he had given it for the last half-hour. But Max anticipated Mr Attaway's reaction and dismissed his limp with:

"I slipped on a step."

Mr Attaway accompanied Max through the bank where the police were still taking statements and tape marked no-go areas where the two bodies had landed. The doors at the main entrance were unlocked for them by a policeman standing guard, but behind them, Jason had seen Max about to depart.

"Hey - Butch!" he called out before noticing Mr Attaway. "Sorry sir, I didn't recognise you, I just wanted to say goodbye to my compadre." Jason had an easy ability to smile as he spoke. "Now you come back an' see us all again, you hear?" Jason continued in a mock Southern accent.

"I will - soon."

Jason moved aside for Max and Mr Attaway to step out into the street.

"It doesn't seem to have affected him. It's like, just another day at work," Max remarked as he nodded toward Jason.

"Thankfully not. Never happened to me before either, I'm pleased to say," Mr Attaway responded.

As the chauffeur recognised his manager, he leaped into action, holding a rear door to the limousine open. Mr Attaway removed a business card from his top pocket and handed it to Max.

"If I can do anything to help with your injury, please don't hesitate to contact me, Mr Slater. I think we may well be contacting you in the next few days. I assume we can do that via the hotel?"

"Err - sure," Max agreed, before adding: "If you need to, but please don't worry." With which departing words, Max was about to step into the car when a camera flash drew his attention to one side. And again - flash. Ms Rubitz was taking the photos on a small camera. She now rushed forward.

"Please, Mr Slater, I need a few minutes with you, to finish my interview."

"I wasn't aware we'd started one."

"Ten minutes, no more. Five? Can I join you now, we'll do it in the car? Please, I need some details."

"No, I'm sorry. I just want to get back to my hotel. I'm sorry." Max moved to the car and Mr Attaway raised a protective arm to prevent Ms Rubitz from following.

"You heard the gentleman, miss."

"I don't even have your first name," she called to Max who was now in the car. The chauffeur immediately shut the door and moments later the limousine pulled out into the traffic for the short journey to 54th Street.

At the hotel, the car double-parked close to the main entrance and the driver quickly had the rear door open and bid Max:

"Have a good afternoon, sir," as he touched the peak of his cap. Max had hardly taken ten slow steps towards the hotel entrance when a raucous call stopped him in his tracks.

"Mr Slater, hold on!" Max knew exactly who he would see when he turned. Gaynor Rubitz was frantically paying off the driver of a Yellow Cab that she had employed to follow the limousine. Now she came bounding up to Max like a hound closing on its prey.

"Thank you for waiting. I'm sorry to chase you like this, really, but I'm desperate for some details for my report. Please can I have just a few minutes, please," she implored.

"What more can I tell you? You've got my name, you have photos of me at the bank and you say your friend witnessed everything that happened. And now you know where I'm staying. That's everything you need for your story – for an ace reporter."

"Almost - just some background information - on you."

"I don't understand why you're chasing *me*? The guard did more than me and he's your local hero. I'm just a visiting Brit."

"Really, you're a Brit?" she interrupted. "I thought you was Australian. Is that a British accent?"

"Yes," Max stated wirily.

"Yeah, but the guard's paid to do his job - that's not the story. You're the vigilante, the man-in-the-street fighting back - unarmed. That's what my readers will be interested in. That's a big story here in New York and it's mine right now if you will just give me some background please. It's the difference between page four and page two – perhaps even the front page."

"Page four in The New York Times sounds good to me."

"Not as good as the front page." Ms Rubitz retorted immediately. "Just your first name then, how can that hurt – as you say, I have everything else? Please?"

"That's all, yeah?.... It's Alex, okay? That's your lot." With that, Max began to walk up the steps of the hotel entrance. As he did so, Ms Rubitz followed, then noticed his limp for the first time.

"What d' you do to your foot?" she asked, but before Max had time to reply, Ms Rubitz thought she had another detail for her story. "You didn't give that guy at the bank a good kicking as well, did you?" Max found the suggestion and Ms Rubitz's enthusiastic delivery more amusing than he wanted. He couldn't contain a smile that turned to a chuckle.

"No, I didn't."

Ms Rubitz watched Max laughing.

"What's up? What did I say? Why's that funny – you might have done – I dunno." She was now laughing at Max laughing without understanding why.

"Here, let me help you up the steps at least." Max didn't resist the offer. Ms Rubitz took his arm and supported Max's weight as he negotiated the few wide steps in his slippery shoes, but then didn't break away as the two entered the lobby.

"Are you okay now? Can you make it to the elevator?..... Or would you like to sit for a minute - for a drink, perhaps?" There was no mistaking Ms Rubitz's blatant flirting or intent. Max assessed what damage that prospect could do and found it more inviting than dangerous. After a very brief hesitation...

"Okay. You win."

Now that she had made the kill, Ms Rubitz's pace slowed considerably. They both settled into a plush sofa in the lobby next to the bar and ordered two soft drinks when a waiter approached. Max charged them to his room despite Ms

110

Rubitz's offer to pay. The conversation was easy despite it clearly being designed by Ms Rubitz to provide some background details for her news item. Max, for his part, invented a concoction of facts that came to him in response to the stream of soft questions that his interrogator was remembering without taking or referring to notes.

Eventually she apparently had enough, checked her watch, thanked Max for his time and patience, then:

"What are you doing later this evening? Have you got any plans?" she asked as she rummaged in her bag.

"Plans? No. Only to rest my ankle."

"How about eating?"

"Room Service, I expect. Why do you ask?"

"I was going to ask you out to dinner. It's the least I can do – as a 'thank you' – if you would like."

"That's not necessary."

"Are you sure? I'd really like to buy you supper."

In fact, Max wasn't at all sure – the idea of dinner with Ms Rubitz was suddenly very appealing.

"But you've got to write your report."

"That won't take long. It can't, my deadline is in less than an hour. I work quickly and I've got most of it in my head already. I could be back here by eight-thirty. What d'you say?"

"Okay, that sounds great. Thank you."

Ms Rubitz bundled up her last possessions, glanced at her watch once again and set off.

"Good. Dress casual – we'll go to the Village. See you at half eight."

Max's first concern on reaching his room was to telephone Bo Garrick to check that Mickey had given a good report of the visit to the bank. After buying his wardrobe of new clothes and paying his bill at The Alamo Motel, Max only had enough money left to stay at The Roy for another two nights. He wanted to know that Bo's next payment was secured. He also had to buy a little time to sort out the problem with the batteries at the bank and to let his hand and ankle recover. All of which would make the idea of scheduling the raid for this weekend somewhat optimistic. Then there was the problem of the attention he had drawn to himself because of the incident at the bank. He anticipated a rough ride from Bo and the others, having argued that he needed their money to enable him to smarten up to avoid just such attention. He rebuked himself when he reflected back on how easily a pretty face had breached that line of defence.

Max got through to Bo on his cell phone almost immediately, but was then surprised when Bo told him he hadn't heard from Mickey. Max began his report with the good news.

"Everything checks out. It's all operational – exactly as it should be," he reported in an upbeat tone.

"That's great. No problems at all?" Bo sought reassurance.

"A small problem with the kit when we arrived, but nothing to worry about and I sorted it out easily enough."

"What sort of problem?" Bo was concerned.

"A nothing problem, honestly. Nothing that had affected the equipment's performance – and I sorted it out with a bit of reprogramming. It took one minute."

"Great, so the job's on then?"

"Yeah, Mickey will tell you – he saw the whole thing working."

"Where's Mickey?"

"I don't know. We left the bank separately. I thought he'd have been in touch by now."

"So he'll bear all this out will he?"

"Of course. But…well, there was another problem that he'll tell you about," Max said cautiously.

"Like what?" Bo responded abruptly.

"There was an attempted bank robbery while we were there, would you believe?"

"No shit?"

"Yeah." Max knew he had to expand on this. "And I…well…we got involved. I couldn't believe it – just in the wrong place at the wrong time, I guess."

"What d'you mean *'involved'*?"

"Oh it was nothing really. One of the gang tried to rough me up and…well, I hit him."

"You *hit* him? You didn't?" To Max's relief, Bo thought it was amusing. "You hit some hood on a fucking bank raid? You serious?"

"Yes. And there was a reporter there so you may ….you will see something in the paper tomorrow." Max expected a bad response to this, but Bo seemed to miss the significance of the remark.

"It won't change our plans or nothin'?" Bo asked.

"No, absolutely not, but we just need to let the dust settle at the bank. I imagine their security will be a bit tighter for a few days – perhaps we should schedule the job for the weekend after next. Is that all right with you?"

"That's great with me. More time to prepare – that can't be bad. We'll have all the equipment we need by this weekend, so you just say the word when we should get back together for another meet to start the training like you said."

"Will do." Then Max added: "One thing I need right now is the next payment on your schedule. I'm right out of funds." The request was followed by several long seconds of silence.

113

"No trouble. Providing Mickey confirms what you just told me, it'll be with you tomorrow."

"Err... you couldn't make it tonight, could you, please. Only, I haven't even got enough to eat out," Max lied, but he was still concerned that Bo might change his mind when he saw the newspaper report in the morning. "I'm really sorry to ask, but I'm completely broke."

There was another silence from Bo until:

"You know I'm taking a helluva lot on trust here, Max."

"That's not how I see it," Max replied innocently. "I've told you, everything checks out. Mickey will tell you."

"So you say, but you know that I ain't seen nothing yet. I'm taking yours and Mickey's word – and Dennis's who I'd have trusted with my life. That's your ticket at the moment. But you let me down and I'll break you into little pieces, you should know that."

"I'm not about to, Bo."

Another pause.

"Where you staying now?"

"The Roy on 54th West – used to be The Viceroy."

"Are you now? Very nice too. What's your room number?"

"926."

"The cash'll be there about seven...providing I can get hold of Mickey and he confirms what you just told me."

"Thanks - I appreciate it."

"I'll expect to hear from you every day – progress or no progress – I want a report, right?"

"That's fine."

"So I'll hear from you tomorrow."

"You will – and thanks again for the money."

As Max put down the telephone, he felt the weight of responsibility lying in the pit of his stomach until he became pleasantly distracted by a more imminent concern for what he should wear for his evening out.

Max left his room ten minutes early to limp down to the reception where he had arranged to meet Ms Rubitz. Bo had been true to his word. A youth who Max had never seen before, had knocked on his door soon after seven o'clock and handed Max a brown envelope, saying only that it was from Bo Garrick, before departing. Max had locked most of its contents, along with his CD, in the safe in his room and now carried a small sheaf of pocket money.

At 8.25, Max took a seat on one of the sofas in the hotel foyer, still glowing from his hot shower and a vodka and tonic from his mini-bar. He was comfortable to sit and watch the activities of the hotel staff and guests while he awaited the arrival of his date. As he casually looked around the stylish new reception, he momentarily surprised himself when he glimpsed his reflection in one of the large mirrors, but didn't recognise it. He looked back to study it surreptitiously, concluding that he liked the image he saw there. That led him to reflect on everything that had happened to him since his arrival in New York. Could it really be less than a week – just five days since he left London last Friday night? Even the Alamo Hotel seemed like another chapter in his life – and Luisa. He pondered her for a moment, then moved on to consider Bo Garrick, the stash of money in his safe upstairs, his meeting with the gang and his visit to the bank today, Dennis's equipment and the prospects of the robbery. And now he was waiting for a lady who had asked him out on a date. Max glanced back at his reflection. This was the Max who had no social life, virtually no contact with the opposite sex and no desire for adventure, in London. His life in the last few weeks had become as unrecognisable as his image. Whatever it was that was happening to him, he was very comfortable about it. He hadn't felt so sharp, so alive or so good about himself for a long time. All apart from his ankle.

Max checked his watch, suddenly aware that he had been sitting for longer than he had expected. 8.45. Surely Ms Rubitz wasn't going to stand him up?

As the hour ticked up on the four clock faces behind the reception desk, Max decided that he'd given her long enough and was about to return to his room, when he remembered that he had her business card with him. He had put it in his wallet when she presented it to him at the bank. As he hoped, it showed her cell phone number that he promptly tapped out on his own, then listened to it ringing several times. Just as Max expected an answering service to respond, Gaynor's voice answered. She sounded rushed and breathless.

"Hi, Gaynor here."

"Gaynor, it's Alex Slater."

"Oh, hi," she replied with the hint of surprise in her voice.

"I'm waiting for you at the hotel."

"Yeah, I know." Her voice had calmed down. "And I guess you're in reception - and wearing a blue jacket over a white tee-shirt."

Max looked across the foyer to see Gaynor approaching him from the doors. She looked stunning even at that distance; and the broad smile now across her face suggested that she was as pleased to be here as Max was to see her.

"I'm sorry," Gaynor protested. "It took a bit longer than I thought, but guess what?" Her voice had jumped an octave.

"Not only did we get page three, but we got nearly an inch on page one. That's my first ever front page."

"Well done." Max responded with genuine appreciation for the achievement, checked only by the realisation that his story and his profile was about to be front page news, but Max managed:

"Must be the way you wrote it."

"Oh you charming Englishman. I don't know about that, but I do know that we've got something to celebrate – come on I've got a cab waiting."

"Am I dressed okay for wherever we're going?" Max asked for reassurance.

"Perfect."

Doberman's on 49th Street, exactly matched Max's mood - energetic, boisterous, noisy and crowded. He quickly concluded that Gaynor was a regular customer when she was greeted by a muscular, camp waiter who called her 'Gay-Baby' as he air-kissed her on both cheeks, before telling her how stunning she looked. Gaynor introduced 'Alex' to 'Patrick ' who was *charmed* to meet him, shook hands then gestured to their table in an alcove.

"Do you have a bottle of Champagne on ice?" Max asked Patrick, then thought to check with Gaynor. "I'm sorry, do you like Champagne?"

"I *love* Champagne."

"On its way," Patrick informed them.
Max anticipated Gaynor's reaction.

"This is on me. We have to toast your first front page."

"That's a sweet thought." Gaynor seemed genuinely touched by the gesture.

"You realise you will have to do all the talking tonight," Max stated.

"Why's that?"

"Because I've told you everything there is to know about me already today – now it's your turn."

"I think it would take a lot more than ten minutes to find out everything about you, Alex Slater. I think you're a man of hidden depths."

"Not me. What you see is what you get."

"Really? Well I'll settle for that." Gaynor flirted her response.

Patrick arrived with an ice bucket containing a bottle of Champagne, which he proceeded to open without ceremony.

"You two young things celebrating something I should know about?"

"Yes," Gaynor replied without looking away from Max. "And you'll see the results in the morning – my first front page!"

"Well done darling. About time. So what's the story?"

"Alex here. I'm going to make him famous."

"For what?"

"You'll have to read about it in the morning."

"Can't wait. Your last night of anonymity, eh Alex?"

"Perhaps," Max replied with a smile, but knew that the remark could be too true to be funny.

The Champagne set the tone for the evening. There was never more than a few seconds break in their conversation while they ate a meal that neither of them would remember in the morning. Max started with some caution that had been his companion since arriving in New York, managing to deflect tricky questions about his past by asking another question about Gaynor's. But as the evening wore on and the heady mood took its toll on Max's defences, he found it easier to be honest about his background and upbringing. So he told his story as if it were Alex's. About the death of his parents and his life with Dennis and Molly and his time in the services with computers and helicopters and Hannah and buying his way out of the services. Then a slight adjustment when Alex left her Majesty's Services to join the games marketing firm. The story served very well for this evening's purposes.

At eleven thirty, they left the restaurant and walked slowly up Lexington Avenue, arm-in-arm to a newspaper vending machine that Gaynor knew would have an early edition of The Times before midnight. They bought a copy each and Gaynor read her report aloud by the light of a streetlamp.

They eventually hailed a passing cab that Gaynor insisted should drop Max off first because Fifth Avenue was closer than her apartment in Greenwich Village. As the car pulled up at the hotel entrance, Max thanked Gaynor for a lovely evening with all the sincerity that the joint effects of fatigue and alcohol permitted.

"Shall I call you in the morning?" Gaynor asked as Max was still considering the next move.

"Sure, if you like. But not too early – it's been a long day by my standards."

"I'll be your wake-up call. What time?"

"Nine o'clock…ish. Is that okay?"

"Of course."

Max leaned forward to kiss her on the cheek as he bid her 'goodnight', but Gaynor turned her head and met Max's lips full-on with a kiss that Max would relive repeatedly until he fell asleep soon after one o'clock.

ELEVEN

By nine o'clock the next morning, Max was already nearly two hours into the craziest rock 'n' roll week of his life. Or perhaps it would be ten days. Max lost count in the spin that was to follow. The telephone had woken him at six minutes past seven, which he struggled to register on the clock beside his bed, before he answered the call.

"Hi, is that Alex Slater?" an excited young woman enquired, as if surprised to hear his voice.

"Yeah," Max croaked in reply.

"Oh, great! My name's Tanya Dronan - I'm from NBC. We would like to interview you about your amazing encounter at First National Bank yesterday. Would that be possible? We'll send a car to pick you up. We'll do the interview at our studios in The Rockefeller Centre – that's real close to your hotel..."

"Hold on, hold on!" Max broke into her excited monologue.

"You've just woken me up Miss..."

"Tanya."

"....Yeah, I'm sorry, I'm not interested. Thank you for asking, goodbye." Max dropped the phone back on the cradle and collapsed into his pillow.

"Ring!... Ring!... Ring!...

There was no point in Max pretending to ignore it.

"Hello."

"Mr Slater, please can you reconsider. I'll call you in…what? An hour when you're awake. Please! This is such a great… such an *important* story."

"Please don't bother." Max groped the phone to its cradle and dropped into his pillow once more.

Next came CNN about twenty minutes later, followed closely by someone representing a syndication company with a name that Max didn't register. He gave them each similar answers:

"Not interested, please leave me alone."
Enough was enough. Max called the hotel switchboard to hold all calls. They could log them and he'd pick them up later.

It wasn't yet seven thirty, but the damage had already been done to Max's sleep pattern. He lay in bed with his eyes closed but his mind wide open to the consequences of his adventure at the bank and Gaynor's news item. There too were the memories of last evening and the novelty of waking up in one of the swankiest hotels in New York. Max considered the unreality of the last few days. The longer he lay thinking about the extraordinary events that got him here, the more appropriate it seemed for him to get some recognition for his actions in the bank. He had to admit to himself that he was flattered by the attention from the likes of NBC and CNN. What harm could another interview do? But Max knew the answer only too well.

As he got out of bed, Max registered some pain in his right foot which he had forgotten about until now. That reminded him of his hand. He flexed and tested both and concluded they were somewhere above ninety per cent operational. He washed, dragged on some jeans and last night's tee-shirt, then phoned down to the switchboard to check if any calls had been held.

"Yes sir, quite a few, shall I read them or I can get a boy to drop a print-out up to your room?"

"Why? How many are there?"

The operator counted under her breath.

"…Thirteen in total."

"Thirteen!" Max exclaimed. He glanced at the clock that showed 07.53. "Blimey. Can you run through the names for me please?"

The operator recited the name of each caller and company in turn until she read out 'Jason Winchester – First National Credit Bank'.

"Jason Winchester?" Max recalled.

"Yes sir."

"Did he leave a message or number?"

"Yes sir – *Sundance to Butch – call me on 207 1437 – cheers!* "

Max scribbled the number on the pad. The operator finished running through the list of TV stations, news services, radio stations and others unknown to Max that he guessed were hunting interviews. Max asked her to hold all calls except Gaynor Rubitz from the New York Times, then hung up and fell back onto his bed to lay star-shaped staring at the ceiling.

"Bloody hellfire!" He laughed as he contemplated the media interest in him. But why had Jason Winchester phoned? He sat up and dialled the number off the pad. It rang once before Jason answered.

"Jason Winchester?" Max asked.

"Yeah – is that you Butch?"

"Yes – hi! You called."

"Yeah man – wow, what a hive you've stirred up my friend. I hear you're all over The New York Times."

"Not exactly. Have the press been onto you this morning?"

"A couple of TV stations and papers called the office and the office called me. They want me to do some interviews. They've got to clear it with the bank though".

"I'm not with you. You work for the bank don't you?"

"No – I work for Atom Security – they want the publicity, but they've gotta get permission from the bank. But I told them I didn't want to do no interview on my own, but I'd do it with you. You're the main man – I'll do it if you will. What d'you think?"

"I don't think so."

"No? Really?" Jason was clearly surprised. "NBC called first and my head office want me to do their interview, minimum. You know NBC? They're about the biggest - them and CNN."

"Yeah – Tanya someone called me first thing."

"Right – well there you go. Come on, it'll be a laugh – your fifteen minutes of fame."

"No. Sorry, I don't think so."

"Come on man, just think about it, yeah? I'll call you back when I hear from the bank, okay? You'll think about it?"

"Okay, but don't hold your breath."

"Right. I'll catch you later."

As Max put down the phone, it rang almost instantly.

"Hello," he answered wearily, expecting it to be the operator.

"Alex?"

"Gaynor – hi!" He sprang to life.

"I know I'm early, sorry if I woke you but you'll never guess the stir over here. Tell me, have any of the press found you yet?"

"Too right they have."

"I thought they would – what's happened?"

123

"Crazy time. It started an hour or more ago with NBC, now the world and his wife have been on to me. I've got the switchboard holding the calls."

"I know, they wanted my name before they'd put me through to your room."

"NBC want me and the guard from the bank to do an interview – and I guess the rest want about the same."

"Well, what d'you think – could be a bit of fun?"

"That's what Jason - you know, the security guard - that's what he said."

"You've spoken to him?"

"Yeah, he called me."

"So? You going to do it?"

"No I'm not… I don't think so."

"I'm coming over. I got you into this, the least I can do is help sort something out."

"That'd be nice."

"I'll see you in twenty minutes - half an hour tops. Don't speak to any horrid press people till I get there."

Max hid in his room, ordered a breakfast of coffee and toast from Room Service and waited for Gaynor. He was sure the telephonist's reaction to him was particularly respectful today and sensed that the boy delivering his breakfast only stopped marginally short of asking for his autograph.

The phone rang as Max was playing with his toast. Reception asked if someone called Gaynor Rubitz was expected - could they send her up to his room? The present distractions had demoted her to the back of Max's thoughts, until he opened the door. There was the working Gaynor – hair back, slightly formal clothing with her trademark satchel. Max thought she looked great.

"God, it's good to see you. Come in."

Gaynor beamed a smile.

"That's nice, you too." She kissed him quickly on the lips then noticed Max's slight limp. "How's your ankle? Sorry, should have asked earlier."

"Much better, thanks."

"Good. Now listen, I've had a thought," she spurted out. Gaynor was in working mode, just as Max had met her. She walked straight to the small sofa in the room, dropped her bag on the floor and sat formally as if in a business meeting. "As I see it, you've got two choices – you can hole up here for two, three days, maybe more while the hotel protects you from the calls and callers. Or, you can do an interview and pop the bubble."

"Meaning?" Max asked as he sat on the edge of his unmade bed.

"If you do one high-profile interview, such as the NBC one, all the other news services will probably back off. You will have lost any 'exclusive' tag. You're soiled, right? You'll still get the general interest rags and mags on to you for a while, but that won't take long. The majority of heavyweight interest is in your news-worthiness." Gaynor raised her eyebrows and widened her eyes in a *'what do you think?'* expression.

"Will it work, to calm things down quickly?"

"Certainly."

"Otherwise how long will it take?"

"No idea. A few days, I guess – until something else happens by to take their interest. But it's a quiet news time at the moment and I did tell you, this is a big story here in New York – vigilantes, Joe Normal against the mob…."

"Do you want a coffee – there's some in the pot?"

"Thanks."

"How do you take it – black isn't it?"

"Thanks."

Max poured the coffee and emptied the dregs of the pot into his own cup. The two sat side by side on the sofa staring ahead at a blank grey television screen. For a moment, the only sound was Max's spoon stirring milk into his coffee.

"I really enjoyed last night," Max said slowly.

"So did I," Gaynor replied, as if it had been their sole topic of conversation since she arrived.

"No, I mean, *really* enjoyed it. I wanted to tell you that as soon as we spoke this morning. I'm sorry I didn't say it earlier."

"That's okay." Gaynor turned to Max, raised her left hand, kissed her forefinger and put it to Max's lips. He wanted to ask if it was a special night for Gaynor, or had it been just another date with another hot interviewee, but it came out as:

"This coffee's nearly cold, shall I order some fresh?"

"Not for me," Gaynor replied as she emptied her cup in one long gulp, put it down on the coffee table then revved up her energy as if the intermission had just finished and it was time to get back to the plot.

"Right then…" she began. Max sensed a lecture coming on, but Gaynor's pitch was interrupted by a sharp double knock on the door. Max answered it to find a bellboy in his hallway.

"Reception sent this up, sir," the boy announced as he handed over a large white envelope and immediately turned and departed. In the envelope, Max found several smaller envelopes and a single sheet of paper containing a printout of the calls logged by the switchboard. He scanned down the list, registering those he already knew, but then beyond that, another nine calls, most being repeats of the original list. They included a second call from *'Jason Winchester – First National'* and two with no names attached.

"Jason has called back," Max informed Gaynor as he walked back into the room to join her. He now began to open the smaller envelopes to find proposals for interviews and guest appearances on various programmes. Two offered to negotiate a fee, one suggested Max provide the name of his agent for a contract to be drawn up. A couple were from agents offering to represent him. Max handed each sheet of paper to Gaynor to read as he finished it. He laughed and made exclamations at the quantity and quality of the callers while Gaynor offered a somewhat more professionally-informed critique on each one in turn, on the lines of:

"…Don't go near these bastards, they'll shaft you soon as look at you ……. Bloody cheek ……. Fuck you, Mr Slimeystein!" and such like.

Max returned to the list of telephone calls.

"Okay, let's see what Jason wanted." He dialled his number again and listened to several rings before it was answered.

"Hi!"

"Jason – it's Alex."

"Hi man! – how you doing?"

"Okay – you called, what's occurring?"

"Well, the bank have given us the green light. More than that, they're insisting I do the NBC interview. Someone called Daniel O'Malley has been trying to call you to speak to you about it."

Max looked down the printout and found the name.

"That's right, who is he?"

"He represents the bank somehow, I dunno, PR or something – but he's told my boss I gotta do the interview

127

regardless of whether you come. But I don't wanna do that. You gotta do it man, you was the hero – you're the one they really want from the newspaper stuff."

"Why's it so important to the bank?"

"Course it is – it shows their security works. It's great for them – they protected their customers' money, but they want it to look like I was the hero. It's real embarrassing if you don't pitch up man. But if the two of us do it....Butch *and* Sundance – well, that'll be real cool."

"Perhaps I'll call this O'Malley guy."

"You do whatever, but do it quick man, 'cos I gotta do the NBC thing with or without you later this morning. It's all arranged for eleven-thirty at their studio. Come on man – what's the harm? I don't know what your job is, but mine's fucking boring one hundred and fifty per cent of the time. This is the only bit of excitement I'll ever see and I'm up for going along for the ride. Can't you see that?"

"Yes."

"Phone O'Malley, tell him you'll do it. Come on man – please."

"I'll call you back – no promises mind." Max hung up as Gaynor finished a call to her office on her cell phone.

"They want me to arrange a follow-up interview with some more background, lifestyle stuff, for the weekend," she told Max tentatively.

Max blew air through his teeth as he considered the situation and Gaynor's remark.

"Do you really think the NBC thing will diffuse some of this?"

"I'd guess."

Max picked up the phone and dialled the number for Daniel O'Malley that he read from the printout. A switchboard put the call through to his extension and O'Malley answered briskly.

"Mr O'Malley, my name is Alex Slater – you called me at The Roy Hotel."

Immediately Mr O'Malley changed his tone, thanked Max profusely for returning the call and for his actions at the bank yesterday. He went on to explain that the media interest in the incident was understandable, given Max's heroism and the public's regard for crime prevention in New York – he corrected himself to *'anywhere in the US'*. Max said very little as Mr O'Malley continued to explain how the bank would understand if Max wanted to keep out of the public spotlight, although that looked unlikely for the immediate future. He, Mr O'Malley, on behalf of the bank group that he represented, would like to persuade Max to join their security guard for the NBC interview. He admitted that the publicity was good for the bank, but that shouldn't distract from an act of heroism that should be celebrated. His tone changed and he emphasised his words:

"I don't know what it's like for you in the UK, Mr Slater, but I can tell you that the people here in New York are fed up to here with crime. Big crime and the daily little things that make life in the city so tedious. Your act yesterday, Mr Slater, was an example to everyone that wants the good guys to win over the bad guys. They'll wish they had your guts to make a stand. What you did was remarkable – people want to celebrate that with you. I'm sure you can understand that. They want to…. I don't know…. want to share what you did, to send a message to the… .the bastards in our society – *'up yours, you bastards!'*…"

Max suspected that Mr O'Malley was losing control, but his apparently genuine emotions conveyed their message.

"Okay. I'll do the interview," Max broke in to announce with a sigh of resignation.

"You will? Excellent. I'll call the station for you. We'll have a car pick you up at half ten, will that be convenient?"

"That's fine," Max sighed again in a tone that sounded far from *fine*. "Will you tell Jason Winchester what's happening?... Thank you."

Gaynor was watching him from her seat on the sofa as he hung up the phone.

"You could try to sound a bit happier about it."

"Happier? Why the hell. I don't need all this. I wish I hadn't gone near the bloody bank yesterday, or done your interview."

Gaynor sat back with a start.

"Well you did – and you did something pretty amazing, so don't blame me for all this. I don't understand you. I think you're secretly enjoying this attention, but for some reason you're afraid to show it. But whatever, you can't put the clock back and if I hadn't reported it, someone else would, so fuck you if you don't like it." Gaynor was throwing her phone and a book back into her satchel. Max watched her briefly before getting up from the bed where he had been perched to make his phone calls.

"I'm sorry," he said to Gaynor's face as he held both her shoulders to slow her down in her apparent haste to leave. "Really, I'm sorry - I was out of order - didn't mean to sound as if I blamed you. And I appreciate your help - really I do. But this is all happening too quickly. I'm not used to all this attention - I'm having trouble adjusting. You have no idea quite how far this is from my normal life in London."

"Well let's just get through the NBC gig and see how things work out. Okay - you can handle that?"

"Yeah."

"You'd better get dressed - smart casual. They'll redress you if they don't like what you're wearing anyway. I'll sort your car out, then I must go."

"You don't need to do that, they're sending a car for me."

"Yeah, to the front doors. That's no use - the front street's crawling with reporters." Gaynor dialled reception. "Security please...Hi! This is room 926, Mr Slater has a car arriving for ten-thirty; can you arrange for him to get out through a goods entrance or somewhere at the back please? He shouldn't go through reception.... Thank you."

Tanya Dronan was pretty, black and mid twentyish, with more energy than a puppy and a clipboard that she used constantly as a variety of props – one moment a fan, the next a direction indicator, a notepad, a lift-door jammer. She was waiting for Max in reception as he arrived at NBC's studios then guided him through the security procedures and the corridors to make-up department with a constant running commentary. Max hardly said a word, but followed dutifully at a fast limp and took in all her instructions even though he assumed the director would repeat them in due course.

Jason was already getting his makeover in a large seat in front of a large mirror with a large cloth over his shoulders just as at a barber's, when Max arrived in the brightly-lit room.

"Hey, Butch - you made it," Jason exclaimed with obvious relief as he recognised Max in the mirror. His right hand shot out from under the cover for Max to slap. "How is it?" he asked, referring to Max's hand.

"Much better, thanks."

131

Jason turned to Ms Dronan.

"War wound this. Sustained in the heat of battle. You should get your man to ask him about it."

Ms Dronan made a feverish note on her pad, excused herself and shot out of the room saying she would let the show producer know they were here.

"What a darling! What I could do for her!" Jason exclaimed the moment she left the room, then checked the reaction of the make-up lady powdering his face.

"Don't mind me, honey, you wouldn't believe what I hear in this job."

"Is she attached - in a relationship?" Jason asked.

"Tanya? I don't know - you should ask her."

"I will."

"That's it, you're done," she announced as she swept the shroud off Jason's shoulders. "Next."

Max stepped forward and took his seat just as Tanya returned with a man that she introduced as: *'your director – Don Puccini'*. He made a series of pleasantries about how grateful he was to have secured Max and Jason's interview then went on to explain the proceedings that would follow. They would do two interviews, if that was all right with them. The first would be with one of the network's top current affairs presenters, Karen Faith, for her late night show, *'Karen Faith Tonight'*. That should take about twenty minutes to record, but they only needed seven minutes for the programme. Then a news reporter would like to conduct a very short interview to be cut into the station's regular news spots throughout the day. Both Max and Jason nodded their approval and were immediately presented with a form to sign. Jason scribbled his signature while Max read quickly down the single typed sheet.

It all seemed in order until he noticed that a space reserved for a fee had not been filled in.

"I'm sorry," Tanya apologised when it was pointed out. She picked up a phone from the countertop, dialled an internal extension number and spoke openly about the fee she should offer. It occurred to Max that this was somewhat casual for an organisation that must do this many times every week.

"Would $500 be acceptable?" Tanya asked as she turned from the phone to address Max and Jason. They looked at one another and shrugged agreement, both seemingly pleasantly surprised. Tanya returned to the phone. "That's fine, shall I write the fee in by hand?... Okay." She picked up both forms and filled the sum of $500 on both, then returned them for approval.

Jason was first to register the sum.

"$500 *each*! Wow."

Karen Faith was more polite than Max had expected, the studio was smaller and the atmosphere more relaxed. But then, Max's knowledge of television studios had been gained from watching Saturday morning children's TV programmes that ran on hyper energy in barn-like spaces with hand-held cameras and manic activity. He was now witnessing the other end of the spectrum and was surprised by the intimacy of the small current-affairs set up. He quickly relaxed to Ms Faith's well-informed approach as she asked a few questions, made notes of their replies and explained how she intended to conduct the interviews. Jason, by comparison with Max's growing confidence, suddenly appeared overwhelmed by the whole occasion. Max was aware of Jason's tension and began to worry that he would clam up and leave him to do all the talking. Karen Faith had made the same observation and tried her best to reassure Jason that everything would be fine. He should try to relax and just be himself.

Once proceedings got underway and the floor-manager had given Ms Faith her cue, she began by directing most of her questions to Max. Nothing too difficult, starting with his recollections of the incident. Ms Faith's approach was non-confrontational and respectful. Max felt good, confident, in control - and it showed. Jason appeared to be overcoming his nerves as he answered the same question and recalled his memories of the event. Then Ms Faith moved on to their backgrounds, asking each in turn how they could have been so well prepared and adjusted for such an extraordinary incident. Had Max seen action during his period in the Army? How well had it prepared him for the prospect of defending himself against someone threatening him with a gun? And how well had it prepared him to cope with the after-effects of maiming his assailant?

It was when she addressed the same question to Jason that the interview took an abrupt turn from the conventional interview to an altogether more intimate exchange. Jason admitted that he had been physically sick last night when he got home and heard about the death of the robber who he had shot. He related his reactions when the adrenaline had stopped pumping up his defences. The others listened sympathetically, as did everyone in earshot in the studio, struck by the force of Jason's simple words to express the most sensitive emotions that had overwhelmed him when he realised that he had taken the life of another human being. It was not Karen Faith who prompted the next question when Jason finished, but Max who hadn't heard that one of the robbers had died from the bullet wounds. Max picked up the mood and consoled his new friend without consideration for the formalities of the interview. The next few minutes would have made powerful television viewing had they been part of a drama produced elsewhere in the NBC organisation. The two men talked candidly to one another of their feelings and reflections on the incident. They spoke in quiet voices just loud enough to converse between themselves only a few feet apart, Max drawing Jason's intimate explanation of his feelings as if in a confessional. At one point he even reached across to touch Jason's hand when he felt instinctively that Jason needed the reassurance of the contact from a comrade, as Max considered their relationship at that moment. Gone was Jason's usual bravado; in its place was the vulnerability of a child. In the control room, the production team had become aware of the impact of this peculiarly gentle exchange of views and sympathies as they watched the bank of monitor screens in near silence. The group of hardened professionals in the gallery and on the studio floor, that were too used to producing quantity before quality, recognised now that they were witnessing a rare piece of television. The director instructed two cameras to tighten their close ups on both Jason's and Max's face, another onto a two-shot of the pair, then he cut systematically between the three angles for the next three minutes - an eternity in television terms. Karen Faith, to her great professional credit, quickly recognised that she had no part in the exchange until, as it became obvious that it had run its course, on instructions from the director through her earpiece, she interjected with an appropriately sensitive question before looking for the opportunity to wrap up the interview.

Immediately the floor-manager confirmed that the recording had ended, there was a ripple of applause from the crew. Applause? In a current affairs studio? Unheard of. Instead of calling over the intercom to the studio floor, Don

Puccini was down from the gallery like a shot to thank his guests and Karen Faith personally for their contribution. He introduced the second journalist who would conduct the shorter news interview, then while they were being briefed, Don Puccini stepped aside with Karen Faith to converse in a whisper.

"Did you catch any of that on a monitor?" the director asked.

"No, but I could see it was special. How did it look?

"Bloody amazing. You could cut the atmosphere with a knife in the gallery. Stella had tears in her eyes at one point."

"No - Stella?"

"I swear. So, thanks K, you were terrific."

He turned back to Max and Jason talking to the journalist.

"Excuse me Joe - have you gentlemen got any plans for lunch or can I take you for something to eat. Karen can you join us?" Everyone agreed to meet in reception in thirty minutes, which gave Joe McInnis time for his short interview, then Max and Jason time to get the make-up removed and Jason time to harass Tanya Dronan into joining them for lunch. He failed. But only because as a lowly PA she couldn't gate crash a director's lunch with Karen Faith in attendance. Jason didn't push the point, but managed to line up another date on a rain check and exchanged phone numbers. By the time the group met in reception for the short walk to Yellow River restaurant, Jason was full of bonhomie and evidently back to his old self.

Lunch was great fun. Max sparkled with the attention paid by his hosts and Jason was in his element as soon as he and Don Puccini discovered their mutual interest in The Giants football team. There was no shortage of conversation even though much of it revolved around the gossip, anecdotes and activities of TV Land during which Max and Jason were relegated to onlookers. But they were drawn back abruptly when Karen asked about the approaches of the other news services to them, then if they had received any party invitations yet. Jason's ears pricked up immediately.

"You will – especially after the programme goes out tonight," Don said with certainty. "You'll have every party organiser and PR agency in town onto you – you're celebs – and for the right reason, so you can be on anyone's list for any occasion."

"Really?" Jason was wide-eyed with anticipation.

"Yeah, of course. In a town where you only have to cut your husband's dick off…"

"Or have your dick cut off by your wife…" Karen interjected.

"Yeah," Don agreed. "Or know someone that knew someone who helped O.J. escape, to be on most party lists, then you guys are very hot property at the moment."

"Really?" Jason exclaimed again.

Don was amused by Jason's evident excitement at the prospect.

"You could be out every night – and day if you wanted."

"Really. Do you get them?" Jason asked Karen.

"Sure. Tonight it's an opening to some new musical off Broadway. I might go after the programme. Some good friends going to this one. Come along if you want, I'll get you some invites."

A few minutes sifting through her diary and Karen had produced invitations to two awards events, another opening night and a handful of assorted parties. She could get Max and Jason the relevant invitations for any that they wanted to attend. The media interest in them would apparently guarantee them access to the inner sanctums of New York's party set.

The moment Max and Jason shut the door of the cab that they were sharing to get across town from the restaurant, they suddenly became two school children who no longer needed to be on their best behaviour in front of teacher. They both laughed aloud as they tripped over themselves to recall their individual sides of the story of the day so far and their respective performances in front of the cameras. Max ribbed Jason about his slow start and how he had thought he may have had to do the interview alone. Jason was more interested in the $500 fee and getting his date with Tanya Dronan. This was clearly going to be a pre-occupation for him.

"She is such a doll, isn't she?" he recalled, then turned abruptly to Max. "Do you believe in love at first sight?"
Max laughed.

"I suppose so – but it's never happened to me. I'm more of a slow burn sort of guy."

"Really?"

"Yeah, why's that so surprising?"

"Oh man, I tell you, I fall in love at least once a week with chicks I don't even speak to. It could happen right now just looking out of the window."

"That doesn't count – that's not 'love', that's 'lust'. That's falling in lust – we all do that occasionally."

"Even you?"

"Even me."

"So what do you think of Tanya? She's a doll isn't she?"

"Yeah, a sweetie."

"Sure is. I could suck her dry." Jason reflected on the prospect. "So come on lend me your phone, man – we got all these party invites, I'm going to fix up a date right now. Tell you what, let's do a foursome – you got someone you could bring?"

"Possibly. For which party?"

"All of them, man."

Immediately Max switched on his phone, it signalled three messages. The first was from Gaynor checking how the NBC gig had gone. The other two drew Max abruptly back to reality the instant he recognised Bo Garrick's voice. The first message was for Max to call him. He didn't sound happy. The second was sharp, abrupt and possibly angry as he *demanded* Max phone him immediately he got this message.

"You okay, man?" Jason had sensed Max's change of mood as he listened in silence to his phone.

"Yeah, just some business messages - some things I've got to sort out, that's all. Let me make one call." Max dialled and listened to the ring of another mobile phone.

"Hi."

"Gaynor, it's Alex."

"Alex, I've been trying to call you."

"I know, I just got your message."

"That was an hour ago. Since then I've seen your interview on the NBC news. Have you seen it?"

"No. How does it look?"

"It's very short. You and the guard…"

"Jason."

"…Yeah. I think you both answered a couple of questions each. But you both looked fine. You know they're trailing a full interview on *'Karen Faith Tonight'* – how did that go?"

"I think it was okay - you'll have to watch it tonight. But that's why I'm calling. What you doing later - sorry, let me rephrase that - would you like to come to a party tonight with me and Jason and…a friend. I'm with Jason now and we've been invited to a party. What do you think? Would you like to come?"

Gaynor thought for moment.

"I'm not sure," she hesitated. "I've got something on this evening. But don't you want to watch the interview?"

"Yeah but I thought we could go afterwards. It's an 'after show' party for an opening night – a new musical or something."

"Karen Faith is on at ten-thirty. I could come to your hotel at ten."

"If you make it eight we could have dinner together."

"I can't. I'll see you at ten. Got to go now. Bye." She was gone. Max suddenly felt a little deflated and unsure about Gaynor but he had no time to reflect before Jason's energy interrupted his thoughts.

"Right, so it's all over to your place for the Karen Faith show then we can go to the party."

"Aren't you forgetting something?" Max asked.

"What?"

"You haven't got a date yet."

Jason laughed.

"Shit. Here give me your phone will you." He fidgeted in his pockets until he found the sheet of paper with Tanya's contact numbers then dialled one. It rang for a while somewhere in the NBC offices until it was answered by a man who told Jason that Tanya wasn't around then suggested he call later. Undeterred, Jason tried Tanya's cell phone but got no response. As the cab drew up outside The Roy Hotel, Jason was frantically dialling another number.

"Hold on a sec," he instructed the driver who was expecting to take Jason on to his company head office down town.

"Jason, please," Max pleaded. "Give me the phone. I've got to go."

Jason hung on, listening for a response to his last call. This one was to Tanya's home phone number. When nothing happened he shut down the call with a sharp stab on the keypad.

"Not even an answerphone dammit. Okay, look, I'll call you later. Your place for the show then off to the party, right? I'll see you at ten with Tanya – otherwise I'll get someone else."

"You do that. I'll see you later." Max took back his phone and the cab pulled off.

In his room, Max sat at the desk and stared at his phone. He needed to compose himself for the call to Bo and didn't want to feel or sound apologetic. He still felt a little light-headed from the wine at lunch and it worried him that this might make it more difficult for him to handle the confrontation he expected. He stood up, walked across the room to compose himself, then back and took his seat again. He dialled Bo's cell phone number.

"Yeah," Bo barked abruptly in his usual manner.

"Bo, it's Max."

"Where the fuck have you been? No, I know where you've been – talking to the TV – you and the guard – been interviewed, I hear. Now you can tell me why." But before Max could compile an answer, Bo was straight back in. "It was you that wanted to be anominous, yeah? This is your idea of staying anominous is it?"

"I didn't have any choice, Bo."

"No choice?! No fucking choice?!"

"No, I didn't."

"You fucking stupid or what? You just say '*no*'- or say nothing. You think I'm stupid?"

"Bo, will you please listen. You know I got caught up with that incident at the bank - Mickey must have told you it wasn't my fault but it happened and the news people got onto the story really fast. I told you that last night. You didn't seem too worried…"

"That was last night – you hadn't been interviewed on TV then – and what about the paper – fucking front page and a fucking photo for fuck's sake – that's real anominous, that is."

"I know, I know it wasn't ideal but none of it was my fault for fuck's sake, Bo, you can see that. Mickey must have told you that. A reporter was at the bank and took the photo as I left. Today I got so bugged here by the press that I was advised to do a TV interview to get the rest of them off my back."

"Advised by who? Karen fucking Faith I suppose."

"Bo. Give it a rest. I'm sorry I attracted attention but I can't change it and I think I'm doing the best under the circumstances. Please give me credit."

"For being a fucking jerk - yeah. You on some fucking drugs or something?"

"Oh for God's sake grow up. I don't deserve this. It isn't going to make any difference to the job or the whacking great haul you're in line for as we both know – bloody millions more than likely – so give it a rest." There was silence for several seconds. "Are you there?"

"Yeah. I still want you to keep in touch. Every day. Developments or no developments."

"Of course."

"And we're still on for the weekend after this, right?"

"I think so."

"You fucking know so!"

"Okay. Next weekend."

"Call me tomorrow. About this time."

"I will. Cheerio."

Bo was gone. Max put down his phone and sat back with a sigh.

By nine-thirty that evening, Max was surprised how bored he had become with his own company as he sat in his room channel-hopping TV stations, waiting for Gaynor. He had also surprised himself by how much he was looking forward to seeing her again, but worried that his growing interested in her was not reciprocated. This was Gaynor's home town, her ordinary everyday life that Max had just stepped into for a passing high-profile moment. Max, by comparison, was living out the most extraordinary time of his life. Everything that came into it now was exciting, frightening and yes, romantic. Try as he might to deny his true emotions, several times during the last few days, he had felt like screaming into the sky above Manhattan just to release some of the pressure. His pent up excitement was enough to burst him at times. Keeping it in check under the stiff upper lip of an English businessman was almost too much.

Reception called Max's room before ten o'clock to enquire whether he was expecting a 'Ms Rubitz'. The moment he saw her at his door a few minutes later, he realised that she had been upset. Her face was puffy. He was sure she had been crying but was now trying to put on a brave face whilst avoiding eye contact with Max.

"Are you all right?" he asked.

"Sure," Gaynor replied as she pecked his cheek and walked into the room. "No really, it's just been a bad day," she continued. "But nothing a drink won't put right."

"You sure – nothing more I can do?" Max asked as he unlocked the door to his mini bar. Have you eaten?"

"Yes…well, no but I'm not hungry."

"You've got to have something. We'll get something on Room Service when the others get here. What would you like to drink?"

Gaynor cast her eye around the contents of the mini bar.

"Campari and soda or lemonade please."

"Do you want to talk about your rotten day?" Max asked as he opened the miniature bottles.

Gaynor appeared to think about the question before reconsidering.

"No. Tell me about yours."

But before Max could answer, there was a loud bang on his bedroom door. Through the spy glass, Max could see two people standing in his hallway. One was Jason but Max couldn't see if the lady with him was Tanya.

"Hi Butch," Jason greeted Max with a slap on the arm. He had obviously been drinking. "This is Chrissy." He gestured for her to enter.

"How did you get past security?" Max asked.

"Famous face, I guess," Jason replied as he spotted Gaynor. "Hi, I'm Jason, this is Chrissy. Don't I know you?"

"Yeah, I work for The New York Times – we met briefly after the raid at your bank yesterday," Gaynor replied.

"*My* bank – hey, I like that." Jason laughed. "But listen, it could happen. Today I got invited to try out for a job at Head Office - to help with promoting the company and that sort of stuff 'cos of the publicity around the raid. Just a trial, but if it works out and it's made permanent, I'll get more money. Not bad eh?"

"Well done," the others agreed.

144

Max ordered a selection of food and drink on Room Service that was delivered as they settled down to watch 'Karen Faith Tonight'. Their babble only stopped as Karen Faith introduced the item using the morning edition of The New York Times.

"A news story that has been catching considerable attention today was covered under an 'exclusive' tag by The New York Times this morning. A quite remarkable story of a bank raid here in Manhattan that was foiled by a member of the public and a security guard in the most extraordinary circumstances. The bank is First National Credit where a gang of would-be robbers entered yesterday afternoon with guns blazing by all accounts. The two men involved were Alex Slater, a visiting British businessman and security guard, Jason Winchester. I interviewed them earlier today in an exclusive television report for this programme. I first asked Alex Slater to explain exactly what happened…"

As Max's face appeared on the screen and he began to answer the question, there was a jeer from the others in the room that quickly subsided. Two questions later and Karen Faith introduced Jason into the interview. Another smaller jeer from the audience. He looked nervous at first but Max appeared completely at ease. For a couple of minutes the two described the incident in response to Karen Faith's questioning. Then, very quickly in this edited version of the full interview, came the questions relating to Max and Jason's ability to handle the aftermath of the killing. As their answers, then their intimate dialogue progressed, the group sprawled around the bedroom, watched in complete silence. Max and Jason seemed as surprised as the other two at the sensitivity of their conversation. The occasional shot of Karen Faith as a virtual onlooker, only heightened the drama of their exchange that was played out in full, unedited.

As the pre-recorded sequence ended, Karen Faith summarised it in the live studio with:

"A remarkable story - and two remarkable men…"

In Max's hotel room there was silence. Max blew air through his teeth and looked across to Gaynor with a *'what do you think?'* expression.

"*Remarkable* about sums it up," she stated.

"That was terrific. You were really good," Chrissy volunteered.

"I'd no idea it was going to look like that." Jason seemed to be in mild shock. "I don't remember it like that with just you and me talking."

"That was…excellent, really excellent, both of you… but I don't think that's put the story to rest exactly." Gaynor concluded with a sense of foreboding.

Max hadn't expected too much of the party which he assumed would consist of lots of people standing around making small talk with glasses of wine in their hands. Not that Max drew on much experience of such gatherings - he would have avoided them at all costs in the past. But he was happy to use it as an excuse to spend time with Gaynor. To Max's surprise he was swept along with the energy and excitement from the moment he and the others arrived. Jason and Chrissy were off into the restaurant to play *spot-the-star* which, at a minor level wasn't too difficult. And Gaynor immediately identified faces that she knew through contacts on the paper. Max had no idea if anyone recognised him; they all seemed very welcoming regardless.

Apparently the opening night for the musical had gone well and everyone was on a wave of relief and anticipation for the reviews that would be in the papers within hours. The mood was upbeat and celebratory. At one point a group even broke into an impromptu routine from the show. Max couldn't believe this is what he had been missing when he turned down the occasional invitation to a cocktail party at home in London.

After a short while of Max being swept from group to group in non-stop conversation, Gaynor attracted his attention to Karen Faith who had just arrived. She was delighted to see that Max and Jason were there. She couldn't wait to tell them that the station had already received more than forty calls praising the interview and Max and Jason's performance, even before the show went off air. Undoubtedly there would be more. She wanted to introduce them to everyone in the room as her new best friends.

Max and Gaynor left the party in full swing before one o'clock – quite late enough for Gaynor who had to be at work by eight in the morning. They walked for several blocks before hailing a passing cab to take Gaynor home. The walk gave Max the time he needed to prompt a few sensitive questions. The more time he spent with Gaynor the more he wondered, but the more it was frustrating him that he couldn't read her feelings for him. Then there were the tears earlier tonight. He knew that she had been crying before she came to the hotel and sensed that she was close to telling him the reason. It took only a few well-directed prompts for her to open up and tell Max what he assumed to be her full story.

Gaynor had lived with a boyfriend for more than a year until they split up during the summer. He had been, and still was, an officer in the NYPD called Jonah Lewins. They met through work many years ago but only began their relationship two years back. But he's a workaholic, Gaynor felt their relationship was going nowhere, their work had driven them apart so she split up the relationship. The problem is that Jonah doesn't see it so simply. He's still very much in love with Gaynor and keeps pestering her to get back together with him which she has no intention of doing. But because she's still fond of him, she agrees to keep in touch and provide a shoulder for him to cry on but nothing more. She senses that Jonah needs her as a prop and a complete split severing all contact would be dangerously cruel to him. So she's trying to let Jonah down gently, but that can hurt – as it did when they met earlier tonight.

Max listened as they walked arm in arm. He could be a good listener and Gaynor seemed to get relief from sharing her story through a slow trickle of details. But as she drove off in the cab, leaving Max to walk the last few blocks back to his hotel alone, he realised he felt no closer to her than he had at the start of the evening. He now knew more about her background and understood why she might be reluctant to expose herself to a new relationship, but try as he might to think of any tell-tale signs of her true feelings for him, he realised he had nothing to grasp. Perhaps he should back off and concentrate on the real reason he was in New York.

Don Puccini and Karen Faith's predictions were spot on. The next morning it seemed that every party organiser in New York knew where Max was staying. His post was full of companies with 'PR' in their names or 'public relations' listed in their services. Max's instinct would have been to file them all into his waste bin but buoyed by the success of the night before and egged on by Jason who seemed to want to share the entire experience with Max, he sifted through all the proposals, invitations, parties and events with a keen eye for a continuous supply of entertainment. And so it was that Max's schedule and profile moved up a gear, as did his circle of friends - or acquaintances. Through the week, Max was surprised at the number of times he saw the same people at the various parties. On reflection, he found it difficult to differentiate one occasion from another. Once the premiere was over or the function had opened, the parties began to look very similar. Not that he didn't enjoy them - he did. During the week, more people recognised him and prompted conversations about the bank raid. His photo appeared in three daily papers and at least as many magazines that he knew of; there were undoubtedly more. He was offered more drugs than he'd ever heard of, propositioned more times than he could remember - by both sexes - and been invited to the most diverse parties he could imagine; including skiing at Lake Tahoe, a private cruise in the Caribbean and a hunting weekend in the Rockies. A shame to decline them but Max managed to remind himself that he had a job to do next weekend here in New York.

In a week that began to blur in Max's mind, two events stood apart from what was becoming the norm. One was the night he slept with Gaynor and the other was the night he went to see a New York Giants match with Jason.

Someone at The Giants had recognised Jason Winchester's name on a supporters' list and spotted a promotional opportunity so called him to offer a VIP evening at a pre-season game against the other New York football team, The Jets. Jason was welcome to take a couple of guests. He was beside himself with excitement as he tried to explain the story to Max one morning on the telephone. He invited Max to make up his party that would include Jason's son.

"Your son?!" Max exclaimed.

"Yeah - Benny - he's eight - lives with my wife."

"You're wife?" Max exclaimed.

"Yeah - well, sort of - nearly not - she lives with a friend - I'll tell you later. You coming?"

"Sure!"

Jason picked Max up from the hotel in his car that evening. Max knew nothing about cars but recognised it as something familiar from home.

"It's a Saab, man. It's Swedish. That's near you isn't it?" Jason announced when Max showed a casual interest.

"What Sweden near the UK d'you mean?"

"Yeah, isn't it?"

"Well about ....I don't know....about two hours flying time."

"Yeah well there you are. She's my baby," he said, caressing the bodywork while unlocking the doors. "The best car I've ever owned – and built for battle," he added. "Gorgeous, isn't she? An' goes like a bat out of hell, bless her." Jason kicked the accelerator to demonstrate the *'turbo coming in'*, whatever that meant, as he pulled away from the hotel forecourt. Even Max could admire the condition of the car from the outside as the bodywork gleamed in the city lights. But inside Jason had created a shrine to everything important in his life. It was like sitting in a scrap book. Every surface had photos, magazine pictures and memorabilia stuck to the paintwork and roof lining. As they travelled across town, Jason explained what various pictures meant as he pointed them out at random. Pride of place was his son, Ben. Jason's conversation returned to him repeatedly as he spoke with endearing affection about the son he could no longer see every day since his marriage broke down and Ben lived with Sabrina, Jason's wife.

"She's a fucking bitch," he announced abruptly when Max asked about her.

Max was shocked.

"I've never heard you swear before."

"That's nothing man, she really is. She was screwing around with my best friend for years till I found out. Now she lives with the little shit."

"Don't you mind Benny living with her?"

"Course I do, but I can't do nothing about it, yet. But I will, when I can get more sorted, Benny will come and live with me. But I work bad hours. I can't be there when he needs me. So it's for the best right now." Then his voice cheered up as he remembered: "Perhaps if this new job works out - you know, if I'm gonna be Mr Nine-to-five, who knows."

Benny was not what Max expected, mainly because he was nothing like Jason. He was quiet and very polite, telling 'Mr Slater' how pleased he was to meet him as he offered his right hand for Max to shake. Max tried not to show his surprise. But once at the match, Benny and Jason were both as excitable and animated as one another. Their VIP entertainment included a reception in a hospitality suite, buffet refreshments and a dedicated PR lady called Greta who was determined to ply Jason and his guests with every comfort at her disposal and every item of merchandise in the club catalogue. Jason and Benny were overwhelmed. Every new sweatshirt, pen knife or beanie hat drew a bigger smile; and when Greta produced a photo of the team signed by all the players, Max knew the next problem would be deciding who was going to keep it.

Max surprised himself by getting into the atmosphere of the game and even beginning to understand some of the rules. As he said 'Goodnight' to Jason back at his hotel at the end of the evening, he reflected on what a great time he'd had, what good company Jason and Benny had been and how the whole occasion had reminded him of his own outings with his father to follow The Arsenal back in London. It had made a refreshingly pleasant change from the succession of parties.

Then there was the night he slept with Gaynor. And that was exactly what he did – slept. Max had deliberately not phoned Gaynor for two days. It had been as hard as giving up smoking, his mind being drawn back to her more than he expected or wanted. So he was very proud of the strength of his will power when she phoned him first to ask when she could do her second interview for the paper. Max hoped he sounded suitably casual as he arranged to meet that evening, as long as it didn't take too long because he was going out. To his surprise, he thought he sensed Gaynor's disappointment and without a moment's thought he invited her to come, then was completely thrown when she asked where and what it was. Max couldn't remember anything about the occasion for a moment until he managed to find the invitation as he fumbled for words to cover the gap. It was a party. No excuse for this one, just a party. Gaynor sounded almost keen to accept, but perhaps Max was imagining it.

Gaynor arrived at Max's hotel at six o'clock already dressed for the evening. Max dropped his defences the instant he saw her and told her that she looked *'great'* and burbled on about how great it was that she could go to the party. He recalled using the word 'great' a third time before he shut himself up and offered her a drink. Perhaps that was their first mistake - to start drinking so early. They finished the interview and a couple more shorts. Max washed and changed. They went by cab to a restaurant a short distance down town, where they arrived in a ready-to-party mood mid-evening.

Lots of champagne cocktails, not much food and two hours later, they tried to find a cab before deciding to walk back to the hotel for a night cap. The fifteen minute walk was not enough to sober them up. Max recalled thinking that he was seeing a new side to Gaynor as the alcohol anaesthetised her defences for the first time since their dinner at Dobermans.

Max only remembered the briefest of visits to his bathroom as soon as they arrived in his room. But by the time he emerged, Gaynor was fast asleep on the bed. She looked so peaceful that Max eased off her shoes, pulled a cover over them both and collapsed beside her.

Shortly after three o'clock he was woken by Gaynor covering herself with the duvet before switching off the bedside light; so Max did the same.

They woke at about the same time as one another soon after seven o'clock, both looking and feeling wretched. Max managed to co-ordinate the most movement and made his way to the bathroom to take a shower after ordering lots of coffee and orange juice from Room Service.

Ten minutes later, Gaynor managed to answer the door to the waiter and direct him to the small table where he placed the tray. She scrambled around to find some change for a tip that she spotted in the contents of Max's pockets that he had emptied onto the small informal table. Then Gaynor collapsed into a chair to pour coffee and sip the fresh orange juice. She placed her head in her hands while she waited for the cold juice to take its affect in her stomach. As she took the coffee cup and saucer from the tray, she pushed the remaining cash, a room key and Max's passport aside to make space to put it down beside her. Almost instinctively, she flipped open the back page of the crisp new passport and turned it to focus her blood shot eyes on the photo. For a moment, she didn't register that the portrait she was staring at was not of Max. Still Gaynor wasn't thinking clearly about why Max had someone else's passport – then she did. Her journalistic instincts were aroused. She focused her eyes on the portrait of a young man's face with a scruffy beard and long unkempt hair. She checked the name – Alex Thomas Slater. Now she returned to the portrait and, looking past the hair, she realised this was the exact same Alex Slater who she thought she knew. She was about to call out to him something about his former life as a hippie, but when she checked the date she realised that the passport was less than a month old. What? How can that be? She studied the date again – no mistake. So which was the real Alex Slater – the clean-shaven businessman in the shower – or the tramp she was looking at in the passport? She was still pondering the oddity of the portrait and date when the lock on the bathroom door clicked. There was no logical reason for Gaynor to be so suspicious of the passport photo that might well have had a logical explanation. Or perhaps her journalist's instincts were sharper at that moment than the rest of her senses, but she instinctively flicked the booklet closed and pushed it away as Max came back into the room with a towel around his lower half.

Even through her hangover, Gaynor's mind kept returning to Max's passport photograph all the way into her office. She reasoned that perhaps he had decided to tidy himself up for his trip to New York…but why? That didn't seem plausible. Wouldn't he have anticipated that and cut his beard and hair *before* getting a new passport photo a few days before his trip? Wouldn't immigration have given him a hard time when he arrived with an unrecognisable picture in his passport? Her alcoholic haze even concocted a version of the options that involved him wearing a false wig and beard for the photo. *'Don't be so stupid. There's bound to be a simple explanation. You should have asked him,'* she rebuked herself. But try as she might, Gaynor could not stop herself from puzzling over the Jekyll and Hyde identity she had stumbled over; and that frustrated her.

She sat at her desk staring at her computer screen that awaited her command while a colleague who had noticed her fragile state, organised a coffee. When she focussed her eyes, the first e-mail message was from Jonah Lewins asking if he could take her to the cinema that evening. Gaynor sighed with frustration at his constant attention and was about to ignore it for a while before replying to the email to decline his offer, when she checked herself. She picked up the phone as her coffee arrived in a plastic beaker.

"Jonah, hi it's me..... No, sorry, not tonight, impossible. But can you do me a favour please?..... A check on a British businessman. See if he has any form, here or in the UK.... I know, I know.... That's not true, I haven't asked for ages.... Come on, that was as much for your good as mine – you got an arrest didn't you? In fact, come to think of it, you still owe me for that one.... Please it's important.... Yes, I know, but your systems'll do it better in half the time I can....... Thank you.... His name's Alex Thomas Slater. He works for a company called Astrodome Games. Don't worry, I'm going to e-mail you all the relevant info, okay?..... You're a dear, thanks.... Yeah, me too but maybe next week. It'll be on for ages yet..... Bye."

Throughout the last week, the shadow of Bo Garrick had lurked close by, never far from Max's thoughts for very long. He had kept his promise to contact Bo every day, even though

155

that normally took the form of a very brief message on his answer service late at night. But as Max lay in bed nursing his mother-of-all-hangovers in the darkened bedroom, his cell phone rang from his coat pocket somewhere close by. It hardly ever rang because the only three people who knew the number were Gaynor, Jason and Bo Garrick. Before he could be bothered to find out which one it was, the ringing stopped. Then it started again, creating a sense of urgency that roused Max to track down the phone.

"Hello," he croaked when finally locating it.

"Fuck me, you're taking your calls at last." It was Bo Garrick. "You never called me yesterday – or replied to my calls for two fucking days!"

"No, sorry Bo. But there's nothing to report."

"Now you listen to me. I want a meet – this morning."

"Not this morning, I can't."

"Yes you fuckin' can!" Bo's simmering had instantly hit boiling point. "I've been fucking patient so far! Have you any fucking idea what day it is party-boy?" Max tried to think but before he could answer, Bo was back in. "It's Thursday – fucking Thursday. That's three days before fucking D-day. I want a meet – and I want it at eleven this morning at Santini's. You be there with everything we need for the run through or I'll come to *you* this evening - and you don't want me to do that. You understand me?"

"Yeah. I'll be there."

"You fucking better be. You hear me?"

"Yeah, loud and clear Bo. I'll be there for eleven."

Bo was gone with a click but the message was still reverberating around Max's head. He lay on his back in bed in the semi-darkness as if asleep, but his brain was trying to function by contemplating the situation that he had created for himself. He knew Bo was right to be anxious; he knew he had let himself become too distracted. He now tried to concentrate on the task, thinking his way around everything that must be done before Saturday night and everything he needed for the rehearsal in a few hours time. He could get that together. It should be just a matter of working systematically through the rehearsal program menu that Dennis had created on the disc. More of a problem were the batteries in the equipment at the bank. Max had to get some new ones and go back to the bank today or tomorrow to replace those in the deposit box. Where the hell was he going to buy the special batteries that he needed?

At one point in Max's deliberations, he even considered walking away from the job. He found himself thinking his way through a series of consequences, of telling Bo that the equipment could fail, which meant they could be in the bank when the alarms went off at Atom Security's monitoring station. The idea began to gel in his mind until he considered that at the very least he would have to return the money to Bo, which he couldn't do because he'd spent most of it. Then there was Molly, he'd be letting her down so badly. Molly! This was the first time he had thought about her all week. He hadn't called her since he'd been in New York. Max felt terrible that he'd forgotten all about her. He hadn't checked that she had recovered from her sleeping pill overdose; then there was the high blood pressure problem.

Max sat up, switched on the bedside light and immediately picked up the phone and dialled Molly's home number.

"Please be in," he whispered to himself as the digits clicked then the ringing tone started. The phone rang for what seemed to Max to be too many times....until suddenly the phone was answered:

"Hello." It was Molly.

"Mo – it's Max."

Molly was overjoyed when she recognised his voice.

"Max – oh Max – where are you?"

"I'm still in Los Angeles. How are you?"

"I'm fine. I was so worried about you".

"I'm sorry Mo. I should have called before, but it's been a bit crazy here since I arrived. I feel dreadful…"

"Oh don't worry," she interrupted. "It's just lovely to hear from you. Are you all right?"

"I am – more important, how are you, Mo? What's happening there?"

"I'm fine. I'm very good, in fact. I got the house valued. Do you know it's worth £850,000?"

"Wow, as much as that? What are you going to do?"

"I'm putting it up for sale. The agent thinks it could sell very quickly, so I've got to look for somewhere for myself. Maybe when you come back you can help me find somewhere. It'll be such a relief - though I'm going to miss The Gables dreadfully."

"Of course you will. But Mo, promise me one thing - under no circumstances must you do anything with The Gables until I get back. You promise me? Don't agree the sale, even on the phone – nothing. You understand? It's really important that you promise me."

"All right, but it's not likely that I'm going to get a buyer in the next few days. I haven't even got a sign board up yet."

"Okay, perhaps it's better you don't. Do nothing until I get back, then I'll help you."

"I don't understand." Molly was confused.

"I'll explain it later. I must go now but I'll phone again in the next few days when I know my plans for coming home."

"When will that be?"

"Not until next week. After the weekend - perhaps Tuesday."

"All right, dear. You take care now – please."

"Of course Mo. It's really good to hear you so well. I'll speak to you after the weekend. Bye for now."

Max had needed to end the call. An overwhelming wave of nausea had welled up from his stomach, demanding his attention and a race to the bathroom where he vomited painfully and loudly.

By ten-thirty, Max was nursing his third wave of nausea and his second pounding headache of the morning. He had been so sick that he couldn't imagine that there was anything left inside him to make him feel so ghastly. He sat on his bed, dressed ready to leave for his meeting, with his head in his hands, waiting for the aspirins he'd just swallowed to take effect. He knew he couldn't possibly phone Bo to cancel the meeting. He would just have to go through with it.

Even in his fragile state, as Max walked through the hotel foyer, he suddenly became aware of a potential problem that he had so far overlooked – that of his modest celebrity. Several of the hotel staff had taken to greeting Max by name as they thanked him for dropping off his room key and bid him:

"Have a nice day, Mr Slater."

Now the lady arranging the flowers looked away from her work to say 'hello'. As he returned a passing smile it suddenly occurred to him that there was a very small chance that any cab driver may also recognise him. Remote, but possible.

Max walked a few blocks down Fifth Avenue with his raincoat collar pulled up to partially hide his face, with the intention of hailing a cab at a safe distance from his hotel. But it was as he walked in his daze, with his mind trying to concentrate on how he would run the meeting at Santini's, that a pin spot of colour arrived in his peripheral vision and dinged into his conscience.

Max was standing at an intersection waiting for the lights to change when across the road, amid the crowd, his eyes had fallen on a pea green straw hat - identical in shape and vivid colour to Jia's in Hong Kong. It instantly took him back to the incident at the airport with the beautiful Jia and the debacle on his last project that now seemed like a world and lifetime away.

When the lights changed, signalling that Max and the hat-wearing woman could cross, they passed in the middle of the road - a brief moment that would have meant nothing to the anonymous blonde lady, but had made a profound and almost sobering impact on Max. He stopped when he arrived at the opposite sidewalk, stepped out of the crowd and turned to watch the hat while he reran his memories of Jia until it and its owner disappeared from view.

A few minutes later, Max hailed a cab and asked to be taken to The Alamo Motel on Queens Boulevard, then kept out of the sightline from the driver's mirror all journey until he paid with a single twenty dollar bill. As the cab drove away, Max began to walk to the restaurant with only a passing glance at The Alamo and a passing thought for Luisa.

Max became aware that the brisk walk in warm summer air had helped refresh his senses a little as he sat in Santini's Restaurant waiting for the others. They all arrived as a group and greeted him politely but with little enthusiasm. Max chose to ignore the jibes about him giving them his autograph and making time in his social calendar for such a trivial meeting. He wasn't in the mood to take them on, so picked up his laptop bag and walked away towards the stairs as Bo ordered Mickey to wait behind for a tray of coffees.

Upstairs, they assembled around the large table and Bo gestured for Max to sit at its head. This was going to be Max's meeting and he would call the shots. There was no way that he could sit it out and let anyone else do the work. It started slowly, as Max tried hard to summon up his thoughts and to concentrate on the running order of procedures listed on the screen of his laptop. The pace and the gang's enthusiasm picked up as responsibilities were identified for each member in turn. Max even sensed that Bo's curt, abrupt mood was relaxing as he was reminded of the comparative ease with which he should be getting his hands on a lot of money in the next few days. The rehearsal covered every detail of the raid, from the preparations and alibis for each member of the gang, through to fencing the stolen property and distribution of the money some time after the event. Max wouldn't be involved in that process, but such was the detail of the run-through that it demonstrated to everyone present just how thorough Dennis had been in his preparations.

As the afternoon wore on, without the ever-threatening bouts of nausea, Max would have enjoyed the exercise as he worked through the programme of events that he knew so well, then organised his squad with military precision.

As the briefing neared its conclusion, Max realised that he must tackle the thorny problem of his celebrity. He wasn't looking forward to raising the subject - expecting some discerning back chat which he got as soon as he asked if someone could get him a false beard, moustache and glasses with non-magnifying lenses. There was a general snigger amongst everyone at the table, but over it came the sound of clapping. It was Joey. He'd been appropriately attentive throughout the meeting but now a simmering irritation with Max found an outlet.

"Fucking great. This is the jerk what wanted our money to make him anonymous. Fucking well done. Now we've got to worry about a disguise 'cos he's so fucking famous."

Max decided to take the criticism. He had expected it and he knew it was justified.

"Okay, I know," Max acknowledged with a show of resignation. "But I need someone to get the stuff for me by the weekend. I can't do it myself – I'm sorry."

"I'll do it," Mickey volunteered. "I know where I can get it. I'll drop it at the hotel by tomorrow night."

"Thanks Mickey," Max replied.

As the meeting was breaking up, Bo suggested Max leave by a back door.

"And don't hail a cab for at least a block," he ordered as he shook his head. "False fucking moustache and glasses – fuck me!"

The process of drawing Max's attention so firmly back to the raid, the program and the problem with the batteries, had been essential. He wasn't about to admit it to Bo, but he was grateful to him for demanding that he concentrate on the task ahead. Now that Max was focused on the robbery once again, he knew that he must check and double check every detail of the plan, the building and the systems that would get them all in and out of the bank. That was his responsibility. If he was too sloppy or if he overlooked one vital detail now, that could be the one thing that blew the plan apart. It also reminded him of the prize that he was about to take for himself and Molly. As he thought about it for the first time for over a week, it made him smile. The more he contemplated it, the more excited he became. And the more surprised he was at himself for becoming so distracted. In the next forty eight hours, he was going to make himself rather wealthy. He would have solved Molly's financial problems and hopefully, have pissed Jack Briggs off big time. Which was a very sobering prospect.

By the time Max returned to his hotel room, he was feeling better than he had all day. He checked his messages to find the now familiar list of names inviting him to events over the weekend and beyond. But nothing from Gaynor.

As Max sat on his bed sipping orange juice from a bottle from his fridge, his thoughts were again tugged back to his earlier brief encounter. Despite his considerable distractions during the day, he had experienced repeated flashbacks to the image of the green straw Derby hat. With them, on each occasion, his mind had returned briefly to events in Hong Kong which resulted in Max examining his conscience.

Max crossed the room, removed his laptop from his shoulder bag and logged into his email. Before checking any incoming mail, he called up a new page and typed.

To: **ari.sumeer@bssystems.com**
Subject: **Hong Kong**
Hi Ari
A favour please. Send 2 x new BSS435-2K boards to Feng Lui at Feng Electronics in HK (address on file) with instructions for replacing old boards at Celestiel and Tempest Hotels pls. <u>ASAP</u>.
Cheers
Max
Send

In the same moment that Max watched the mail depart, he felt a rush of relief. Job done - case closed. It was the right thing to do. He reflected for another minute before his thoughts returned to the present. He began to contemplate everything he still had to do before Saturday night. And as he thought how close it was, he experienced the first tremor of fear about it since he arrived in New York. Two full days to go now. This was not how it was meant to be. He had promised himself that he would only go ahead with the raid if he was completely prepared and if he was convinced that the plans were totally watertight. He couldn't claim either. For a moment he sensed a real anxiety, before reminding himself that nearly every thing was in good order. The rehearsal had gone well; the gang had all the equipment needed; their alibis were sorted; everything from their side was ready to go. So that left two problems for Max.

The first was relatively simple – to create his alibi and the excuse for him to disappear for the weekend. The only person who he hoped would ask, was Gaynor, but that was looking unlikely. And if Jason came up with anything for Saturday night, Max knew he would take some putting off. But the business meetings that Max was planning out of town would solve that.

The bigger problem was to replace the old batteries at the bank. Perhaps he should have arranged that one of the gang bought the new ones - he wouldn't have needed to admit there was a problem. But he'd missed his chance to sort it out at the meeting, so now he had to find them himself and get them installed tomorrow; it was now too late to organise anything today.

After the best night's sleep Max had had all week, he got up early enough to spend time planning his alibi before setting off from the hotel to buy the batteries. There was no risk of them providing a link between Max and the bank raid, so he took a cab to two specialist stores advised by the hotel concierge as the most likely places that would stock them.

By 10.40, Max was in his third taxi of the morning, rushing to yet another store. He hadn't appreciated just how difficult it would be to locate the exact batteries that he needed. Now Max was getting very nervous and very angry with himself for leaving this so late. He tried to think of some alternative plan by using different batteries that he could buy easily, but they would all be too big. There was no space in the box for larger batteries - for larger anything. They had to fit the exact space in the equipment.

Just when he didn't need the attention, Max was recognised by the cab driver who thought he was an actor from some TV soap that Max had never heard of. But to Max's great good fortune, when he told him that he had something of an emergency on his hands, the cabby took charge.

"You want electric stuff – you want my cousin." He pulled over by the sidewalk, produced a cell phone, called up a number from its memory and spoke to his cousin for long enough to introduce Max.

"Here, you speak to him, his name's Tozo." He handed Max the phone.

"Hi, I'm trying to find some D27 Luna batteries. Can you help - please?"

Within a couple of minutes, they were on their way to a shop in somewhere called Hell's Kitchen that Tozo assured Max would have them - and it did. Back in the cab, back to the hotel for Max to pick up his laptop and the CD, then off to First National Credit.

Max's celebrity status took on a new dimension at the bank. It seemed that everyone knew he was coming and instead of a clerk meeting him, Mr Attaway, the manager, arrived to welcome Max and show him to the room. Max was afraid he may be too attentive but Mr Attaway politely left him alone with his box and the assurance that he could take as long as he needed to sort out his business in private.

It took Max no time to rig up his laptop and join it by umbilical cord to the equipment in the security box. He moved through the menu to the point in his program that showed the batteries' life. The scale hardly registered, it was now so low. Max sighed as he stared at the package of equipment. He had worked out, as best he could remotely, the safest way to change the batteries without causing harm to the system. Now, faced with the equipment, he was less sure of himself. But it had to be done and now was not the time to make new plans. He disconnected the laptop in case he sent a spike back into his program, loosened the old batteries in their holders then took the new replacements out of their plastic wrappings. He tested each of the old batteries in turn with a small meter which showed that both had exactly the same morsel of life left in them, so it made no difference which he changed first. Once again he stared at the equipment and planned his next moves in his head. He carefully pulled the first of the old batteries from the casing and removed the connections which snapped off, making Max start. Now the system was running on the one old battery. If its power wasn't sufficient to prevent the system from shutting down, the kit could scramble its memory as it started up when the new battery was fitted. Max cleaned the connections with a cotton handkerchief and snapped them onto one of the new batteries. If the program was going to get damaged in this manoeuvre, the harm would already have been done. He repeated the process with the second battery, more relaxed now, as he knew that this would have no effect. Max slotted the two new batteries back into their holders and quickly set up the laptop once again, immediately running through his program to measure the power of the new batteries. It showed virtually full strength. Then Max ran some other checks, trying to identify any damage, but he already knew this was impossible until the equipment was working. The only real test would come on Saturday night.

With a heavy sense of uncertainty, Max packed away the contents of the box and his laptop then pressed the bell to signal that he'd finished.

To Max's shock, the head that came round the door was not Mr Attaway or one his clerks – it was Jason.

"Hi Butch!" Jason said sheepishly with little suggestion of his normal enthusiasm.

"Jason – what're you doing here?" Max asked in surprise as he then realised that Jason was in his familiar uniform and must be on guard duty. "What's happening?"
Jason looked embarrassed

"I'm back at my old job, ain't I?"

"Why - what about the office job?"

"It wasn't me, man. It was only a trial and, well, me an' paperwork were never good buddies. I should have known. No this is better - even got some stripes up now." Jason pointed to the three stripes on his arm. "So they pay me more." He was coming back to life, but Max felt uncomfortable for him. He didn't seem at ease telling Max.

"When did you start back here?"

"Yesterday."

"Right. Well I'm glad – if it's for the better."

"Yeah – it's good to be back. Come on, I'll show you out. Hope you don't mind, they want to take a picture of the both of us for the staff magazine. Butch and Sundance back together."

"No problem." There was a short silence before Max added: "By the way - I've been meaning to say - you know Butch Cassidy and Sundance Kid were bank *robbers*, don't you?" Jason considered that for a moment then laughed his familiar laugh that broke the tension.

They walked through the corridors to the concourse where Mr Attaway and a photographer met them and took a couple of posed portraits at the scene of the crime from Max's last visit. Jason had cheered up a little by the time Max left the bank, especially when he remembered to tell Max that he'd tracked down Tanya Dronan from NBC and she'd agreed to a date tomorrow night. He was so happy at the prospect.

"Let's make it a foursome with that foxy lady from the paper," Jason suggested enthusiastically.

"Sorry - can't do it. I'm out of town on business for the weekend."

"Oh man, that's too bad." Jason seemed genuinely disappointed.

"Come on - you don't need company. You're a big boy now – you've got to learn to do these things on your own. Besides, I'd be too much competition for you on a first date."

"Get outa here will you?"

TWELVE

This was to be a very big weekend in Max's life. One of the biggest when measured by his actions and their outcome for him and his family back in London.

Max had planned that his countdown would begin at 9.30 on Saturday morning. But by the time his alarm went off, he was in the shower washing away the effect of a very disturbed night. He'd slept in fits and starts between prolonged periods awake, playing through the entire process of the raid. He was annoyed at himself for not taking better control. This would be his last night's sleep until Sunday and he dare not be off the pace tonight.

His body clock and a hearty breakfast combined to provide Max with some energy, but with it came a heady state of nervousness. It was important that he take control of his emotions – he must relax. He felt anxious about feeling anxious. He'd been taught a mix of breathing and yoga exercises in the army, intended to calm nerves. He hadn't used them for years, but now tried to recall some of the routines. This at least diverted his attention and forced him to concentrate for a few minutes on something other than his day's agenda.

Max threw the cover back over his bed, smoothed it flat to present a large clear area, then systematically began laying out every item of clothing, every gadget and every piece of equipment that he needed for the next thirty six hours of his life.

Despite the chaos that appeared to surround Max in his London persona, he liked order. He had taken great pains to design stress out of his normal lifestyle over recent years, but whenever he sensed a pressure from work or in his private life, Max found comfort in compiling all the facts of the case into a neat order. He'd sit at his computer or scribble all the known data into 'pros and cons' lists on a sheet of paper. When he found himself confused by a problem with some equipment, he'd blitz his work area to clear it of all the rubbish that was distracting him, then lay out his tools and the components of the equipment on the work bench to help him focus on the task at hand. He knew that order worked for him and now, as he stared at the neatly arranged piles of clothing and equipment laid on the bed, Max began to relax. He felt in control. He felt good. More importantly, he felt confident.

At 10.15, Max left his hotel room with his bag and laptop over his shoulder and made his way to reception. This was one occasion lately when he was pleased to be recognised and ensured his departure was noted by involving one of the reception staff in a brief conversation about the weather that he should expect in Philadelphia, as he dropped off his key.

"Much the same as this, I think, Mr Slater. Perhaps a summer storm – all this recent hot weather brings them on. Are you checking out sir?"

"No, just away for the weekend. Back on Monday."

"Very good sir."

At La Guardia Airport, Max collected his ticket from the US Airlines desk, checked in and took his seat on the plane as soon as the gate opened.

The flight arrived on time in Philadelphia at 12.50, giving Max plenty of time to reach the Sheraton Hotel on the airport perimeter before making his three o'clock appointment with a certain Mr Adam Ranyard-Green from A.S.Staging. Max had chosen A.S.S. at random from a business directory at his hotel in New York and phoned to arrange a meeting on the pretext of needing the company's audio-visual services at an exhibition in Philadelphia next spring.

Mr Ranyard-Green was appropriately polite and attentive as he presented his company credentials over drinks in the hotel bar, never once suggesting that he recognised Alex Slater or suspected his motives for calling a meeting at short notice on a Saturday afternoon.

The meeting over, a company brochure and business card to add to the evidence of his trip out of New York and Max could plan the next phase of his alibi.

In his bedroom, he applied the false moustache and beard that Mickey had bought for him. To his relief, they looked good. He trimmed them a little, put on the new heavy rimmed glasses and became 'James Turnbull'. The original James Turnbull had been a friend of Max's at secondary school. Essentially, it was a name he could always recall.

'So far, so good,' Max thought to himself as he admired the finished affect in his bedroom mirror while dialling the number for Delta Airlines to confirm his - or rather, James Turnbull's - booking for the evening flight to JFK Airport.

"Yes, that's confirmed, Mr Turnbull. Your ticket will be ready for collection at our ticket desk. But there is a weather warning issued for tonight's flight."

"Sorry – what does that mean?"

"The forecast is bad for JFK – some very heavy storms, by all accounts - so we're warning all passengers that there may be delays to flights into New York – even cancellations."
Max Panicked.

"That's impossible - I've got to get to New York tonight."

"I'm sorry sir, we are doing everything we can to keep flights on schedule but you appreciate we can't control the weather. We're advising all passengers to arrive at the airport on time as flights are pretty much running to schedule as of now."

This wasn't in Max's plans. He had no back up arrangement and could only think to hire a car and drive. But if planes couldn't fly, there was every chance he wouldn't get through by road – or not by midnight at least. He had to stick to plan 'A' and trust to his luck. Moreover, all the other members of the team were doing the same in much the same manner so they would be travelling back into Manhattan tonight.

Max killed an uneasy hour by channel-hopping between sports coverage and old movies on the television in his hotel room until it was time to leave to catch his flight. He rustled up his bed, laid out his wash things in the bathroom and left the clothes he had arrived in, over the back of a chair and on a hanger in his cupboard, just in case a maid decided to by-pass the Do Not Disturb card that Max hung on his door handle as he left the room.

Fortunately, Saturday evening was a busy time in reception and James Turnbull slipped out unnoticed, even queuing up for the courtesy bus back to the airport without drawing undue attention.

All the way to the departures terminal and during his wait for a flight that may not take off, Max forced himself to remain calm. Max's chips were all stacked on one number. If the plane didn't leave, he had no alternative plan in place as backup. Bad mistake – he chided himself for such a misjudged oversight.

Whatever was going on behind the scenes, the airline staff appeared to be in control. Apart from a repeated warning when Max picked up James Turnbull's return ticket, arrangements appeared to proceed as normal. Even so, as the flight was announced for boarding, Max sensed a great relief, so as it left the runway just thirty minutes behind schedule, he closed his eyes briefly and muttered a near silent "thank you."

The weather in New York was foul, but the plane landed without apparent problems and Max was in a cab on his way to Santini's Restaurant within half an hour of touch down.

He was surprised to find Bus already in the upstairs room when he arrived.

"My wife thinks I'm working on a building site in Boston this weekend. I didn't have nowhere else to go," he explained. Max had wondered how much of the gang's family-members knew about the job and now hoped the others had been as thorough as Bus with their alibis.

Max carefully removed his James Turnbull identity then placed his disguise away in a small box. He changed out of his smart clothes and packed everything up ready to move on. The plan was to disperse immediately the raid was over. No one would be returning to Santini's so everything would go with them tonight. As Max systematically transformed himself from businessman to bank robber, Bus looked up from a magazine he'd been reading.

"That's what I'm going to buy with some of my money from the job." He held up a picture of a gleaming motorbike.

"Uh-huh, very nice," Max replied politely. He knew no more about motorbikes than cars, but he had heard of Harley-Davidsons and it was easy to appreciate the appeal of anything with so much chrome.

"Not too soon after the raid, though," he added.

"Nah – course not." Bus went back to the magazine, then put it down and asked Max directly what he was going to do with his share of the haul. Max had no cause to be evasive, so found himself telling Bus the full story of his passage to New York and what he was about to retrieve from the deposit box. Bus was fascinated, admitted that he had wondered what could possibly be in a single deposit box that made so much work worthwhile. Max's explanation satisfied that curiosity before Bus went on to prompt Max with more questions about his background, his time in the services, his work and the bank's security systems. Physically, Bus was big. He gave the impression of someone burdened with a body too large for comfort. But now Max sensed a delicacy of touch and a sensitivity in Bus' character that made him easy company for the time they were together awaiting the arrival of the others.

Just after eleven o'clock, Bo and Joey came bustling upstairs followed ten minutes later by Mickey who was very nervous to have left the van with all their equipment in the back street.

"Well go and sit in it. We'll bring you some coffee," Bo ordered, then checked: "Have you got your gloves on?"

"Yeah course." He took his hands out of his pockets to show Bo as he turned and scurried off back to the truck.

Midnight was zero hour for the countdown. Everyone was happy to follow a military-style schedule, which demanded that they were at the bank by 0.30 hours and inside within fifteen minutes. Max sensed that he was not the only one of the

174

group trying to control his nerves. He was increasingly anxious to get started and observed how the other three in the room with him handled the waiting time. Bus had gone back to his magazine that Max knew he'd already read from cover to cover several times over. Bo paced around chewing a cigar and looking at his watch every few minutes, suddenly firing off random questions to the others about aspects of the preparations. 'Had Bus remembered this? Had Max got that? What happens to something or another....?'

Joey lay across three chairs and appeared to be asleep, but Max suspected he was as alert to the pressure as the others. Max sat quietly with his various bags and his laptop in its case at attention by his seat. He spent most of the final thirty minutes thinking through each step of the job. Not a trick learned from the army, but from his schooldays and his time playing rugby for his county. Now his nerves were in much the same sense of tension as they were pre-match.

11.55. Bo announced it and the other three silently gathered themselves and the few items in the room, tidied the chairs, checked they had left nothing behind, then Bus switched off the lights and shut the door behind them without a word being spoken.

The small grey truck with false security company livery on its sides and a black Range Rover on hire under a false name, pulled away from the back of Santini's Restaurant at precisely midnight and headed towards their destination in Manhattan. Max wanted to get on with the job. Now, moving was helping to calm his nerves. He alone knew the significance of the first few minutes when he opened the program and made his connection with the equipment in the bank. He had no idea whether that connection would be clean or if the information passing between his computer and the kit in the vaults would be corrupted.

There was rain in the air as the van pulled up in an alleyway a block's distance from the rear of the bank and the Range Rover parked in view some hundred yards away. In the van, Bus, Joey and Mickey fitted their headsets with earpieces and microphones, then switched on their receivers. In the Range Rover, Max and Bo repeated the procedure then made contact to check the reception. It was good.

"New gloves," Bo ordered and each member of the team responded by removing their heavy gloves and rolling on a latex rubber pair.

Max removed his laptop from the bag, set it up and plugged in his mobile phone. He removed the CD case from the inside pocket of his blouson jacket, inserted the first disc into his laptop then tapped the unique password onto the keyboard and watched the program open onto the screen. Joey and Mickey were already making their way up a series of fire escapes to the roof of a building so far from the bank that they were unsure if the route would take them over the roofs to the rear of their destination. Two years earlier, Dennis Buchanan had casually mentioned to the fire officer at the bank that the escape route from the rear of the building would be very precarious in the case of an emergency. At the time, the officer was grateful to Dennis for drawing his attention to the problem and immediately ordered extra walkways be installed between adjoining buildings.

'How considerate for them to provide such good access,' Dennis had thought when he checked it out on his next visit to

the bank. Now, Joey and Mickey were two of the only people ever to have used it since it was constructed.

Five stories below in the black Range Rover, Max tentatively pressed keys on the laptop to make contact with the transmitter in the deposit box. He felt tense as he approached the final tap and hovered for a brief moment. Bo looked across the car and caught Max's eye. Both men watched Max make the pronounced tap.... then the screen come alive with data steaming like a waterfall down the screen. Max turned back to Bo whose face he could see was beaming brighter than the street lights that partially lit the interior of the car.

"Well, we have contact," Max explained. But Bo remained speechless until the cascade of data stopped abruptly.

"What's happened?"

"It's finished downloading."

"Right."

'Please God it's the right information,' Max thought to himself. Over his earpiece, Max heard Mickey announcing in their agreed shorthand, that he and Joey were in position at the exit door on the roof of the bank. Dennis had chosen it as their entry point because it was hidden from the view of other buildings and it was about the furthest position from the vaults, so would certainly get little attention by the police investigating the false entry method that the team would create later.

Max had assembled the downloaded data and began to run some checks. He pulled up a small frame area on his screen that slowly filled with a black and white picture of an empty room.

"What's that?" Bo asked.

Max pointed to the word 'Security' on the screen.

"The security office on the lower ground," Max replied.

177

" J to base…" Joey's voice came over the headsets. "…What's happening? Can we move? It's fuckin' wet up here."

"Base to J… Shorthand!" Max hissed abruptly. "No, standby"

He ran the cursor down a list of locations on his screen that signified the various cameras around the building. He clicked on 'Upper rear 15'. Another black and white picture slowly scanned into the small frame area.

"Where's that?" Bo asked.

"That's the camera covering the top door." Max replied as he pointed to a door in the picture of an empty corridor.

"What now?" Bo asked again.

"We freeze it." The egg-timer symbol sat on the screen for a few seconds then changed back to an arrow. "That's done."

"What is?" Bo asked.

Max tapped the screen.

"That's the picture the security company's receiving from that camera. It's frozen, but they can't tell 'cos there's nothing moving in it – and that camera's fixed – it doesn't have a moving head."

"That's lucky," Bo responded with genuine innocence. Max turned to look at him in the dim light, wondering if he really believed that luck had any part in the plan so far.

"Yep, lucky, eh?" Max responded pointedly. Realisation suddenly showed in Bo's expression.

"Oh - right."

"But for the moving cameras, we'll feed in moving pics. Not a problem," Max added reassuringly. Bo smiled with only the slightest suggestion that he was embarrassed at having under estimated Max and Dennis's preparations.

"Right."

Now Max pulled up another set of images on his screen. Columns of numbers and icons appeared and Max began to move from page to page, knowing exactly where he was going in the program. He stopped.

"Okay," he said as he stared at a new page of numbers. "That one's the alarm on that door," he told Bo, pointing to the middle of some columns of figures.

"Really?"

"Yeah. So we'll isolate that." Again the egg-timer appeared…Then disappeared "…..And we're ready…..Base to M," Max called to Mickey on his mouthpiece.

"Receiving."

"Clear to go."

Over the headsets, the team could hear Mickey and Joey wrenching open the door. Max's heart was racing. This was the test. If no alarms were triggered in the next few seconds, all was well, but Max wasn't confident. The sound of tearing wood seemed to take too long. Max flipped between the frozen image of the corridor and a page of security code numbers on his screen. Nothing was indicating that the door was being forced. Suddenly the noise over the earpieces stopped.

"In. Making good."

"Understood."

Max quickly checked that nothing had been triggered. All was clear – as still as a secure bank should be at midnight. He said a silent prayer of thanksgiving and blew out his cheeks with a sigh.

"A problem?" Bo asked with a snap.

"No, thank God. I think we're okay."

"Okay, okay." Bo was beaming with pent up excitement. "Let's go then."

"Hold on." Max was pulling up more camera images which he systematically froze one after the other. Bo smiled and caught Max's eye as he recognised the view of the interior of the vault as it was being scanned on the screen.

"Our destination, eh young Alex?"

"That's right," he replied. Then into his mouthpiece: "Base to M."

"Receiving."

"Clear to the ground floor."

"Understood."

Max went back to his pages of numbers.

"Just three internal security doors to the car park," he told Bo as he pointed out anonymous groups of figures. "Those are the four figure codes for the keypads. Low security, these. That's a clear route to the outside doors."

"B - Come in," Max called to attract Bus, but he got no reply. In the van, Bus was fumbling to find the switch for his microphone. Bo flicked his on first.

"Bus – wake up!" he shouted. Max turned and glared at him in silence.

"B here. Sorry boss." Bus called through in a fluster. Max took over.

"Stand by."

"Okay."

The others could hear Bus start up the van's engine.

Within a few more minutes, Mickey and Joey had made their way to the underground car park using the various keypad numbers fed to them by Max at each stage of the route. They soon had the roller door open for Bus to drive the truck into the building, followed by Bo and Max on foot. The Range Rover was left parked by the sidewalk in an adjoining street 'just in case of a problem'.

The group was so excited in the car park that Max felt his task was complete. They congratulated him and one another as if they had finished the job until Bo reminded them that they needed to get moving. Calm returned along with the sense of teamwork. The van was emptied of its contents that were laid out in a regimental order according to when each item would be needed.

The plan now was to gain access to the outer sanctum of the vault, which Max could do without the need for more force. He had all the security codes for each lock on each door in the building. Once in the vault, they would use the next few hours to create a false entry by cutting large holes through a series of walls to an outside sewage system, thus creating the appearance that this was their entry route. Bus immediately began work on the walls with an enormous industrial drill with diamond cutting head. Meanwhile Mickey and Joey returned to the door on the roof that they had damaged as they forced it open, to change it for an identical copy that they had brought in the van.

They had until 07.30 to complete this relatively routine work, at which time they could get into the secure vault. The last doors were designated a 'Status One' security level, so incorporated a time lock that made Max's task far more difficult than getting through all the other lower status doors. But, by changing the date in the computerised control system, Max could kid it that today was tomorrow, so the time lock would release at seven-thirty this morning just as it was programmed to do tomorrow, Monday. With its major defence down, Max's program could easily get past a lower level security lock that only required a keypad number code.

181

As the night wore on and each task was completed without problems, the atmosphere relaxed. Max even sensed evident boredom setting in as seven o'clock approached and the team assembled for another round of coffees to kill time before they could get into the security vault.

"Tell me Bo, how did you know Dennis?" Max asked as they sat on the floor a few feet apart.

"He never told you?"

Max shook his head.

"Originally, it was in Belfast in 1974."

"Yeah?" Max was intrigued.

"He always said that I saved his life, but I don't know about that."

"You were at The Grand Hotel when the bomb went off?" Max suggested as he recalled the story that he'd been told many times by his uncle.

"That's right," Bo confirmed. "We were both there on business. There was no warning and some fucking terrorists blew the front out of the fucking place. Our rooms were next to each other, but Dennis's got the worst of the blast. I was first on the scene and got him out of the mess just before his bed fell two floors into the street. The joke was that we spent the next week in bedrooms next to each other in hospital. We got to know one another quite well then - and a bit about one another's business. At the time, I was working with NORAID – you know, the charity support group? All legal - just about - but, well… between you, me and Dennis, we were gun-running. Dennis knew that…..and I knew that he knew. Your uncle wasn't as squeaky clean as you may've thought. You need a devious mind to think up this scam for God's sake. Anyway, we just hit it off – you know, like some people do.

"We kept in contact for a lot of years, but not so much lately, till a year or more back when Dennis needed help in New York and he looked me up."

When 7.30 clicked up on the clock on Max's laptop, the group was sitting on the floor around the entrance to the vault. The sound of the locks moving in the thick secure door was imperceptible to anyone except Max who was listening closely for evidence that the time lock had been activated.

"Okay gentlemen. Next phase," Max announced. "The time-lock's off."

They all looked to one another for reassurance as Max continued. "The numbers you need are zero-one-zero-four-six-three on the keypad." He couldn't believe that they weren't eager to get in. They couldn't believe it was so easy.

"Really," he urged. "It's open."

"Okay, okay. I'll do it," Bo announced as he quickly stumbled to his feet before tapping the numbers onto the steel touch pad as Max repeated the sequence. From inside the heavy metal door, they could hear a servo operate the last lock. Bo pushed down the handle and tugged…and the door eased open.

"Fuck me!" he declared.

The team swung into action once again, systematically moving equipment into the vault, running power leads to operate tools, piling collapsible boxes in neat stacks inside the doors.

"New gloves!" Bo announced and without comment each member of the group ripped off their latex gloves and replaced them with new ones from a box that Joey handed around. All was set for 'collection time' as Bo was calling this phase.

"Well Alex, here we go. Give us your box number again."

"One hundred and thirty-five," Max said precisely without needing to check that this was Jack Briggs's deposit box.

Bus pulled up the electric hammer drill with its trailing power lead, dropped his eye shield and put the drill to the face of box 135. He immediately began to operate the drill, but for Max the moment stretched in his mind. He hadn't realised that it would have quite such significance. As he watched Bus working the drill-bit around each edge of the box, Max's heart rate increased with impending expectation. This was the focal point of all his work, anxiety and adventures of the last few weeks. Max would never claim to be religious or even to have any well-defined beliefs about the afterlife, but since the death of his parents, he would occasionally wonder if they were with him at an important moment in his life. In the same way, his thoughts now went to Dennis. Could he possibly know that they were about to realise the result of all his work? Was he there in the vault with them?

Suddenly the box jumped loose from its housing. Bus pulled it out without ceremony and passed it to Joey who immediately began work with another drill to break into its lock which gave way with little effort. He looked across the lightweight folding table that Joey had set up as a work bench, to Max, then pushed the box across the vinyl surface for Max to open. Bus switched off his drill, pulled his eye shield up to his forehead and watched Max as he nervously lifted the lid. From their positions, no-one else could see the contents except Max who was looking at white tissue paper wrapped around a package that he removed with due ceremony, appropriate to its significance in his thoughts. Max carefully removed the tissue paper to see a red velvet presentation box that he opened with a flick of the catch. As he lifted the lid, a gleaming set of jewellery sparkled in the work lights. Max had never seen

anything so beautiful or more valuable in such a small space.
£2,000,000.

'So that's what £2,000,000-worth of jewellery looks like?'
Max thought. He was exultant.

He closed the red velvet lid, gently picked up the case and
carried it out of the vault as Bus started up his drill to continue
work. Mission accomplished, at least thus far.

"Thank you, Dennis." Max looked up and mouthed the
words that no-one could hear over the cacophony from the
vault.

By midday, it was clear that progress was on track. The gang
had modified their systems to what was now a conveyor–belt
operation. As each box was opened, the contents were sorted
and anything vaguely valuable removed, then the box went
back into an empty slot in the racks to save space. Its contents
were placed in one of the crates which were stacked outside
the vault, then taken to the van one floor below. Max had no
part in this operation except to monitor the program on his
laptop which demanded little effort on his part. Max had the
velvet case beside his laptop and would occasionally open it to
gaze upon its contents. It brought a smile to his face and into
his heart every time he opened the case during the course of
the morning.

At precisely one o'clock, the team stopped work, downed tools
and sat outside to eat sandwiches and drink lukewarm coffee
from flasks. Not surprisingly, everyone was in high spirits.
They had seen enough recognisable valuables to know that
they were taking a very sizeable haul. Then there were the
oddities that people stored in deposit boxes. They agreed that
the strangest had to be a glass eyeball. As if to illustrate they

185

were not without some feelings for their victims, they had, where possible in their haste, returned everything they didn't want, back to its original box – including the glass eye.

Max was surprised and impressed with the team's professionalism, if that was the right word to use for a bunch of crooks, thieving the contents of safe deposit boxes. But Max considered that their systematic, well-disciplined approach in this military-style operation was admirable.

Lunch over in less than twenty minutes and operations resumed. The team was back in the vault, leaving Max to clear away the debris from the sandwiches and drinks.

The cut off deadline for all work in the vault was to be five o'clock. By the time they had cleared up and packed the van, they would be leaving the premises at six o'clock. Max was wishing away the time. He wanted to tidy up all the loose ends here in New York and go home to England as soon as possible. His adventure was almost over, but he knew he had to be careful not to drop his guard. He had to get back to JFK airport to complete the process of creating his alibi in Philadelphia. He would collect the final payment of $13,000 from Bo tomorrow to pay his hotel bill, then catch the first plane he could get back to England, perhaps on Tuesday. The prospect was overwhelmingly appealing.

Max woke abruptly. He had drifted off to sleep gripping his prized possession beside his laptop on an upturned crate. He glanced at his watch and was embarrassed when he realised that it showed four-fifteen. No-one else seemed unduly worried that he'd been asleep for so long - they were too busy racing to get all the boxes opened before the five o'clock deadline.

Max immediately checked through the program again but was not surprised that nothing had changed. He would certainly have known if any alarm had been triggered.

With nothing else to do, he casually began to scroll through some of the data he had downloaded from the bank, more to kill time than for any other purpose. He was amazed at the volume and detail of information that he could access, even though much of it was routinely uninteresting. It seemed that everything to do with security at the bank was there. Max sifted deeper and deeper into the files until he found a full list of all the customers for the deposit vault – or at least, a list of the names in which security boxes were rented. Max scanned them for any names that could recognise apart from 'Briggs' and 'Slater'. It appeared to be a mix of nationalities, even a Lord who he assumed to be British, but that could have been a Christian name. And there were two Sirs that weren't recognisable to Max. He then thought to check how Jack Briggs had registered his box. 'Briggs.J.' As simple as that. But as Max was about to move on to find something more interesting, his eye was caught by the numbers of Briggs.J's deposit boxes – 135, 301. Two boxes? Yes, there was no mistake. 135 and 301. Max jumped up and through the door into the vault. They hadn't opened box 301 yet. Seeing Max in the vault for the first time since early morning and clearly trying to tell him something, Bus switched off his drill and raised his ear-defenders.

"Bus - 301 next - okay?"

"Sure." Bus replied and went straight to it. A vigorous attack and the box was free in a few seconds. Then Max stood over Joey as he drilled through the lock. As it popped open, Joey flicked the lid automatically as he had the previous two hundred and seventy boxes. He and Max now stared at a

187

collection of papers and envelopes. Max pushed them around to check underneath the top layer but could see nothing of any obvious value. Just some papers, some old floppy computer discs and an even older sound tape on a small reel. Max poked around in the papers thinking how uninteresting they appeared by comparison with his gems. But then the words '*Private and Confidential*' on one envelope reminded Max that perhaps anyone with such a dubious background as Jack Briggs must have good reason to lock such items in a deposit box. He picked up the box and left the noise of the vault to sit outside again.

Max skimmed through the papers quickly. Many were in foreign languages, but those he could read didn't immediately strike him as particularly interesting. They were also quite old, the most recent date he noticed was five years earlier. But still the thought kept occurring to him that Jack Briggs wouldn't have locked them in the vault if they weren't important. But why?

Max put the documents to one side then turned his attention to the three floppy discs – one, three and a quarter inch, but two very old five and a half inch discs, well past their use-by dates. All three had simple, quite anonymous hand-written notes on them, but again nothing to infer that they had any particular importance. Max wanted to check through them on his computer, but was nervous about coming out of the bank's security program. Nothing had happened all day, but if it did, warning systems in the program would have raised an audible alarm, then identified the problem. Max contemplated the situation for a few minutes, then stepped through all the relevant checks to put his mind at rest that he could break the link with the bank's security systems for a few minutes. All was as normal as it had been for the last sixteen hours. He shut down the link and immediately pushed the smallest disc (which was the only one of the three that his computer would accept) into his A-drive. He quickly identified its word processing language and opened it within a few moments. It appeared to contain a lot of letters and a variety of documents with unremarkable identifications. He opened some at random. The first two documents were written in what Max identified as Spanish. On a quick review, Max spotted the occasional name that could have been English or American which included references to London and Washington in the text and addresses. To his greater surprise, he recognised the name Aldermaston. He returned to the menu of folders to look for any idents in English. As he checked them more closely, he became aware of the names of several companies known to Max as competitors of Briggs-Buchanan. He chose a folder at random and opened it to find a lengthy list of correspondence between the Managing Director of one of Italy's biggest Security companies named Zindomi, and the chief executives of several other organisations. At first glance, Max couldn't find any reference to Briggs-Buchanan or any correspondence to or from Jack Briggs. The majority of the letters were written in Italian, but Max checked them for names and found none that he recognised. So why would Jack Briggs have them on a disc and why were they so important to him that he had to lock them up for safe keeping?

Had Max not been so distracted, and had his laptop still been on-line to the bank's security system, an alarm would have sounded to signal the side door of the bank at ground level had just opened. Had he then monitored camera 14A, he would have recognised the tall man who entered wearing security guard's uniform, as Jason Winchester. The guard duty roster showed that the shift wasn't due to start until seven o'clock that evening, by which time, the gang would be long gone.

It was now four forty-two in the afternoon and in the basement, Max and the team were less than twenty minutes from their scheduled cut off-time. But why had Jason chosen today of all days to come to work over two hours early? Because The Giants were kicking off at five o'clock and the match was being televised live from St Louis. This wasn't the first time Jason had watched a sports event on the large television in the comfort of Mr Attaway's office on the top floor. If Jason had come to work on time at seven o'clock, he would have missed the middle of the match while he was travelling. So this way, he could watch the whole game then clock on duty at seven. As Jason set himself up in the manager's office and turned on the TV to catch some of the pre-match coverage, he was totally oblivious to the activities five floors below him.

When Max realised the time, he pulled the floppy disc out of his computer and returned to the bank's security system. He quickly checked it to find everything as peaceful as when he left it fifteen minutes earlier, oblivious to Jason five floors above.

As five o'clock clicked silently onto the laptop clock and Max called a halt to all activities in the vault, the hooter sounded to signal the kick off by The Giants.

In the secure room, just seven boxes remained unopened.

"How long to do those?" Bo asked Bus who was packing away his drill.

"Ten, fifteen minutes," Bus answered.

"Go on. Finish them," Bo ordered.

Bus wasn't sure. He looked to the others for confirmation. He wanted to stop.

"Go on!" Bo shouted. "Get them opened."

Bus fed out the cable, switched the power on and fired up the drill once more. He attacked the remaining boxes with a new ferocity, clearly not happy about over-running the schedule. As soon as Max heard the drill start up again, he rushed into the vault and shouted at Bo over the noise.

"What's happening?"

"We haven't finished. Ten minutes – no problem," Bo shouted back.

"No. We have to go – now!" Max shouted again and tapped the face of his wrist-watch. "Now, Bo!"

Bus was vaguely conscious of the argument going on behind him as he wrenched another box from its housing and kicked it across the floor towards Joey, who had already packed up his temporary work table. But in his haste, Bus hadn't switched off his drill which caught the leg of his trouser as he swung his foot to kick the box. The drill instantly gripped his loose trouser leg as it touched the spinning bit, then ripped through the material and into his flesh of his shin in a moment. In the time it took Bus to remove his finger from trigger, the drill bit had shredded his trousers and cut down to the bone. Instantly, blood began spurting from a cut blood-vessel. The noise of the drill was replaced with Bus's cry of anguish. The drill clattered to the floor, followed immediately by Bus falling to his knees clutching his wound.

Max was the first to move to help.

"Hold onto it Bus!" Then to the others: "Who's got a knife – quick I need a knife!" The group seemed paralysed, except Joey who flicked open a stiletto and passed it to Max who instantly attacked the leg of Bus's trousers.

"What the fuck are you doing?" Bus hissed through gritted teeth. He was fighting the pain and a steady flow of blood.

191

"We've gotta stop the bleeding."

"With that?" Bus stared at the knife cutting into his trousers. "Fuck off Alex!"

"No – hold still – you need a tourniquet." By which time Max had sawn off a length of cloth and was tying it around Bus' thigh just above his knee. Surprisingly quickly, the flow of blood slowed and with it, the situation calmed down.

"How's that?" Max asked.

"It's okay," Bus replied.

Max turned to Bo.

"Now can we clear up and get out of here?"

"Okay, okay. Mickey, find some towels or something to clear up here," Bo ordered.

Fifteen minutes later and everything was set for the final phase of the operation. Because of Bus's accident, the original plan had changed. Mickey would drive Bus straight back in the van to a lock-up garage in Queens, not far from Santini's Restaurant, that Bo had rented to store the haul while it was being sorted and fenced. Joey would now complete the work in the bank, then meet Bo in the Range Rover to follow on to the lock-up. Max would make his way to JFK to catch his return flight to Philadelphia.

To complete the mock break-in, Joey had to shut up the garage when the van had left, return to the vault and fire off a charge that had been set on the inner vault door. This would create the impression that the gang had blasted their way in through the last line of defence. But there was a high risk that the vibration caused by the explosion could set off an alarm even with Max taking control of the rest of systems, which was why it had to be the last act before Joey made his escape. Joey would then leave the bank by the same route that they had entered – through the exit door on the fifth floor, across the roofs and down the fire escape.

The van had departed. Joey had secured the garage and was now back in position at the entrance to the vault.

"J. Standby." Max instructed as he checked through the cameras and security doors that Joey would use for his exit. Everything was set.

"All clear J. Switch off your headset – we don't want to be deafened."

"Understood," replied Joey, then a gentle click was heard on the three headsets to indicate that Joey had switched off his microphone. In the Range Rover, Max checked his watch. He was running late on his schedule to get back to JFK in time to catch the seven-thirty flight back to Philadelphia. In the confusion at the bank, Max had not put on his beard and moustache, so now he began to apply them in haste.

In the bank, Joey had run the power line as they had rehearsed and hid behind a wall to detonate the plastic explosive stuck around the lock of the door. They couldn't take a chance that it would fail, so Bus had applied enough to ensure a result. And it did. As Joey made the second battery contact, the power of the explosive blew the door away from its lock and swung it violently on its hinges, smashing it into the adjoining wall. Dust and fragments of plaster blew through the annex and back into the vault.

Joey emerged from his hiding place. He had to brush up the dust around the doorway that would otherwise indicate that this was the last, not the first act in the break-in. He snatched up a broom and swept violently as dust continued to swirl around the rooms. It took less than a minute to complete to his satisfaction, then he threw the broom aside, checked the rest of the scene with the briefest glance, then turned and ran for the exit five floors above. Which was exactly where Jason had set up camp and had been lounging in Mr Attaway's large leather chair, talking to Tanya Dronan on the phone about the success of last night's date that hadn't ended until the early hours. He was half watching the football match with the volume on the TV turned down low.

Despite the sound of the explosion being well muffled from the office so far above, the impact sent a shockwave through the entire building.

"What the...?" he interrupted the telephone conversation and sat up in the seat. "Hold on doll," Jason told Tanya. "Something's up." He dropped the phone on the desk, stood up and rushed over to the door into the corridor. He was on the top floor so whatever had caused the vibration had happened downstairs. He set off down the stairs cautiously, checking each floor in turn. On the second floor, from a distance, he could then hear the sound of Joey running up the stairs two and three at a time. Jason couldn't understand what was happening, but froze on the stairs waiting for whoever was approaching. He had no time to wait or think before Joey turned a bend in the stairs,

"Who are you? Stop right there!" Jason shouted, but before he could make another move, Joey had stopped and turned with the agility of a wild animal then leapt back down about ten steps. Without thinking, Jason followed, assuming he was taking chase. But as he rounded the first bend in the staircase, Joey was standing with a gun raised to Jason's head height - then he pulled the trigger. The sound of a single shot range through the building as the 38mm bullet hit Jason in his forehead at little more than point blank range. Jason's forward momentum carried him down the next flight of steps, tumbling and sliding to a halt at the turn in the stairway where he lay motionless on his back with his eyes open. Joey followed with this gun pointing at Jason's head. He satisfied himself that Jason was dead at about the same time as he recognised him.

"Shit!" he murmured under his breath, then turned and continued on his exit route with his handgun raised at every turn of the stairs and corridors.

At the other end of the open phone line Tanya might have heard the sound of the shot. She couldn't be sure, but now waited impatiently for a short while before shouting down the phone to attract Jason's attention. The longer she waited for him to return, the more she began to worry, sensing that the shot she heard could have been exactly that.

Joey had arrived at the fire door onto the roof and needed the number to use on the security keypad. His hand was shaking as he switched on the microphone in his headset.

"J to base. Come in." Joey tried to sound as calm as possible.
In the Range Rover, Max was still applying his moustache so took a moment to reply.

"Where the fuck are you!?" Joey shouted into his mouthpiece.

"J - okay, receiving," Max replied in surprise, then read off his screen. "Numbers are 3-7-1-3."
There was no reply, but over Joey's open microphone, Max could hear Joey tapping the numbers onto the keypad, then opening the door and closing it behind him. A few moments later he appeared at the top of the fire escape and was racing to get to the car. As Bo saw him, he started the engine, bumped off the sidewalk then drove to the bottom of the fire escape ladder where Joey dropped the last eight feet and jumped into the back seat of the car.

"Go! Let's go!" he shouted before he'd closed the door.

"Okay, okay," replied Bo as he began to drive.

"What's up?" Max asked. "What's happened?"

"Happened? Nothing's happened, you jerk – apart from us robbing that fucking bank – that's all. Let's get out of here."

In her apartment, Tanya was using her cell phone to call the news desk at NBC's studios as she continued to listen to the dead line from the bank. Sensing something serious had just happened, she wasn't sure what to do and wanted some advice. A friend on duty in the news department took down the details with some urgency as he recognised the significance of the story that could be unfolding.

"Give me ten minutes, then call the police – not before. Okay?"

"Okay," Tanya agreed, her voice trembling with tension.

In Times Square, the black Range Rover pulled up beside a line of taxis outside the Marriot Hotel. James Turnbull emerged and climbed into a cab that would take him to JFK for his return flight to Philadelphia.

THIRTEEN

Max's senses were roused from a deep sleep. Alarm! Where am I? Hotel in Philadelphia. Oh God! For a few seconds, Max's thought processes resembled his scrambled bed covers. But as his concentration returned, Max lay on his back while he collected his thoughts in the early light filtering into his hotel bedroom. He rolled over to gaze at the red velvet case containing his precious haul that he had placed next to his bed as the last act before he went to sleep last night. There was plenty to think about as he relived the fantastic exploits of the last two days. He'd actually robbed a bank – and with remarkable ease. He pondered that for a few minutes before his thoughts moved to the task at hand - to the steps he now had planned to get him back to England with his treasure trove.

First on that schedule was to keep an appointment with another would-be business contact for Astrodome Games, for an early breakfast meeting here at the hotel, then to catch the 09.55 flight back to La Guardia. From there he'd go to meet Bo at Santini's Restaurant to collect his last $13,000 on the way back into Manhattan. He needed the cash to settle his hotel bill. This brought a smile as Max realised that he had a possession worth about £2,000,000 that was worthless until it was sold. Max would stay on at the Roy Hotel until he left to catch an overnight flight back to London. Only then did Gaynor come into his consideration. He hoped that he would see her to say goodbye – perhaps for a coffee or drink this afternoon. The precision of that schedule made Max comfortable as he reached out to take the jewellery case, open its lid to gaze on its contents that would change his and his family's fortunes more than Max's life had already changed over the course of the last month.

The clock-radio beside his bed showed the time 07.50. Time to get up and shower before the eight o'clock news. Max was unsure whether the robbery would have been discovered and released to the news services yet. If it was, he assumed it would be at the top of any newscast. So he flicked to CNN on his television and watched a few moments of a business report before changing channels to NBC. There was still nothing to indicate that the news had broken, so Max turned the TV towards the bathroom from where he kept his eye on the reflection of the screen in the mirror as he shaved. Still nothing. Once in the shower, Max relaxed totally under the warm water. It felt good. He felt good. His mind wandered off again along the many strands of thoughts that kept emerging from his subconscious. Max was content to let the hot shower massage his head and back as his thoughts moved to Gaynor. He wondered if he had meant anything at all to her, then wondered if he would give her much thought when he got home to his life in London.

Max had lost track of time until he suddenly realised that the news may have started. He reached out of the shower and wiped the condensation from an area on the bathroom mirror that allowed him to see a distorted reflection of the television screen. As he focussed his eyes and ears on the TV, it abruptly occurred to him that the image on the screen was a still photograph of Jason. Max couldn't hear the commentary clearly enough, but realised instantly that this must be the story of the bank raid. He swept the shower curtain aside and leapt out of the bath and into the bedroom. The portrait had gone, but the picture showed masses of police activity outside the bank at night behind a reporter who was describing the scene. Max hung on every word. The NBC reporter was summing up the little information he had about the raid, then handed back to the newscaster in the studio who simply promised to keep her audience updated on developments as they came in, before moving on to the next item.

Max grabbed the remote control and began clicking though channels until he found another news report. He stopped at CNN and heard the words: "...shot dead." Then continued:

"......We have no further reports from the scene, but we understand this is a major raid that will have reaped a substantial haul." There was one brief shot of the same activity in the street outside the bank that NBC had shown.

'Who's been shot dead?' Max thought. 'Was that something to do with the still photo of Jason on NBC? Jason may well have been on duty last night, but not until seven o'clock.' Max was totally confused, he continued to click through channels looking for another news report. He found two more, but neither mentioned the raid nor anything about a shooting. Max was certain that Jason's mug shot and the shooting and the bank raid were connected. He had to go to his meeting in twenty minutes. Maybe there would be a bulletin on CNN at 08.15 before he left his room.

Max began to dress, his thoughts focussed on the bits of the report that he'd seen and heard. The more he thought about them, the more anxious be became.

"Gaynor - she'll know." He suddenly realised, snatched up his phone from beside the bed and began dialling her cell phone number. It rang twice and she answered.

"Alex, where are you? I've been trying to call you."

199

Max knew immediately he heard the tone of her voice that his fears were founded.

"I'm in Philadelphia on business. I've just seen a bit of a news report showing Jason and a bank raid. What's happened?"

"He's been shot dead, Alex." Gaynor's tone had changed. She was uncertain, sensitive to the reaction this might bring from Max. "I'm so sorry. It was a raid last night. He was on duty at the bank where we all met. The story's really unclear. He seems to have stumbled on a raid in the bank vaults and was shot dead yesterday evening. NBC broke the story last night."

Max had dropped onto the bed. He sat with his head in his hands barely holding the phone to his ear. He was replaying all the events of last evening back in his head. It didn't take him long to recall Joey's anxiety as he fled from the bank. But how had Jason got into the building without them knowing? Could he have been there all the time? No, of course not. So when? And how? The disc! Max realised that he must have arrived when Max was reading the floppy disc. *'Oh God! Oh no!'* That would be too much of a coincidence.

"Alex - are you all right?" Gaynor's soft voice penetrated Max's thoughts.

"Yes."

"I'm so sorry Alex. I know . . ."

"I've got to go. I've got a meeting." Max was numb. The reasons, the consequences of a murder, his responsibility. *'Oh God'.* He couldn't think straight.

"Are you coming back to New York?" Gaynor interjected.

"Yes – this morning. I'll be back later today, but I'm leaving for London tonight."

There was a short silence from Gaynor that seemed like a long one.

"Right. Er, perhaps I could come to the airport with you to say goodbye."

"Yeah, that would be nice. I'd like that." Max heard himself saying the words, but his stomach was churning and his mind was vacant. He was almost totally distracted. "I'll call you when I get back – sometime mid-afternoon," he said finally.

Mr Dominguez from Mokus-Dimway Plastics was polite and punctual. He was also sympathetic to Max's distraction from their meeting as they sat together in the hotel dining room. Max apologised soon after they took their seats and explained briefly why his mind wasn't focussed on their discussion. Mr Dominguez was charming and volunteered to cut the meeting short and leave, but Max insisted he stayed for breakfast, having made such an early start on his account. Mr Dominguez hadn't heard the news, but as Max's story unfolded, he recalled both Max and Jason from their earlier exploit. He wanted to know about the original raid. It was a help to Max, who now found it much easier to talk about Jason than to avoid the subject and pretend to be interested in MDP's services.

Back in his room soon after nine o'clock, Max couldn't bear to put the TV on while he quickly packed. His plans now included the meeting with Bo. He called his cell phone number to check that he would be at the restaurant. It was more important than ever that he get himself away on a plane tonight with the final loose ends tied up.

Bo's cell phone was on answer service, so Max left a brief message about them meeting as they'd arranged at twelve o'clock at Santini's.

The overnight storms had passed, but it was still raining as the cab dropped Max outside Santini's just after midday. There were two or three tables occupied when Max entered the restaurant with his suitcase, hoping to see Bo amongst the diners. Sonny was behind the counter.

"Hi, I'm meeting Bo Garrick here. Has he been in?" Max asked.

"Not yet. You want anything?"

"Just a coffee please. Regular, white."

"Take a seat," Sonny suggested and Max parked himself behind a small table facing the door.

Twelve-fifteen came and went. A second coffee was barely warm as twelve-forty-five approached. Max was very concerned. He had tried Bo's cell phone number twice and only received the answer service. Max's concern was fast becoming something close to panic.

He was only vaguely conscious of a door opening behind him, so as Bo's large hand slapped on his shoulder, Max jumped in his seat.

"I think we have some business in private," Bo told him, then turned to Sonny, "Can we use your room?" Bo gestured up the stairs. Sonny nodded. As Max turned with his suitcase, he realised that Joey was standing behind Bo. He'd followed him in from the back street. Max's emotions moved from the relief he felt at Bo's arrival, to a deep uncertainty about what was about to happen in the privacy of the upstairs room.

"You've heard the news?" Bo questioned as he closed the door behind them.

"Yeah," Max replied.

"So how the fuck did the guard get into the fucking building without you warning us?!" Bo thundered, then checked himself, knowing his voice could carry downstairs.

"I don't know," Max replied with some authority.

"Now we've got a fucking murder investigation," Bo added. "You know that means real fucking heat. Not just a fucking bank raid – the murder of a fucking security guard."

"I don't know how it could have happened. You saw I was monitoring everything till the time we left, he must have come in while we were walking back to the car."
Joey stepped forward.

"He was on the top fucking floor – watching TV. He'd been there for fucking hours."

"No he hadn't!"

"How do you know – you've no idea when he arrived – or so you say," Joey retorted.

"You not telling us something?" Bo asked.

"No. Of course not."
The three stared at one another for several seconds before Bo removed an envelope from the inside pocket of his overcoat.

"A deal's a deal – thirteen grand. You want to count it?" Bo asked.

"No," Max replied. "Can I remind you," Max started to say as he placed the envelope into his own inside pocket, "that the man you shot – the man you killed – was a friend of mine." In turn, Max now looked both Bo and Joey full in the eye as he continued with barely contained anger. "I'm hardly likely to do anything to endanger him."
Under his breath, Joey mumbled something Max couldn't hear, except the last word that sounded like 'nigger'. Max turned on him abruptly.

"You what?!"

203

"I said – he was only some fucking nigger." Joey replied aloud. Not a split second of thought separated the last word coming from Joey's lips and the back of Max's right hand making contact with Joey's chin. Joey recoiled as much from surprise as in self-defence or from the impact of the blow, but Max followed through with a second blow from his left fist that caught Joey square on the cheek as he turned away. The force of both contacts sent Joey sprawling back across the large table, followed by Max trying to land more shots to his face. Max had lost it. His anger had surfaced in an uncontrollable, all-consuming rage. It was an outlet for the frustrations that had built-up through the morning since he first heard the news of Jason's murder. Now he launched himself at Joey in an explosion of pent up anger. Joey tried to scramble clear whilst lashing out in Max's direction, but it was Bo's intervention that slowed Max's onslaught with a tug on his collar then a bear hug around his arms. Still Max fought to get at Joey, but the brief remission gave Joey the moment he needed to pull a pistol from inside his leather jacket and swing it at Max, making contact first with his jaw, then a second with his cheek and nose. The contact paralysed Max momentarily, in which time, Joey drove the butt of the gun into Max's right temple, knocking enough fight out of him for Bo to release his grip. Max fell to his knees with blood pouring from his nose. Bo immediately stood over him to prevent Joey from taking another swing at Max's head.

"That's enough!" Bo ordered as he held Joey back. The flurry of action had taken just seconds from first to last blow. Now all was calm with a broken chair, possibly a broken nose and a pool of blood to show from the conflict. The two combatants stood apart, mopping the blood seeping from their wounds.

"That's really going to help – you fucking jerks." Bo scolded both Max and Joey. "Look at you. Joey - go to the bathroom, clean up. Go back to the car."

Joey strutted out of the room as Bo pulled a handkerchief from his pocket and offered it to Max who had found a tissue from somewhere, but it was falling apart in his blood-soaked hand.

"Here - use this - and keep it." Max took the handkerchief. "You gonna to be okay?" Bo asked. Max nodded.

"We're going. Stay here and clean up. Sonny'll get you a cab if you need him to. No-one'll recognise you, that's for sure."

Max said nothing in response. Bo turned away and left the room without another word or a glance back at Max.

A short time later he heard Joey pass the door on his way out. Max made his way to a small bathroom at the end of the corridor, soaked the handkerchief under the tap and dabbed at his injuries, each in turn. Eventually the cold water seemed to take affect and stopped his nose bleeding. A final dab on his weeping bruises and Max decided he could leave. He'd walk until he found a cab to get him back into Manhattan.

Outside the rear entrance to the restaurant, the rain had slowed to drizzle that matched Max's demeanour. Max didn't want to walk far, but before he could look out for a cab, his nose began to pour blood like a dripping tap. Try as he might, he couldn't stop it. He thought about returning to the restaurant, but decided against making an entrance, having just managed to sneak out unnoticed by the diners. Max assumed the bleeding would stop if he just waited for a few minutes, but it didn't. Neither did the light rain. Max felt wretched. He couldn't get into a cab like this; he couldn't return to Santini's like this.....But he could go to The Alamo Motel. It suddenly occurred to him. Not an ideal option, but better than any other he could think of at that moment.

Arriving outside The Alamo reminded Max of his first visit. The door was locked and again he had to ring the bell to attract attention. It wasn't Becky who arrived to let him in this time, but the chubby assistant whose name Max couldn't recall.

"Hello," he said very politely when she opened the door a little. "I hope you can help me, I've just fallen and banged my face. Could I come in and clean up-please?" Max had to immediately return his bloodstained handkerchief to his nose to catch the drips.

"Are you staying here?"

"No, but I have in the past. Can I come in?"

"I don't know," said the lady whilst checking that he had no-one else with him in hiding beside the door.

"Please. I just need some warm water and a dressing. I'll pay you for your trouble."

"I don't think so."

Max couldn't believe she would turn him away. He must look such a bedraggled mess, with bloodstained hands and a bloody handkerchief.

"Is Luisa there – please?"

"Why? You know Luisa?"

"Yes. I told you, I stayed here recently.

"Hold on."

'Good grief,' Max thought to himself as he heard the door being locked against him once again.

A minute later, Luisa appeared and frowned at him through the gap in the door that she held a few inches open.

"Hi. My name is Alex Slater, I stayed here a few days…." But before he could finish his sentence, Luisa had pulled the door wide open.

"Mr Alex - come in." Clearly she recognised the name if not the puffy, bloody face. "My God, what's happened?"

"I had an accident."

"A car hit you?" she asked.

"No, just a fall in the rain."

Within a few minutes, Luisa had stopped Max's nosebleed, had cleaned him up and dressed his other wounds. Max was sitting in a small office behind the dining room. It had no mirrors, but eventually, when Max had to visit a bathroom and saw his reflection, he winced at the image that looked back from the mirror.

He returned to the office and sat alone for a while, feeling sorry for himself and trying to gather his thoughts. In such a short time, his confidence had vanished, his appearance was unrecognisable and his self-esteem was nowhere to be found. He must have looked as downhearted as he felt when Luisa returned with a small tray holding two cups of coffee.

"I hope the other guy looks worse than you," she said without looking at Max for his reaction to the comment as she placed the tray on a table. Max frowned to suggest he hadn't understood.

"Sorry?"

"You're not going to tell me you fell over and hit the front *and* side of your head are you? Don't worry, I'm not prying."

"No, you're not - and yes, I think he did."

"I saw you in the news - I was very excited - so was Becky. You remember Becky, my daughter?"

"Of course. I wouldn't forget either of you."

Luisa smiled. She was calm and mature, less skittish than Max remembered her from his previous visit. But just as attractive. He stole the occasional glance at her features and her figure whenever she turned away. They sat together sipping coffee, Luisa recalling the television coverage of the foiled bank raid and the Karen Faith interview. It had evidently given her and Becky quite a thrill to follow the story, then to see his picture in the society pages of some magazines. Luisa's enthusiasm for Max's exploits was not reciprocated. Perhaps the pain was the prime factor, or the lingering guilt for Jason's death, but Max could not hide his anger at how things had finally turned out.

"Well, all that's over now. And look how things ended."

"Ended?" It was Luisa's turn to frown. She didn't understand, but felt that she was entitled to check Max's statement. "How can it be so bad - a few bruises will be gone in a day or so. What is more important? You don't look so poor. No, things are good - just remember."
Max shook his head and rubbed his eyes.

"You English expect too much. Be grateful for what you have."
Max gave a sigh of resignation.

"I mean it," Luisa chided. "You English always have a good life - through history - and you expect it still. I'm Mexican - we haven't spoken our own language for five hundred years. We've had a bad history, very difficult, much killing. So we're always grateful for what we have - not what we don't have. I think you have a good life - a good family, you told me once. And now you are famous. No, you have much to look forward to."

Max took the rebuke. He drew himself up in his chair and stared at Luisa for several seconds while he again assessed how attractive he found her. Her appearance and her demeanour. She became self-conscious and started to stand.

"I think I've said too much…" she muttered.

"No, please, don't go. You're right. I probably needed that. And besides, I need to ask you a big favour." Luisa sat down and looked at Max suspiciously.

"It shouldn't be too difficult," he added as he reached across to his overcoat and took the plain brown envelope from the inside pocket. He ripped open one end and shuffled the contents out far enough to realise that the money was bound in $1,000 bundles. He removed five, thought for a moment and took another bundle then shook the rest back into the envelope, picked up a pen from the desk and began to write on the brown paper package.

"I want to ask you to get this money to this person. His name is Ben Winchester. He lives in New Jersey with his mother - but the money must go to Ben, *not* his mother. That's essential." Max continued to write. "You can get the address from here. It's a company called Atom Security with offices somewhere in mid-town, Manhattan. You may have to send it there for them to forward, if they won't give you the address. Ben's father was a good friend of mine. He was killed last night. He works – worked – for Atom Security." Max looked up to gauge Luisa's reaction. "You don't mind doing this for me do you?"

"No. I think there must be some reason why you can't do it yourself."

"I'm leaving to go back to London tonight." Max looked at his watch, realising he'd forgotten about his schedule and needed to get back into The Roy Hotel. "There's $6,000 in there that must only go to Ben," he told Luisa as he handed her the envelope, then peeled two $100 bills off another bundle

209

and added: "That should more than cover any costs." He handed them to Luisa who took the envelope and read Max's hand written notes.

"Don't worry, I'll deal with it." They both sensed there was an understanding between them at that moment. Both knew there was more to the story than either wanted to discuss, explain or ask about.

Luisa picked up the phone from the desk and began to call a local cab company. Max watched her fingers with the chipped pink nail varnish, tapping the keys. He suddenly felt such a calmness that he became aware of his own breathing. He gazed at Luisa, unashamedly admiring her speckled arms, her raven hair, her eyelashes matted with old black mascara. She wasn't aware of Max's stares any more than she could have sensed the attraction that Max was feeling for her at that moment.

The cab company wasn't answering. She tried another. And as Luisa began to tap the new number on the keypad, Max reached into his bag, pushed open the envelope and pulled a number of bills from the bundles. Four, five, perhaps more, $100 notes. Luisa was involved in the call as Max rolled up the bills and slid them into the corner of the desk draw without her noticing.

Their conversation continued with small talk about the hotel and Becky for the few minutes until they heard the doorbell ring. Max stood, picked up his coat and suitcase then turned to Luisa before leaving the room.

"Thank you…for everything." He leaned forward and kissed her lightly on the cheek. Luisa squeezed his arm. That would be their last contact.

At the New York Times offices, Gaynor had just returned to her desk from a wasted appointment with a woman promising a story about some skulduggery at the Mayor's office - but she hadn't shown up, so Gaynor was not in good humour.

"Any phone calls for me?" she asked across the open plan work area as she dumped her satchel by her desk. She was hoping that Max would have called so she could plan her evening.

"A Mrs Gorring," replied a colleague, reading a note from a pad. "She left her number and wants you to call her. The number's ..." She realised that Gaynor wasn't listening. Gaynor had been checking her e-mail messages and one had evidently taken her total attention.

"Sorry Barb, what was that?"

"A Mrs Gorring – here's a number to call back."

"Gorring? Never heard of her - thanks." Gaynor took the sticky note and pressed it onto the side of her screen without looking at it. She was still absorbed in the e-mail message. She picked up her phone and tapped in a number with rhythmic familiarity.

The sun was shining and the sticky summer temperature was rising again by the time Max's cab pulled up outside The Roy Hotel. He would like to have slipped in unnoticed, but he had to collect his key and arrange to check out later that afternoon. He was booked onto an eight-thirty flight from JFK, so he'd leave at about five to meet Gaynor. He was looking forward to spending his last hour or two in New York with her. But now he wanted to get back to his room with as little attention from the hotel staff as possible.

"Good afternoon Mr Slater. Nice to have you back," was the greeting from a familiar desk clerk. "Are you all right?"

"Yes thank you," Max replied, trying to make light of his bandaged wounds. "I had an argument with a pavement at the airport."

"You could sue for that. It looks real bad."

"No. Looks worse than it feels."

The clerk handed Max his room keys without needing to ask the number then remembered a package that he retrieved from under the counter.

"This arrived for you about an hour ago, delivered by courier." He handed over a plain manila envelope with a cardboard back and a 'fragile' sticker on the front with a typed label showing his name and room number. At a quick glance, Max couldn't see any identification of the sender.

"That must have been quite a fall Mr Slater. Are you sure you don't need a new dressing or anything," the clerk offered.

"No, I'll be fine thank you. I'll have a rest in my room," Max replied. "Although an aspirin might help - my head's aching."

"Certainly." The clerk rummaged in a draw and produced a small sheet of foil-wrapped pills. "Take this – you might need them all."

"Thank you. I have to check out later this afternoon. About five o'clock. I'd be grateful if you could have my bill ready."

"Certainly sir. It will be with the cashier."

Max's head was pounding by the time he reached his room. He dropped his suitcase and shoulder bag by the door, threw his jacket and the envelope on the bed and went straight to his bathroom to swallow two pills that he washed down with cold tap water. He stood for a moment leaning over the wash basin, scowling at his reflection in the mirror.

'Fell over,' he thought to himself. 'Who the hell are you kidding?' He eased off Luisa's lint bandages and winced as the tape pulled away from his nose and cheek. He didn't look quite as grotesque or dramatic without them - and at least his nosebleed seemed to have stopped. He dabbed his face with cold water in the hope that it may have some effect on the swellings during the next three hours before he saw Gaynor. That reminded him that he should phone her to tell her his arrangements and departure time. He sat on the bed and dialled her cell phone number. It took a while to connect during which time he casually picked up the stiff manila envelope and began to open it.

"Hi," Gaynor replied abruptly.

"Gaynor, it's Alex."

There was a moment's silence.

"Hi."

"Are you alright?" he asked.

"Yeah, why not?"

"You sound...no, nothing. Are you still on for this evening?"

"I suppose so, what time's your flight?"

"Eight-thirty. Can I call for you at about five-thirty?"

There was another silence before Gaynor replied.

"Okay."

"I thought we could eat at the airport - is that okay? There must be somewhere half decent at JFK."

"Yeah, whatever." Another short silence. "Alex," Gaynor continued. "Why were you in Philadelphia?"

"On business. Why d'you ask?"

"Oh, I tried to call you at the weekend - to meet up. I didn't know you were going away."

"No, I only got instructions from London on Friday. My company wanted me to go to check out some prospective suppliers for a new contract."

"In Philadelphia?"

"Yeah."

There was a long silence from Gaynor.

"Right, must go. I'll see you here at five-thirty." Max blew out his cheeks until they hurt. '*What was that all about?*' he thought to himself. He considered calling Gaynor back to ask her what was wrong and to give her a fresh option to cancel this evening's arrangements. As much as he wanted to see her, he didn't relish the thought of their last meeting being as strained as that phone call. As he contemplated, he finished tearing open the manila envelope and pulled the contents out onto the bed. His attention was immediately focussed on four sheets of white paper on which he could recognise black and white laser-printed photographs. In the moment it took him to wonder why anyone was sending him such prints, he had shuffled the pages so that he could see the images clearly. A moment later, his body temperature must have dropped so fast that his ears hissed. A cold, stark fear grabbed him. He could hardly move to shuffle the prints enough to see all four images - images of himself and each of the gang in the bank during the raid.

'*Oh my God!*' The first thought to come to Max's mind before it grasped the situation firmly enough to race through a hundred new thoughts in a matter of seconds. The photos had been taken from security cameras. The same cameras that Max had controlled with his program - or so he thought. Each image had a time and date overprinted and had obviously been chosen to show the five members of the gang at different times of the day. But by whom? Max picked up the envelope and

214

peered into it, but it was empty. He became conscious of a trickle of cold sweat running down the centre of his back.

'What now?' Max was still considering, when the phone beside him rang so abruptly that it jarred him out of his daze.

"Hello," he answered.

"Good afternoon Mr Slater, this is your operator. I have a call for you from someone saying it's important they speak to you about a package that was delivered to you here at the hotel this morning. Will you take the call sir?"

Max was conscious of swallowing before he could answer:

"…Yes."

"Mr Slater?" enquired a chirpy young female voice.

"Yes," Max confirmed cautiously, his mouth so dry he could hardly get the word out.

"I'm just calling about an envelope that was delivered to your hotel earlier today, sir. Can I ask if you've received it yet?" The voice was bizarrely cheerful with no suggestion of threat in its tone.

"Yes."

"Good, so you've seen some photos that were in it?"

"Yes."

"Good, because I've been asked to arrange a meeting for you to discuss them with my boss. Can you do that this afternoon?"

"Who are you? Who's your boss?"

"Pardon me, my name is Sonya Luckman, but my boss said that if you could come to our lawyers' offices in an hour - say, three-thirty - everything will be explained."

"Where's your lawyer's offices?"

"On Third Avenue – very close to your hotel."

"Three-thirty?" Max glanced at his watch. "Okay."

Ms Luckman recited the address and described how Max could find their particular tower block, with a disarmingly bouncy delivery.

"Who do I ask for?"

"Ask for me, Sonya Luckman. We're on the twelfth floor. I'll let reception know you're coming. See you at three-thirty." Max replaced the phone robotically.

The air was getting heavy with typical summer heat as Max walked the few blocks to his destination on Third Avenue. He was still reeling since receiving the photographs that only increased the discomfort of his bruised face. He walked with tunnel vision through the bustling shoppers, rather as if walking to the electric chair, he thought.

The security staff inside the entrance of the office tower on Third Avenue already had a visitor's pass printed with Max's name and directed him to the bank of elevators to take him to the twelfth floor to meet Sonya Luckman.

As Max arrived, a smart young lady with platinum blonde hair, greeted him with a glance at his badge to check his name.

"Mr Slater?… Hello, I'm Sonya." She shook hands with an almost imperceptible grip. "Thank you so much for coming at such short notice. Did you find your way here alright?"

"Yes, no problem."

"It's quite a landmark isn't it – you can't really miss it?" She was everything Max had imagined from the short telephone conversation - above all, she was plainly ignorant of the true significance of the package, the photos or Max being summoned to her offices. Max followed her through a pair of large glass doors into a reception area. A spot lit brass plate at the entrance identified the law firm as Garland-Grimes that meant no more to Max than he would have expected. Sonya asked him to take a seat while she disappeared down a corridor to check that he could go through to his meeting. But with whom? During the last hour, Max had contrived reasons in his mind for just about everyone he'd met or knew about in New York, to be waiting for him with his or her lawyer. Any one of the gang, anyone at the bank, even Gaynor had crossed his mind. At one point he found himself considering the feasibility that Dennis was not really dead, but had master-minded this part of the plot for some sinister reason that Max couldn't fathom.

"We can go through now, Mr Slater," Ms Luckman suddenly announced. "Please follow me."

Max stood up and walked in procession out of the reception area to a door at the far end of a corridor. Ms Luckman gave it one knock and pushed it open for Max to step into a plush office. As he did so, he was conscious of a rush of nerves, heightened by his difficulty to see into the room. The afternoon sun was streaming between the surrounding buildings, through the venetian blinds and into his eyes, preventing him from seeing the face of the person sitting behind the desk. But as the person stood up to greet Max, her head obscured the sun, allowing Max to identify the face that accompanied the familiar English accent.

"Good afternoon Mr Slater – or shall I call you Max?"

It belonged to Tessa Chapman, Dennis's English solicitor. She gestured for Max to sit opposite to her as the door behind Max clunked shut. He looked around the room but there was no-one else to be seen.

"No, Max, no-one else, just me. Can I get you a drink? You look as if you might need it. Are you all right?" She frowned at his appearance.

"Yes. Fine. Sort of." The words came slowly.

"Please. Have a seat." Miss Chapman gestured to the seat across her desk and Max sat down.

"Are you going to tell me what's going on?" Max asked as Miss Chapman stood to poor a beaker of water from a dispenser. She placed the beaker in front of Max as she responded.

"Where do you want me to start? Or should I cut the background and come straight to the demands?"

"Whose demands? Who do you represent? What are you doing here?"

"Doing here?" Miss Chapman frowned at Max. "This is my office - my New York office," she replied as if Max should have known. "And who am I representing…? Right now, no-one - just me." She waited for a response from Max that didn't come. "You really don't understand do you?"

"Understand? What exactly?"

She contemplated the situation for a moment.

"I suppose there's no reason why you would – this must be quite a shock for you. Not the first recently, either." There was a short silence before she continued.

"Let me explain. The photos are mine, the original idea for the raid was mine…" She thought about the next line before adding: "…And for quite a while, I thought your uncle, Dennis, was mine as well."

Max's expression changed abruptly.

"Yes," she continued, "Dennis and I had a relationship for … I don't know … quite a lot of years - perhaps ten, on and off. Eventually I came to realise he was never going to leave Molly, so this was my pay-back for the long wait." Miss Chapman became almost melancholy for a moment. "We hatched the plot together, but the seed of the idea was mine, way back. Dennis worked on it for over two years and I helped where I could. Just the two of us."

"It was you," Max interrupted as the realisation dawned. "You were the one other person who knew about the CDs."

"That's right. But Dennis's health problems changed everything - nearly killed the whole plan, until I thought of you. I wasn't going to let all that work go to waste – not to mention my cut of the take. Unfortunately, that went wrong as well. As your uncle came closer to the end, he… well, he shut me out. I suppose it was understandable. His family won over, so I had to look out for myself."

"And you planned for the photos to be taken so you can blackmail us," Max interjected.

"No - not blackmail," she insisted, then reconsidered. "I am going to ask you for my commission - for all the work I put into the planning - but no, the photos weren't an after-thought - they were planned from the very start. Remember, you weren't in the plan until the eleventh hour. Dennis was going to handle the whole thing with Bo Garrick's gang just as you have - so we built in the photo program as a safeguard in case they decided to double-cross him. An insurance policy, if you like."

"But it wasn't in the CD program," Max reminded her.

"No." She offered no explanation. "So we come to the subject of my commission. This is a pretty straightforward business arrangement and now it's payment time. I set my fee at £1,000,000 but since we're in the US, let's round that to $1.5 million."

Max closed his eyes, then opened them.

"A million pounds?"

"One and a half million dollars." Miss Chapman corrected. "Let's work in dollars and it has to be in cash - used currency - or a direct bank-to-bank transfer to this account if you prefer."

She pushed a sheet of paper across the desk. "Whichever, but I want it paid within thirty-six hours."

"Thirty-six?"

"Please stop repeating everything I say...... Yes, that's right," Miss Chapman replied as she stood up and walked to a side cupboard by the wall of her office. "You expected thirty days?" she asked, but got no reply. "I'd be more patient had this not become a murder investigation so I want to get out of New York before the end of the week - sooner if possible." She slid back a door of the cupboard and removed some books to reveal the front of a safe which she opened by tapping a series of numbers on a keypad, then produced another manila envelope identical to the one Max had in his briefcase containing the photos. She brought it to the desk and pulled out another sheaf of prints that she fanned out to show Max the full range of the images documenting their activities in the bank.

"Quite a choice eh?" She delved into the envelope and pulled out a disc that she held up for Max to see. "There's even more on here," she added.

"So what you're saying is - you want the Geraldine Diamonds."

"No. I want cash. Used, paper cash or a bank transfer, pure and simple."

"Simple?! Huh. I haven't got any cash."

"Not my problem, Max. We both know that the take from your haul will be many times greater than my fee - at least, I hope it is, for your sake. So you have until the end of tomorrow to pay me my money. I assume Mr Garrick got the lion's share of the take."

Max nodded.

"Well I suggest you contact Mr Garrick and arrange to get my money before the deadline. I'm not joking Max. I haven't gone to all this trouble, or worked so hard for so long, to be fobbed off. One and a half million dollars by tomorrow night or these go to the police on Wednesday morning. I think we can both imagine their reaction to these with their murder investigation...... Murder," she sighed as she contemplated the word. "That was careless of you, Max. I expected better of you. By the way, the guard arrived just after half past four and went straight up to the fifth floor. I don't know what you were doing at the time, but I could see you had no idea he was in the building."

Max felt chilled by the memory of Jason's murder and the realisation that Tessa Chapman had been watching their every move in the bank.

"I'll expect you to phone me tomorrow to let me know how you're making the payment - or to arrange where and when to hand it over if that's how you want to do it. You can bring it here or we can meet wherever you want as long as it's in a public place. That's a detail. But believe me, Max, when I say 'deadline' I mean 'deadline'. And remember, I have nothing to lose but the money - you on the other hand ... Well, I think you get my drift."

She stood up to shake hands.

"I look forward to our next meeting."

"I'm sure you do." Max stood and turned to leave without accepting Miss Chapman's out-stretched hand, but then he turned back. "Tell me, why don't you just want the Geraldine Diamonds?"

"Why do you think?"

FOURTEEN

The death of Max's parents had devastated his young life and changed him forever - changed his character, his outlook, his direction. He only later realised that he'd enjoyed something close to a perfect upbringing to that point. And yes, as an only child he'd been spoiled by doting parents. A small loving unit within an extended loving family.

Then it all changed. A marker was driven into the calendar of Max's life on that night in December 1988. Thereafter, he would reflect on time as being before or after the disaster. With it, came the guilt - the constant, nagging guilt that his parents had been on flight 103. And the recurring nightmare. Swimming in a river on a perfect, sunny summer's day, shouting and splashing under a blue cotton wool ball sky. Then a current in the river, almost imperceptible at first, getting stronger and stronger. Play turned to fear. The harder Max swam, the faster the current took him downstream. The sky darkened, the water became cold and the current became a whirlpool. Max was drawn, powerless into the vortex, into darkness that suddenly became light. He was under the blue sky again, but the cotton wool balls were all around him. The ground was thousands of feet below and Max was falling. He once heard that the night you hit the ground in such a dream, is the night you die. He couldn't remember where he heard the theory - perhaps he had read it. He certainly never talked to anyone about his nightmare. But he never landed. He'd wake up with a start, or his dream would spin off in other directions. But the swim that ended in a fall from the sky was a regular companion at night. Even now, eleven years later, Max found it easy to relive those terrible, punishing memories. It was the most agonising time of his life. He never thought anything could cause a repeat of the pain he'd felt at the time of his parents' death, or the torment that he'd put himself through over the months and years that followed.

Just recalling the hurt of so long ago, helped Max to convince himself that he could cope with the pain he was now feeling. The worry, the guilt and the anxiety crushing Max's insides were all sensations he recognised of old. He knew that he was as guilty as Joey for Jason's death. He felt as responsible as he had for his parents being on that fateful flight. He would have to live with that guilt forever; and the pain that he knew Jason's son Ben would now be feeling. He knew it - he felt it constraining his stomach. Tears welled in Max's eyes as he relived the memory. If he could change places with Jason - such a pointless thought, but he would have, right now without another moment's consideration. He lifted his head from his slumped position, to look at his reflection in the mirror just across the small desk in his hotel bedroom. He'd almost forgotten about his injuries. But nothing that had so far happened during this extraordinary day, came close to the hurt Max felt for his part in Jason's murder. Not the beating from Joey, the revelation of Tessa Chapman, the photos or the blackmail. Max took in a breath and drew himself up in his chair. He stared back at his forlorn image in the mirror.

'You have two choices,' he told himself silently. 'You can turn yourself in, tell all and face the consequences ...' Max tried to imagine exactly what those consequences might be. Prison certainly, but here in the US or back in England? Then there was the gang. Within two days, the photos would be with the police, Bo and the others would be arrested in a matter of hours and they would blame Max. Could they end up in the same prison? Max had no idea, but it was becoming clearer that he had to take his second option.

'... or fight it - get the ransom, pay off Tessa Chapman, then go home. Bo will be making a helluva lot more than the $1,500,000 she's demanding,' Max assured himself. 'He can afford it. He won't like it, but he'll have to pay. Two days from now it'll all be over.' Max gained some strength from the thought. Luisa's nagging earlier in the day suddenly came to mind, reinforcing this new positive attitude. He had to fight. He couldn't buckle under the strain, however difficult or however painful it was going to be to get Bo to pay the blackmail demand. Only then did Max realise that another consequence would be that Bo would demand Max give him the Geraldine Diamonds in return. And with that thought, Max recalled Miss Chapman's sneering dismissal of payment with the diamonds.

"Why do you think?"

'Why?' Max pondered that thought then walked over to the safe in his wardrobe, tapped in the numbers and removed the red velvet case. He studied it for any markings, but there were none. He sat back at his desk and removed the large, heavy necklace, looking for markings on the reverse. He quickly found some stamped into the silver. Had he seen something on the discs to verify their authenticity? He vaguely recalled some images of hallmarks.

A few minutes later, Max had located the information on number two disc. He held the necklace up to compare the image on the screen with the hallmark in his left hand. They didn't match!.... THEY DIDN'T MATCH!!

Max was mesmerised, rerunning the revelation over in his thoughts. He was holding a fake. Probably a next-to-worthless fake.

FIFTEEN

"I came with nothing. I have to at least leave New York with nothing. That includes a prison sentence."

Max had moved into 'damage limitation' mode. It had taken the best part of the last hour to overcome his crushing realisation that the diamonds - the fake Geraldine Collection - were worthless, he was not about to solve his family's financial problems. But he had a bigger immediate problem that was to pay off Tessa Chapman.

"Right," he told his reflection, aloud. "We need a strategy." He glanced at his watch. 4.50. By five o'clock, Max had formulated a plan which unfortunately had to start with a phone call to Bo. Max had to face the music. He knew Bo would become apoplectic with rage - and that was assuming he believed the extraordinary development that Max was about to explain. At least the photos must convince him.

Then Max had to check out of the hotel. However long this took to sort out, he certainly couldn't afford to spend it at The Roy. He'd calculated that after paying his hotel bill and his flight, he would have taken a little over $1,000 back home with him tonight. That wasn't enough for bed and breakfast for a few more nights at The Roy, but it was at The Alamo Motel in Queens - he'd move back there. On contemplating the prospect, Max realised that he'd miss his now familiar comforts, but seeing Luisa was appealing and The Alamo was near Bo's centre of operations so that might help to speed things up.

Max almost forgot about Gaynor in his plans. They were supposed to meet at five-thirty, but now that he wasn't leaving tonight, that wouldn't cause such a problem. He could catch up with her later - or perhaps just let the contact drop unless she called him.

Max settled down to make the various phone calls starting with Bo. In his renewed mental state, Max felt that he could handle the situation, whichever way Bo reacted. Max had nothing, but that meant nothing to lose – all except his freedom. He composed himself, then dialled the cell phone number that he knew by heart. It rang several times before an answer service cut in.

"Bo, it's Alex. I'm not leaving New York. Something serious has come up. Call me any time - I must talk to you immediately you hear this. It's serious - an emergency." Max hung up, a little relieved to have the opportunity to prepare the ground without speaking directly to Bo.

Next, a call to The Alamo Motel. It was answered by a female voice other than Luisa's. She confirmed that there was a room available that Max reserved in the name of Alex Slater. Then a call to the airline to cancel his booking in the hope of transferring it to a later date. Then to Gaynor at her office.

"Gaynor. Hi, it's Alex."

"Hi there."

"Look, something's come up. I can't leave New York tonight. I've got to stay on for a couple more days. So we could meet up sometime later if you like."

"Sure. How much later - do you mean later tonight? Or later during your stay?" There was a silence while Max tried to think whether he wanted to make the effort this evening, then both he and Gaynor tried to speak at the same time. Another halt, then Gaynor tried again.

"I think we should meet today. I need to speak to you about something important. But not on the phone."

'*What now?*' was Max's first thought, but he said: "Okay, I could come over in half an hour or so," he replied cautiously. "You sure you don't want to tell me anything now?"

"No. I'll see you in reception here about five-thirty."

"Right. See you then." He hung up.

'*She wants to see me,*' Max contemplated. Yesterday that may have raised his hopes, but today the prospect just meant that he wouldn't have to get himself over to Queens early, which did, he admitted to himself, have some appeal.

Bo still hadn't returned Max's call by the time he arrived at The New York Times offices. He took a seat in the reception and waited for Gaynor, his mind still running through the options, problems, eventualities that could upset his plans to get out of this mess, then get out of New York as fast as possible.

'*What if Bo's left town?*' He'd thought earlier. '*He could have left the country to escape the heat. What then? Will Tessa Chapman extend her deadline? Surely she only wants the money. As long as that's the end result, there's nothing for her to gain by turning us in before she gets it. What difference will a few days, or even a week or two make if you're about to get $1,500,000? But she may take the money, then hand the photos over to the police. What guarantee do we have that she won't do that? None!*'

Max's thoughts were jolted back to the present by Gaynor's arrival.

"What have you done?" She was shocked at Max's appearance which he had forgotten about.

"I had a fall at the airport this morning – in the wet. It's not as bad as it looks."

"I hope not."

"What do you want to do now?" Max asked.

Gaynor checked that no-one was listening.

"I need to talk to you - somewhere quiet - not here. Around the corner, Dandini's will be quiet for the next hour or so."

They made small talk for the short walk to a bar down the street from the office block during which Gaynor made it plain that she didn't believe Max's explanation for his injuries, but Max was indifferent. In the bar, they ordered the first drinks that came to mind, with little consideration, then took seats opposite one another at a corner table. Gaynor appeared to be considering her next words carefully.

"Look Alex," she began, "I don't want you to take any of this the wrong way. I'm ...well..." She paused for thought. "Alex, tell me, why were you in Philadelphia?"

Max was puzzled, but answered:

"On business. I thought I told you. So what?"

"You never mentioned it last week."

"It came up at short notice. I got a call on Friday from my office in London to go to see some prospective suppliers. What's so special about that?" Max made his answer sound plausible if rather too well rehearsed, but he was more worried by the question, knowing that Gaynor must be asking for a reason. There was a silence from Gaynor. She diverted her eyes from Max then drew in a long breath.

"Alex…" Gaynor paused for a moment. "I know you're lying…and I'm afraid I might know why."

Max stared blankly at her while his mind tried to identify anything he'd just said that she could contradict.

'*She can't know I'm lying,*' he assured himself. Max tried to look relaxed. He smiled as if bemused by her certainty.

"Why do you say that? Why would I lie about such a thing?"

"I don't know - not for sure." Gaynor checked over her shoulder. The bar was so quiet, she was conscious that her voice had risen. She looked back at Max who was waiting for her lead.

"Alex…your company - Astrodome Games - it ceased trading last month. It's gone out of business - something to do with its bankers foreclosing …… and……" She took a longer pause. "I know you haven't worked there for more than two months."

Max disguised his shock by taking a long gulp of his tomato juice. He put it down and wiped the corners of his mouth.

"That's not all," Gaynor continued. Again, she took her time, considering her words and Max's likely reaction to the next remark. "I know the police have you on their list of suspects in connection with the big bank heist over the weekend."

Max picked up a drinks mat and began to play with it. It allowed him to divert his eyes from Gaynor and gave him something to do other than talk. Nothing was said for what seemed like a long time. The longer the silence lasted, the more Max felt sure he looked guilty. But then how could he look anything else? His resistance had gone. He didn't want to push Gaynor away. He didn't want a fight or to put up any more barriers. Perhaps he wanted her sympathy, even her respect, if she knew the full story.

"How do you know that – about the police?" he asked eventually, but Gaynor was reluctant to answer.

"I just know - I'm a reporter for God's sake - it's a big story. I know, okay?"

"No, it's not okay. You make these wild accusations, suggest I'm involved in some bank robbery, then duck back to hide behind your press badge or oath or whatever you call it. How can you make such an extraordinary accusation?"

"I've only accused you of lying," Gaynor said calmly. "Are you going to deny that?"

"And what about the police?" Max asked.

"What about them? They know you were visiting the bank when the robbery took place, of course – who doesn't? They know you were visiting the vaults and that you made more visits the following week. More than any other client. Perhaps sussing out the layout."

"So what? None of that makes me a bank robber, for God's sake." Max thought for a moment. "Is there something you're not telling me? Why would they make such an odd connection? Between my visits to the bank and a heist….a heist in which a really good friend got shot dead?" Then he added: "I hope they also know I was in Philadelphia all weekend."

"Were you? Why? On business for a company you don't work for that stopped trading last month - before they asked you to go to Philadelphia to find new business, or whatever?" Max had no reply. He looked away. Was there any point in continuing this charade? They both knew he was lying. He wanted to confide in Gaynor, but he wasn't sure enough of her motives - or her reaction to the truth. He just knew that the longer the exchange lasted, the more pointless his excuses seemed.

Gaynor broke the silence. She reached across the table and took his hand.

231

"Alex. You have every right not to believe me - I know I haven't been ... well... approachable or as responsive as you may have wanted. You know a little about my last relationship with Jonah - just believe me that it's more difficult than you know to put that behind me, so I didn't want you to get caught up in it. Believe me, please, that's the only reason. I want to help if I can. Judging by the look of you, you need some TLC before any more pavements attack you." She smiled. It lightened the atmosphere.

"I'll tell you what," she continued. "I'm going to tell you as much as I know - and how I know it. I wouldn't consider that normally, but I....I want you to trust me. I want you to confide in me, not so I can use it, but so I can help. Do you understand?"

"Yeah." Max replied.

"I saw your passport photo when I stayed overnight last week..."

Max blew air through his teeth and rocked back in his seat. He knew exactly what she was talking about before she explained.

"...the hippie photo, dated last month?"

"Yeah," Max said with a resigned sigh.

"So, I made some enquiries. I cared, for Christ's sake. I didn't want to think you had some sort of dark past. I hoped we had a future." She stopped for a moment to compose herself. "The problem was I got Jonah to make the enquiries .... through his police channels at the NYPD..."

Max let out another sigh.

"Oh no."

"Yeah, 'fraid so. He told me earlier today about your company going bust and your resignation a couple of months back. They're investigating anyone who visited the vaults over the last month, as a matter of course, so now you're very high

232

on that list because he knows you've told all the press that you're here on business – for a company that's gone out of business. You get the picture?"

Max nodded. Gaynor continued:

"Other than that, I don't think they particularly suspect you, but you can imagine how any policeman would react when they suddenly spot a flaw in someone's credentials." Gaynor stared at Max for this response. He was playing with the drinks mat again. Eventually he spoke without making eye contact.

"You realise that if I did have anything to tell you, I'd make you an accessory to anything I told you about."

"Yes."

"That wouldn't be very fair of me, would it?"

"Alex, I'm a reporter for Christ's sake - I live with that responsibility every day of my working life." Then she added: "And I'm never normally emotionally involved."

Max looked directly at her, as if questioning her last statement.

"Yes Alex, I am. I'm fond of you - *very* - and I don't want to see you hurt. Look at you. You look awful. I want to help - it upsets me to think that I could do something but you won't let me. And now I might be responsible for adding to your troubles with all the exposure I started. So it's over to you Alex. I've told you my side of the story. Are you going to trust me or not?"

Max was about to speak when, from inside his jacket pocket, his phone began to chirp. The sound jarred Max's attention back to his pending conversation with Bo about the blackmail payment. He answered the call to hear Bo's familiar growl, a little less aggressive than normal, Max thought - probably because he was contemplating his fortune from the haul.

"Hi," Max replied without using Bo's name. "Can you hold for a moment - I must talk to you, but I'm in a bar. Hold on." He turned to Gaynor. "We have to finish this conversation. Don't go, I'll be one minute."

Outside in the street, Max slipped into a doorway.

"Bo - we've got a problem - a very big one."

"So you said. What's happened?"

"I need to see you."

"Tell me - what's happened!" Bo barked in his more usual tone.

"We have to meet - where are you?"

"Brooklyn right now."

"Can we meet in an hour? Sooner the better."

"Where?"

"Anywhere you say - I'm in mid-town, but I've checked out of The Roy Hotel. I've got to move back to the motel on Queens Boulevard tonight."

"I'm coming into town in an hour. Meet me where we dropped you by Times Square at seven-thirty. This better be important cos you're worrying me."

"It is," Max assured Bo, then added: "And Bo, is Joey driving you tonight?"

"Course."

"I don't want any more grief from him, right?"

"Okay, okay." And Bo was gone with a click on the line.

Back in the bar, most of the tables were now occupied and the atmosphere was getting more boisterous.

"Do you want another drink?" Max asked, but was glad when Gaynor declined the offer.

234

"Just the truth Alex," she added, "or I might as well drop out of your life. I don't want to be strung along any more than you want me making my own investigations or assumptions."

"Was that a threat?" Max asked.

"No, it's fact," she hissed in a loud whisper. "I'm inviting you to confide in me as a friend. That's a confidence and I don't betray confidences. If you want to shut me out, then I can carry on my investigations as a reporter. The paper may or may not want me to cover the story of the heist - I don't know. I won't offer my services, but that's the best I can promise."
Another couple came over to sit at the next table. Max watched them sit down then turned back to Gaynor.

"Let's get out of here."
They left the bar and stood in the street looking around for somewhere to continue their conversation with some privacy.

"Come on, I know where we can talk," Gaynor announced. Bryant Park is a formal green oasis just a short walk from the bar. Gaynor took Max's arm and they walked in the clammy heat without saying a word until they arrived in the park and found a bench.

"Has it been worth the walk?" Gaynor asked. "Have you got something to tell me?"
Max had decided to tell Gaynor everything, so he did. It started slowly with background about his uncle, the will, the CDs, Jack Briggs ... and so it went on. The whole story flowed from Max's lips in a continuous uninterrupted monologue. Gaynor listened intently without uttering a word or interjecting with questions. Max was sitting a little apart from her, telling most of the story without making eye contact. After a few minutes, the story came up to date.

"… so I assume Jack Briggs still owns the real collection or my uncle would have known if he'd sold something so famous as the Geraldine diamonds."

Gaynor looked across to Max as she measured the weight of his extraordinary story.

"Now what?"

"I'll go back to the motel in Queens tonight and hopefully, with Bo's co-operation, I'll leave for London by the end of the week. That's the best I can hope right now."

Gaynor slid along the bench and kissed his cheek.

"Thank you," she whispered in his left ear. "That can't have been easy."

Max looked her in the eyes.

"Oh yes it was. You don't know how good it feels to tell someone."

"That's a hell of a story."

"And it hasn't finished yet," Max added.

"No – and I might be able to help sooner than you thought," Gaynor announced. "I've got a spare bedroom in my apartment."

Max stared at her.

"It's small, well, tiny, but it's yours if you want it. You can pay me rent if you don't want to take my charity," Gaynor added.

"I can't let you do that. I can't involve you so directly."

"You already have - because I insisted. I'm involved, right? So if you want to stay at my apartment, you're very welcome."

Max was shocked. How many more surprises could today offer, he wondered?

'Perhaps Bo will hand over $1,500,000 with his blessing later tonight?' But in reality: "I don't know if I can let you do that for me," he suggested.

"Alex, I wouldn't offer, if I didn't mean it. It's up to you - but I'd like you to stay… because I want to help."
He knew what he wanted to do and couldn't be bothered to deny the urge.

"Okay - if you're sure."

"I'm sure." In truth, Gaynor wasn't sure why she'd made the offer. She realised it was foolhardy. It was a mix of emotions, including a genuine concern for Max. But no-one gets to her status as a reporter on such a prestigious newspaper without a talent and instinct for the work. Max's story had gripped Gaynor's imagination. While she had no intention of breaking her promise to Max, she sensed that the adventure had some way to run and she wanted to witness it at close hand.

SIXTEEN

Max cut a lonely figure as he waited at the meeting point just off Times Square. His attention was drawn to Bo's Lincoln Continental by the sound of its horn. To his surprise, it had arrived almost exactly on time. Max crossed the street and climbed into the back without a glance at Joey in the driver's seat.

"What's this about?" Bo asked as the car pulled out into the traffic. Max unzipped his shoulder bag and produced the brown envelope containing the photos.

"This was at the hotel when I arrived back there earlier." Bo pulled the sheets of paper out of the envelope and squinted at them. Max could see from his expression that it took a moment for him to work out what they showed. Bo reached into his pocket and took out his glasses case, put on his spectacles then rushed from print to print. The full horror of the images was now expressed on Bo's face.

"What the fuck are you showing me here?"

"Dennis's solicitor - his lawyer - a woman named Tessa Chapman, sent them. She's got the originals - and more."

"What the fuck's going on?" Bo couldn't grasp the implications or understand how the photos had been taken. Max started to explain:

"This Tessa Chapman woman was… she had a relationship with Dennis. She helped to plan the raid. Dennis had included a facility in the program to download feeds from the security cameras - probably onto the Internet. So she could watch us in the bank and now she has a file of these images

238

that she's threatening to send to the police unless we come up with $1,500,000 by tomorrow night."

"Huh! One and a half mill by tomorrow night? Fuck off!" Bo removed his glasses, rubbed his eyes. "How do you know all this?"

"She phoned me for a meeting after I got the photos – when I got back to my hotel this morning. I met her at her office here in Manhattan, this afternoon."

"Well, you'll just have to give her your diamonds won't you, sonny boy? You fucked up so now you can pay up."

"I wish it were that easy - really I do, Bo, but…. well…. they're fakes. Worthless."

In the driver's seat, Joey sniggered. Bo turned to stare at Max.

"Fakes? Your precious diamond ain't - precious? They're fakes? Fuck me. You got any more nice surprises."

"Really Bo, I'm not messing with you - I'm serious – I've got nothing from the raid but I'm here to sort this before I leave New York. I could have done a runner this afternoon, but I want to sort it for all of us."

"Fuck! Fucking hell!" Bo shouted at the top of his voice and slammed the flat of his palm down on the leather armrest. "I knew it was too fucking easy. Stop the car!"

"Boss?" Joey responded.

"Stop the fucking car!" Bo repeated at a higher volume. It pulled into the sidewalk.

"Out! Get out - go on, fuck off and take these fucking things with you." Bo threw the prints at Max. "You find a million and a half fucking dollars."

"Bo, you know I can't do that," Max tried to reason with him.

"Get out or Joey'll throw you out."

Max bundled up the prints and his laptop shoulder bag.

"Bo - these prints are going to the police on Wednesday morning if she doesn't get the money." Max was shouting into the car as he climbed out into the traffic on Broadway. He stood with his arms full of his belongings as the rear tyres of the Lincoln screeched briefly and the car shot away. Max stepped onto the sidewalk ignoring the glances of a few passers-by. He stood packing the prints into the envelope, then the envelope back into his bag.

'What now?' Max was thinking to himself, but he couldn't find an answer. He hadn't considered that Bo would be so unreasonable or so stupid, as to do nothing.

'Get a cab to The Roy, pick up my suitcase, then down to Gaynor's.' It was all Max could think to do. *'Then wait, I guess. Hope Bo comes to his senses….Or perhaps, just get out of here while I can.'*

As Max pondered, while scanning the traffic cruising down Broadway, looking for a cab with its light on, he became aware of a car moving slowly against the flow of traffic on the side of the road behind him. He turned to see the dark blue Lincoln Continental, its hazard lights flashing, creeping in reverse towards him. The rear window slid down and Bo glimpsed a look at Max, just a few feet from the side of car.

"Get in."

Bo had calmed down enough to realise something had to be done.

"If I thought you knew anything about this fucking scam…"

"Bo - I swear. I don't want this anymore than you do? I just want to get out of here and go home."

"I ain't got no fucking one an' a half million dollars. Nothing like. I don't know how much cash we've got, but it sure ain't close to a million…and the rest could take weeks to

240

convert." Bo was thinking out loud as much as he was talking to Max. "You'll have to tell her that - she can't have even a fucking million - not now."

"When?" Max asked. "And how much can she have by the end of tomorrow?"

"I don't fucking know." Bo was getting irritable again. Then he added: "I want to meet this broad. You set it up for tomorrow. I'll get what I can by tomorrow afternoon, then I want to meet her. You and me. I want to know she's for real. She knows me, so I want to meet her, the bitch."

"Okay. I'll set it up and let you know the time. I'll call you."

"Use a new cell phone number. Take it down, I'm dumping my last one while it's still clean."

Max scrambled in his bag for a pen, then scribbled the new phone number on a book cover. Bo watched, then flicked his head toward the door on Max's side of the car.

"Go on."

Max was out on Broadway in the muggy summer air again.

Gaynor's flat was charming, feminine and cool. Max arrived with his baggage to see the small round dining table laid for two.

"You expecting a guest?" he asked.

Gaynor laughed in surprise.

"Yes, you."

"Oh - wow. This is…this is great. You shouldn't have bothered."

"No, right. That's your room," she told Max, pointing at a door, "and the bathroom's there," pointing at another door. "Do you want to clean up? We can eat soon. You like fajitas?"

"Yeah, terrific."

Max began to make settling in motions around the apartment, carrying on a conversation with Gaynor as he moved from room to room.

"How did the meet go?" Gaynor asked and Max explained the events of the evening since they left the park.

"What are your plans for tomorrow?" Gaynor asked.

"Apart from setting up the meeting with Tessa Chapman and Bo, not many. But I've been thinking about the papers and some old tapes that were in the second safe deposit box I told you about. I need to track down somebody that can translate Italian and Spanish. Will that be easy?"

"Are you kidding? This is New York. If you put a billboard on the front stoop, you'll have a queue in ten minutes. For any language, I'd guess."

"I've also got to track down an old computer that takes five and a half inch discs."

"Can't help there. But Gerry who runs the corner shop is the best place to start, for the translators and the computer. He knows everyone round here."

Gaynor brought two plates to the table. The smell and the atmosphere of the apartment was intoxicating. Max drew in the aroma of the fajitas and the comfort of his surroundings.

"Do you have any house rules?" he asked.

"No. Haven't had a guest for a while. Haven't needed any. I can tell you that I'm not good in the morning, so best you keep out of my way. But I'm out of here before eight most days. I don't have breakfast, so if you do, you'll have to get it in. I'll trust you to keep a record of phone calls - roughly, so I can put that on your bill. I'll charge you ten dollars a day and we split any food. Otherwise you have the run of everything that's here. So you can do what you like in your room, providing I don't have to decorate it when you leave." Then

242

Gaynor thought for a moment. "There is one problem – what do I call you now? Alex or Max?"

Max smiled. It was the first time he'd smiled all day and a sharp painful reminder of his bruises turned the smile to a wince.

"Best we stick to 'Alex'. Safer or you could let my cover slip if anyone hears you call me Max – besides, I've grown to quite like it."

SEVENTEEN

A note on the dining table read: *'Good morning. Make yourself at home. Gerry's shop is on the next block for provisions. Left out of the entrance. See you later. G'.* Max assumed that the keys lying beside it must be for the front doors.

Breakfast was a new habit to Max, only recently developed since he arrived in New York. He pulled some clothes out of his suitcase, tested the key to the apartment door then set off to buy something to satisfy his hunger.

Gerry was middle aged, cheery and Greek - or perhaps Turkish, Max decided as he stood in line to pay for a few provisions and a magazine of free ads called 'Loot' that he was surprised to recognise from London. As he paid, Max checked that he was speaking to Gerry, then asked if he could help by finding some translators.

"No problem around here, Mister," he replied with a smile across his face and in his voice. "What languages you want?"

"Spanish and Italian."

"No problem. Give me your phone number. I'll get a reply later today for sure. When everyone wakes up." He laughed again.

Back at the apartment, Max scanned the columns of ads in Loot magazine, looking for an old computer for sale. He marked two that may have taken five and a half inch discs, but he wasn't optimistic. Two phone calls later and he'd crossed one off his list and left a message on an answerphone telling the seller that he was only interested if their computer took large floppy disks.

'*This really is very comfortable,*' Max thought to himself as he crunched on a slice of toast in the cool of the apartment. Looking around at the furnishing and décor, he decided he would blitz his flat in London with a serious make-over as soon as he could afford it. Thinking of London suddenly brought Molly to mind. He remembered that she thought he would be back yesterday and she had no contact phone number for him. He had to phone her. He also had to call Tessa Chapman to arrange a meeting later for Bo to deliver the first instalment of the money. Things didn't seem so bad this morning. Perhaps an end to his problems here in New York was in sight.

There was a certain comfort in the sound of the UK ring tone as Max waited for Molly to answer his phone call. But it wasn't Molly who answered.

"Hello."

"Sam?" Max asked as he thought he recognised the voice of Molly's daughter.

"Max?!"

"Yeah. Hi. How are you? Is Molly okay?"

"No. Where are you?" The anxiety in Samantha's voice was unmistakable.

"Er - still in LA." Max was trying to think which lie he had told his family. "What's up with Mo?"

"She's in hospital. She's had a breakdown. I've been trying to call you. We need you back here. When're you coming back?

"Soon. What d'you mean a breakdown?"

"She's...*we* found out last week that she doesn't own The Gables."

245

"What?!"

"It was the last straw – mum collapsed at the weekend."

"What do you mean, she doesn't own The Gables – she doesn't own her own house? How come?"

"The estate agent or someone dealing with the sale discovered that the deeds are in Jack Briggs's name and he now has them – presumably somewhere in the US. It turns out Dennis signed them over to Jack in 1995 for a loan of £500,000 using the house for security. Molly never knew any of this till last week."

Max was rigid with tension.

"Oh shit!"

There was a short silence before:

"There's worse, Max……. Buchanan's effectively stopped trading last Friday."

"What? It's gone bust?"

"Seems so."

Then another realisation occurred to Max.

"Which means Molly's money will stop."

"In two months according to Jim Wandle."

"Shit."

"Yeah, right. It's awful, Max. Mum can't take any more of this, she's too frail now. I don't know what to do, Max."

Nor did Max. He had no answer but mumbled something about getting back as soon as possible - hopefully at the weekend. Then he cut the call short. He felt wretched. He knew he should be there but couldn't tell Samantha the truth about his efforts to sort Molly's financial problems from New York. It was all getting too heavy. Too complicated. Max sat with his head in his hands after the call until he summoned fresh energy.

First priority right now - he had to tackle Tessa Chapman. Max retrieved her business card from his coat. It gave all her contact details in New York and London. On the reverse of the card were listed associate companies in various parts of the world including 'Scrimiger & Co. - London'. Travelling between her offices in the two cities would have given her easy opportunities to help Dennis with his plans - and with her own. Max tapped out her number, spoke to an operator at Garland-Grimes and was put through to Miss Chapman after a short wait.

Max sensed that she was not alone.

"Good morning, Miss Chapman. We need to agree a time and place to meet this afternoon." Max spoke without emotion.

"Certainly. As early as that? I trust that gives you enough time to prepare everything for the meeting?" She replied with equal formality. Whoever was sitting across the desk from her would not have suspected the true relevance of the call. "I suggest you come here to my office at… sometime between three forty-five and …..four-thirty. How about four o'clock?"

"Okay. And Mr Garrick wants to come," Max added.

"Really?" She was surprised. "That'll be fine. I'll see you then. Thank you for calling."

Max knew that his call to Bo would be less straightforward. He was right.

"Well she ain't getting no fucking one-and-a-half million dollars at four-a-fucking-clock, that's for sure!"

"How much can she have?" Max asked.

"I don't fucking know. She'll have what I can get. Fucking broad!"

"I'll meet you in reception. You know where to go, right?" Max checked.

247

"Yeah, Yeah... And I want those fucking photos. You sort that. See if you can do that without fucking that up as well!"

"Okay...I'll ....I'll see what I can sort out. But she's not going to hand anything over till she gets her money."

"You sort it - that's all." The line clicked dead.

Max contemplated his next moves as he made himself a coffee. There was little he could do now except wait - for contact from Gerry's translators, from the computer sellers and for his meeting at four o'clock.

He idled the morning away, playing with the letters from Jack Brigg's safe deposit box until his boredom was broken by two phone calls in quick succession; the first from a Juan Minguez who arranged to call in to the apartment to look at the letters; the second from Gaynor checking on developments and telling Max she'd come back to the apartment at lunchtime with *".....something that might be useful at the meeting."*

"What sort of something?" Max wanted to know.

"I'm trying to get one of our miniature cameras, but failing that, a recorder. You never know, it could be useful to record the meeting."

"Right." It hadn't occurred to Max, but now seemed like a good idea.

The doorbell rang as Max ended his call from Gaynor. In the hallway were a man and woman. The man introduced himself as Juan.

"We just speak on the telephone," he explained, before introducing Alina, who was an Italian friend who could help with the translations. Max invited them into the sitting room where he had the letters sorted into piles. He explained briefly that he'd been clearing out a dead relative's affairs and come across these business papers, but wasn't certain if they were important. He wanted to know what they contained before he threw them away.

"...so if you can tell me what they say, I'll know whether my company needs to keep them or not," he explained without suggesting they had any true significance.

Max passed out the two small piles and Juan and Alina immediately began to read. Juan quickly moved on from the top letter to check the others in his collection. "These isn't Spanish - eet's Portuguese," he announced.

"Really?" Max was a little embarrassed. "I'm sorry, I don't speak either. I thought it was Spanish."

"No, I can understand a leetle Portuguese, but not enough to give you a good translation. I have friend from Brazeel. He'll do good translation for you. He lives near here. I'll send him over."

"Thank you," Max said with a resigned smile. "I'm very sorry to waste your time."

"Ees no problem." Juan stood up and Max showed him out, waving aside Max's offer to pay for his time.

Alina was well into her pile of documents and letters. Max had put what appeared to be a contract with names of locations that Max recognised, on the top of the pile.

"Mr Slater, you want me to write a complete translation for you, or just to tell you what these say?"

"Can you tell me now and I might ask you to write it out for me later. I'll pay you for your time."

"That's okay. These is all pages from a contract, I think. This company, Zindomi, is going to install big security facilities in some government buildings in Milan and Turin. These are details of the agreement." She flicked over the pages of one of the documents. "It stops here. There's no costs - no money. Perhaps other pages are missing."

"Does it say what buildings?" Max asked.

"Yes." She pointed at some addresses in the body of the text. "Here. They may be military, I don't understand some of these expressions and names. They are very important - here it says about the security equipment being 'very highest specification,' er, right for very important building - you understand?"

"Yes. That's good - thank you. Can you see anything else that might be interesting?" Max asked. Alina read quickly in Italian under her breath. Max watched as she ran down the sheets of A4 paper.

"No. it's not very interesting," she laughed. "Just a list of all the things they will provide in the contract. But it stops in the middle of a sentence." She pointed to the bottom of the last page. "There must be more pages."

"That's very good of you. Thank you for coming over, Alina." Max pushed two ten dollar notes across the table. "Is that enough for your time?" he asked. Alina looked a little awkward, but took the notes and thanked him. Max then wrote down her phone number and showed her out.

Within the hour, the process was repeated with an elderly gentleman named Miguel who arrived unannounced, but he'd been well briefed by Juan Minguez. It took Miguel only the time needed to scan over the first page to look over his glasses at Max. "Theez is not from Portugal or from Brazeel."

"Can you read it?" Max asked.

"Oh yes, but eet has some words I don't know. Ees that a problem?"

"No. If you can tell me roughly the meaning."
Miguel sat absorbed for some time while Max made him a coffee. Eventually, he put the papers down, removed his

glasses and began to stir several spoonsful of sugar into his drink.

"What kind of business you say your relative ees in?"

"He was in security before he died."

"Thees ees a contract - but not real - how would you say - it's rough, not complete."

"A draft?" Max suggested.

"Yes, I theenk so. It ees contract for a company to supply military planes and guns and munitions for contract with Government of China."

Max's expression must have changed as he absorbed the significance of the words. Miguel smiled. He realised how strange it may sound.

"Yes. That's what eet say. Eet's a very big contract if the company get it." He turned to the back pages with columns of numbers listed in US dollars that had already caught Max's attention. Now Miguel explained their context.

"These is the costs that the company will want the China Government to pay."

Max looked at the pages.

"So it's more of a pitch - you know, like a proposal. It's not a contract yet, but this company..." He flicked to the front to find a name he could recognise. "Amber International - they are proposing these prices for payment for the planes and things listed here. Is that right?"

"That's right," Miguel confirmed. "Exactly."

Max leaned back in his chair and stared out of the window, oblivious to Miguel who was now slurping his sweet black coffee noisily. Max was trying to recognise any significance in the two documents. A contract for the supply of security facilities by one of Briggs-Buchanan's competitors and a proposal for supplying armaments to the Chinese Government by a company that Max had never heard of. What did they mean? And why would Jack Briggs lock them in a safe deposit vault? Nothing registered in Max's mind.

"I'm sorry, Miguel," he apologised when he realised that he was ignoring his guest. Max thanked and paid Miguel for his trouble, took his phone number and showed him out. He then returned to the papers and the letters and laid them out on the small dining table in date order. But try as he might, Max couldn't identify any logical link between them, or any reason for their apparent value to Jack Briggs. He was beginning to consider that he was in a dead end.

'*Perhaps there is no relevance to them,*' he thought to himself. After all, they were all so old. '*I think you're barking up the wrong tree here Max!*' he told himself. He packed the papers into a neat pile and put them into a cardboard folder which he flapped closed with a sense of finality. And there they may have stayed had Gaynor's telephone not chirruped, had the voice at the other end of the line not been the owner of a 'Tan-Dem' computer, as he pronounced it, that operated with five inch discs, and had the said computer not happened to be located a couple of minutes' cab ride away from the apartment.

By the time Gaynor arrived back at lunchtime, Max had his $20 computer set up and almost operating, with the aid of a set of well-fingered instruction manuals.

Gaynor hadn't been able to get the miniature camera from work, but arrived with a Dictaphone connected to the smallest microphone Max had ever seen that fitted into any one of a selection of imitation buttons, a brooch or a wrist watch strap. He chose the watch strap, set it up and tested it in preparation for his meeting with Tessa Chapman and Bo. It worked perfectly.

Gaynor hung around long enough to make herself a sandwich and catch up on news of Max's exploits of the morning, before leaving in a rush. Max promised to call her later with a report on the meeting, then went back to his instruction manuals.

By the time Max had to get ready to leave the apartment for his meeting up town, he'd tried everything he could read and remember about the operating procedures of an old computer. He had to conclude that the move and the cab journey had probably performed the last rites on the old equipment. He shut it down for the last time, tested his recorder again and set off for Third Avenue.

As he approached the tower block, Max was relieved to see Bo climbing out of his car. Joey was at the wheel and immediately pulled away, leaving Bo on the sidewalk. He was as curt as Max had expected, when he recognised him. Max's first question was:

"How much you got?"

"Eight hundred fucking grand."

His worst suspicions confirmed, Max dropped his head and sighed.

"What about the rest?" He asked with evident discomfort at pursuing the point.

Bo looked hard at him.

"I don't fucking know. But it won't be by tonight - if at all."

"We're going to die," Max muttered under his breath. "Bo, she's not bluffing. I know it."

"Well, if she's as bright as you obviously think, she's not gonna get us locked up before she gets paid is she?" Bo spoke as if Max had overlooked the logic of this reasoning.

"I hope you're right."

They made their way through security at the entrance then to the twelfth floor where they were asked to take a seat while Miss Chapman was informed that they had arrived.

"Bo," Max spoke in a little more than a whisper. "There's every chance she'll record the conversation - so be careful what you say - right?"

Bo didn't reply, but stared at Max as he took in the concept that he clearly hadn't considered.

Miss Luckman appeared a moment later, greeted both men by name and invited them to follow her to Miss Chapman's office. As he walked in procession, Max reached into the inside pocket of his blouson jacket and flicked on the small recorder just as he'd rehearsed several times on his bus journey to the meeting.

Miss Luckman showed them into an empty office.

"Miss Chapman, your guests are here," she announced.

From an open door, they heard her voice:

"Be right with you."

A minute later, Tessa Chapman appeared from what Max guessed was a small adjoining washroom and apologised for keeping them waiting. She shook hands, using their names to welcome them, then suggested they sit.

"I'm surprised to see you so early. I thought you might need a little more time to raise the money, Mr Garrick."

"Yes, well another few hours won't change nothing. So I've got your down payment, as we might call it and you'll get the rest when I can sort it."

Miss Chapman's expression moved from accommodating, to uncomfortable, to stern, in as many moments as she glanced between Max and Bo.

"I'm sorry, has there been some misunderstanding here? Are you telling me that you're not expecting to get the money by tonight?"

"No," Max volunteered.

"Max, didn't I make it clear that the deadline for *full and final* payment is tonight? My words to you were 'a deadline's a deadline'. I don't think I could have made it clearer."

"Now listen to me, lady," Bo jumped in. His irritation was unmistakable. "I've got eight hundred thou in here, I think that's a pretty substantial down payment. You hear what I'm tellin' you? We're not talking peanuts here - an' you'll get the rest when I convert my funds to cash - you got that?"

"How dare you raise your voice to me. Let me remind you, Mr Garrick, that without my involvement - without the plan that *I* - yes *I* instigated, you wouldn't have a penny. So, Mr Garrick, don't get so high and mighty with me."

"Well in your plan, didn't it occur to you that the haul from safe deposit boxes ain't cash? And it takes time to convert?"

"Yes, I did consider exactly that. But I *didn't* consider anyone would get murdered. That changed the rules of play, don't you think? I'd have been more flexible, but now I don't want to be in New York any longer than I need to be." But then Miss Chapman calmed and assessed the situation as the others looked on.

"Look - as an act of good faith – I'll take this as a down payment and extend the deadline…" There was an almost audible sense of relief in the room. "But if you don't get the rest to me by…. shall we say tomorrow at 4 pm? Sixteen hundred hours - four o'clock New York, Eastern Time, the police get the photos. I can't be more precise – that's my final deadline for the full payment. The $700,000 remittance, here

255

in cash or direct into my Swiss bank account – you have the details, Max. Do you understand that, Mr Garrick? Tell me if you don't, because I don't want any misunderstanding."
Before Bo could answer, Max interjected.

"You didn't tell me *you* planned the robbery at First National Credit Bank, Miss Chapman. So it was your idea and your plan?" The remark cut across the flow of conversation. The other two couldn't have looked more surprised if Max had just passed wind loudly.

"Yes," she replied cautiously, "just as I told you yesterday." Miss Chapman seemed to be waiting for Max to recollect their previous conversation. Apparently he didn't.

"So the robbery was your plan?" he persisted.

"Yes, originally. Then Dennis developed it to…"

"Okay, okay." Bo cut into the conversation. He had no idea why Max was playing dumb when he'd already reported exactly what Miss Chapman was telling them about her role in the job. Nor did he care. He was getting impatient. "What guarantee you giving me that nothing else will happen when we hand over the money?" Bo wanted to know.
Miss Chapman considered the question for a moment.

"My word."
Bo sneered. Miss Chapman added:

"What do you expect, a written guarantee?"

"I want the photos and the negs."

"They're on disc," Max interjected.

"Okay, okay. The disc then. Whatever." Bo added.
Miss Chapman thought about the request.

"Fine, but you know I'll keep a copy under lock and key here." She nodded in the direction of the safe at the foot of the side cupboard. "I think you're going to have to trust my word, don't you? Honour among thieves and all that…?"

Bo grunted something unintelligible.

"…Still don't mean I can get the money in the next twenty four hours. So you'll have to take this as a down payment and I'll get the rest when I can. You have to take *my* word on that."

"Sorry Mr Garrick - not good enough. I'm not going to say it again - but if you want to test me on this, you'll find out tomorrow. Believe me, I'm, not joking."

"You don't seem to understand, lady. Read my lips - I ain't got the money - when I do, I'll pay you. If you don't like it that's just tough shit 'cos if we go down, you're coming with us. You hear what I'm tellin' you?"

"No Mr Garrick, I don't think so. *I've* never robbed a bank or murdered anyone. Now I think this meeting's over. There's nothing more to be said - especially in that tone. But just think about the consequences over the next twenty-four hours, Mr Garrick. It's what we might summarise as 'your money or your life'."

Gaynor was already back at the apartment when Max arrived. She sensed his agitation immediately. After the meeting, Max had tried to impress on Bo that Miss Chapman was going to make a point. She couldn't let Bo win even one round in this contest, so she'd send the photos to the police. Bo wouldn't have it and ended the conversation with Max when his car arrived. The last words Max heard from Bo as he climbed into the Lincoln, were his threats of reprisals if Tessa Chapman tried anything stupid.

Gaynor listened to Max's explanation of the afternoon's activities and his frustrations at Bo's attitude. He admitted being preoccupied, frightened and totally out of his depth in a situation so unfamiliar that he felt powerless. Max talked briefly of making a run for London which led to his account of his telephone conversation with Samantha. At least he would be there to try to comfort his aunt - even if he provided no financial solution to the anxiety that was killing her. Reality returned when Gaynor reminded Max of the consequences of such a short term plan. They discussed the options, but that served to confirm that they had none that were beyond Bo's or Tessa Chapman's control. And what about Jack Briggs? Surely Max should trace Jack Briggs who lives somewhere in or near New York, to try to get him to release his hold on Molly's house. Max could see the sense in that, but he found it hard to summon any optimism for any part of the scenario.

As a distraction, Gaynor asked about the computer that Max had bought and received another bad response as he recalled his frustration with the equipment that was many years past its best-by date. Gaynor walked into Max's tiny bedroom where he had managed to set up the equipment. She switched it on and watched it warming up with a familiar whirring and wheezing. She called back to Max.

"What's the problem with it?"

"I don't know," Max replied from his seat in the sitting room. "It's a load of pants."

"Excuse me?"

"Knackered… rubbish…a load of crap."

"Seems all right to me," Gaynor replied.

Max pulled himself out of his chair and strolled to his bedroom. He couldn't believe his eyes.

"Bloody hell. How d'you do that?"

"I just switched it on and opened Word Perfect." Gaynor was as surprised as Max.

"That's brilliant." Max's mood changed. He pushed the first of the two large discs into the machine. But Max's frustration was not to be so easily satisfied. The discs didn't

258

contain any program recognised by the computer. He was faced repeatedly with screens full of unrecognisable data. An hour ago, Max had lost interest in Jack Briggs's possessions convinced that they contained nothing of importance. Even the reel-to-reel tape that Gaynor had volunteered to get copied tomorrow, held little interest. But now, the frustration of not being able to read whatever this was on the discs, had set a challenge. Max wasn't going to let it beat him. He sat at the computer for long enough to satisfy himself that it was never going work - but somewhere he felt, not a million miles away, there was a machine that could and would unlock the codes.

"Are you eating in?" He suddenly asked Gaynor.

"Sure. Are you?"

"Yeah. I'll go and get something from Gerry's." Max picked up his keys and headed for the door.

"Alex, I've got food here."

"I'll get some wine then." And he was gone.

At the corner shop, Max chose a couple of bottles of wine without much consideration and hovered until Gerry wasn't so busy at the checkout. Then Max reminded him of the two translators who he'd sent around to the apartment and thanked him for his trouble before quizzing him about anyone in the area who mended or bought and sold old computers. Gerry thought about the question, called to a lady at the back of the shop, speaking in an unrecognisable guttural language.

"Two blocks down, above a delicatessen. It's got a green or maybe red and green door. Ask for Geronimo. Everyone calls him Geronimo, he's got televisions, computers, that sort of thing."

Max was away. Two blocks down to a delicatessen and beside it, a green and *yellow* door. A lady in the shop confirmed that Geronimo worked upstairs but he didn't open until about ten in the morning.

On his arrival back at the apartment, Max was surprised to find a candle-lit table set. Gaynor had changed out of her work clothes and the stereo was playing some melodious 'hillbilly' music, as Max would have described Gaynor's choice of Country and Western ballads. He instantly took in the mood of the setting.

'*Oh yes,*' he thought to himself. Sensitive to the atmosphere, he wasn't going to talk shop. It was Gaynor who, perhaps to cover a slight embarrassment, volunteered that she'd listened to the tape recording of the meeting with Tessa Chapman and Bo Garrick.

"You never know, it could be useful. It can't hurt to have some odds on your side." Gaynor was talking over her shoulder as Max washed in the bathroom "And I'll tell you what," she called to him, "at least you now know where she keeps the disc with the photos." Max came to the table as Gaynor arrived with a casserole dish in gloved hands. "I suppose it's out of the question to break in and rob her safe?"

"Yes, it is." Max replied. He would have been more interested in the proposition had he not been grappling with an unfamiliar corkscrew at that moment.

Unsurprisingly, Max's predicament and any possible solutions, were the topics of conversation for most of the first course of the meal, until Max refused to talk about it anymore. He wanted to enjoy the atmosphere of the evening and Gaynor's company. He couldn't believe that she went to all this trouble over supper every evening, which she agreed, admitting that he made it worth the extra effort.

The change of topic was reflected in the selection of music. Max sorted through the CD's in his bag and produced a

Mozart compilation. They opened a second bottle of wine whilst exploring one another's true history, their expectations, dreams, politics - but that didn't last long as a topic, replaced abruptly by their exploration of one another's desires and hates then by their individual fantasies about inheriting very large sums of money. The conversation and sense of wellbeing took Max's memory back to their first date at Dobermans the day they met.

They sat at the round dining table until the candles burnt themselves out then collapsed onto the sofa in a tangle of limbs. The desire for physical contact seemed so natural to both of them, as if they'd spent countless such evenings together. Neither suggested that Gaynor snuggle under Max's arm nor that Max would respond with a sensitive bear hug. Their explorations continued, the conversation now moved naturally to their feelings for one another, their plans for the immediate future. Each assumed the right to question the other without apology or explanation. The gentle hushed atmosphere was more intoxicating than the wine. The feel of Gaynor's body, her smell, her voice, were suddenly overpowering. Max was hardly aware that Gaynor had stopped talking. She raised her head from his shoulder to look at his face, thinking perhaps that he was dozing. Max turned to make eye contact then readjusted his body as he leant forward the few inches to kiss her lips. It was the most natural action, but the first contact was so gentle that Max felt the sensation throughout his body. He cupped his right hand under her ear and neck to support her head as his lips touched hers as lightly as kissing a sleeping child. Max traced the line of Gaynor's lips delicately with his tongue, before aligning his with Gaynor's soft, full mouth. He was lost in the contact, barely conscious of the sound of Gaynor's breathing, the feel of her breath on his cheek, or the

261

knocking on the door… The door! They opened their eyes, released their contact as the doorbell rang, followed immediately by a voice from the other side.

"Gaynor, it's me, Hilda."

Gaynor stood up with a shrug and an apology as she adjusted her clothes and her hair. She flicked on a light in the entrance and opened her front door to a small lady who was clearly upset.

"Hilda, what's up?" Gaynor asked.

"Oh, I'm sorry to knock at this time…" Hilda noticed Max. "Oh, you've got guests. I'm sorry."

"Hilda, tell me what's wrong," Gaynor insisted.

"It's my mother. She's just called me. I have to go over, I think she's very ill this time. But please, don't worry….I'll….I'll…"

"Do you need me to baby-sit Mira and Josh?"

"No, you have a guest."

"This is Alex - he's staying with me for a few days. You must go and see to your mother. Go on, I'll sit with the children," Gaynor ordered.

"I'll do it." Max stated as he stepped forward to join Gaynor in the doorway. "You've got to be up earlier than me."

"No, I can't let you do that," Gaynor said.

"You can. It's no problem." Max smiled at Gaynor knowingly. Hilda looked away, realising that perhaps she had disturbed their evening, but she was too grateful for their help to insist otherwise. Max got his key, then squeezed Gaynor's hand as he passed her in the doorway with instructions for her to get an early night. He then followed Hilda across the passageway to her apartment.

EIGHTEEN

Wednesday. This was going to be yet another big day for Max - one way or another. By this time tomorrow he could be planning to go home or planning his defence in court.

He woke in a very sober mood. A hand-written note on the dining table from Gaynor read simply:

'Good morning. I'll call in later, G.' Now in the cool reality of morning, the comfortable excitement of last night felt rather distant. Gaynor's note served to confirm it. Max found it difficult to summon up any enthusiasm but knew he had to contact Bo to do whatever he could to get the money to Tessa Chapman.

'And if Bo doesn't make the payment...?' Max became anxious at the thought.

The call to Bo verified Max's worst fears.

"Fuck the broad!" Bo thundered into his cell phone when Max asked about the next payment.

"Bo, what the hell good is it to have millions in your bank when you're locked up for robbery and ..."

"Murder? You were goin' to say *murder*?"

"Yeah,"

"She ain't going to get us locked up is she? Not till she's got her money. Probably best I never give it to her - that's our best fucking protection right now."

"Bo - she's going to do it. I know she'll do it to make the point."

"What fucking point? Oh fuck it. I ain't got time for this. I ain't got the money, period. That's all there is to it. You wanna call her and tell her that - you do it. I'll get the rest to her when we've converted some cash."

"When?" Max asked.

"Dunno. A week, maybe two. Dunno."

Max felt sick when he put the phone down. He immediately picked it up and dialled Tessa Chapman's office number from her card and was surprised to be put straight through to her extension."

"Yes Max, good morning. Or is it - have you got some good news for me?" she asked.

"Sure." He tried to sound reassuring. "Mr Garrick's doing everything he can to get you the money, but he might need a little extra time."

"Is this supposed to be the good news?" She sounded threatening. Max sensed that she was alone and he was hearing her unfiltered reaction.

"Of course. We'll get this all finalised in the next few days." He delivered his answer in a tone that suggested the logic to be self-evident. Apparently this was not so for Miss Chapman.

"Max, are you taking me for a complete idiot or are you just refusing to listen to me? The deadline's the deadline - remember? And that deadline's four o'clock. I'm not going to say it again. If you or Mr Garrick think this is an empty threat, just carry on doing nothing until four o'clock and you'll find out."

"But he hasn't got the money. He can't give you what he doesn't have. This is the best we can promise. Please, be reasonable."

"Oh, so a declaration of some intent from the likes of Bo Garrick is supposed to reassure me is it? No Max, you may be honourable - you may even believe him - but from my experience, the only thing people like Mr Garrick understand is strength. They're bullies. He's a street fighter, Max. The strongest wins - weakness is deplored. He'll walk all over you - and me if I let him."

Max had no instant reply.

"But how are we going to get you the money once we're locked up?"

"Don't let it get to that stage. You've got until four o'clock." Max was silent again. Miss Chapman broke it. "So if there's nothing more to be said, I'll expect your remittance - that's $700,000 - by four."

Max put down the phone in slow motion. He knew it wasn't going to happen. He had no answer, no solution. He was blinded by the headlights of inevitability. Max sat at the dining table almost motionless, staring at an anonymous point on the tablecloth while his anxieties scurried about in his head, investigating all the facts that he could recall, darting down every path that presented itself, exploring every avenue that might reveal a solution. His thought processes resembled the urgency of his aunt's spaniel following the scent of rabbits on Wimbledon Common. Where could he find $700,000 today? Who could help? How could Bo be persuaded to see sense? How could Tessa Chapman be persuaded to see sense? To give them more time? Grasping at straws, he again considered if the tape recording could be used in any way, but again concluded that it was not possible without incriminating themselves…could it?

'*Hold on.*' Max sat up. He thought about it - and some more. '*What's it matter if we're all on the recording?.... It's only the treat to her that's important......If she carries out her threat to shop us, our fate will be sealed anyway.*' Max contemplated that thought for a moment. '*That's it!*' he realised. He picked up the phone and dialled Tessa Chapman's number. His call was routed to Sonya Luckman who took a message for Miss Chapman to call him back as soon as possible.

"But it won't be until lunchtime. I'm afraid, Mr Slater. She's just gone into a meeting that won't end until then. But I'll be sure to pass on your message," Ms Luckman assured him.

Max had bobbed to the surface like a fishing float. He was suddenly buoyant, his mood instantly upbeat. He had the antidote to her sting. He stood up and walked around the apartment replaying the recording in his thoughts. Yes, it was the solution. If Tessa Chapman sent the photos to the police, Max and the others would have nothing to lose, so they'd send the tape recording of Miss Chapman admitting that she planned the heist and was now blackmailing the gang. Surely that made her complicit in the robbery and the murder – an accomplice, at least. At best, her career was finished; at worse, she faced a prison sentence.

'*Yes*' Max knew he'd found the answer. '*Checkmate, Miss Chapman.....Or should that be 'stalemate'?*' Pondering the thought brought a smile to Max's face before he laughed aloud with the relief.

The phone rang as Max was crunching on a piece of toast a short time later. He glanced at his watch, thinking Tessa Chapman must have received his message early. It was now only mid-morning. But it was Gaynor's voice that greeted him once he'd composed himself and answered the call.

"Hi - good morning." She had the most seductive tone when she turned it on.

"Hi," Max replied with evident surprise.

"You were expecting someone else?"

"Yes, Tessa Chapman - but how are you?"

"I'm fine - how about you? What time did you come in last night?"

"About three."

"Oh Alex, I'm so sorry."

"It was no problem - really. I was glad to help. Hilda was still upset when she got back, but she got her mother into hospital, so it was okay."

"What's this about Tessa Chapman?"

Max told her the potted story of developments during the morning.

"I am right aren't I?" he asked Gaynor for her assurance that he hadn't overlooked anything.

"Yeah, seems so," she replied.

"You're brilliant," Max exclaimed. "Your tape - what a life saver that's turned out to be."

"What about the floppy discs? What're you doing about those?" Gaynor asked. Max had forgotten about them. He glanced at the clock on the cooker.

"Yeah, that guy'll be there now. I might walk round and see if he can help," he said with little suggestion of urgency.

Half an hour later, Max was back at the green and yellow door studying a panel of bells for the name Geronimo. As he spotted one marked 'Ronnie Mo' and was considering whether to try it, the door opened and two men appeared carrying a large television.

"Is this the right place for a guy named Geronimo?" Max asked as they pushed past him into the street.

"Second floor," one answered.

On the second floor Max couldn't miss the fluorescent yellow doors with scuffed paintwork on which was a large sign announcing: 'Ronnie Mo's Electronics Warehouse'. The letter G had been graffitied with red spray paint in front of the name Ronnie.

Through the fluorescent doors was an electronics grotto. There were racks from floor to ceiling on which televisions, videos, hi-fis and computers of every description were stacked in regimented order. Through the racking Max could see the top half of a swarthy man with jet-black hair pulled back into a ponytail. He stopped whatever he was doing and looked up as Max approached.

"Can I help?" he asked.

"Yeah, hi," Max replied. "Are you Mr Mo?"

Behind Max, the two men from downstairs had returned to collect another TV. They laughed aloud at Max's question.

"Mr Mo?" one of them spluttered.

"Hey, fuck off you guys - take a hike," the man behind the counter ordered before turning back to Max. "Everyone calls me *Geronimo*. What can I do for you?"

Max removed the two discs from an inside pocket of his jacket.

"Someone's told me you might be able to read these for me."

Geronimo took the discs and studied the labels for identification.

"Do you know what program's on them?"

"No. I think it might be CAD."

Geronimo stood up and invited Max to follow him into a room behind the counter. Here were more stacks of equipment, but these were all powered up and working. Every inch of available space seemed to be taken by machines, monitors, speakers and tape decks. A small man wearing a kaftan was feeding videocassettes into a stack of recorders. Max nodded at him, but Geronimo ignored him and pulled a desk chair along the floor to sit in front of a collection of computers. He reached behind and re-patched some cables then switched on a large IBM terminal. They watched it warming up.

"You Australian?" Geronimo asked.

"English."

"Uhu. Where from?"

"London. You know London?"

"Never been. Like to someday." He pushed the first disc into the computer then clicked his way into the program. In no time, he identified the software and opened the relevant program. They both watched it downloading.

"Fucking slow these old things," Geronimo mumbled as he stood up, walked back to his reception counter and picked up a metal box. The program was still downloading as he opened the tin to reveal the contents for rolling joints.

"Big file this," he declared then licked the cigarette paper and sealed his roll-up. The screen icons froze. Geronimo tapped a couple of keys and a green wire-framed image began to build slowly onto the screen. Both men stared at it as more and more details continued to appear. It now held Geronimo's full attention.

"Fuck me, man. Where d'you get this?"

The question was unexpected.

"From a...my uncle. Why? What is it?"

"What's your uncle do, man? Is he in the forces?"

"No, he's dead. He *was* in security."

"Right. I ain't seen nothing like this since I was in the army." Geronimo didn't take his eyes off the screen. He was using a mouse to move around the three-dimensional image. He moved to the bottom of the frame area. "This is high security rated. Look."

The small man in the kaftan had now joined the others. They were all looking at a US Government stamp and the words 'Classified. Security A.'

"That's the highest," Geronimo explained. Then he pointed to more data. "See this, it looks like this was some prototype design."

"For what. What is it?" Max asked.

"It's a missile. Looks a bit like a Scud."

"How do you know?"

"I was in electronics in the army. We never saw things as high rated as this though. When was this dated?" He scrolled through more data until he found a date suffixed '94'. "Well it was highest security in ninety-four. That was after I left. I never seen nothing like this. What's on the other disc?"

He exchanged discs, then lit his lumpy cigarette as he waited for the program to download into the computer hard drive.

The first image to appear resembled an electrical wiring diagram. Max studied it and identified familiar symbols and codes. But there was much of it that meant nothing to him. He took the mouse and scrolled through the rest of the information. Geronimo knew exactly what they were looking at before they reached the US Government logo, the security rating and other data.

"This is the wiring and control systems for that Scud thing." He pointed to the same identification that read 'Model: IRONMAN S10'. "That's the name: Ironman. Never heard of it, but must have been important in ninety-four." Geronimo had the mouse and was scrolling through the rest of the information on the screen, sighing periodically in astonishment at what he was viewing. "This is fucking amazing man. You've no idea. Do you mind if I copy these?"

"Oh, I don't know about that." Max answered, then thought. "Well…if you make me a couple of copies of each, onto three and a half floppies or CD."

"You got it," Geronimo replied and began to fiddle with leads to reconfigure the equipment for duping the discs. "I'll tell you who'll know…" he suddenly announced. "Here Jimmy," he addressed the little man. "You set this up to do some dupes."

Jimmy took over the wiring while Geronimo rolled his chair along the floor to a telephone on the worktop and called up a number from its memory.

"Katie? Geronimo…is Dougie there?" He waited. "Hey man, how you doing?…..... Good…… Listen man, what you know about a bit of military hardware called Ironman or Ironman S10?" He listened. Max couldn't deduce anything from Geronimo's end of the call. "Someone's just come in the shop with some old discs an' there's an I.D on 'em…..... Uhu…. Right….." Geronimo stared across the room to Max, who still couldn't read anything from Geronimo's reaction. Eventually Geronimo ended the call.

"Well Mr Englishman. You've got yourself something interesting there. Maybe I don't want a copy."

"What? What've I got?" Max asked.

"Ironman was a development from Scud, back in the early nineties. But the Chinese got the whole thing - espionage or something. So the military dropped it. Cost a shit load of money too."

Max thought for a moment.

"Can you make my copies - please?"

"Sure."

"Two of each disc."

"Sure. Fifty in cash. And I've never seen you, right?"

Max couldn't wait to call Gaynor. He wanted to tell her about his discovery and to check that she could get the sound tape transferred as she hoped. Suddenly the prospect of getting something on Jack Briggs – and perhaps something *from* Jack Briggs - was back in the frame. Now that he'd neutralised Tessa Chapman's threat, Max could plan to leave New York, but he wouldn't if there was a chance that he had some hold over Jack Briggs. At least he would get him to sign back the deeds to Molly's house.

Gaynor wasn't at her desk, so he left a short cryptic message on her voice mail to remind her about the sound recording, then turned his attention to Jack Briggs's letters. It was obvious that he'd been mixed up in espionage, even spying, back in the early and mid-nineties. The arms contract, or whatever it was from Alder International and now the blueprints for the Ironman missile. Not conclusive proof perhaps, but Max was convinced he had some highly incriminating evidence that Jack Briggs wouldn't want to fall into the hands of the authorities.

Max cast his eyes across the papers and discs that he had laid out on the dining table. An innocent pile of correspondence that should give Max the firepower he needed to get Jack Briggs to release his grip on Molly's home. There was one apparent problem that had been bugging Max. It was still irritating him that he couldn't find Jack Briggs's name on any of the documents to connect him with these pieces of evidence, if that's what this was. But evidence of what? Max couldn't even prove that this had come from a deposit box owned by Jack Briggs. If Jack Briggs chose to call Max's bluff by denying all knowledge of the papers and the discs, Max's leverage was lost.

'What's the good of knowing he was involved in espionage if I can't prove it?' Max considered. But his thoughts were interrupted by the chirrup of the phone that Max answered, expecting to hear Gaynor's voice, instead he heard Sonya Luckman.

"Mr Slater, hello. This is Sonya at Garland-Grimes. I have Miss Chapman for you."

Max was almost thrown for a moment. He readjusted his concentration in time to answer Tessa Chapman when he heard her voice.

"Mr Duncan - good morning. You called me earlier."

"Yes. It was about a development in our arrangements." Max paused, but Tessa Chapman said nothing. "I'll come straight to the point. You see, I recorded our meeting yesterday - a sound recording. I thought it might be useful and of course it is." Still Tessa Chapman made no response. Max pressed on. "You might recall some of the conversation when you explained briefly, but very clearly, that you had initiated the bank heist, as you called it, and that you now wanted your cut. You recall that?"

"Yes. So what's your point?"

"My point is that I don't think you would want that tape to find its way to the police any more than we would want the photos to. You understand?"

"Are you blackmailing me?"

"I didn't think you like that word, but yes."

Tessa Chapman seemed to consider her response before replying.

"An interesting dilemma. Interesting, because it only occurred to me after you left that perhaps that's why you were asking daft questions. But it doesn't change the situation as much as you obviously believe."

"You think not?"

"Certainly."

"How do you reckon that?"

"Well Max, think about what you have. A recording with three voices - yours, Mr Garrick's and mine." Max said nothing. "Right?" Tessa Chapman prompted.

"Yeah, right."

"So it incriminates all of us equally, right?"

"Yeah."

"So if I sent photographs of four of you to the police, but not Bo Garrick's then you can't release the tape because it'll incriminate him. *You* will have incriminated him. Alternatively, I could send photos of everyone except you, Max, then you will have to incriminate yourself to implicate me. Now that seems pretty stupid, don't you think?"

Max said nothing. He was desperately trying to think straight - to think of an answer that would give him back the initiative.

"If you're considering whether you could edit the tape, well my recollection was that we were talking over one another – names were used frequently in quite a short exchange then Mr Garrick interrupted me mid flow at one point, as I recall, which would make that exercise pointless because to cut either or both of you out, will cut most of me out as I recollect. Besides that, as a lawyer I can tell you categorically that a heavily-edited tape would lose its credibility as evidence - it would certainly not stand up in court as the police know all too well."

Max had no reply. He couldn't think of anything to say, his mind still desperately trying to come to terms with the consequences of the riddle Miss Chapman had just posed along with the consequences of his own oversight.

"Are you there?" Tessa Chapman asked.

"Yes."

"So, Max. I think we return to the status quo. The money by four - that's within two and a half hours - or the photos go to the police. I'll decide later exactly which ones to send, but thank you for bringing it to my attention. So, I'll expect the money by four o'clock, yes?"

Max wasn't quick to reply.

"No, almost certainly not. You know it's impossible to get that much money so quickly. We need time."

"That'll be a great pity. So I suggest you do your very best Max. I must go. Goodbye."

Max put the telephone down.

'Fucking hell! Fuck. Fuck. Fuuuuuuck!' He couldn't think past the barrier that had re-appeared from nowhere in the last few minutes. He sat with his head in his hands listening to his own breath, trying but failing to think of any solution. Bo couldn't or wouldn't make the payment - he had no way of finding so much money in so little time - Max had to assume the worst. If Tessa Chapman carried out her threat, by the end of the day he and the gang or Bo and the gang would be arrested. Max knew she would do it - the end was inevitable. When he thought more about her threats, Max realised that of course she would not get Bo locked up or she would never get her money. He was her only source for the $700,000. So it would be Max that she sacrificed.

Max hardly noticed the phone ringing. Eventually he moved to pick it up and answered in monotone.

"Hello."

"Alex, what's up?" It was Gaynor. Max sighed.

"Bad news. Very, very bad news,"

"What?"

275

"Tessa Chapman." Max sighed. "She's going to send all the photos except Bo's. That means I can't use the tape without pointing the finger at Bo. His voice is on the tape in the middle of her admission. I couldn't even edit it out. She has just told me that she only intends to send one or two of photos to the police - a human sacrifice to make her point - and it almost certainly won't be Bo's photo or she won't get her money, so I think that may be one of me."

"Shit." Gaynor realised the significance immediately. "What can we do?"

"We? It's not your problem. And right now I can't think of a bloody thing."

"I don't suppose you want to think about this tape I've got copied?"

"No . . . Why, what's on it?"

"I haven't listened, but Stephan, the guy that copied it, says it's a recording of some phone conversations."

"Between who?"

"I don't know. Stephan didn't listen to them - not in detail."

"Well, if I'm still here when you come back, I'll listen to it this evening."

Gaynor sensed that she couldn't say much to reassure Max, so cut the rest of the call short, leaving him alone with his thoughts.

The cosseted, calm atmosphere of Gaynor's apartment resembled a cell. Max wanted to break out, fight the depression that was gripping him from his inside, defend himself against the inevitable. He tried for a while to contact Bus, Mickey and even, in a moment of greatest desperation, Joey. He wanted them to know the danger they were in. Maybe they could put pressure on Bo to find the money. Max only had phone numbers for Bus and Mickey, but neither answered his calls. He left a message for Mickey with a lady who had no idea where he was, nor did she know anyone called Joey Garrick. No one answered Bus's number. Had Max got through to any of them, there was an outside chance that he could have persuaded them to pressurise Bo into finding the money to meet Tessa Chapman's demands. Was this the last throw of the dice of a desperate man facing imminent disaster? Max knew it was.

He watched the clock on the cooker tick up 4.00 pm. With it, Max was surprised to feel a wave of calmness. That was it. He could do no more, but wait. Running was pointless, as was denial. He imagined what a meal the news services would make of the story. Hero turned villain. Hero to zero in a little over a week. The true price of his fifteen days of fame.

Max was making himself a pot of tea as the thought came to him. The process always calmed his nerves. But suddenly, as he realised the consequences of his arrest in Gaynor's apartment, he knew he had to get out or he'd cause her unimaginable embarrassment. If he was getting out, he may as well try to get away, back to London. He glanced at his watch. He'd go to the airport and catch the next available plane home. It didn't matter if it took all night, even until tomorrow morning. By the time the news broke, the chances were that he would be on a plane and he'd rather be arrested in London than here in New York. Decision made. Time to go.

He finished his packing and was writing a note to Gaynor as the doorbell rang. Max froze. He glanced at his watch. Four-twenty. Surely not.

'No, the police can't have acted that quickly - unless she's jumped the gun and sent the photos early'. A series of knocks pounded on the door. Max straightened himself, crossed the room and peeped through the spyglass to see two men on the landing outside. *'Oh fucking hell.'*

"Hello," he called through the door.

"We're looking for an Alex Slater," came the muffled answer.

Max opened the door onto the security chain.

"Who are you?" he asked.

"Police, sir."

He saw two identity wallets pushed forward into the gap between the door and jam.

'Shit,' Max thought to himself as he released the chain. "That's me, I'm Alex Slater - what can I do for you?" he asked in the most innocent tone that he could muster.

"I'm Lieutenant Baker. This is Officer Timmins. We're investigating the robbery at First National Credit Bank last weekend. We just need to ask you a few routine questions. Can we come in?"

Max managed to contain a rush of relief to invite the men into the apartment. Now the relief was replaced by concern that the police had traced him to Gaynor's apartment so quickly. The explanation came with:

"We got your forwarding address from The Roy Hotel…"

'Really?' Then Max recalled giving the address to the concierge to book a cab to Gaynor's apartment. *'Idiot,'* he chastised himself.

"We're interviewing anyone that visited the deposit vaults in the last few weeks. You know about the robbery and murder I assume?" Lieutenant Baker asked, but Max was still distracted so hardly registered the question.

"Oh, err, yes. Terrible. I couldn't believe it when I heard. I knew the guard who was killed. I was stunned - completely gutted." Max was collecting his thoughts and summoning up his original defence. "Do you want a seat?" As he offered, he saw the note on the table and swept it up before either officer could see it, but he then realised that his suitcase and bags were on view in the bedroom. He moved to take the seat facing them at the table. The police sat with their backs to the open bedroom door. Lieutenant Baker checked his notes.

"You visited the First National Credit twice recently Mr Slater." He looked up from his notebook. "Is it right that you got caught up in the robbery there, on the 30th June?"

"Yes."

Officer Timmins spoke for the first time.

"I told you," he reminded his superior. Then to Max: "You hit the guy - one of the raiders - and shot another."

"The guard that got killed at the weekend - he shot one of them. That's how I met him."

"Then you was on Karen Faith's show."

"Yeah."

"I saw it…" Officer Timmins couldn't hide his enthusiasm.

"Can you tell me why you visited the bank's deposit vaults twice in as many weeks, Mr Slater?" Lieutenant Barker drew the conversation back to the subject of their visit.

"My father passed away a few months ago. I've been tidying up his affairs. He had some business papers and files in a box in the vault."

"That needed *two* visits to clear up?" Lieutenant Baker questioned.

"Yeah."

"Is that why you came to New York?"

"In part. But mainly because I had some business meetings here, so I came to do both things at the same time."

"Right. Can I ask where you were last weekend - were you in New York?"

"No, I was in Philadelphia."

"Why?"

"I was on business. Not very productive as it worked out. I had a couple of meetings there."

"But not very successful?" the Lieutenant suggested.

"Probably not. My old company went into administration about a month ago and I've been looking into setting up a new enterprise here in the US using its remaining assets, but I don't think it's gonna work out." Max had to get the closure of Astrodome into the conversation in case the police were about to make the same investigations that Jonah Lewins made just a week previously.

"I'm sorry to ask you this, sir, but do you have proof of your trip – airline ticket, a hotel bill, that sort of thing?"

"Err, sure," Max replied with mock surprise. "Do you want to see it?"

"It'll speeds thing up - you know, paperwork and that." Max picked up his laptop case and retrieved the relevant papers that he'd kept handy. He fiddled about to suggest that he hadn't made them too ready for this moment, then passed them to the Lieutenant and explained briefly the background to each receipt, business card and brochure that he'd kept from his two meetings.

"That's very helpful of you Mr Slater," the Lieutenant told Max as he noted down details from the paperwork. He was making time-to-go movements. "If we need to speak to you again, can we contact you here?"

"Probably. But I'll leave forwarding details when I go."

Lieutenant Baker began to stand up and was about to close his notebook when he remembered something.

"I nearly forgot. A Mr Gonzo," he read from his notes. "He was with you on your first visit to the bank. We can't trace him or the address he left."

"Really?"

"Can you tell us where we can contact him?"

"No, sorry. He was a contact of my father's. He called me when I arrived in New York and told me that my dad may have left some papers in his safety deposit box belonging to him. We arranged to meet at the bank. I never needed a number or address for him." Max was aware of how unlikely this sounded.

"Did he?" the Lieutenant asked, but Max didn't understand the question. "Did he leave some papers for Mr Gonzo?"

"No, nothing - not what he hoped to find. I never saw him again. Don't expect to."

Officer Timmins had apparently been taking no more than a casual interest in proceedings, or so Max assumed, until he now chipped in:

"You did nothing all day Sunday - in Philadelphia?"
Both men looked at him. He appeared a little awkward.

"No meetings on Sunday - just Saturday afternoon and a breakfast meeting on Monday?" he qualified his original question.

"That's right," Max admitted. "I had a migraine. Hardly left my hotel room all day."

There was a pregnant pause while Lieutenant Baker scribbled a note.

"Thank you, sir. Right, well, we won't keep you."
As both men left the apartment, Max was unsure if he should feel relief or concern at his performance.

Gaynor was on the phone at her desk when a colleague's head appeared over the partition between their work spaces. She mouthed the words:

"Jonah - must speak to you - line four."

Gaynor apologised and ended her call quite abruptly then pressed the key to line four.

"Jo, what's up?"

"What the fuck's going on, Gay?"

She was taken aback.

"With what?"

"This guy Slater - I've got your apartment as his current address in town."

"So?"

"So, what's going on?"

Gaynor was close to speechless.

"What's going on? What the hell…? Nothing's *going on* – he just needed a room – my *spare* room - all right? As if it's any of your business now."

He backed off a little.

"Gay - look - this guy's…. well I dunno, but he could be involved with our investigations - and now I find he's staying with you for Christ's sake. I'm worried for you - what if he's mixed up in the raid? What d'you know about him?"

"I know what I know - piss off. Be honest - you're not worried for me - you just don't like the fact that he's staying with me." Gaynor had dropped her voice to a forceful whisper. "But you wouldn't like it if any man was staying with me – especially if you thought I was in a relationship."

"That's just not true."

"It is," Gaynor insisted. "So what do you know about Alex that you're not telling, if you're so concerned."

"What I said."

"Jo?"

"It's true."

"No it's not - I know you - there's more. Tell me, Jo."

"It is...but there could be a press conference called later tonight - maybe tomorrow morning."

"Yeah? Why? Have you got something to tell us?"

"At the press conference."

"Jo - be fair - come on. You know I can't use whatever it is till after the conference. What you got?"

"A big break. Just happened." Jonah was whispering so quietly that Gaynor could hardly hear. She was straining over the noise around her in the office.

"Come on Jo, tell me."

"We're expecting an arrest, perhaps in hours."

"Who?"

"That's enough. No more. You'll have to wait."

"Jonah...? Who? What's this gotta do with Alex? Jo - you're not trying to tell me you're arresting Alex?"

"No."

"So who - how many?"

"Just one guy. That's it, I've got to go."

"Hold on - a name." Gaynor was desperate.

"Can't."

"How do you know all this? In fact, how do you know Alex is staying with me? You on the case now?"

"Yeah. Bye."

Gaynor sat back in her seat and thought about the call.

'One guy - not Alex,' she reminded herself. She tapped a couple of keys on the phone to call her home number. The apartment was empty. The phone rang a few times until Gaynor's pre-recorded voice answered:

283

"Hi, sorry there's no-one here to...."
She hung up and immediately dialled Max's cell phone
number. After a couple of rings, she heard Max's voice almost
drowned out by background noise.

"Alex? It's me."

"Hi."

"Where are you?"

"On a bus."

"Why? Where you going?"

"JFK."

"What for?"

Max was trying to keep his voice as low as the noise of the bus
would allow, but a tubby lady with a small dog on her lap
beside him was making no effort to disguise her interest in his
end of the phone conversation.

"I'm leaving for London. I think it's the best out of some
pretty poor options. Besides, I shouldn't stay on with you
under the circumstances."

"What circumstances?"

"Gaynor ...?" He expected her to make more effort to
understand. He couldn't elaborate over the cell phone with the
fat dog-owner taking such an interest from a few inches away.

"Alex, the circumstances may have changed." Gaynor
whispered as loudly as she could.

"Sorry." Max was straining. "I can't hear you."

Gaynor spoke up.

"Get off the bus and call me back." She hung up
immediately. Max switched off his phone and pushed it into a
coat pocket.

"My husband ran away to Alaska," the fat lady suddenly
volunteered. Max nodded. "Yeah, twenty-three years ago this
spring...with a lady in oil...and it still hurts."

"Really?"

"Yeah. So you do the right thing, young man."

Max realised that the bus was pulling up at a stop.

"I think you're right madam. Thank you for the advice."
He stood up, grabbed his bags and struggled off the bus. His
fat friend glanced around at other passengers, looking for signs
of approval at her evident powers of persuasion. Everyone
ignored her, so she turned to the scrawny dog on her lap that
gazed back with large watery eyes and an expression that its
owner interpreted as admiration.

From a shop doorway, Max called Gaynor's office number on
his phone.

"What circumstances?" he asked immediately she
answered.

Gaynor spoke in a whisper.

"The police think they're about to make an arrest... one,
Alex, only one. Not you."

"How d'you know?"

"I asked Jonah."

"You what?"

"Don't worry, I was discreet."

"You certain about this?"

"Positive. If this has come from your Miss Chapman, you
know what it means?"

"Yeah, she's fired a warning shot across our bow."

"What you going to do? You can't leave. She's giving you
time to get the money."

"If that's what's happened. We can't be sure."

"No, but if Jonah's right, the police will release something
to the press very soon. They're under a lot of pressure to get a
result. They'll want to tell the press, perhaps even tonight."

Max had been thinking what to do.

"A lot of *maybe's* in this. Maybe we're completely wrong."

"Maybe." Gaynor agreed.

"Look, I'll stay out till you tell me what's happening. I can't get back into the apartment anyway - I left your spare keys. I don't want to come back if I might cause you a problem. Call me as soon as you know anything certain."

"Sure."

NINETEEN

By Wednesday lunchtime, Tessa Chapman had formulated her plan on the assumption that neither Bo nor Max would arrive with $700,000. She knew it was unlikely, so in the privacy of her office on the twelfth floor, she scrolled through the images of the gang that she had downloaded onto a disc during the raid. She knew exactly what she was looking for as she munched on one of her regular low-fat lunches while studying the pictures on her screen.

Eventually she came to the end of the selection. She'd printed off three, which she retrieved from the printer beside her desk. Each one showed a different image of Bus Cleveland at work. His was the head that she'd chosen for sacrifice. She suspected that the police would have found the bloodstain on the floor. In his haste, Mickey couldn't have cleaned it up sufficiently with paper towels to hide it. And if the police could see the traces, they would have enough samples for a DNA match with Bus's blood. So Bus would become a sacrificial lamb at four o'clock if the money wasn't forthcoming.

Tessa Chapman now typed out a brief anonymous note which she printed onto a sheet of plain paper. She then clipped it to the photos and fed them into a white envelope. On the front cover, she copied down the name of Chief Inspector Cahill, the name she found from a newspaper cutting about the robbery that also provided an address for his operations room. She sealed the envelope, placed it in a desk drawer and tidied away the evidence of her activities.

287

Between afternoon meetings, she checked with her assistant that no package had been delivered to reception. When, by a few minutes to four, nothing had arrived, she removed the envelope from her desk drawer, put on a raincoat then made her way down to the street to wait in reception until her watch showed four o'clock. She then walked half a block, pulled her collar up to hide part of her face and hailed a passing cab. She checked that the driver knew the address.

"Immediately. You understand?" She instructed in a phoney American accent.

"Sure, lady." He replied.

She then paid him with a twenty-dollar bill for which she got a receipt with his cab number.

"I'll check, that it's arrived in thirty minutes," she shouted at him through her coat. "If you ain't delivered it by then, you're in trouble, buddy."

"It'll be there lady," the driver assured her.

Miss Chapman returned to her office. The package went to Chief Inspector Cahill. And Bus was on his way to the sacrificial altar.

Headquarters for all investigations relating to the robbery and murder had been set up at the police department buildings on Madison Street in Lower Manhattan. When Tessa Chapman's package arrived, it was immediately opened by an officer working on the case. Within a matter of minutes, Chief Inspector Cahill had given instructions for the police machine to swing into action to trace Bus Cleveland and bring him in for questioning. Not knowing if Bus had any previous record, Tessa Chapman had conveniently provided his name. Locating his home in Morningside Heights was a simple formality, then staking it out until he arrived later in the evening was almost suspiciously simple.

Bus couldn't believe what was happening to him, as twenty heavily armed police officers in plain clothes surrounded him on his doorstep, then trussed him with plastic cuffs before leading him away with the sound of screams of abuse from his wife and daughter resounding through the apartment block.

At the police operations HQ, a blood sample was taken for DNA-matching that would later confirm his guilt. He was read his rights and charged with robbery and accessory to murder.

The police couldn't believe their good fortune. A result from nowhere, within a matter of hours. Neither could they wait to tell the press. The story was officially released soon after nine o'clock in the evening. By that time, Max was sitting in a bar somewhere in mid-town, a few minutes' walk from the stop where he'd left the bus some four hours earlier. Max had taken up residence in a corner of the room with a view of the television. It was tuned to a sports channel, but between games and at some commercial breaks, it ran the news headlines. Max was bored and a little drunk from the four beers that he'd stretched out to keep him company.

The nine o'clock news had come and gone with no reference to the robbery investigation so Max was beginning to worry that nothing decisive was going to happen tonight. He had telephoned Gaynor over an hour ago, but she knew nothing more by then.

Max hardly heard his phone ringing through the noise that now surrounded him in the bar. When he answered, he had difficulty hearing or understanding Gaynor's news as she spoke from her desk in a hushed voice.

"Hold on - I'll get out of here," he told her. He gathered up his possessions and struggled into the street.

"Gaynor - talk to me. What's happening?"

"The police have made an arrest and charged someone with the robbery and a connection with the murder. That's all they've told us. No name yet."

"Just one?"

"Yes."

"It wasn't on the nine o'clock news. I just watched it."

"Where are you?"

"Mid-town. I was in a bar."

"What you going to do now?"

"I'll call Bo - he's got to listen now. She's done it as a warning. Tomorrow it'll be another photo to the police, I'll bet that's her plan."

"You've got to come back to the apartment then. I'll meet you there. I'll be back in half an hour."

Max knew he shouldn't return to the apartment. Anything could happen over the next few days. This was a short reprieve, possibly *very* short. If Bo didn't pay up, then it was still just a matter of time. But Max was tired. The thought of Gaynor's comfortable apartment was too much to resist.

"Okay, I'll see you back there later," he agreed.

The atmosphere in the apartment was subdued. Max and Gaynor ate a bowl of pasta each, with long silent breaks in their conversation. Max had left two messages for Bo, hoping he had seen the item that was leading each late night news bulletin. The police had now named Bus so the TV stations were evidently trying to piece together a profile for him. Max was convinced that Bo had left New York and gone into hiding. But Gaynor was equally certain that he hadn't, reasoning that with his police record, Bo wouldn't get far and while he had so much money from the robbery, he could afford the remaining $700,000 price tag to secure his freedom.

"You're crediting him with more sense than he deserves," Max told her. "Besides, he hasn't got the cash and Tessa Chapman will only accept cash. She's not going to take jewellery or silver bullion - or glass eyeballs."
Gaynor gave him a sideways look that Max passed over without explanation.

In reality, Bo would certainly have gone to ground, or at least put some distance between himself and New York if he could. Disappearing to avoid the police was one thing - avoiding his creditors in a real estate scam that had gone badly wrong and left him owing some very nasty acquaintances some very large sums of money, were more powerful influences on his decision – firstly to do the raid and now to see through the consequences. Had those creditors suspected that he was trying to dodge his responsibilities to repay his debts to them, Bo would be stirring up serious trouble for himself, his family and his businesses. So he had to stay in New York to face whatever was going to happen for as long as it would take to convert the haul into cash to pay off his debts. Facts unknown to Max.

"I must leave here tomorrow," Max suddenly announced between mouthfuls of pasta. "It's only a matter of time. I shouldn't even be here now. I'll go in the morning - get myself on the next plane…"

Max was interrupted by his cell phone ringing somewhere. He jumped up from the table and pounced on his jacket in the bedroom. He knew it could only be one person.

"Bo. Have you seen the news?…. Yeah…. Yeah…. Okay…. No, not here. Hold on." Max turned from the phone to Gaynor, whose attention was already focussed on the call. Under his breath, Max asked:

"Somewhere to meet… quiet… near here?"

Gaynor thought.

"Small park – may be called Vincent's or something like Vincent – where 7th and Greenwich Avenues cross."

"Did you hear that… a small park called Vincent where…."

Gaynor filled in the gap.

"7th and Greenwich meet."

Max repeated it.

"…How long?.... I'll be there." Max dropped the phone to his side. He was stunned.

"What's happening?" Gaynor was desperate to know.

"I don't believe it." Max was in shock. He then began to laugh. "I don't believe it."

"Alex - what?"

"That was Bo. He's got the money. He wants me to deliver it to her tomorrow first thing. He wanted Joey to drop it here tonight. I'm going to meet him at that park in an hour." He laughed out loud.

"My God." Gaynor was as shocked as Max at the development.

"*Thank* God." Max added. His mood had changed abruptly, but his relief was tinged with caution. "You don't think there's a catch? Huh - is the end really in sight?" He was asking himself as much as Gaynor across the dining table.

"Let's hope so - apart from the police investigation and your friend Bus being in custody." Gaynor added her sobering afterthought.

The news had transformed the mood of the meal. Conversation even came around to Max's investigations into

Jack Briggs's discs and Max's theory that he was involved in espionage. Gaynor produced the sound tape and cassette copy that she'd made at work, but Max put it to one side as a task for tomorrow. His enthusiasm for that chase, to pursue Jack Briggs for Molly's deeds and perhaps something more, had been rekindled by the prospect of delivering Tessa Chapman's blackmail demand in the morning.

Max was preparing to leave for his late night rendezvous, when he became aware of Gaynor putting on her shoes.

"You don't need to come?" he told her.

"I know, but I'll keep you company."

They walked the few blocks to the meeting point, with Gaynor gripping Max's arm. It was another clammy hot evening. The air was made heavy by lack of wind to move the heat and fumes from the city. They arrived at the corner of a small park at the intersection of the avenues a few minutes early. Jack Briggs's discs and the tape had become their main topic of conversation during the walk. They explored the evidence that had so far come to light, its relevance, its blackmail value and what it all meant. Gaynor hadn't listened to the tape. Perhaps that would reveal something to explain the rag-bag of other bits in the collection. Max had to admit that what he already had was pretty circumstantial. If Jack Briggs denied all knowledge, it would be hard to make a case strong enough to get him to sign back the deeds to The Gables, let alone any more of his wealth.

Max held his watch to see the time in the street lighting. Joey was already half an hour late. Max started to worry that he wasn't going to show. They decided to wait for a few more minutes before phoning Bo, their conversation, meanwhile,

293

moving to the prospect of Gaynor coming to London - perhaps during her Christmas break.

"God, it's too hot - we need a storm." Gaynor declared as she fanned her face with her hand.

Max pulled his phone out of his pocket and tapped out Bo's cell phone number. He listened then announced:

"It's his answer service."

"Let's walk. One circuit, in case he's parked the other side of the park," Gaynor suggested.

They were nearly back to the start when the headlights of a car parked in a side road flashed to attract their attention. The car was Bo's dark blue Lincoln Continental. Max and Gaynor turned and crossed the main road towards the Lincoln. As they reached the car, Max could see two figures in the front seats. When Joey recognised Max, he immediately pressed the central lock button which Max and Gaynor could hear from outside. They stood waiting for Joey to do something, but he only responded by waving through the window, making signs to suggest he was comfortably cool from the aircon inside the car. Max recognised Joey's companion as the guy who had delivered a package to his hotel room on his first night at The Roy. He and Joey were evidently having a good time at Max and Gaynor's expense. Max could feel his anger rising to the surface and knew it was just a matter of time before he snapped. He tried to appear casual as he turned Gaynor away to lean on a wall across the width of the sidewalk in an attempt to disguise their growing irritation. Joey and his mate were now jigging in their seats to the sound of the radio with the volume turned up. That was enough. Max marched up to the car and slapped the window.

"You got something for me or not?"

Inside, Joey lifted a colourful sports bag for Max to see. He slid the zip open to reveal its contents of neatly bundled notes. Max pulled his cell phone out of his pocket and redialled Bo's number that he pointed at Joey.

"Bo," he said, pointing to the phone then made a big gesture of pressing the 'call' button with his finger hovering. It worked. Immediately, Max heard the central locking click off and Joey try to open the door. On the other side of the car, his mate was having more success getting out of the passenger seat. As they emerged, it was obvious that they were either drunk or high or both. Joey had dragged the sports bag out of the car with him, but now kept it out of Max's reach.

"This is the mother-fucker that's fucking my uncle over." Joey slurred to his mate. "Aren't you a fucker? Fucking my uncle real good?"

Max checked around to see if anyone was witnessing the scene, but the street was empty.

"Joey, I don't want any trouble. Just give me the bag. Let's not attract any attention, shall we?" Max tried to reason.

"No fucking attention - just give you all this money. That's what you want is it?"

Gaynor now stepped forward to join Max.

"Who's she?" Joey wanted to know.

"A friend," Max answered. "Now come on Joey. Give me the bag and we can all go home."

"How's a mother-fucker like you got a pretty friend like that? Or is this your mother?" Joey and his mate both laughed. Max said nothing, but reached forward to take the bag.

"Not so fucking quick, fucker. We got an eager beaver here, Bing." Joey told his companion. Then he turned to Max.

"You want this so bad, we'll have to think of how you can earn it Mr Beaver - Mr Eager Beaver." He and Bing seemed to think the prospect of Max *earning* the money was very amusing. "How about you run round that park over there?"

"Twice." Bing added, then laughed.

Gaynor stepped past Max.

"How about you fuck yourself?" She announced into Joey's face as she raised a small gun clenched in her right hand. "Stop fucking us about, give us the bag and fuck off, Shit-for-brains."

Joey seemed to sober a little in an instant.

"Well, Eager Beaver's got a fucking minder." Then to Gaynor: "What you going to do with that - kill me, eh?"

"No," Gaynor replied. "I'm going to shoot you in your knees - then you can tell the law and your uncle, whatever you want – from your hospital bed."

Max shook off his shock at Gaynor's action, stepped forward and took the sports bag out of Joey's hand.

"No trouble, Joey. Now go home."

Joey released his grip on the bag.

"Fuck you. You're fucking dead meat. You hear what I'm saying?"

"Yeah. Tell Bo, why don't you - before I do. Now fuck off home and try not to attract any more attention - as if I give a toss." Max prodded Joey's chest and felt his gun through his jacket. He unzipped it and quickly pulled out the pistol from its holster.

"And yours," he ordered Bing who had his hands raised.

"I'm not packing. Honest." He opened his jacket to show his shirt. Max considered what to do with Joey's gun for a moment, then pushed it into his own jacket pocket. "I'll give it to Bo next time I see him. Now get in the car and go home," he ordered.

Gaynor was still holding her gun to Joey's temple. She moved with him as he turned to get into the car, then stepped away before Joey could slam the door onto her.

"Let's go," Max suggested. Both he and Gaynor set off down the street. "Where did the gun come from?" Max asked.

"Insurance. Meeting shits like them in places like this is an occupational hazard."

Joey had started up the Lincoln and pulled it away from the sidewalk when, in his mirror, he could see Max and Gaynor crossing the street behind the car. He stepped on the brake then grappled the car into reverse and floored the accelerator, sending a puff of smoke from the rear tyres that squealed before gaining some grip then catapulted the car down the narrow road in reverse. Max was first to react as it charged towards them. He pushed Gaynor ahead of him to the opposite side of the road.

The Lincoln wavered as Joey tried to aim the car at his moving targets then sped past Max, missing him by a few inches. Joey immediately slammed his foot on the brake and swung the wheel towards his target in preparation to make a second charge. But his movements were so violent, that he lost control of the two ton monster that slid in reverse for more than its own length before crashing hard into an old Volkswagen Beetle at the end of a row of parked cars. Joey fumbled with the gear stick until he found 'drive' and pushed his right foot down to the floor to make his getaway. But the Lincoln had ridden up over the bumper of the Volkswagen, effectively locking the two cars together as one. The Lincoln had the Beetle in tow and was jumping and gyrating it out of its parking space. The violent movement began to snap the bumpers, but still the cars remained locked in tandem. Joey

297

quickly realised the problem, stamped on the brake and pushed the gear into reverse. He slammed the Volkswagen backward and was intending to hit the brake in an attempt to release it, but Joey couldn't see beyond his unwanted trailer and both cars powered back into a small truck with a loud crash. The Beetle was now stationary, but the Lincoln, still driving backwards, rode up the curved bonnet of the Beetle, digging its nose into the road and lifting the limousine's rear wheels almost clear of the tarmac.

Inside the car, Bing had been screaming at Joey to slow down. When he realised they weren't going to get the Lincoln back on the road, he jumped from the car. Further down the street, Max and Gaynor had been watching the scene from a safe distance. They expected to see Joey follow his mate out of the car then make their getaway on foot, but he didn't appear.

Joey refused to believe that he couldn't prize the Lincoln apart from the Beetle, but the only way he had of controlling the car was with its automatic gears. In turn, he banged it into 'drive', then 'reverse', pushing his right foot into the floor mat each time. Without the weight of the car fully on its wheels, the engine quickly revved through the red danger line on the tachometer dial. The rear wheels spun furiously, sending up clouds of burning rubber smoke from their light contact with the road. The Lincoln began to bellow smoke from its exhaust into the night air. Bing approached the car cautiously as it thrashed around. He opened the front passenger door and shouted at Joey.

"Get out man! It's not gonna move. Come on - let's get outa here!"

Joey ignored him, still frantically pumping the gear stick back and forth and revving the engine until it screamed. Now, adding to the burning tyre rubber, smoke began to blow out from the front grill - perhaps it was steam - perhaps it was petrol vapour....

K A B O O M !

The power of the explosion blew Bing down the sidewalk then immediately engulfed the front of the car in flames. From some way off, Max and Gaynor witnessed the explosion and flinched away from the brightness of the fireball. In the car, Joey had been knocked nearly unconscious and was trying to regain his senses amid flames that were now surrounding him, inside the car and out.

"Stay here!" Max ordered Gaynor as he forced the sports bag into her hand and set off down the road.

"Alex, don't!" she called after him, but Max ignored her and kept running.

The heat coming off the car was so fierce that Max could barely keep his eyes open. He made his way down the side of the Lincoln, protecting his head with his right arm as he reached for the handle of the driver's door with his other hand.

B A N G ! .... B A N G!

Two smaller explosions came in fast succession under the car, driving Max back. He returned a moment later, lunged at the handle, managed to grip it and wrenched it with a jerk. As the door flung open, Joey's body slumped through the gap. Max could see that his trousers were alight as he dug his fingers into the shoulders of Joey's blouson jacket, took two handfuls of leather and dragged his body back, away from the driver's seat. The dead weight wouldn't give at Max's first pull. The heat was almost too much. Max tried again with another pull. He put his foot against the door. His lever worked and Joey's body slid over the leather seat and flopped onto the tarmac. One of the onlookers who had now come out of nearby apartments, rushed forward to help Max drag Joey's lifeless body along the road to a safe distance from the cars that were now totally engulfed in fire. Someone began to beat out the flames from Joey's trousers with their coat as the Lincoln exploded for a third time, sending a shower of fresh glass and pieces of bodywork flying high into the air.

From another direction, the sirens signalled a police car or fire engine approaching. The flashing lights, rounded the end of the street. Through the line of parked cars beside him, Max noticed Gaynor waving to attract his attention. He didn't need a second call to make himself scarce before the law arrived. In the confusion, Max found it easy to slip away from the group around Joey's body and catch up with Gaynor who was already heading for home with a particularly tight hold of the sports bag.

At the apartment, they couldn't wait to count the contents of the holdall. Max fanned every bundle to find a mix of ten, twenty and hundred dollar notes. But they checked out and added up exactly to $700,000. Max and Gaynor both looked at the neat stacks on the dining table.

"Shame to hand it all over." Gaynor voiced exactly Max's thoughts at that moment.

"Don't even think about it. That's the cost of my freedom right now," Max stated as he began to load the money back into the bag. "First thing in the morning, your new owner will be a certain Miss T. Chapman," he told the bundles.

"You think so," Gaynor said behind his back. It took Max the briefest of moments to register the statement. But as he turned to question her, his actions were frozen by the sensation of the cold metal barrel of Gaynor's small Derringer handgun touching his temple.

"Gaynor…?"

"Yes."

"…If this is a joke, it's not funny."

Gaynor said nothing. She slid her hand around Max's waist band searching for Joey's gun that he might have put in his trousers, but it was on the small table with the bag of money within Max's reach.

"Undo them." she ordered, referring to his trousers. Max tried to turn his head to check what she meant, but she forced him to look forward by pushing the barrel of her pistol along his cheek.

"I mean it Alex. Drop your pants."

Max lowered his hands and slowly undid his belt, then the waistband of his jeans and the fly buttons. His trousers fell to his ankles.

"Now in there - into the bedroom," Gaynor ordered.

"I can't move like this."

"Precisely - I don't want you running anywhere - just make an effort Alex."

Max raised his hands to shoulder height, then shuffled towards his bedroom.

"Not that one," Gaynor instructed as she nudged him into her own bedroom.

"Gaynor, this is crazy, don't do it!"

"Please - shut up, Alex," Gaynor ordered as she frisked him again, running her hand up his back then around the waistband of his boxer shorts until her hand was at the front, then her hand dropped inside his boxers.

"Hmmm, you are packing."

Max was confused and tried to look at her again but received the same impact from her gun muzzle. But before he could question her again, Gaynor had clicked off the light and a moment later, dropped her pistol as she hit Max with a bear hug that sent them both sprawling onto the bed with a burst of laughter peeling from of her body. Gaynor was in near hysterics. Max was less amused for the first few moments, but then began to see the funny side of it all.

"You ....you mad bitch."

"Yeah," Gaynor managed to spurt out between taking breaths and creasing up with more laughter.

"You're crazy. What if I'd hit you?" Max soon began to laugh. "Where's that bloody gun now? It's not in here with us is it?"

"Bang!" Gaynor mimicked.

"What the hell are you on, woman?"

Gaynor was preoccupied with unbuttoning Max's shirt and pulling off the few items of clothing that he was still wearing. The action of grappling with fastenings had a calming effect on her near-hysterics. She stopped laughing and began to search for Max's mouth with hers, then locked their lips in a massaging and passionate kiss. Max responded by groping to undo Gaynor's clothing until, when his progress was too slow for her, Gaynor assisted by undressing herself, as far as possible without releasing the contact between their mouths. By the time they were both naked, they were as aroused as one another. Max was desperate not to shame himself by losing control, but the sensation of Gaynor's body against his, her smooth skin, her caressing touch - it was all becoming too much for a man who hadn't made love or even felt a woman's body next to his for such a long time. Max felt the sensation welling up inside. He tried to control himself, but knew it was beyond him.

'No. No. No.' He pleaded with himself, but a moment later his body throbbed and bucked with the over-powering, all-consuming natural urges of an ejaculation. Gaynor sensed it coming and held him in a gentle hug, her arms around him like those of a consoling mother. The sensation peaked and fell away from Max's body and with it all his energies drained, all his passion spent. He was as weak as a baby and embarrassed beyond description.

"It's all right." Gaynor whispered her assurance, still hugging him in the half light.

"I'm sorry. I'm really sorry."

"It's not a problem." Gaynor repeated, without loosening her grip. And so their two bodies remained intertwined until Max fell asleep just minutes later and Gaynor soon after.

TWENTY

It had been patently obvious to Max from the outset that
Sonya Luckman had no idea of her boss's darker business
dealings. Having now been sitting in Garland-Grimes's
reception for the best part of an hour waiting for Tessa
Chapman's arrival, he wondered if Ms Luckman had any
better knowledge of her boss's diary. He'd phoned into the
office on the dot of nine o'clock to be told that Miss Chapman
had a morning meeting with a client and would be in at ten. It
was now nearly eleven. Had Max known that he would be
wasting his time, he would have spent the morning listening to
the new cassette copy of Jack Briggs's tape. He'd become
excited at the prospect of this providing some answers to the
mixed bag of paperwork and apparent evidence of espionage.
Without it - without something more tangible - Max knew he
had very little to frighten Jack Briggs into releasing his claim
on Molly's house, let alone any additional payment for his
trouble.

Max continued to wait with the sports bag at his feet;
sipping his second coffee, impatient to finish the business. He
needed to ensure that no more photos were dispatched to the
NYPD. He began to think through the entire scenario for the
remainder of his stay in New York, regardless of whatever the
tape might reveal. But regular flashbacks to last night kept
derailing his train of thought. Even the drama of Joey and the
fire was overpowered by thoughts of Gaynor. A heady mix of
excitement, amusement and embarrassment followed. He
found himself smiling and grimacing in turn, so much so that

he checked around the reception to see if anyone was witnessing his involuntary reactions. But the reception was empty for most of the time Max had been there. A lady only appeared from an adjoining office when the glass doors opened and a visitor or member of staff arrived.

Max was bored. He wanted to leave, but knew he couldn't. He had finished his coffee and the one newspaper on the side table. Bus's arrest was covered in detail on page three, serving as a reminder to Max, if it was needed, as to why he was here. While still wondering just how long this vigil would last, Max's attention was drawn to a flash of bright colour through the double glass doors. It was Little Red Riding Hood, or so his imagination suggested. Approaching reception from the elevator, Max could see the figure of a woman wearing a bright red oversized raincoat, complete with hood, who had evidently modelled her look on the nursery rhyme character. On closer inspection, Max realised that it was Tessa Chapman and she was clearly not in good humour. She pulled open the glass door, marched straight through reception and disappeared down the corridor towards her office without giving Max a glance. A moment later, the part time receptionist appeared from the office, realised that nobody needed her attention as soon as she recognised Miss Chapman then disappeared back into her lair. Max was alone again wondering what to do.

Sonya Luckman emerged a couple of minutes later looking a little flustered and full of apologies.

"Miss Chapman was held up at her last meeting, but she can see you now for a few minutes," she told Max. They set off to her office where Ms Luckman announced Max then immediately left them alone.

"Well, what have you there?" Tessa Chapman was shuffling the paper on her desk and working through her first housekeeping tasks of the morning. She gave Max her divided attention.

"I think you called it *the remittance,*" Max replied.

"Excellent." Miss Chapman stopped fiddling with her computer keyboard and concentrated on Max as he lifted the bag onto the desk. Miss Chapman expected to take it, but Max kept hold of the handles.

"I want a copy of the disc with all the photos."

"Of course. It's here." Tessa Chapman turned to the wall cupboard and slid back the door to reveal the safe, tapped some numbers onto the keypad and swung open the door. Max could see the bag that Bo had left previously, still pushed into the small cavity. From under it, Miss Chapman pulled the familiar manila brown envelope. She brought it to the desk, tipped out two discs onto her desk then pulled some photos into view to show Max what was in it.

"I'll keep the original disc - for insurance purposes. You can have the rest. I assume that'll satisfy Mr Garrick."
Max shrugged.

"I think so. And I need your word - your assurance - that this is the end of your involvement."

"If that bag contains $700,000 then yes, you have my word that no other photos will go to the police. As far as I'm concerned the case is closed."
Max unzipped the bag to show the contents.

"To the dollar - seven hundred thousand."
Miss Chapman's face cracked in a smile for the first time today.

"Excellent." She pushed the photos back into the envelope, dropped one of the two discs in and passed it across the desk to Max.

"Nice doing business with you, Mr Duncan."

Max left the room in silence.

Molly had once said to Max in passing that she considered there was no greater relief than getting out of debt. It was a sentiment that he occasionally recalled, just as he did now, sitting on a bus on his way back down town to Gaynor's apartment. He was aware that the euphoria he was now experiencing was more from the relief of being saved from impending doom than the responsibility of paying off his dues. This was a chapter in his life that he could now close, but he had to plan his next moves. He could leave New York - just pull stumps on the whole affair and go home to London. He had to admit to himself that the prospect was very appealing. Distancing himself from the police investigation into the bank raid and Jason's murder seemed his most logical option. But while his head was telling him to run, his heart and his conscience wouldn't let him. He owed it to Molly to at least try to retrieve the deeds to her house. Max could only guess at the pain and anguish she must be experiencing right now, with her debts still as great as ever and her sole modest income due to end in a matter of weeks. No, running for home wasn't an option, he knew that as a certainty. Molly deserved to experience the relief that Max was now feeling.

Max was planning to spend some time listening to the cassette that Gaynor had brought home last night. He wasn't planning to spend the next hour and a half in the company of the NYPD at their offices in Lower Manhattan. As he climbed the stairs to Gaynor's apartment, Max met Lieutenant Baker on the way down.

"Mr Slater," he exclaimed as they came face to face at a bend on the staircase. "The very person."

"What can I do for you...?" Max had forgotten the officer's name and rank.

"Lieutenant Baker," the officer volunteered, before explaining: "I have a few more questions relating to your company and the bank's security. More routine stuff, I'm afraid, but I was hoping you could come down to the station with me."

Max tried to think what he would do had he been innocent. Object or agree?

"I am rather busy. Do I need to come to the station?"

"It'll speed everything up. Hopefully then we won't need to bother you again."

Max thought for a moment - then another moment.

"I suppose so - if we can make it as quick as possible."

At the temporary headquarters for the investigation, Max was shown into an interview room and offered a drink that he declined. Lieutenant Baker had slipped away to find some documents as soon as they arrived. When he returned, he was accompanied by another plain clothed officer who he introduced as 'Sargent Lewins'. Max nodded at the man who hovered in the background, before Max recalled the name that sounded familiar.

"*Jonah* Lewins?" Max asked.

"That's right," the Sargent confirmed.

"Hi." Max was trying to gauge whether or not Jonah Lewins' presence was ominous, but decided it was probably just chance that he was investigating the case. It was when Lieutenant Baker casually announced that he would be recording the interview that Max abruptly experienced a sense of unease. The situation suddenly seemed serious and Max felt vulnerable. If he asked for a lawyer to be present, he would look guilty - and anyway, who would he contact, Tessa Chapman?

'No, let's press on. Stay relaxed,' Max told himself.

The questioning was just as the lieutenant had indicated, concerning his reasons for his two visits to the bank. Once underway, Max relaxed into the interview. He had answers for everything - most of which were true. Sargent Lewins stood to one side of the room out of Max's eye line, observing without a word or gesture, until Lieutenant Baker's questions appeared to have run their course. Then, to the apparent surprise of his colleague, Jonah Lewins suddenly entered the dialogue with:

"Would you know why the raiders would want to take your uncle's deposit box with them?"

Max knew that the question referred to the gang's random choice of deposit boxes that they took away after the raid along with Dennis's. They removed another ten or fifteen boxes to disguise the important one. Max had anticipated the question, but was now surprised that Sargent Lewins was asking it so late in the interview, as if Lieutenant Baker had either overlooked this piece of evidence or simply hadn't been made aware of it.

"Did they?.... No... no idea," Max replied.

"Of course, you knew what was in the box having only checked the contents a few days earlier. Can we ask if there was anything of particular value in it?"

"Sure you can - and no there wasn't. Some documents and a stack of computer discs with clients' confidential systems information," Max answered.

"Heavy are they - the discs?"

"Yes quite. There were a lot packed in." Max had also anticipated questions about the weight.

"But not especially valuable to the casual thief?"

"No."

Silence and some exchanged glances followed. Jonah Lewins pulled a plastic chair to the desk and sat down as he asked:

"Tell us about Philadelphia - why were you there?"

"I had to meet some prospective contractors."

"For what?"

"I'm trying to decide whether to get funding to recreate my old firm – Astrodome Toys and Games so I wanted to meet some contacts for distribution."

"Will you."

"Will I what?"

"Be starting up a new company?"

"It's looking unlikely."

Sargent Lewins made a note.

"Can you tell me why you left that firm two months ago?"

"A disagreement. I anticipated its downfall - could see it coming for the last year because of bad management. But I was a small percentage share holder so, since it went into receivership, I've been considering ways to get something from the mess. But it's looking like a pretty hopeless case, to be honest."

Sargent Lewins made some more notes and appeared to ponder Max's answers then returned to his position at the back of the room.

"Well, I think that's about all for now," Lieutenant Baker announced, before switching off the tape recorder. "If we need you again, I assume you'll be at the same address, yes?"

"Yes." Max replied

"For how long?" Jonah Lewins jumped in with the question very abruptly "…How long before you leave New York, in case we need to interview you again?" he added hastily to hide the suggestion that he had any particular interest in Max's accommodation address.

"As long as I'm welcome, I guess." Then Max couldn't resist a silly urge to irritate his interrogator and added: "On present form, that may be quite a while."

It was mid-afternoon before Max arrived back at the apartment. Gaynor had left two short messages on the answerphone, wanting to know what he'd found on the cassette and where he was. It reminded Max that he'd forgotten to switch his cell phone on all morning.

Max set up his cassette player in the dining area, slotted the tape in and turned up the volume, before making himself a sandwich while the tape started to play. As Gaynor had reported, it was evidently a recording of a telephone conversation – very poor hissy quality, but discernible enough. It began with some long ringing tones followed by a female voice that announced the name Tudor Technologies. From this end of the recording, a man with an American accent asked for 'Todd Graham.' There were some more rings on the tape, then a click, before a voice answered.

"Graham," came the answer.

"Todd - Hi, it's Jack."

"One moment."

In the background, Max could hear Todd Graham finishing a conversation with someone who apparently then left the room.

"Sorry Jack."

"Can we talk?"

"Yeah, you're okay."

"Have you received the files?"

"Yeah, they look good. I'm impressed."

"But are you convinced?"

"Not entirely. Don't get me wrong Jack, what you sent was good, but you're asking for a big fee on trust. You can't prove that these files came from S83 - you know that."

"Sure, but does it matter where they came from. In fact, let's be precise - they did come from S83, but that's not the issue here. The issue is that I can get this level of information for you on the Alder contract. It's my problem to deliver."

"Sure, but before you do, you want me to pay the half a million dollars. I've got to be pretty damn certain you're going to deliver the goods for that sort of down payment."

"I know that, Todd. And you agreed this was the best proof I could get you. Now if you want something else, then you tell me, but time's ticking, my friend. Your deadline's in less than two months. You know this could take some time and it's running out while we're talking."

"Yeah I know."

There was a short hissing silence on the tape. Jack was apparently considering something.

"But I'll tell you what I'll do. I'll change the split to the deposit being two hundred and fifty thousand dollars - that's quarter of a million up front - then half a million when we deliver. Same price, less up front risk to you."

"Let me think about it. Sounds like it might help me here. What does your S83 contact say? How long do they reckon for them to get a result?"

"Hey, come on Todd, you know it's not up to them. They'll begin the monitor immediately I get the deposit. But then it's down to Alder."

"You're going to have to leave it with me. Twenty four hours, perhaps overnight your time. I'll have an answer. I think it's a go, but it's not up to me."

"Okay, but that's my best offer. Two-fifty now, five hundred on delivery."

"I know. I'll be back to you. Thanks."

"Okay."

Max had brought his snack to the table and now sat beside the cassette player listening for the next instalment as he swigged beer from a small bottle. Just as he was wondering if that was the end of the recording, the silence was broken by a fresh ringing tone. But that seemed to be a false start. Jack Briggs asked for Todd Graham who wasn't at the office and the recording ended. A short time later, the same start, but Todd Graham answered the call.

"Todd - Jack Briggs."

"Hi."

"So, do we have a deal?"

"Yeah. I got the green light this morning. The money will be in your account by the end of the day. Can we start the monitor now?"

"Tomorrow. Let's let the money arrive first."

"Okay."

"And your people know that's non-returnable - results or no results?"

"Yeah, they understand that."

"And half a million when we get a result. That's the deal right?"

"Yeah, that's agreed."

"You get nothing more from me until I get the five hundred thou once I prove we have a result to hand over. That's understood?"

"Sure. Jack what's up? You don't trust me?"

"No - I don't want any misunderstanding later."

"Okay. And Jack, I need you to keep in touch with me. Any developments from S83 - anything helpful from Alder, right. That's in the deal, right?"

"Sure."

"Okay."

"I'll be in touch. Good to speak to you Todd, have a good day."

"Yeah, and you."

Max lost track of time. He sat through another five, maybe six, such recordings of telephone conversations with a variety of men, with a variety of accents, about a variety of financial deals, much on the lines of the first two calls. It seemed clear to Max that Jack Briggs was using the tape to record the agreement to various dubious deals with these business contacts. The sums of money involved were always clearly discussed and always large - never smaller than a quarter of a million dollars. It was evident that Jack Briggs had some way of supplying information to his various clients and prospective clients. From what Max could deduce, these were all corporate companies working in a range of unrelated market sectors that included security, automotive and armaments. But the one constant reference throughout the recording was the mention of 'S83'.

'What is S83?' Max thought to himself. *'Could it be the codename for someone, or the name of a building, even a communications system?'* Max rewound the tape and began to play it again, this time with a notepad beside him to jot down all the names and any details that he assumed to be important as he listened to the recording. He'd become excited when he first heard the tape, convinced that he now had proof that Jack Briggs was involved in espionage. But on re-running the recordings, he became aware that these could - just *could* - be

legitimate deals. Jack Briggs was offering the services of some monitoring agency. So what? Plenty of companies around the world monitor market trends, legislation - even press cuttings - for large and small companies that want to keep ahead of, or keep an eye on, their competition. Max knew full well that this was not what Jack Briggs was offering, but still, if he wanted to call Max's bluff, Max might have trouble putting a cast iron case together to show categorically that Jack Briggs was trading in industrial espionage. If only he could identify 'S83' that might well hold the key.

The phone rang as Max was near the end of the recording. He glanced at the clock on the cooker and was surprised to see the time was four twenty-five.

'Where's the day gone?' he thought as he answered the call from Gaynor.

"Hi. Where have you been?" she wanted to know.

"Sorry. Forgot to switch on my cell phone. Long story - which includes a trip to police HQ for the raid."

"Really? Everything all right?"

"Not sure. Think so." Then Max remembered. "Hey, I met your Jonah Lewins. He was at the interview."

"Why was he there?"

"He's obviously investigating the case – but he seemed to be just as interested in my plans to stay here."

"Do you have any?"

"I'm working on them. I've been playing through the cassette."

"And?"

"I dunno," Max replied despondently. "You might disagree when you hear it, but I don't think it's exactly conclusive. You're right about the phone conversation -

several of them - but I don't know how incriminating they are."

"I'm sorry." Gaynor's reaction reinforced Max's suspicions that this was his last hope to find a lever to force something from Jack Briggs.

"How about the letters or the stuff on the floppies. Any connection?" Gaynor asked.

"Yeah. But there's nothing to link him to the Ironman blueprints and they're the only real heavy things here. There's no doubt that we have something, he's obviously trading in espionage - at least, I'm pretty sure he is - it's just that nothing here proves it conclusively. I'm just about to look up some names on the Internet. There's a codename he uses that I need to track down."

"Can I help with it?"

"Maybe, but it's a bit of a long shot. It's S83 - that's S for Sugar. It's someone or somewhere or something that Jack Briggs was using to get the material he was selling. He refers to S83 as 'monitoring'. Whatever or whoever S83 is, supplies the information he's selling."

"Could it be military surveillance?"

"Could be. If it is, that would be brilliant – all the proof we need to confront Jack, but it could be something else…like a mole's codename. I don't know. But S83's in a pretty good position to get a mix of information on commercial contracts, a deal on a car plant - all sorts including arms, but it's not all military."

"I'll see what I can do. I'll call you."

Gaynor had written just the three letters and numbers - S83 - on a sheet of her note pad. She left her desk and walked through the open plan confusion to an older colleague the far side of the office area.

"George, got a moment?" she asked.

George stopped leafing through a large manual and looked over his glasses at Gaynor.

"Yes. What can I do?"

Gaynor perched on the side of his desk.

"Does the codename S83 mean anything to you?"

George thought.

"S̲83?" he asked, emphasising the S.

"Yeah."

"In what context?"

"I'm not sure - espionage of some sort. It may be an individual - perhaps a mole - or it could be a monitoring centre or a computer program."

George raised his eyebrows.

"A bit broad don't you think?"

"Sorry. The best I can do. I thought perhaps all that work you did on your industrial espionage series might have thrown up something."

"Leave it with me. I'll come back to you - give me half an hour."

"Thanks."

Max, meanwhile, was sitting at Gaynor's computer, on-line, working systematically through every name he'd noted. He'd found Alder International quickly but the company web site only provided a guide to its services and some addresses of premises in the US, Hong Kong and Macau. He suspected that their liberal use of the word 'Security' in the profile of services was more to do with arms and munitions than Max's understanding of the definition. He was about to move on to search out Tudor Technologies when he noticed their addresses again. *Macau* suddenly assumed an importance that he'd overlooked, but now he recalled from his time spent in Hong Kong.

'Of course - it's Portuguese. Hence the Portuguese letter,' he realised. Another piece of the jigsaw was in place. He then shut down the link and hunted for Tudor Technologies. Amid all the Tudor name variants he found what he was looking for. Here was a much bigger presence. Pages and pages downloaded. Tudor was a holding company for twelve subsidiaries in construction, real estate, financial services and security. Max was on the scent with all the focus of a hungry bloodhound. To his surprise, he quickly realised that his prey could not have left a more pungent trail. Under 'History', the site conveniently listed all major contracts undertaken since 1980. And in 1994, Tudor Securities won just such a contract to supply *'security products and services to the People's Republic of China'.*

Max referred back to the letters, pulling them out of the file to check the dates. The correspondence from Alder, written in Portuguese, was dated January 1994. The pieces fitted. If Jack Briggs had Alder's pitch document then presumably so did Tudor, giving it an unassailable advantage in a competitive pitch. Not surprising then, that Tudor Securities won the contract to supply the Chinese Government with *'security products and services'.* For *security* read *arms,* of which the blueprints of the Ironman missile might have been part of the package and suddenly another large piece of Max's jigsaw might have just fallen into place.

'Fuck me.' Max could see the scenario as clearly as if it were written as bullet points in Jack Briggs's prosecution - evidence against an industrial spy.

'Okay - we know what he traded and who to - but how? Who the fuck's S83?'

Gaynor's friend George had drawn a blank.

"Sorry Gaynor, just not enough to go on. You don't even know if it was in The States. He, she or it could be operating anywhere in the world and all my contacts are just here in the US."

"Okay George. Thanks for trying."

"You could post it on an internal e-mail. See if anything comes up. Someone else might know something."

"Good idea. Thanks again." Gaynor watched George depart then tapped her home number on her phone. It rang as she began to type an e-mail message requesting help.

"Hello," came Max's voice.

Gaynor picked up her phone off its cradle.

"Hi, it's me........ No, not yet, but I haven't given up. I'm still hunting. How about you?........ Uhu......... That's great........ Yeah?... Cool - real cool. Doesn't that crack it?........ Why not?...... Okay I'll keep trying. I'll call you. Bye."

Gaynor hung up the phone, typed a few more words into an internal email with refreshed energy, then she stopped abruptly, thought for a moment then stood up.

"Right. Attention here!" she shouted over the top of the ambient noise level. The volume dropped. "Need your help here people. I need a lead on something or someone known as S83 that's S for Sugar. Something to do with espionage, information tracking, industrial secrets - that sort of stuff. Could be an individual, organisation or even a computer program. Something to do with monitoring services or facilities. Anything you've got is gratefully accepted. Okay? Come on - anything. Bit desperate for a lead. S83. Does anything come to mind?" Gaynor ignored the mutters and small pockets of laughter that her somewhat unorthodox approach had triggered. She was still looking around the open-plan area, a lone figure, as everyone turned back to whatever they were doing before her interruption. Gaynor sighed with exasperation then caught the eye of her workmate, Barbara, over the partition separating their desks.

"Don't look at me like that - it was worth a try."

"Yeah, well try your friends first, next time." Gaynor stared down over the low partition between their desks.

"Why?" she asked, suspicious of the answer.

"I know how to find them."

"You do?"

"Uhu." Barbara looked away and began dialling a phone number. "Or I know someone who will," she added, then broke off to speak on the phone. "Julie, it's Barb. Check your e-mail as soon as you get this. I need some help pronto. Love you." She hung up then immediately began to type an e-mail. S for Sugar eighty-three you said?"

"That's right," Gaynor confirmed, then added: "Thanks Barb," with her surprise still evident in her voice.

It was after six o'clock when Gaynor phoned her apartment with the unexpected news. Max had assumed he needed to make his case against Jack Briggs using only the material that he'd accumulated on disc, on tape and in the letters. But now with the assistance of the information he'd gleaned from the Internet and some reliance on Jack Briggs's poor memory after so many years, Max was feeling a little more confident that he had enough to frighten him into parting with Molly's deeds. He'd duplicated nearly everything of importance and was in the process of copying the letters through Gaynor's fax machine when the call came. As soon as he heard Gaynor's voice, he knew something very good or very bad was about to follow. She was almost breathless.

"Alex. Well – I've got nothing on '$\underline{S}$83' – drawn a complete blank."

"Uhu." Max sighed "No problem."

"But . . . you ready for this?" Gaynor was finding it difficult to remain calm.

"For what?"

"I think I've got it!" Her voice was now trembling with excitement. "It's not S for Sugar it's F - F for Freddie, Foxtrot whatever - check the tape again – it's gotta be cos $\underline{F}$83's a US Government surveillance station – a big one by all accounts - somewhere in a place called Yorkshire in north of England. It's also known as Menwith Hill. Get this, it's owned by US Intelligence and feeds straight into Fort Meade in Maryland here in the States. It's run by the NSA - the National Security Agency."

"Fuck!" Max uttered as he realised the significance of the discovery. This had to be right.

"It gets better," Gaynor continued, reading some notes passed onto her by Barbara. " *'It's equipped with state-of-the-art global monitoring systems capable of intercepting millions of telephone conversations, faxes and e-mails across Europe'.* 'Echelon'….listen to this. *'Echelon, a global system for electronic eavesdropping, thought to be used for commercial as well as military spying, uses computerised systems to locate and monitor targets of interest by origin, destination, language or key words'.* It goes on - I've got a pile of stuff here. *'Voicecast'* this is another bit of kit it uses. It says it's *'an advanced voice recognition and processing system that can be programmed to recognise the voice prints of specific individuals'*. State-of-the-art or what?"

"Brilliant. You are absolutely bloody brilliant. And I'm a div. The tape's such bad quality, you gotta be right. I'm gonna check it again."

"Do that – then check it out on the Internet there's loads of stuff there."

"It all falls into place. Fits perfect. If you're right, you realise what we've got? We've got the proof that he had someone inside this monitoring station feeding him whatever his clients requested - whatever they'd pay for - essentially competitors' pitches, even bloody state secrets. Serious state secrets - like top secret missiles. And we've got him on tape admitting it all. No wonder he locked it in a safe deposit vault. Bloody hell, this could get him locked away for the rest of his born days." Max laughed out loud at the thought. "What a bloody result? You're brilliant."

A pause as Max pondered the news.

"Hey - you got any plans this evening - after work?"

"No."

"Let me buy you dinner."

"Okay - why?"

"Why d'you think - a thank you for all this…..and a sorry for last night."

"Don't worry about that - not about last night."

"I am. Well, you know - a bit embarrassed…*very* embarrassed, actually."

"I'll be back by eight. We could walk over to Sol's on Washington Square. That'd be good. Call them and book a table. There's a card on the pin board. It's called 'Sol's Kitchen'."

"I'll do that - for eight or eight thirty."

"Sure - great. When you going to call Jack Briggs?"
"First I'll check the tape – check we're right."
"Then what?"
"Call him I guess."

Moments after coming off the phone, Max had the tape playing and replaying over Jack Briggs's voice stating "S83". It wasn't conclusive – it could still be S but now it sounded more like F every time Max heard it.

'Huh – result!' he thought to himself. *'Fantastic!'*
He sat with the collection of papers, discs and tapes that he'd accumulated and began to sort them into piles. One of each for Jack Briggs, the rest as his insurance policies. He reflected on the contracts while sifting through the letters and recalling the information on the discs and the tape. Suddenly with the one keystone in place, it all held up. One piece of evidence supporting another. His Rosetta Stone that provided the code to break the impasse. Max stared at his neat piles of incriminating evidence.

'Right, Mr Briggs,' he thought. Then suddenly, for the first time, Max realised that he had no way of contacting Jack Briggs. *'How bloody stupid,'* he told himself. He knew that he lived, or had lived, somewhere outside New York, but where? And who would know? Molly? Buchanan Security? Tessa Chapman? It was then that Max recalled a page on his CD that he'd stumbled on a few times, giving all the contact details for everyone and every location involved in the plot. He'd never had to use it, so hadn't studied it before. But now to his great relief, there was an address and phone number for Jack Briggs - or at least, it was a year or more ago.

"Thank you Dennis," Max whispered with the briefest glimpse to the ceiling as he identified it in the list on the screen of his laptop. Max put the computer beside the neat piles of evidence and placed the phone beside that. There he sat at the dining table in front of the shrine of neatly-ordered objects. He was collecting his thoughts before making the call.

'*So how do you call an ex-business colleague of your dead uncle and tell him you have enough evidence to lock him away for the rest of his life unless he pays you not to?*' An interesting prospect, Max admitted to himself.

'*Hello Mr Briggs, my name's Max Duncan. We met several years ago when you were working with my uncle, Dennis Buchanan, who's just died....No, too long.*'

'*My name's Max Duncan, my uncle was Dennis Buchanan. You have something of his that I want you to give me back please...Please? ... No.*'

'*My name's Dennis.....No it's not.*'

'*My name's Max Duncan - give me the fucking deeds to my aunt's house, you fucking slimy toe-rag or you're in big fucking shit!*'... *Hmm – that could work ...*

No, this wasn't helping. Max picked up the phone and dialled the number off the screen. It rang.

"Good afternoon. Can I help you?" It was a female voice with a non-American accent.

"Yes, hello. I'm trying to contact a Mr Jack Briggs. Is that his home?" Max asked.

"Yes sir."

"Is he there please?"

"Let me find out. Who shall I say is calling?"

"My name is Max Duncan. Mr Briggs used to work with my uncle."

"One minute, please."

Max blew out his cheeks. He became aware of his pulse-rate increasing as he waited, trying to anticipate the conversation to follow.

"Hello?" The reply eventually came in a cautious tone.

"Hello," Max responded. "Is that Mr Briggs?"

"It is."

"My name's Max Duncan, Dennis Buchanan's nephew."

"Sure. I think we met once. How are you? What can I do for you Max?"

"I'm fine. I'm calling about some business that you and Dennis had a few years ago involving his house in London - 'The Gables'. My aunt is trying to sell the house and has just discovered your loan arrangement with Dennis. Do you know what I'm talking about?"

"Errr, yes." There was a note of suspicion or perhaps uncertainty in Jack Briggs's reply.

"You remember Molly?"

"Of course I do. How is she?"

"Not well. Very unwell, in fact. Partly because she's just discovered that you're holding a charge on her house deeds. Do you still have them?"

"I think so - I assume so. Frankly, I'd forgotten about them. But what's your point Max?"

"The point is that she needs them to sell the property to clear a lot of debts. I'm in New York and I'd like you to release your interest in the house – to release Molly from the debt to you."

"I'm sure you would. So what about repayment of the loan - as I recall it was a $500,000…"

"Pounds," Max corrected him.

"Right."

325

"Well she's got no income now and can't afford to pay you so I'd like you to relinquish your claim on the house and sign it back to her, please. I need you to sign a legal document to that affect."

Jack Briggs laughed.

"Are you seriously asking me to forget about a debt of half a million pounds?"

"Err, yes."

"Extraordinary." Jack Briggs took a while to grasp the notion. "Why - why would I do that?"

"Because she hasn't got the money to pay you, or any of the rest of her debts, without selling the house - and it's making her ill with worry."

"I'm sorry to hear that, really I am. But your uncle, you haven't mentioned him – do I assume Dennis has passed away?"

"Yes, a few weeks ago. Leaving a monstrous problem for Molly that's making her ill with worry."

"Yes, you said. I'm sorry to hear that." Jack Briggs appeared to consider that news for a moment before he spoke. "But I don't see why it's suddenly my problem to get Dennis, or his family, out of the mess he created. The fact is that I bailed Dennis out of trouble with a fair business arrangement backed by the value of The Gables. All fair and legal. "

Max hadn't planned this approach. He was letting the conversation take its course, but now he felt his old anger welling up inside him. He knew he had to keep control.

"I'm sorry you see it like that Mr Briggs, because that's not quite how I see the situation."

"Oh wouldn't you?"

"No. My uncle worked long and hard to the very end to save Briggs-Buchanan, while you were distracted by other business ventures. You took advantage of him and his very good nature. Had you had the company's best interests at heart, perhaps it wouldn't have gone bust."

"How dare you speak to me like that? If you really think that's going to persuade me to hand over the deeds, you're wrong. So if that's all….."

"No Mr Briggs it's far from all. I hoped you would show some compassion, but evidently it's beyond you. So we have…."

"What are you talking about?" Jack Briggs broke in.

"I haven't finished!" Max shouted into the phone. His anger had got the better of him and flared into life. He calmed his voice. "I have some property of yours that I think you will want back. I'm prepared to do an exchange."
There was a short silence before Jack Briggs spoke.

"What sort of property?"

"A mixed bag of items - some papers, computer discs and a very interesting tape. Lots of references to the business you were doing with Alder International, Tudor Technologies, The Chinese Government, Zindomi and, oh yes - F83." Max knew he didn't need to say more for Jack Briggs to understand the significance of his words or his intentions. For Jack Briggs, these were some trappings from a former life that he'd left behind since he retired. He'd forgotten they even existed. But now Max had just exploded a small device in Jack Briggs's memory bank.

"And where are these items?" he asked slowly.

"Here, in New York. Some with me, some in safe keeping."

"What's your proposition?"

"Well Mr Briggs, you just heard it. Had you been reasonable, I just wanted you to write off Molly's debt and hand back the deeds, but…well, let's keep this on a business footing. I'll give you back all your original possessions – your extremely valuable possessions - for a finder's fee of the debt and deeds, plus the Geraldine Diamonds." Max had just thought of this.

"And if I tell you I can do without them - in other words, tell you to go to hell…" His voice had risen. "…what then?"

"Oh come on. You must remember what's in this bundle of things. Do you want me to be more explicit? Do you remember the name Todd Graham and some very interesting conversations about how you would use your contact in F83 - that's the tracking station in Yorkshire isn't it, the US Government establishment? Your contact there could get Mr Graham all the information on Alder International's pitch to the Chinese Government for the supply of arms back in ninety four…"

"All right!" Jack Briggs broke in abruptly, but Max wasn't finished.

"That's not the best. Remember the Ironman blueprints?" Jack Briggs had forgotten but now this new missile hit his memory bank with decisive impact.

"Okay. What's your suggestion?"

"A meeting. Shouldn't take long. I'll bring your possessions and a document for you to sign to release your interest in The Gables - you bring the deeds and the diamonds and we'll never have to meet or hear from one another ever again. It really can be as simple as that. You have my word."

"Okay. I'll have to get the items you want."

"Where are they?"

"Around. Here in New York."

"Good. So let's meet tomorrow. No time like the present," Max suggested. "And I'll be out of your way by this time tomorrow night."

There was a silence.

"Okay, but you come here." Jack Briggs insisted.

Max considered it for a moment. To get the deeds and a couple of million pounds-worth of diamonds, he'd have travelled to California.

"Okay. Is that the Trant Hill address?" He read it off the laptop.

"Yeah. Be here about lunchtime. I'll get what you need by then. You be sure to bring everything if you want this over real quick."

"Don't worry, I will."

Max and Gaynor's meal that evening was a celebration. At last they believed the end was in sight and some rewards were almost within Max's grasp. A few boring details to worry about, such as how Max was going to get himself to the other side of New Jersey. He was planning to hire a car but Gaynor announced that she could borrow one, as long as she drove.

"Of course I'm coming. You don't think I'm going to miss out on this bit of your adventure?" Gaynor insisted in reply to Max's surprise that she was assuming to go with him. Max thought about putting up a fight but decided against it. Besides, he reasoned, it shouldn't be dangerous so why not? Gaynor was as excited at the prospect of the adventure ahead as Max was concerned. He was suspicious that there were still some pitfalls to come. Perhaps a double-cross. Maybe Jack Briggs has a minder who will use force to steal back the evidence; although Max had that covered by duplicating everything he would be carrying to the rendezvous. After everything that had happened in the last few days, he couldn't believe it could be so easy to get a man like Jack Briggs to part with anything as valuable as his precious Geraldine diamond collection. But how to prepare for the unforeseen? Very difficult, he concluded, with a sense of foreboding combined with his excitement.

They left the restaurant in high spirits talking again about Gaynor coming to London during her Christmas break. Perhaps they would both stay with his aunt in Wimbledon. Gaynor had few family ties and still fewer plans. Max's were always big family affairs that he dare not miss, especially this year. Molly would need the family around her. By the time they reached the apartment block a few minutes later, Gaynor had all but promised to be there, finances permitting.

"If tomorrow goes to plan, I'll pay for everything - it won't cost you a penny – a dime, cent, whatever." Max promised.

As they climbed the few steps to the double front doors to the apartments, neither of them were unduly concerned about the young guy who followed them, or the other one they could see through the glass panels who looked as if he was about to leave the building. Max pulled the door ajar to let the man out. But as he and Gaynor stepped aside, the two figures burst into a brief frenzy of activity. From behind him, the first man pounced on Max and threw him to the floor. The second man burst through the gap in the open door, grabbed Gaynor by the throat then powered her backwards into the wall so hard that the air was pumped out of her lungs in a moment. Max seemed equally powerless to defend himself with the larger of the two men pinning him to the floor, face down and dizzy from the impact of his head against the concrete steps. He couldn't see that his assailant had produced a knife, but Gaynor could. She struggled to get away from her captor but, with his hand over her face and her arm forced behind her back, she couldn't break free.

"This is from Mr Garrick for Joey." The man on Max's back spoke into his ear from a few inches away.

"You put Joey in intensive care - so that's where you're...." But suddenly both assailants were distracted by the brief but piercing sound of a police siren from somewhere nearby. They looked across the road to see a man scrambling from the car that had made the noise and was now running straight towards them.

"Police! Stop right there!"

In the street lighting, they could see a man wielding a gun. The two men froze. The larger one made a distracted lunge at Max with the knife that ripped into his loose blouson jacket. A split second later both men had sprung up and raced away in different directions. Max and Gaynor were trying to regain their senses as the policeman arrived at the steps. He now held the gun in one hand and his police I.D. in the other. Everything went quiet.

"Jonah? What're you doing here?" Gaynor asked in bewildered shock.

"Are you all right?" the policeman, Jonah Lewins, asked.

"Yes...thanks. But why were you here," she persisted.

"Just as well I was. Who were they?"

"I don't know," Gaynor answered.

"Do you know?" he called to Max.

"What d'you mean 'who were they?' They're muggers or whatever you call them here. Just a couple of fucking thieves." Max was inspecting the rip in his jacket as he replied.

"Are you okay?" Gaynor asked when she saw the knife cut.

"Yeah. He didn't cut me."

Gaynor turned back to Jonah and walked down the steps to talk to him without raising her voice.

"So why were you here?"

"Just as well I was. What the hell would've happened? I've told you he's bad news." Jonah nodded to Max and hissed at a volume that Max might have heard from a distance.

"You're not answering me, Jo. Why were you here?"

Jonah averted Gaynor's gaze.

"No reason."

"What, just passing were you? No, you were watching the apartment weren't you?" She could see into Jonah's parked car with the driver's door still hanging open. "And it's not official or there'd be two of you," Gaynor told him forcefully. "Shit Jo..." She spoke a little louder than a whisper. "What am I going to say to you?" She turned away, then back to him. "Look, you just saved us from something, who knows, something horrible, so I'm grateful - we're both really grateful. But honestly Jo, you can't … you can't do this. You can't look after me or follow me or … or … or anything me anymore."

Jonah continued to avoid eye contact.

"I know that."

"Do you? Honey, please, you've got to stop it."

He sighed and swallowed.

"I know."

"No more."

"Okay, okay, okay."

"Promise me. No more."

"Yeah okay." Jonah put his badge and his revolver away, glanced back at Max at the top of the steps and turned away from Gaynor.

A minute later he pulled his car into the empty street and drove away, leaving Max and Gaynor to watch him go before making their way into the apartments.

TWENTY-ONE

Max wouldn't have chosen a fifteen-year-old camper van as his means of transport this morning, but then, why not? It came with a chauffeur and more important, it was free. By the time Gaynor discovered that her friend had sold his big Buick and replaced it with the camper, it was too late to make other plans. So she and Max now sat a few feet apart watching the world drift by outside the vast windscreen as they bobbled along in the heavy traffic heading out of Manhattan. Gaynor was concentrating on her route. Max was concentrating on the task ahead, thinking through his plans for the meeting with Jack Briggs in the methodical manner that had become so familiar to him of late. Having run through the entire scenario before they reached a bridge to take them over the Hudson and out of Manhattan, Max's mind moved on to other subjects of which Gaynor's visit to London was the most satisfying. He planned where they would go, how long she could stay and he wondered how the family would take to her. He thought about what Christmas present he would buy her.

'How about some diamonds? I wonder if she'd see the irony in that.' Max looked across the width of the van to consider if Gaynor was a diamond-wearer. *'Probably not,'* he concluded.

Now the grimy heat haze hanging over New Jersey dominated the view ahead. And beyond that, what appeared to be a bank of dark grey cloud. Hopefully, rain-bearing cloud to end the oppressive hot spell.

Having exhausted the run-throughs of today's proceedings in his mind for the third time, Max's thoughts drifted back to last night. Immediately they arrived in Gaynor's apartment, Max had telephoned Bo Garrick and shouted at his answer service with a message that shouldn't have left Bo in any doubt about the strength of his anger - more than anything, that Bo would allow his hatchet men to involve Gaynor. He told Bo to check his facts and speak to someone called Bing who was with Joey when he wrecked the car and nearly incinerated himself.

"The only reason Joey's still alive's cos I pulled him out of the car after he'd crashed the bloody thing trying to run us down!" Max was shaking with anger when he ended the call.

Once he'd calmed himself with an almost neat vodka, he continued preparations for his meeting with Jack Briggs, dragging them out to avoid an awkwardness about going to bed. Max was unsure whether Gaynor assumed they would sleep together. He didn't want to appear presumptuous by going to her room, nor did he want to look disinterested by going off to bed in his own if that wasn't what Gaynor expected. In the event, Gaynor solved his dilemma when she departed with the order for Max not to be long before 'coming to bed'. That problem averted, he was now faced with another - Gaynor's expectations of him and his ability to satisfy them. He couldn't bear the prospect of embarrassing himself for two nights in succession. But Max needn't have worried. There followed the most sensitive and sensual experience of Max's life. His more recent carnal experiences were limited in the extreme. One serious and a small handful of passing relationships for an unmarried man in his late twenties could be considered surprising, even shocking. Certainly, for Max now trying to make comparisons with similar nights in his past, it was a very short trip down memory lane. He'd never experienced anything close to the high that his senses had hit sometime in the middle of last night.

Max stared across the van at Gaynor who was preoccupied with watching for road signs. He was struck by her ability to look so different from mood to mood, day to day, just by the way she wore her hair and the clothes she chose. Whatever she did to herself, she was always striking - stunning - pretty.

'*No, not pretty,*' Max thought. '*Attractive. Yeah, strikingly attractive,*' he settled on. Even today, in a tee-shirt and old ex-army fatigues, Gaynor in manoeuvres-mode still managed to look gorgeous. Gaynor became aware of Max looking at her and stole a glance at him quickly then back to the road.

"What?" she asked.

"What, what?"

"Why are you staring at me?"

Max paused for thought.

"Have I told you how attractive I find you?"

"No."

"Good."

"But you can."

"No…I don't think so. It'd make me too vulnerable if you knew just how much I fancy you."

She smiled at him.

"What's the time?"

"Eleven-thirty. How we doing?"

"Okay. About an hour away I'd guess."

"Do you know what really pisses me off about this?" Max asked, but didn't wait for a response. "It's that Jack fucking Briggs was swanning around the world back in the early nineties - and for God knows how long before - at the company's expense, on the pretext of setting up deals for

336

Briggs-Buchanan when really he was setting up all these scams for himself. It was the perfect cover for him. The marketing director of a leading security firm - perfect. He had all the right connections - all the right doors opened for him to give him the right introductions. And meanwhile my uncle's back at base trying to bail out a sinking ship with a very small bucket and his own money. The company's on its fucking knees and Jack fucking Briggs is creaming it. And when my uncle runs out of funds, his beloved fucking partner takes the deeds to his home as blood money. What a shit?" Max went back to gazing at the passing suburban landscape as Gaynor gazed at passing direction signs.

"Has it occurred to you," she asked without looking away from the road, "that your language has been heading down the toilet since you've been hanging out with New York's criminal fraternity?"

Max reflected on the remark and wondered whether to tell her to '*go fuck yourself*' but decided it was a bit too obvious.

Trant Hill is an exclusive, secluded mound dotted with equally secluded homes of the very well-heeled. Mansions hide behind gates, security walls and woodland. The verges are as well manicured as its residents, as is the golf course that boasts a membership of the great, the good and the not-so-good. Gaynor had been driving through a Stepford landscape since she turned the van off the motorway. Now the large beaten-up box-on-wheels looked very out of its comfort zone in Squeakyville.

Finding Jack Briggs's particular pair of metal security gates took a few wrong turnings but Gaynor eventually pulled the camper into the verge within sight of the gates just after twelve-thirty.

"What time's lunchtime round here do you think?" Max asked as he checked his watch.

"About one, I guess."

Max considered.

"I could wait - or could get it over quickly. No harm in being a bit early I suppose."

He and Gaynor were running through their plan when Max's phone rang. It startled him, especially as he knew it could only be Bo Garrick.

"Alex...?" came the familiar growl plus a lot of background noise.

"Yeah," Max responded.

In his car, Bo was straining to hear.

"Hold on...Mickey, stop the fucking car, I can't hear myself think here." Mickey had been drafted in as replacement chauffeur of Bo's replacement limo. He pulled the featureless white sedan into a side street.

"That's better... Alex - can you hear me?"

"Yeah," Max replied.

"I got your message last night - well, this morning. Look, I might have been a bit premature - a bit hasty - sending Tom and Jerry round to visit you. I didn't know Bing was with Joey the other night. I've spoken to him now and ... well, he's explained what happened." Bo waited for a response that took a moment.

"That I saved Joey's life, you mean?"

"Yeah ... right."

"So...?"

"Well I'm just phoning to tell you, so you don't have to worry that they'll be back."

"And...?"

"That's it. What the fuck you want me to say?"

338

"*Sorry* would be nice. You scared the shit out of me and Gaynor - and she's nothing to do with any of this. You know that," Max shouted.

"Okay, okay!" Bo retaliated with similar volume. "I'm sorry, all right?"

"Yeah."

"Yeah, right." Bo had calmed down. "So I'll see you round."

"Yeah, maybe. Cheers." Max shut down the call and looked across at Gaynor who was slumped in her seat behind the steering wheel watching him.

"One door closes…" She nodded towards the gates to Jack Briggs's house. "…Another one beckons."

They carried on checking their plans from where they'd been interrupted. Then Max checked the contents of his bag and leaned across the width of the van to kiss Gaynor.

"Wish me luck."

She cupped his face in her hands and kissed his lips.

"Just be careful then you won't need luck."

"Don't you believe it."

Max climbed out of the camper and made his way to the gates along the road as the rumble of distant thunder arrived from the west.

The same female voice that had answered the phone now spoke to Max on the Intercom at the gate. She evidently expected him. Immediately he introduced himself, the motorised gates began to swing open.

The house was palatial. As Max rounded the corner at the end of the drive, before him sat a magnificent pile with a double storey Palladian entrance. Two large cars were parked on the gravel drive that swept in an arc past the front doors.

Max had assumed that Jack Briggs was worth a few dollars but this was a shock nonetheless.

The large wooden front door opened as Max arrived. Inside was the lady with the accent. She welcomed him then showed him through the reception area to a drawing room.

"Mr Briggs will be right with you," she assured Max as she left.

A few minutes later a tall suntanned man with very short-cropped grey hair entered the room. Max hadn't seen Jack Briggs since a few brief meetings almost ten years previously. Both men recognised one another but it would be difficult to say which of them had to make the greatest adjustment for the appearance of the other.

"Well hello Max." Jack Briggs's greeting was impressively charming as he stretched his hand to shake Max's.

"Good afternoon sir." Max never considered his use of the title 'sir', but at times it seemed appropriate when he addressed someone evidently more senior. He was hoping that this encounter would be as painless, as civilised and as quick as possible, so the last thing Max intended was to irritate Jack Briggs, however much he despised the man. In fact, he surprised himself how easy he found it to keep calm. His polite approach was reciprocated. A good start. Jack Briggs was calm, attentive and urbane.

'*Perhaps he's taking the same approach,*' Max reasoned. '*Or perhaps this is the cobra making ready to strike.*'

"Have you been offered refreshments?" Jack Briggs asked.

"No, but I'm fine thank you."

"Well this may take a little time. You're early and I'm waiting for some of the items you requested."

"What d'you mean?" Max asked with evident concern.

"Don't worry, they're on their way. But it took my people a while to locate the deeds. Please, let me order you something to drink. I'm having tea, would you like some, or coffee perhaps?"

"Thank you - tea would be fine."

Jack Briggs left the room briefly. When he returned, he fiddled with the controls of an imitation log fire which burst into life in the grate. Given the outside temperature, this was entirely unnecessary, but it instantly enlivened the amenable atmosphere in the room.

"You must forgive us, we didn't expect you to arrive quite so early," he volunteered, as a reason for the fire not being lit in advance. He then adjusted a high-backed chair the other side of the hearth to face Max as the lady arrived with a large silver tray laden with tea, sandwiches and some fruit.

"Thank you Maria." Then to Max: "I assumed you could eat a snack."

"Thank you." This was all so disarmingly civilised that Max found it unsettling. He was supposed to despise the man sitting a few feet from him, but it was proving difficult.

Max was wondering how and when to redirect the conversation to the true reason for his visit, when his host took the initiative as Maria left the room.

"Right, so let's get down to business. And let me just say, Max, that if you have what you tell me you have, then I'd like to sort everything out as amicably as possible. Do you understand?"

"I think so. That suits me fine."

"Good." He stared at Max for a moment, his thoughts elsewhere. Then he turned his attention to the tea on the low table between them. "The way I see it, Max, is that I may well have made a rather silly mistake – a stupid oversight that

341

allowed these things to get into your hands - and I'd like to put it behind me as quickly as possible - for once and for all, period. So I'm prepared to pay whatever that costs, within the range you indicated on the phone last night. But a word of warning, Max. Once we've done the deal and made the exchange, that's the end. That's how I want it. If you even thought about taking this any further after today, don't. It would be the last thing you ever did." Max felt his eye contact like two lasers. "Do I make myself clear?"

"Absolutely clear," Max replied.

"Good." He handed Max a cup and saucer then gestured to the sugar and milk on the tray. "Please help yourself. Okay, so would you like to show me what you have?"

Max placed his cup and saucer back on the tray, opened his bag and removed two envelopes which he handed over. Jack Briggs opened the first and pulled out the letters which he sorted through slowly enough to register their content and to identify them as some he recalled from long ago. He pushed them back into the envelope and repeated the exercise with the second, this time tipping out the collection of discs and the white cardboard box containing the reel of quarter inch sound tape. He noted the names on the box in his own handwriting before opening it to check the contents.

"I have a copy of the tape on cassette - and copies of the Ironman blueprints from those discs if you would like me to show you." This felt bizarre. Max heard himself sounding like a salesman trying to close a deal. This was not how he had envisaged the meeting.

"No, that won't be necessary. I recognise the writing. I know they're mine - there's no point denying it - I know what's on the tape. I suppose you have copies."

"Yes. In safe keeping."

"*Very* safe, I hope."

"Yes. But not so safe that if anything happens to me now, that they won't be in the hands of the authorities very quickly." Max was still not certain that Jack Briggs didn't have some plan to betray him. He removed his cell phone from his trouser pocket and pressed some keys while he was talking.

"Here, this is my answerphone in London." Max leant forward in his seat as he listened for a few seconds until he identified his own voice, then handed the phone to Jack Briggs to listen.

"Okay, I believe you." He handed the phone back. "There's no chance anyone else will listen to that before you return to scrub it, I assume."

"Not as long as I cancel it today. Otherwise various safeguards kick in, here in New York and in London." Jack Briggs began to select sandwiches and transfer them to a small plate.

"Please help yourself," he suggested to Max. "There's no problem with the deeds," he began to explain as he glanced at a clock on the mantle above the fire. "They should be here any minute now. But I'd like to make a suggestion about the diamonds. I'm prepared to offer you $2,000,000 in cash as an alternative. But it must be cash. No transactions that can be traced."

"How about a transfer to Dennis's bank account in Jersey?" Max asked.

"No, it has to be a cash deal."

"I can't carry $2,000,000 back in hand luggage on the plane." Max was still calculating the transfer between sterling and dollars, trying to work out if that was a good deal, when Jack Briggs moved the conversation on.

"You could put it in a bank here in the States and transfer it once you're back home."

"I don't have an account here."

"That's easily rectified."

Max thought about the proposition but he had now realised that this was not a good deal when the collection was worth two million in sterling, that should be more than $3,000,000.

"No, thanks all the same, I'll take the diamonds please, then we can get everything sorted fast. They're what I came for - they'll be easy to carry. Besides, you're going to give me an official receipt so they're legally mine." Max put down his plate and pulled two sheets of paper out of his bag. "I've made these out for you to sign the collection over to me and also your interest in The Gables' deeds back over to Molly along with the cancellation of any loan repayments." He held them for Jack Briggs to see.

"This all looks very thorough." He looked down both sheets then put them aside. "That's fine." Jack Briggs took a small bite of a sandwich as he thought he noticed a reaction from Max to his last remark.

"Max...It occurs to me that you may be wondering why I'm making this all rather easy for you. Yes, you're holding a particularly strong hand of cards with which to negotiate, but that's not all." He looked across to Max whose mouth was full of food, so said nothing.

"You see, Max, I suspect Dennis created the impression that I'm some sort of insensitive monster responsible for his demise. And that of BBS. I'm no angel for sure, but nor was your uncle. He knew what I was doing to get the contracts we needed to build the company as fast as we did. Not in detail, perhaps, but he knew that we were often sailing mighty close to the wind. We even had a slush fund of money for bribes and the like, except it went down as 'entertaining' in the books. But the difference between your uncle and me was that I was a businessman and Dennis wasn't. He made some serious blunders that he blamed on me, so I know I got cast as the villain when the shit finally hit the fan while I was out of the UK. I'm not and never was the ogre that you and Molly may think I am. I just wanted the chance to say that to you to put some of the record straight." Jack Briggs contemplated his words for a moment then took a breath.

"So we come to here and now......Max, I'm a man who likes a quiet life since I've retired. I have my routines. I like routines - I don't like anything to disturb them. But you've just happened by to disturb them - or to *potentially* disturb them. So, as I said, I'm prepared to pay whatever it takes to correct the problem – and to help Molly in the process. I can afford to pay you what you're asking without it affecting my life in the slightest. I have no dependants, so one day, some faithful friends and employees, some charities and, of course, the state will be my beneficiaries. Anyway, the point is that the cost isn't the issue here - my problem is that I've sort of promised the Geraldine Collection to a friend and I'd like to honour that promise. Yes Max, honour. I am an honourable man so if there's some way we can sort this out by me making payment in some other form, I'd like to do that."
Max considered the request.

"Can I see them, please?"
Jack Briggs showed a moment's surprise at the sudden request, then stood up, walked to a low cupboard at the side of the room on which a white cloth was draped over something the size of a box containing a collection of precious gems. And so it did. Jack Briggs had placed them there earlier in the day and now revealed a dark blue leather presentation case with a

flourish of the cotton napkin. He picked it up, brought it across the room and opened it for Max to see the contents set symmetrically into the velvet-covered interior. As a child, Max had been taken to The Tower of London to see the Crown Jewels - the insignia of the British Monarch. Their beauty had left a lasting impression on his young mind. He'd never seen anything that radiated such apparent value. And now the gems in the navy blue box in front of him made the same instant impact the moment he saw them. But then, what did he know about precious stones?

"Do I have your word that these are the originals?" Max asked.

Jack Briggs couldn't disguise his offence at the question.

"Of course," he snapped abruptly and, for the first time today, Max witnessed the petulance that he'd heard on the phone last night.

"They are absolutely beautiful," Max stated quickly to hide his discomfort from the previous question.

"Too beautiful to live out their lives in a safe…" But his attention was distracted by a droning sound coming from outside the house and quickly getting louder. He closed the box and put it on the table then stood up and turned towards the tall windows that overlooked the gardens to the rear of the house.

"Good," he proclaimed. "These will be your deeds. They were at my lawyer's office." The noise had grown so loud that it nearly drowned out his voice. A moment later Max could see the source, as a bright green helicopter came into view through the top of a window, descending towards the lawn. As it dropped closer, the down draught blew up dust and leaves, creating a veil that hid most of the plane from their view.

As the sound of the engine cut and the dust and debris began to settle, Max and Jack Briggs could see the doors of the aircraft open and a pilot climb out. He crouched and ran round the front of the aircraft to the passenger's door. It took only the briefest glimpse of the figure in a Red Riding Hood raincoat for Max to realise the passenger was someone he hadn't expected to see again - at least, not on this trip.

'Well there's a turn up for the book. What's she doing here?' Max pondered, as he watched Tessa Chapman being helped out of the helicopter by the pilot. She apparently needed that assistance as she stumbled before regaining her composure then pulling up her hood against rain that had just started to fall. The pilot handed her a briefcase that she grasped closely to her chest as she set off across the lawn towards the house. Max was aware that Jack Briggs had become visibly agitated the moment he saw her. He was more animated than he'd been all afternoon, quickly excusing himself then hurrying out of the drawing room, presumably to greet her.

Tessa Chapman had entered the house through a side door into an annex, followed by the pilot. She was marching purposefully down a corridor when Jack Briggs opened a door at the end to greet her.

"Tessa honey, what a pleasant surprise. I thought you were on your way back to London."

"Not until tonight, darling," she replied with the suggestion of impending confrontation in her voice.

"What are you doing here? Not that it's not great to see you, but you didn't need to come. Bruce could have brought the papers." Over her shoulder, he caught the pilot's eye. He shrugged a gesture that suggested he didn't know why she'd insisted on coming. Bruce, the pilot, and Jack Briggs both knew how much she hated flying in the helicopter and had vowed never to repeat the experience after her first and only trip that had made her violently ill. She must have a good reason to break her pledge.

Jack Briggs addressed her as Bruce turned away.

"Have you brought the deeds?"

"Yes," she replied as she set off towards the drawing room with Jack Briggs in tow.

"Hold on, where're you going?" he asked.

"I'm guessing that there's only one person that could want these - only one person who's here in New York right now, anyway."

Before Jack Briggs could prevent her, she'd opened the door to the drawing room to see Max still standing by the window. He turned as she entered.

"As I thought. Good afternoon, Mr Duncan."

"Hi there."

"Can I have a private word with you please Miss Chapman?" Jack Briggs asked. Then to Max: "Excuse us one minute please, Max." He ushered her out into the reception hall and shut the door behind them.

"What's going on, Jack?" she asked.

"You're extraordinary," Jack Briggs told her; the expression on his face conveying the same shock as his tone of voice. "Nothing's *going on* as you put it. I'm trying to sort out some business - a bit of a problem involving Molly. She's in trouble and needs to sell the house in Wimbledon, but I have a charge on the deeds that I'm about to relinquish. That's all."

Tessa Chapman had calmed down, considered the situation and now looked a little sheepish.

"Jack, you're getting soft in your old age."

"A small favour. I'd forgotten I even had them."

"So it's nothing to do with the robbery?"

Jack Briggs mocked a surprised expression.

"How could it be? But now he at least knows that you and I know one another and that doesn't help. He's not daft – I expect he'll put two and two together."

"Nonsense. I'm your lawyer from the old days just clearing up some old business." She tried to make light of what she now realised was an over-reaction on her part. To cover her discomfort, she changed the direction of the conversation.

"Why do you need the deeds? It's only the charge that you're rescinding."

Jack Briggs was confused.

"Don't I?"

"No, it's not essential to hand the physical papers over." Jack Briggs sighed at the realisation that the situation had been created by his own ignorance.

"Okay, well they're here now – and so are you, so we'd better go through with this. He'll expect to see you now. Just hand over the deeds, be polite and make your excuses - you've got your flight to catch - you need to leave immediately," he ordered, then opened the door for her to enter.

"Sorry about that Max. A small private matter to sort out," Jack Briggs explained as he closed the door behind them.

"These are for you." Tessa Chapman pulled a large brown envelope from her briefcase and handed it to Max who immediately unwound a short length of string that held it closed. He removed a bound document that, as best he could see with his untrained eyes, contained the deeds to The Gables in Parkland Gardens, London SW19.

"Don't worry, they're the deeds to your aunt's house," Tessa Chapman assured him.

"Thank you." Max pushed them back into the envelope. "Now if I can have your signature please Mr Briggs." Max moved to the table to retrieve his sheet of paper with the pre-prepared note assigning full ownership of the house back to Molly at no cost. In doing so, he drew Tessa Chapman's attention to the collection of papers, envelopes and the dark blue leather box. Jack Briggs suddenly appeared very uncomfortable and jumped into action.

"Of course, Max," he said too loudly. "And perhaps Miss Chapman could give her professional opinion on your wording – then provide the witness signature." He took the paper from Max's hand and flourished it in front of her. But she was focussed on the leather box and was not going to be distracted. She alighted on it with a disarmingly gentle approach.

"The Geraldine Collection," she said in a clearly suspicious tone. Then she saw Max's second document, assigning ownership of the diamonds. "You're expecting to sell it?" She made no effort to hide her shock at the notion. Max was a little surprised at the tone of the question.

"I was just showing Max the gems." Jack Briggs was attempting to appear disinterested in her actions by calmly signing Max's paper which he then turned for Miss Chapman to add her signature. Tessa Chapman obliged but was obviously distracted.

"So why the bill of sale?" Tessa Chapman held up the second word-processed sheet. Now Max was *really* surprised by her abruptness.

"I don't think that's any of your business." Jack Briggs insisted - obviously shocked by her audacious behaviour. "Thank you, I'll take that." He tried to snatch the paper from her grasp, but she was too quick and pulled back.

"Oh really, Jack? None of my business?" she snapped. Max was transfixed by the confrontation, trying to read the interplay between the couple.

"Cut the crap, Jack," Tessa Chapman continued, now standing with the paper held at arm's length away from Jack Briggs's reach. She tightened her grip on it and screwed it into a ball that she threw at him, hitting his shoulder. He sighed with resignation and dropped his head as if considering his next move. Miss Chapman turned and snatched up the navy blue box.

"You see Max, these aren't Mr Briggs's to give - not in the strict legal sense - because he promised them to me. A verbal contract."

Jack Briggs caught Max's eye then turned to Tessa Chapman.

"I was telling him exactly that before you arrived to put your dainty size twelves right in it." He shook his head with exasperation as he bent to pick up the crumpled paper. "Yes Max, Miss Chapman here was to be the beneficiary that I told you about - for services rendered over the years." Max sensed that now was not the time to question what those services had been, when he'd always understood that she worked to defend his uncle *against* Jack Briggs.

Tessa Chapman had clicked open the box to check the contents.

"Well that's fine then Jack. Why don't I just take them with me now - for safe keeping?" She closed the box and gripped it tightly under her arm.

"I can't let you do that. I've still got some business to settle with Max here." Then he raised his voice. "And frankly, I don't see why I should." Jack Briggs moved to take them from her. "So I'll thank you to hand them back." He had his hands on the box, but Tessa Chapman tightened her grip.

"That's enough. I haven't got time for this," she announced as she dug her hand deep into a pocket of her red rain coat and pulled out a small pearl-handled pistol that she

351

levelled straight at Jack Briggs's head. "Let go Jack or I will. I mean it. And you back off Max." She tugged away from Jack Briggs's grip while waving the pistol between both men.

"Bloody hell," Max uttered under his breath as he raised his hands in submission. "Has everyone in this country got a fucking gun?"

"Tessa…" Jack Briggs sounded as incredulous as he looked, completely dumfounded by her actions. "Have you gone crazy? What the hell are you trying to achieve. We can sort this out."

"Can we? How do you reckon that? Max here obviously has some hold over you, to be demanding the collection - and for you to even consider handing it over. What is it Jack?" She waved the gun, to suggest he should answer.

"Something from my past." He nodded to the envelopes on the low table beside her, hoping that she would drop her guard to pick them up, which might provide an opportunity for him to jump her. But she never took her eyes off the two men with their hands raised as she groped for the envelopes and brought them up to her eye line.

"Your past catching up with you, Jack? You want me to get you out of another scrape? Sorry, can't help this time, darling. I don't think I'm going to be back in New York for quite a while. In fact, I think under the circumstances, you should assume that Garland-Grimes will be resigning your business." She had peered into the envelopes briefly as she spoke.

"Time to go," she announced as she gathered up her briefcase then swept all the papers and documents from the table into it. Max watched in shock as his papers and the deeds disappeared from view.

"No, not the deeds. Please?"

"Sorry Max. Insurance." She showed no sympathy for his pleading before adding: "Jack, you're going to drive me."

"What?"

"You heard. You're going to drive me back into town."

"Look - let's just calm down, shall we. We can sort this out - without the gun - then Bruce can fly you back." She took only a split second to consider the offer.

"Oh no, not the chopper. I'm happier with my plan. Come on Jack, we're going."

"Tessa, is that really necessary? You've got what you came for. Here - here are the keys to the Jeep. Take it - take the diamonds - I'll find another way to pay Max. Only, please, leave the envelopes." She hadn't assumed they held much of any importance or value, but now she realised that whatever they contained afforded her some leverage against him.

"Oh - that important are they Jack?" She thought for a moment. "Hmmm, good. Now let's go Jack."

"Why do you need me?"

"Because you know the way and I'm in a hurry to get back to the office. Come on."

"I need a coat. It's pouring with rain now."

"Stop messing me around - let's go - now, Jack!" She flicked the pistol at him and moved backwards to open the door. Jack followed. As the door closed behind them, Max was motionless, still dazed by the turn of events, not knowing what to do. His first reaction was to follow them. He heard a muffled squeal coming from outside the drawing room - it was Maria. She had dutifully hurried into the reception hall to offer her services to a departing guest, only for Tessa Chapman to wave her away at the point of her revolver. When Max emerged cautiously, Maria was cowering at a window watching her master and his captor leaving through a downpour of rain then climbing into a red Jeep at the front of the house. Jack Briggs started the car and cautiously swung it onto the drive and headed towards the main gates. Maria turned away and began screaming for:

"Bruce! Bruce!"

The pilot pounded from a corridor.

"What's up?"

"It's Mr Jack. Miss Chapman's taken him with a gun." Bruce looked confused, disbelieving. He turned to Max for confirmation.

"It's true. She's taken him hostage. They're in one of your cars - heading back to her office in Manhattan, I think."

"Quick, you must follow. Quick, hurry!" Maria ordered. Bruce rushed around collecting the car keys then banged through the front door. Max and Maria watched as he grappled his way into a silver Mercedes sports car and spun the wheels on the gravel in his haste to chase them through the rain that was now falling heavily. Max became aware of his cell phone ringing from somewhere nearby.

Outside on the road, Gaynor had become bored and a little concerned by the long wait. She had been considering whether to phone to check that Max was all right, when she noticed the gates start to open and the Jeep edge through. As it turned past her and headed up the hill, Gaynor could see a man and woman in the front seats, but didn't recognise either. She was calling Max on her phone when the gates stopped closing and began to open again. This was too much. She grabbed her bag, nearly fell out of the van onto the wet road in her haste, then watched the silver Mercedes bounce out of the gates onto the road and roar off down the hill at speed as she collected her bag and senses. Gaynor ran to the gates and squeezed through as they clicked shut behind her. At the end of her phone line, Max could hear her rustling and running and panting.

"Gaynor! Gaynor...!" He was shouting to attract her attention, which at the time was taken with her race to negotiate the gates as they closed on her. When she came on the line, she was breathless.

"Alex. I'm here - what's happening?"

"Tessa Chapman's just done a runner with Jack Briggs and all the..." He suddenly became conscious of Maria at his shoulder listening to his conversation. "... with all the things I'd come for. Where are you?"

"On the drive. I'm coming up." She hung up.

"We must call the police," Maria announced as she rushed off through an open door into the kitchen where a telephone handset was lying on a worktop. Max wasn't sure. He had no time to think - he just suspected that this wasn't the best course of action under the circumstances.

"No - hold on." Max snatched the phone from her hands forcefully, upsetting Maria still more than she was already. She began shaking.

"Sorry Maria. Let's just see what Bruce does? Has he got a phone with him?"

Maria was barely in control of her actions or senses now.

"I think so."

"The number. Maria, where's the number?"

She pointed at a sheet of paper on a small pinboard.

"Here, here." She was pointing at Bruce's name followed by a number that Max immediately dialled. It took several rings before Bruce answered.

"Bruce - this is Max at the house. What's happening?"

"Nothing. Haven't caught them yet and I'm halfway to the freeway. I can't see them - must go."

The front door bell rang, frightening Maria who couldn't move.

"It's okay," Max assured her, "It's probably a friend of mine." He ran through and opened the door to find Gaynor bedraggled and panting on the step, soaked through from the torrential rain.

"You okay?" Max asked.

"Yeah. You?"

"Yeah. They're in a car on their way back into Manhattan. And the guy here's chasing them in another car, but he can't catch them."

Gaynor was still catching her breath.

"Well he's not going to catch them - they went left out of the gates and he went right."

"Oh shit." Max swore as he searched for the re-dial button on the phone. But Gaynor's attention was taken by the view though the drawing room door and out to the lawns.

"Bruce. They're on a different route," Max shouted into the phone. "They went left out of the gates...... I don't know. Well, do what you can...... let us know." As Max ended the call, Gaynor tugged at his sleeve to turn him towards the window to view the helicopter.

"Look." She was wide-eyed expecting Max to realise the significance of her discovery.

"What?" he replied innocently.

"The chopper - a helicopter. Come on. You can fly that." Gaynor was serious. Max was speechless. Gaynor began to bundle up her bag. "Let's go!"

"Hold on - I can't fly that."

"Why not? You told me you could."

"I haven't flown for years."

"So what? Must be like riding a bike."

Max was trying to think if it would be possible.

"Well at least try. You got a better idea? Come on!"

"The keys Maria?" Max asked, trying to recall if he needed any. "I don't know. Maybe they're in it. He was going to fly back soon."

"Oh shiiiit," Max uttered under his breath as Gaynor pulled him towards the front door.

"No - that way." Maria pointed to the back of the building, then rushed ahead to open the doors onto the lawn.

"No police Maria." Max called over his shoulder as they braced themselves against the pouring rain and set off from the rear entrance, squelching across the lawn towards the waiting helicopter. To Max's surprise, but not to his relief, it was ready to fly, but getting a helicopter airborne takes a few minutes during which time Gaynor was getting more impatient and agitated. Max was thinking more about the flight than his predicament, but he did briefly question why they were about to take chase.

"I'm not sure we need any of the papers she's got."

"What? Why?"

"Err… well I don't know we need the actual deeds… And Jack Briggs has agreed to sign the house back, so he can do it later."

"Assuming he has a *later*. What about the diamonds?" But the exchange was cut short as all the helicopter gauges showed that it was ready for take-off. Now Max was prepared to give this a go. He was finding his way around the controls, trying to remember procedures, safety checks and the meaning of all the dials. Unbeknown to Gaynor, he was close to ordering her to get, considering it could be too dangerous but, to his own surprise, the controls felt familiar and his confidence was returning. There was just an outside chance that this could provide some sort of solution. Max ordered Gaynor to put on her seat belt and headphones.

From inside the house, Maria was barely able to see the helicopter through the rain and clouds of spray blown up by the rotors once they had crawled into life then wound up to a rhythmic throbbing.

"Here we go. This could be a bit bumpy," Max announced, then took a firm grip of the two control levers and lifted the plane vertically from the lawn in a slightly wobbly manoeuvre. They were airborne, gaining height and a view at a steady speed. Gaynor had never been in a helicopter. She was unsure about the noise, the movement, the vibration. Max was finding his confidence.

'This feels good,' Max thought to himself.
Gaynor wasn't so sure.

'This feels scary,' she thought to herself.
They were over the entrance.

"Which way?" Max called into his mouthpiece.

"They went left," Gaynor replied. "Over the hill there." From their vantage point, they had a view for miles in all directions, so set off, nose down, following a likely route heading towards the main highways back to Manhattan. The windscreen wiper was already battling against the rain, but despite their limited visibility, Max began to cover ground very quickly.

Jack Briggs had no plan when he set off at the controls of the Jeep, other than to take as much time as he could to get her back to the freeway, to give the others time to find them. But, to do so, he'd taken a devious route that Bruce obviously hadn't anticipated. Once in the heavy motorway traffic, Jack Briggs knew there was very little anyone could do to stop them. Tessa Chapman had only driven herself to Jack Briggs's home on two occasions and had got lost on both. She was only now beginning to question the time it was taking to reach the highways and the sedate speed that Jack Briggs was driving – slow even for the deteriorating weather conditions.

"I never drive myself these days," he replied to her demands for him to speed up. "If you want to drive dear, please do. This ain't easy – believe me."

"Let's just get this over with Jack, then I'll get out of your life, for once and for all."

"Why the hell? I never wanted that. You know this is crazy, you must realise that. None of this is necessary. Look, let me take you into your office, pick up your things and I'll even drive you to the airport if that's really what you want. You take the diamonds, I'll take the two envelopes and the deeds. It can all be sorted very easily."

Tessa Chapman was softening, considering that this was a safe and sensible option. She had her stash of cash back at the office, so she should be feeling chipper with her success - and perhaps she had over-reacted a little and let things get out of hand.

"No reprisals - no recriminations? And I keep the diamonds to do with whatever I want?" she asked. But before Jack Briggs could answer…

WACK – WACK – WACK – WACK – WACK !!!

The car was suddenly enveloped by the violent sound of the helicopter that thundered into view from behind the Jeep, filling the sky in front of the car that had shielded its approach until it was almost over them. Now it burst into their view so abruptly and in such an explosion of noise and blown spray, that Jack Briggs momentarily lost control of the Jeep, hitting a verge and losing traction on the soaking wet grass. He fumbled to find the wiper control to speed it up to maximum to clear the water from the windscreen. Tessa Chapman screamed with surprise, then shouted a string of curses.

In the helicopter, Max was trying to invent some way to stop the Jeep without killing himself or Gaynor. As soon as he saw the effect of their first pass, he realised the potential ally he had in the volumes of rain and standing water now lying in puddles along the lane. Perhaps he could make it impossible for Jack Briggs to drive - even give him an excuse to stop the car.

Gaynor had been excited when she spotted the Jeep a minute earlier. Now as Max threw the aircraft into tight turns, she fell silent. Max swung it around again, approaching the Jeep from behind and dropping so low that the skids were just feet from the vehicle's roof.

In the Jeep, Tessa Chapman had become very agitated, waving her gun at her driver, ordering him to speed up, to get to the freeway as fast as possible. Jack Briggs was protesting.

"It's too dangerous - I can't see." The car's wipers were beating away the clouds of spray driven up by the helicopter now overshadowing them - its dark shape tracking above them, increasing the tension in the car.

"What the hell's it doing?" Tessa Chapman asked while craning her neck to see the helicopter through the top of the windscreen. The noise and the pounding spray heightened the drama, making it more difficult for Jack Briggs to see the road. Max pulled slowly ahead of the Jeep, the helicopter's shadow creeping along the road in front of the car, driving up so much water that the wipers were losing the battle to clear it. Jack Briggs could barely see the hedges and certainly not the road ahead or any oncoming vehicle sharing the narrow lane. He had no choice but to stop. From his view in the mirrors under the body of the plane, Max could see the Jeep pulling back.

"Alex! Look out!" Gaynor screamed into the microphone on her headset. Max looked up to see lines of power cables looming ahead. He pulled hard on the controls, accelerated and banked the helicopter. It stood on its tail, then dropped sideways so violently that Gaynor gripped ferociously onto her seat to prevent her from falling into Max.

When Tessa Chapman saw the helicopter banking away and the flurries of spray stopped pounding the car, she ordered Jack Briggs to get moving, shouting at him with a mix of panic and anger in her tone.

"Tessa, let's just think about this…" Jack Briggs attempted to reason.

"As we drive. Go!" She ordered while peering into the pounding rain, trying to locate the helicopter. Jack Briggs put the car in gear and set off again.

In the helicopter, Max was gathering his reactions having frightened himself by such a close miss. He'd pulled away to assess the scene and could now see the Jeep begin to move once more. From their height, they could also identify the freeway only a couple of miles ahead.
Gaynor had been silent since nearly hitting the power lines.

"I think I'm going to be ill," she suddenly announced. Max looked across to her. She was as pale as she sounded.

"Don't you dare," he warned, then reached into her footwell, pulled out her satchel and dumped it on her lap.

"The best I can do as a sick bag, I'm afraid."
He then turned the plane once more, dropping a few hundred yards ahead of the Jeep to sit immediately above the narrow road, high enough to see it without the rotors stirring up spray.

"Keep going, Jack," Tessa Chapman ordered as soon as they saw it ahead of them. Jack knew there was no point arguing though they both knew what was about to happen. As they approached, the helicopter dropped like a hunting hawk, swooping along the road toward them.

"Go on!" Tessa Chapman screamed.

"I won't see," Jack Briggs protested as he slowed the car, anticipating the complete white out as bellows of heavy spray pounded the car with a torrent of water, causing Jack to stop the car again.

Max had turned the plane and set it up for another pass as clouds of spray were still settling. But he could see that the Jeep had stopped. He pulled the helicopter into position, ready to start another run, but the only movement from the car was the driver's door opening then Jack Briggs climbing out into the storm. He had tried to reason with Tessa Chapman that this was all stupid and dangerous. He didn't want to drive any further. But her exasperation boiled over and she ordered him out of the car.

"Tessa, don't be crazy," he tried to protest.

"Get out," she insisted, with a wave of the gun barrel. "The end of the road for you Jack."

"I haven't got a coat."

"You better hope they pick you up then."

He stared at her across the width of the car.

"You really are a nasty piece of work." And with those his last words to her, he opened the door, tugged vaguely at the collar of his shirt for a modicum of protection and stepped out into the storm.

Across the field, Max was positioning the helicopter for another encounter, as a knight composing his steed in a joust.

In the Jeep, Tessa Chapman had clambered across into the driver's seat, gathered her trusty steed, then dug her spurs into its side with a violent jab at the accelerator. Her mount twitched as it found grip on the saturated road surface and set off through the downpour.

The helicopter dropped, pounded along the lane, then clattered over the roof of the Jeep. The blanket of spray hit the car, but Tessa Chapman had seen that the road ahead was straight. She slowed a little, held the wheel with a vice-like grip and drove blind with the car wipers fighting to provide some visibility. The helicopter pulled up to view the cloud of spray that Max had stirred up behind the plane. To his and Gaynor's surprise, they could make out the roof of the Jeep pressing ahead through it, occasionally hitting a verge, twitching and bucking, but keeping to the road.

Gaynor braced herself for the expected swoop, but instead of chasing the car, Max turned back towards Jack Briggs who they could see standing bedraggled, pressed into a hedge by a gateway with his back towards the driving downpour.

"One more." Gaynor managed to call into her microphone.

"No. I have to get the old man. He'll get hypothermia out there."

"Alex - one more - there's time before she gets to the freeway."

"I don't want any more deaths. I've got to get him." Gaynor puzzled about Max's motives, but only briefly because, very quickly, Max had swooped down to the field and was about to land the helicopter within a hundred yards of where Jack Briggs cowered.

At about the same time, the Jeep was driving up the slip road onto the freeway. Tessa Chapman peered up through the windscreen to check that the sky around her was a helicopter-free zone, which it was. She afforded herself a rye, satisfied smile. She was feeling rather pleased with herself.

Max, by comparison, was feeling deflated. Gaynor was nauseous and Jack Briggs was soaked to the skin, but grateful. A somewhat sorry trio.

"Thanks Bruce." Jack Briggs managed to stutter as he climbed into the rear seats of the helicopter, where he pulled a blanket from under the seat and wrapped it around his sodden frame. As he looked up, Max was staring back at him over his shoulder.

"Max!" Jack Briggs was trying to make a mental adjustment when he recalled Max's background. "Right. You used to fly choppers didn't you?"

"Uh-huh."

"Where's Bruce?"

"Not sure. He took chase after you in a car, but went off in the wrong direction."

"Right…. Well thank you Max. I appreciate this."
But Max had turned back in his seat and slumped as he reflected on the situation.

"So that's it," Gaynor suggested.

"You gave it your best shot, Max," Jack Briggs told him over his headset. "But she's got all the aces and she knows it – or certainly will when she checks the contents of the envelopes. I can't touch her while she has all the evidence on me and the photos from the raid are her protection from you."
Max didn't respond. He had been trying to think of any way they hadn't yet tried to stop the Jeep. But Jack Briggs's words now drew his attention. He turned to look back at him.

"You know about the photos?"

"Sure." Jack Briggs replied.

"And how much more?"

"Pretty much everything, I guess. About Dennis's plans, the CD program. Why do you think the real diamonds weren't in the bank?"

"A mole," Max suggested, "named Tessa Chapman?" Jack Briggs nodded.

"You got it in one."

Max was more confused than shocked by the revelation.

"Why? Why did she involve you - she had nothing to gain by involving you?"

"Pillow talk, you might say," Jack Briggs admitted.

"You and Tessa Chapman?"

"Yeah."

"But what about Dennis?"

"That was over two years back. No, our Tessa's a little gold digger all right, no question. Always follows the money - and knows just how to get what she wants."

Max blew out his cheeks and glanced at Gaynor who was recovering now that the plane was on the ground. Gaynor shrugged as if lost for an appropriate remark then offered:

"Time to lick your wounds, regroup and find another approach."

"For what?" Jack Briggs asked from the rear seat.

"I have to get Molly's deeds back."

"Do you?"

"Yeah, course - don't I?"

"I dunno - do you, now that I've agreed to assign them to you?" Jack Briggs suggested.

"I assume so.....oh, I dunno." Max was confused. "Fuck it, I don't want her to win, anyway."

He pulled his headset off, retrieved his phone from his coat pocket and called a number from its memory.

A cell phone lying on the leather upholstery of a featureless white car parked somewhere in Manhattan, began to ring. Mickey Gavini picked it up.

"Hi," he answered.

Max was having trouble hearing over the noise of the helicopter engine that was still ticking over. At least the rain had eased, but Max could hardly hear his call being answered.

"Who's that?" he shouted into his phone with his hand over his other ear.

"Is that you Alex?" Mickey shouted back.

"Mickey?"

"Yeah."

"Where's Bo?"

"He's here - in one of his shops."

"Where are you?"

"The Bronx."

"Where?" Max shouted.

"The Bronx." Mickey shouted back louder.

This was getting too difficult for Max.

"Hold on. Can you get Bo to the phone?"

"Yeah. One minute."

Max was grappling with his seat harness. He pulled it over his shoulders, climbed out of the helicopter and squelched off across the field, leaving Gaynor and Jack Briggs confused by his actions.

On the freeway, Tessa Chapman had plenty of time now to contemplate her next moves and her good fortune - quite a sizeable fortune.

'*A good day's work,*' she reasoned. The diamond collection worth millions of dollars lay on the passenger seat beside her, another one-and-a-half million in cash was locked in her safe at the office; and she suspected that she had all the protection she needed against the few people who could spoil her plans. She laughed aloud with smug satisfaction as the Jeep plodded back towards Manhattan in a steady flow of freeway traffic throwing up a wall of spray that Miss Chapman hardly noticed. She picked her cell phone up from the seat beside her and pressed a couple of keys.

"Who's that?" she asked abruptly when it was eventually answered. "Where's Sonya?.... Oh yeah, I forgot. Is she coming back today?.... Well thank you for standing in - you'll have to do something for me, Ms Ellery. I need you to confirm my flight tonight - to London .... I don't know - look on Sonya's desk - the ticket's there somewhere .... Well get someone else to do it then. But just get it sorted out. I'll be back in an hour to collect my things from the office and I'll be leaving immediately for the airport.... No, I'll drive myself." She hung up, dropped the phone on the passenger seat and turned on the car radio to be greeted by a music channel that she accompanied in full voice.

She looked at her watch as she swung the Jeep into the underground car park below the office block. Miss Chapman was on schedule to make the airport by six if she didn't hang about. She snatched up her briefcase, stuffed her phone and the blue leather presentation case containing her diamonds into the pockets of her Red Riding Hood coat and set off into the building. As she hurried through ground floor reception, she hardly noticed the slight figure wearing a Visitor Security Pass who stood up from one of the leather sofas and shadowed her into one of the eight elevators. She was too pre-occupied to notice him making a call on his cell phone, that he then hang up as it was answered. Nor had she registered that he'd pressed

367

the button for the sixth floor, so when they stopped and the doors opened but he didn't move, she had no suspicion of impending danger. It took her a moment to register the bulky figure of Bo Garrick stepping forward to join her, but by then the doors were already closing. Her brief concern was subdued by reasoning that they had company in the elevator, so what would he do to her in public?

"Good afternoon, Mr Garrick - are you here to meet me?" But before he should have answered, the man behind Tessa Chapman slapped his hand over her mouth as Bo looked on with no change of expression. He was removing a roll of black carpet tape from his jacket pocket before tearing off two lengths - one for her mouth then, after removing Miss Chapman's red raincoat, another piece of tape secured her wrists. Bo and his colleague, one Mickey Gavini, had rendered their victim powerless to scream or to defend herself during the journey to the twelfth floor where the view from the elevator looks straight through the glass doors into Garland-Grimes's reception area.

All was quiet as a figure in the Red Riding Hood raincoat, hurried through the doors and headed for the corridor towards Tessa Chapman's office. The doors of the elevator had closed as it continued its climb.

The sound of the main reception doors opening into the offices had roused the part-time receptionist into life. She came out of her adjoining room to survey the scene then quickly identified the rear of Miss Chapman by her familiar hooded red raincoat. Had the receptionist looked more closely at the legs protruding below its hemline, Mickey's hairy calves and oversized feet crammed into Tessa Chapman's shoes might have given her cause for suspicion. But she evidently took no more than a cursory glance before returning to her office.

Mickey reached the door at the end of the corridor with his heart pounding somewhere close to his throat. Bo had told him that it was the last door on the right – or at least, he thought it was. So Mickey was already nervous about entering, but if it was locked, their make-shift plan would be blown. But the door was open - and Mickey was into Miss Chapman's office with a sigh of relief.

Bo had meanwhile taken the lift to the top of the building where he had held it briefly until directing it back down. He had become aware of the fragility of their cobbled-together plan. If anyone called this elevator on its way to the top floor or during its decent back to the twelfth, they would see Miss Chapman trussed up and presumably raise the alarm. Bo could do nothing but continue with their plan A. Now as it started its descent, he explained politely but firmly to his prisoner that she had nothing to fear if she co-operated. With her mouth covered by a strip of tape and her wrists bound, Miss Chapman was powerless to do more than listen.

"My colleague is clearing out your safe right now," Bo told her. "He's repossessing a few things that you should never have gotten hold of including my money and the file of photos. Once we've got them, we'll be letting you go. And we'll never need to see one another again - ever. But if you're unreasonable… Well, why would you be? Remember, we still have the tape recording of you admitting you planned the bank raid. But you…. well, you soon won't have nothing to bargain with…. In fact, you'll have nothing, period. Funny how things turn out, ain't it?"

To Bo's good fortune, but Miss Chapman's misfortune, the journey to the twelfth floor was uninterrupted. At the last moment, as the elevator slowed, Bo pulled out a small knife from his coat pocket. Tessa Chapman's eyes betrayed her panic, but to her obvious relief, Bo aligned the blade with the tape around her wrists and slit it, freeing her hands as the elevator doors began to open.

"Now just you remember the tape recording," he insisted, but Tessa Chapman was gone from her trap like a greyhound. She ran through the reception doors, down the corridor towards her office in stockinged feet, still with tape across her mouth, preventing her from crying out. She had briefly tried to rip it off her face, but that hurt so she left it. That was not foremost in her thoughts at that moment. She just needed to get to her office and her safe. She rushed through the door into her room where she stopped momentarily to survey the scene. She could see instantly that Mickey had disturbed the normal order of her desk, the wall cupboard, her safe. The door to the cupboard was open and the books that normally hid the safe from view were scattered on the carpet, but the safe door was closed. If she had been thinking straight, she may not have dived straight at it to check that the contents had been cleared out. But she was still experiencing the joint effects of relief and panic.

She fell to her knees on the carpeted floor in front of the safe and instantly tapped the combination of numbers onto the keypad - automatically, without thought. The moment the lock released, she jerked open the door just as she had a hundred times before. At about the same instant that her eyes took in the full contents and her brain began to question why nothing had been removed, or even disturbed - in that same split second, her own pearl-handled revolver touched the back of her head. Mickey was peering down the length of its short barrel.

"Thank you ma'am. Now if you'll pull everything out, that'll be a great help and the quicker I can be on my way." She'd frozen. Mickey jerked the gun into her head.

"Now!" he demanded.

Miss Chapman pulled the contents of the safe out onto the floor including the sports bag that had resided there overnight.

"Everything into the bag," he ordered and she obeyed by unzipping the holdall and cramming the other items on top of the bundles of notes already there.

"Be reasonable …," she tried to say from behind the tape still across her mouth, but Mickey pushed the gun into her head again.

"Just do it."

As soon as she'd completed the task, he ordered his captive to her feet and pushed her ahead of him into the small washroom from where he had just emerged; then he locked the door and threw the key across the room without consideration. He opened the office door tentatively and checked down the corridor. It was empty. He was out and away towards reception at a brisk walk, leaving behind the muted cries of help that were muffled to virtual silence as he shut the office door behind him. Of more concern to him now was the sudden appearance of a middle-aged woman in the corridor ahead. She was making her way straight towards him - surely she would spot his stockinged feet and challenge him? Mickey slowed his pace, whilst preparing to run at any moment, but to his relief, the woman took no notice of him, her attention more absorbed in an airline ticket that she was studying as she headed towards Tessa Chapman's office. As she approached, the woman's attention was drawn to the distant cries for help that became louder as soon as she opened the door into Miss Chapman's office. A short expletive-filled conversation through the washroom door was enough to set Ms Ellery into a headless panic until, to Miss Chapman's good fortune, Ms Ellery spotted the key lying where Mickey had discarded it across the room. The moment she unlocked the door, Tessa Chapman burst past her.

"I've been robbed!" She shouted. "Call security. No-one leaves the building!" she blurted out as she rushed for the door, then turned back to the woman who was totally bewildered.

"No police - just security. No one leaves the building - I'm on my way down. Tell them they have a gun. Two men. Now - do it now!" She screamed at Ms Ellery who jumped into action and seized the phone from the desk.

Tessa Chapman set off in pursuit in her stockinged feet; barged out through the glass reception doors and dived at the buttons on the wall to summon one of the bank of elevators. A moment later, her patience gone, she turned and crashed through a door towards the stairs. Which was exactly where Bo and Mickey were making their escape on another floor. But Bo was exhausted and taking a breather.

"Come on Bo," Mickey was urging. He grabbed the envelopes and blue leather jewellery case containing the Geraldine Collection from Bo and pushed them into the zip-topped bag.

Tessa Chapman was bounding down the staircase two and three steps at a time, her feet hardly making a sound on the vinyl-covered floor.

"We'll have to take the elevator," Bo was telling Mickey elsewhere on the same staircase. "I can hardly fucking breathe," he managed between gasps.

"They'll expect us to be in an elevator – it's too dangerous," Mickey tried to remind Bo, but then worried more about the big man's ability to handle more stairs. They opened

372

a door onto the landing, then made their way to the elevators as casually as it's possible for two men attempting to flee a building whilst carrying a fortune in cash and diamonds, to appear relaxed. Mickey pounced on a 'call' button.

"Come on," he pleaded under his breath.

In reception at ground level, the call to security a minute earlier, had given the uniformed official a start. But now he was taking the order seriously and herding everyone at gunpoint as they left the bank of elevators.

"I'm sorry folks, there's been a robbery. Women can go. All men – hands away from your bodies while we check passes - sorry gentlemen - against the wall. Do it!" he ordered.

On one of the floors above, Tessa Chapman had realised just how demanding twelve flights of stairs can be on shoeless feet. She was slapping the buttons to call an elevator.

On another floor, the doors to another elevator were just closing on Bo and Mickey who were unaware of the activities in reception, or even that Tessa Chapman had made such a quick escape from the washroom.

Down in the reception, the security guard had called on the services of two colleagues to help control a crowd that was growing by the minute. A line of men stood with their arms raised, most with briefcases at their feet. The guards had their guns in their hands, checking security passes before releasing any man who had been trying to leave the building. The situation was getting so tense that the guards were obviously relieved when Tessa Chapman arrived in a high state of exasperation and perspiration.

She ran round the bemused group, looking from face to face for Bo and Mickey. She quickly concluded that they weren't amongst the small group of men. She stopped to catch her breath, frantically wondering where they could be. They should be here – they set off minutes before her. Where were they?...... Then came a sudden realisation!

"The stairs to the car park. Come on!" She shouted at two of the guards who set off behind her on a route towards the underground car park.

Bo and Mickey could sense the end of their marathon was in sight as they rounded a corner in a concrete corridor and spotted a door marked *Fire Exit* at the far end. Bo was gasping for breath. Mickey was encouraging him to keep moving.

"We're there Bo. Come on," he urged.

Tessa Chapman was confronted by an identical exit door at the end of an identical corridor. She banged a release bar and the door swung open into the gloomy light and smoky aroma of the underground car park. She shouted at the men in uniforms to spread out and find their quarry.

"They're armed – shoot if you have to!"

Mickey had reached his exit with Bo limping behind. He hit the bar with his shoulder and the door burst open in front of him, revealing blinding daylight above the Manhattan skyline.

Twenty-three floors below, Tessa Chapman was facing the reality that Bo and Mickey were making their escape by another route. She had no idea how or where but, having run through the length of the car park below the tower block with her posse now at her heels, she was breathless and exhausted, resigned to the inevitable conclusion that they weren't there, nor was her booty. She stopped running, her hot breath pumping into the fresh damp air near the entrance from the street. The guards stood nearby waiting for instructions, but Tessa Chapman had become distracted from them - from the car park - from the hunt for Bo and Mickey. Her ears were now tuned to only one sound filtered from a million city noises, penetrating her senses from some distance away.

She turned and ran up the ramp from the car park, out into the bright afternoon light, then stood in the street, oblivious to the stares of passing pedestrians as she shielded her eyes to squint into the stormy sky above the tower blocks - in time to see a bright green, five-seater helicopter landing on an adjacent building.

Bo and Mickey were watching the same scene from their vantage point on the roof of their tower. Max had landed the helicopter as close as possible, but that had a twenty yard gap between his landing place and his would-be passengers' location.

"What the fuck now?" Bo fired the question at Mickey who was breathless and speechless. "Fucking great." Bo observed between his own gasps.

"Can you hover so they can jump in?" Gaynor asked Max in the helicopter, but then saw Bo. "Perhaps not."
The two groups each had direct line of sight to the other over the short distance, but that was no help.

"So bloody close, but…" Max volunteered without needing to complete the thought, whilst in the back seat of the helicopter, Jack Briggs had been straining to see through his window to study a structure on the other roof.

"I think that could be a fire causeway – there, that thing beside them." He announced into his mouthpieces. "Look - that metal box thing's a sort of folding stairway to this building in case of fire. There must be a way to extend it."

On the pavement, the security guards were trying to contact their colleague in the reception but their internal radios were out of range. Now one was using his cell phone to call in to direct his colleague towards the roof.

Max was on his phone. He could see Mickey on the other roof receive his call.

375

"Hi Alex – what the hell now?"

"That metal thing beside you – we think it'll extend to this building. There must be something on it - a handle or electric switch. It's for emergencies - can't be difficult."

From the helicopter, they could all see Mickey rushing around studying the apparatus.

"Got it!" he announced into his phone then cut the call. He'd found a large red lever with an arrow and the word ON stamped beside it. He wrenched it, but it wouldn't move. Bo rushed, as best Bo could, to apply his weight and eventually the lever clunked through ninety degrees. A motor somewhere in the equipment began to wheeze and the structure creaked into life.

The security guard below had made contact.

"On the roof. They're…. hold on…. Shit - get up there - they're getting away!"

The guard had seen the metal causeway beginning to extend across the space between the two buildings.

Clang! The end landed just yards from the helicopter. At the other end, Mickey pushed Bo ahead of him onto the causeway.

In the street, a small group of pedestrians had joined Tessa Chapman and the two security guards to stare at the activities twenty-three floors above them. They were all craning to work out what was happening at the top of the two towers when they spotted Bo and Mickey scrambling across the metal causeway.

Mickey was pushing Bo who had never had to admit to his fear of heights until this moment. He was fighting the urge to freeze as he looked down through the open-tread grating of the bouncy structure. Mickey was urging Bo to move, but as he pushed at Bo's bulky frame, his feet slipped on the wet metal. He stumbled then fell hard onto his knees. As he reached out

376

to grasp for support he dropped the zip-top sports bag – except the zip had not been closed in his haste to get away from Tessa Chapman's office. Now it fell open on impact with the grating and some of its contents bounced out. A few bundles of money fell - some bursting open as they hit the metal floor, scattering currency confetti into the void between the buildings.

In the street, Tessa Chapman saw the money cloud and realised that something unplanned had just happened. She fired into action and snatched at one of the guard's handguns before he could respond.

At the helicopter, the rear door was open and Bo threw the sports bag into the rear footwell. Jack Briggs immediately pulled it open to check the contents.

"Are the deeds there?" Max shouted into his mouthpiece.

"Yeah, they're here – and my envelopes!" The relief in Jack Briggs' voice was evident.

"Great - what's Mickey doing?"

They could see that he was still on the causeway, but couldn't see why. He was reaching through the railings trying to retrieve the blue leather jewellery case that was wedged in the metal structure at the extent of his reach. As he managed to get his hands to it…

Clang – clang – clang – clang – clang.

Tessa Chapman was firing off rounds from the security guard's handgun in the street below. The first shots hit the causeway some distance from their target.

Clang – clang – clang.

These were too close. Mickey dived away and in doing so, dropped the case from the end of his tentative grasp. He could do nothing to prevent its fall. He watched its descent for a moment then scrambled along the causeway towards the helicopter.

Below, it took Tessa Chapman a few moments to register what was happening - then she couldn't believe what she thought she could see falling from the top of the buildings. She was so mesmerised that she hardly noticed the policeman's bear hug or one of the security guards snatching back his hand gun. Her eyes were locked onto the descending blue jewellery case until its impact with a tree, then with the ground below, where it bust open. As did Miss Chapman. A rush of adrenaline gave her the strength to brake the policeman's grasp as she fought her way to the case's landing spot. She dived on it and snatched up the few items that had scattered themselves across the raised flowerbed.

With equal urgency, high above, Mickey had slammed the door before strapping himself into the last rear seat in the helicopter. Bo handed him a headset as Max started to rev the engine for take-off.

"Sorry Alex, it was a small blue box – I couldn't hold it. I hope it wasn't important," Mickey called into the mouthpiece, but Max showed little concern; his focus was on getting airborne and getting away. Gaynor and Jack Briggs's eyes darted to Max, knowing full well the contents of the blue case and the consequences of its loss.

"Oh Max – I'm really sorry," Jack Briggs sympathised over the headset. Gaynor checked Max's reaction before looking out to see a security guard arriving on the roof of the other building just as the helicopter lifted into the air.

At street level, Tessa Chapman could not believe the good fortune that had befallen her when all seemed lost. She wiped away the remnants of soil that blemished the necklace and brooch, resulting from their impact with the wet ground. The tree had slowed most of its momentum, so now Miss Chapman was marvelling at how she had managed to repossess the

Geraldine Collection – hardly aware of the two policemen who arrived beside her with their guns pointed at her head.

No-one spoke in the helicopter as it swung to the west and set off towards Trant Hill. Jack Briggs eventually broke the silence.

"I must say, Max, you seem very calm about losing the collection."

Max glanced across to Gaynor whose expression was the most sympathetic Max had seen during their short relationship. He left his response for a short time to heighten its impact.

"I haven't." Max smiled, knowing the reaction that the statement would receive.

"Haven't what?" Gaynor asked.

"Lost the collection." Max announced with evident confidence.

"How come?"

"Those were the fakes. I have the real ones in my bag - I swapped them over."

Gaynor and Jack Briggs were astonished. Neither Bo nor Mickey understood the significance of the claim.

"When did you make the swop?" Gaynor asked.

"When Jack and Chapman left me alone with them at the house. More than enough time to make the exchange."

Jack thought about it and laughed when he recalled the time when he and Tessa Chapman were arguing in the hallway outside the drawing room.

"Max, you old dog."

Mickey and Bo exchanged glances and shrugged. Mickey spoke.

"Sorry Alex - I don't understand…"

"Oh, Mickey," Max interrupted in a resigned tone. "I swapped the fake diamond collection that I got from the bank,

379

for the real thing when I was left alone with them at Jack's house. Now Tessa Chapman has the fakes that fell from the tower. Got it?"

"Yeah, I got that - but what I don't understand is - why's he keep calling you Max?"

Max glanced at Gaynor and smiled.

"Ah, yeah. Well that's a bit of a long story."

J R LANDON

Also author of

CANCER OF TIME

Available at the Kindle Store

38934441R10215

Printed in Poland
by Amazon Fulfillment
Poland Sp. z o.o., Wrocław